ALAM

BEGINNINGS

Reader Disclaimer

While the locations, destinations, and icons are real, the names of characters, events, actions, and deaths mentioned in the story are works of fiction. The likelihood of such events, characters, and actions stated in said story are to be considered a coincidence. The events that transpire in the novel are works of fiction and are meant to be taken as such.

Alam Beginnings contains action, violence, coarse language, gore. It is not meant to be read by audiences younger than the age of sixteen. Reader's discretion is advised.

Science Fantasy, Science Fiction, Action, Drama
For Readers 16+
First Edition December, 2023
ISBN 979-8-8690-8219-0

LCCN 2023921488

ALAM

BEGINNINGS

THE NIGHCOS DYNASTY

EVENT: 1

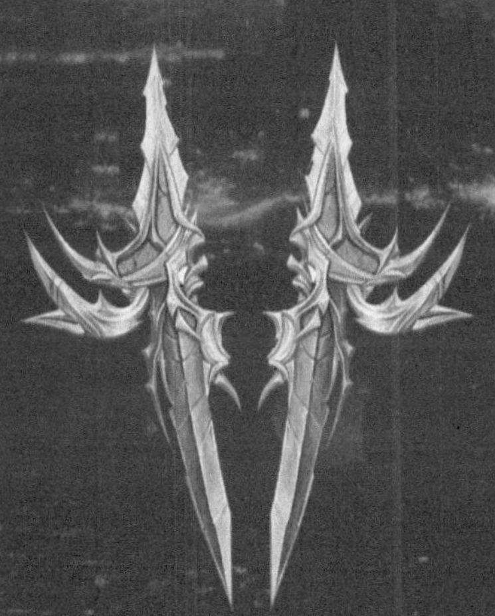

AKIL O. SMITH

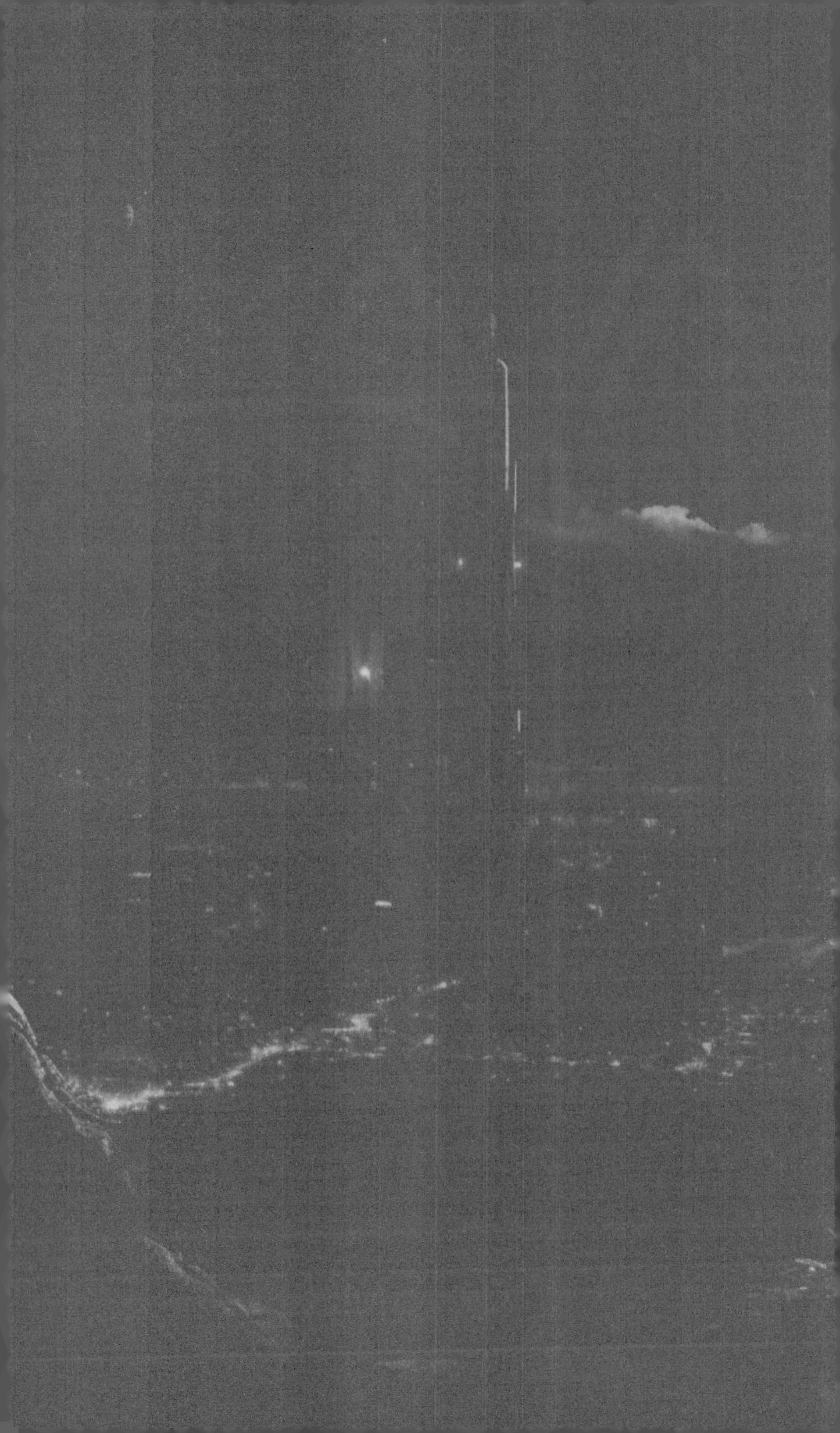

CONTENTS

To you, the reader. Welcome to the world of Alam and
I hope my story inspires you…

PROLOGUE

Ocean waves, at least a sound equivalent to them, reached the ears of one woman amongst the many attendees in the boardroom. Her gaze fixed on the sun as it rose over the faint Midtown Manhattan skyline.

"Ahhh," she breathed out. Each time, the towers became clearer. The action helped to calm her fidgeting. She closed her eyes.

Surrounded by the welcomed darkness, she felt the coldness of the table against her forearm's length. Magnetic-like stares pulled her eyes open again. She looked at her watch. Only a few minutes had passed, though it seemed as if the sun had been rising for hours.

She tapped the shoulder of the woman beside her. "What time was he supposed to come?"

"He should have been here now, but you know how traffic can be."

"Yeah!" She laughed shakily.

She took a moment to look around the room. Some attendees were paired; others seemed odd mirrors of herself, their straight-faced stares following her eyes. Particularly one man; from the corner of her eye, she met his gaze. The hairs on her arm rose. Her fingers began to dance around her pen.

What caught his mind? She wondered. *Was it possibly my elegance?* She looked around, sensing much the same feeling from the others. Today, the reaction must have been caused by her tight dress suit, which accented every curve of her body, or her glossy red lipstick that made her lips appear fuller. With all her peering, she tucked her shoulders down into her chest and lowered her head to study her own mundane action, wiping the dirt off her nails. Though her audience remained seated, she felt their body heat grow. They felt as if drawing closer.

She sighed, mouthing, "Why am I here?" Her musing continued: *"What's the point, anyway? He's not even here, and these people…ugghh! Screw this!"*

She grabbed her purse and raced to the door.

Until, the host, suddenly towered over her in the doorway. She stopped, petrified at the sight of his suited figure, shocked. The genuine smile he gave when she gazed into the void of his red checkered eyes caused her to duck down, feeling uncomfortably drawn to those features. She tightened her grasp on her purse, timidly did a double take, and returned to her seat, her head still drooped low.

His steps and hers marched in unison. Each audience member she passed paused their conversations to look on the host with motionless faces. Slowly returning to her seat, she looked up at him once more. He stared back, puzzled. Her ribs jerked as he signaled her to sit. She couldn't keep her hand from trembling as she obeyed. She didn't feel her actions were her own anymore, continuing to look at him with an oddly welcoming smile.

"I'm sorry to have kept everyone waiting," said the man in the suit, putting his belongings on the table. "Especially you," he added, staring at the woman he'd encountered at the door.

"People," he addressed the group, "I have gathered you here today to tell you that the war will soon come to an end. We have been fighting for years, since nineteen sixty-nine in Earth years." He paused, scanning the room for attention.

"My People, I believe the time has come to draw our attention towards Tiyshio Taylor, or Tiyshio Ioritae. Also known to the people of Zorin as Alam. As we all know, Alam means 'savior' in the Zorian language. The same savior that bore the mark of Alam and who saved the planet from what would have been its destruction! This was near the beginning of time itself, for those of you who don't know! Zorin, the creator of that world, is his father. The boy is strong-willed, We must change that. Does anyone have any suggestions?"

"Sir, I have a question?" a man asked, sitting across the table. "Where can we find the boy this time? Has his appearance changed? How old is he now? Do you know if he is better trained than before?"

The suited man dropped a stack of photographs in the middle of the table as he paced back and forth. The others reached for the pictures to pass them around.

"Tiyshio goes to a school in Long Island, New York. He lives in Manhattan, at his father's place. His guardian is still Kevin Bratt, as he's been known to others for some time now. Many of you may not know who Kevin Bratt is; some may know him as Kino Zara, the identity he gave himself to remain hidden as Tiyshio's guardian. I believe we need our lesser-known affiliates to infiltrate Kino Zara and bring the child here. Without him, all is lost. We keep fighting, and we lose more good people. We need a victory under their noses, or we risk beginning again."

He scanned the room once more, taking in twitching eyes and open mouths.

"You think there would be a risk?" asked an attendee outside of the host's sight.

"Indeed, there would be risk. Remember, silence is our ally," he took a deep breath, scanning his audience. "I am certain the son of Zorin has gotten stronger since we left the planet. Which means he will become a greater threat if we don't act quickly!"

Amongst the ensuing white noise came the squeaking of a chair. The woman looked at him like a puppy. He took a deep breath and stroked his beard, seeing her lips dance.

"Please speak aloud?" he calmly asked.

"Jizen, I have a suggestion. What if we use a method of persuasion towards the boy, rather than his guardian? Because the boy would fulfill the rest of our plans; if the boy trusts us, so will his guardian. Doesn't that seem right?" She sounded shaky.

"Jolla," the man in the suit replied, "being that he is not independent, nothing, except someone his age, will get past Kino. I suggest we gain *Kino's trust* instead. Since we have no one here who is the boy's age… how would you go about this?"

"We can infiltrate the school. Someone can become his teacher, and gain a close relationship with the boy. Someone can start with his studies, gain interest in cooperating with Kino, and we will then have a chance to build an outside relationship with the two. With most of our attention on Tiyshio as a whole, of course."

The man in the suit seemed visibly impressed. Jolla grinned.

"That is not a bad idea. I will consider it. However, people, we are an organization. If we have to plot in order to persuade Tiyshio to join us, we need to do it in a way that will motivate him to fight for us. We know one thing, ladies, and gentlemen. We can follow Jolla's example. Someone can dissect their personal life. We need to know who their friends are, what do they do every day. Any other suggestions?"

Another man stood. "Well, sir. I would volunteer to do this task. I work at the school. I have him as a student. He respects me, well, I think so. I am sure I can build a relationship with him. Then, once I am close enough to him, I can assure him and Kino that we are on his side. That this planet is not a safe place to stay."

"That is true. If you can follow up with this and gain their trust, then he will come to you for protection if Kino does not. Very good, Taylon," the man with a suit looked around the room. "Does anyone have any other suggestions to offer before we conclude this gathering?"

The woman who'd wanted to leave the gathering rose from her seat and smiled slightly at the suited man.

He could see the spark of interest wash over her. He kept watch, waiting for her to speak, though he could tell she was timid, despite her excitement.

He called her over. She walked toward him slowly, as though to her death, yet couldn't contain her smile from her nervousness.

"Aida, what do you suggest?" he asked in a low, naturing tone.

"Well, Lord Nighcos, I suggest we use someone in particular. Someone like my son. What do you say, my lord?"

"She draws the first piece!" Nighcos replied excitedly. Aida's smile grew, continuing the details on the white board behind him.

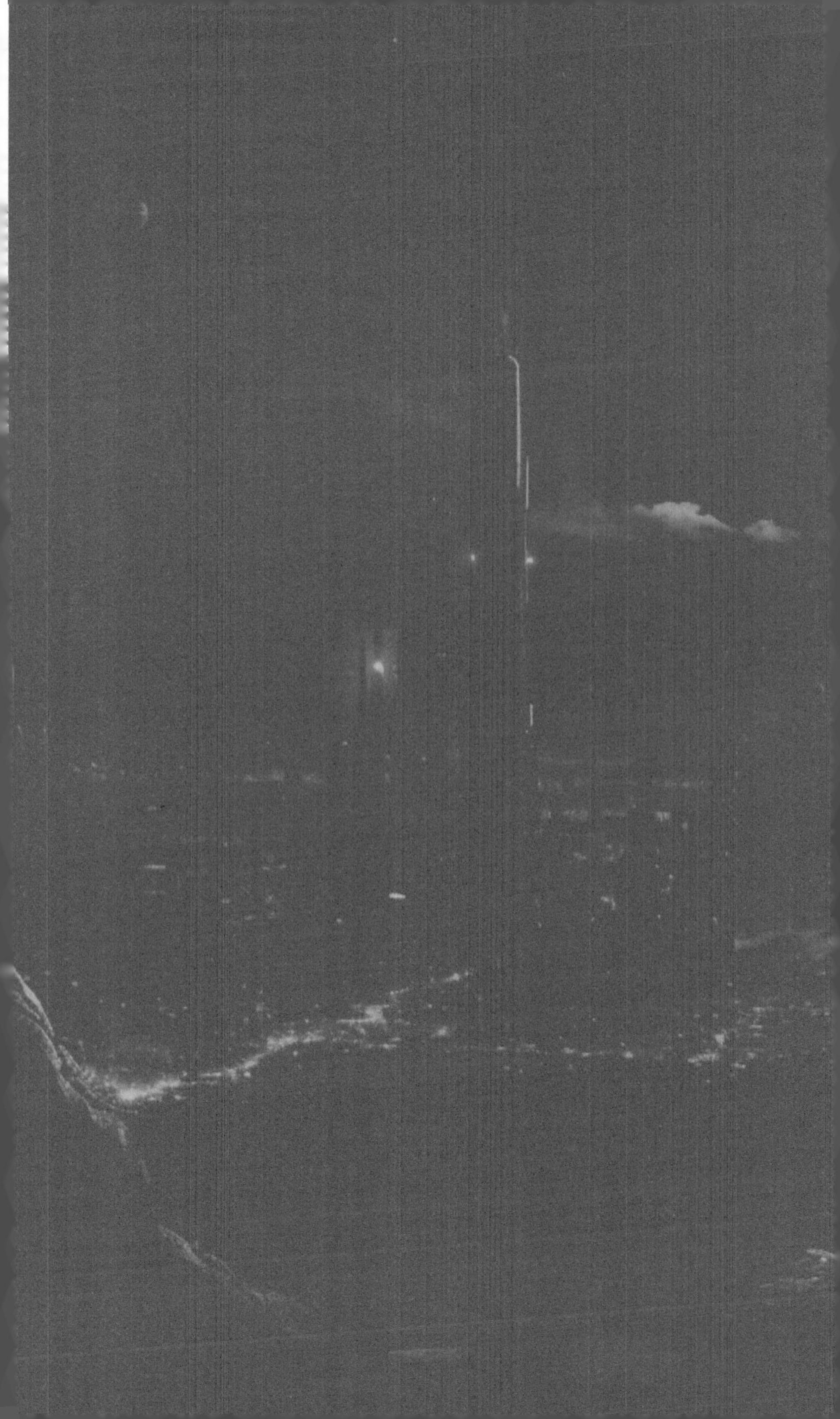

CHAPTER
ONE

BEGINNINGS

A dark orange glow crept through the shadowy room. It engulfed a school bag, then spread across the hardwood floor to the dresser, finally reaching up to a young boy's eyes as he slept opposite the window. On waking, he peeked at the clock. Six a.m.

"Mmmm!" he groaned.

The ambient sounds of cars passing by, their horns blaring through the cracked window, felt soothing as he pulled the covers over his eyes. That complete bliss came to an end when *Mountains* by Prince began playing on the radio of his alarm clock at 6:01 AM.

"Tiyshio! I hope you're up!" he heard in the distance.

"Yeah, yeah, I'm up!" he called back. "Jackass," he mumbled, forcing himself out of bed. He stumbled into his bathroom, walking over the sea of clothes covering the floor. He leaned into the mirror, studying his light brown skin like a vulture, checking for red spots.

"You look like shit," he told himself. He pulled off the hair tie, revealing long, braided, black hair tied in an open bun raised above his head to form a sphere-like crown. His hazel eyes held a hint of gold.

"Hair looks good, staying up, firm. The gel worked." He looked at the bottle of styling gel, with 'extra strength' on the label. He threw off his nightshirt and grinned at his torso, pumping up his arms and flaring his chest. Giggling, he flexed like a body builder, despite his thin but still athletic figure.

He then moved to the next room, grabbed a sword, and looked on the wall at a picture of a fighting routine. He turned to bow to another picture, this one of a man standing atop a wall, looking similar to himself. This man sported a small goatee and robes, with short hair and a stoic look.

"Good morning, dad."

His eyes lingered on the photo a moment more before he took a deep breath and shut them. Dundun, dundun, dundun… dundun… dundun… dundun. His body jolted slightly. The hairs on his arms rose when he smiled and charged toward the red-eyed target below the picture.

"Twenty-nine, thirty, thirty-one, thirty-two, thirty-three…" he spouted a half hour later, doing sit-ups, his eyes focused on the target.

The man in the apartment downstairs scoffed as he readied his cooking pan. He turned up the volume on the news, seeing the tag line, '*Explosion in Home*'

"Last night, a complaint was lodged in College Point regarding an altercation in a home in the area. Neighbors said they heard yelling, banging, and finally an explosion! When first responders reached the scene, they found four mortally wounded victims and this large hole in the back of the home. This homeowner claims to have seen everything."

The man whisked his pan as he walked toward the television. The picture on the screen was dark, with the only light showing an opening reaching to the roof of the home. Yellow tape boarded the entryway.

"The whole thing was crazy!" exclaimed the interviewee. "I was watching TV when I heard yelling in the back of my house. So did my neighbors! We all rushed outside to the yard and then: POOF! A big blue flash came from the window, as bright as the sun! I was blinded. When I could open my eyes again, there was no more window, only my neighbor on the ground. I called for the ambulance."

"Did you see the person who did this?" asked the newscaster. "Was anyone in the area able to track them down?"

"We tried! We circled around to the front of the house. The door was locked. Everyone in the street was looking for the perpetrators. They were gone. Whoever they were, they have some next level stuff, man. I think it could be Russia?"

The interviewee chuckled.

The man cooking looked at the time. It was nearing seven AM. "Tiyshio! It's almost time to go. Are you ready?"

Tiyshio sat on the floor, feet crossed at the ankles, eyes closed. Birds chirping alongside his ears sounded far away; his name being called periodically was only a bit louder. Physically, he enveloped these sounds. What he truly saw was different. As he took in his surroundings, people zipped past him. One, with a faded face, even approached him. The sounds of the city stood out the strongest.

He pressed his hand against his heart: dundun... dundun... dundun. A smile crossed his face, slowing the pace of his breath amid the calm chaos of his surroundings.

The smell of bacon, blueberry pancakes, and eggs finally grabbed his attention. Especially on the first day of school.

When Tiyshio came down to the kitchen, fully dressed in a Hip-Hop band's shirt, jeans, and striped shoes, he was ready for the day. So much so that he grabbed the wrong mug, drinking something he likened to chewing on paper. He rushed to the sink to spit out the pure Colombian roast coffee.

The man who prepared his meal glared at him in awesome fury as he paused on his phone call, "Tiyshio! What the hell, man!? That was my coffee!?"

"Kevin! You know I don't drink coffee! Why would you make me that?"

"Tiyshio, if you opened your eyes in the morning, you'd know I always put your cup of green tea to the right. My coffee is always on the left."

Tiyshio looked to the dinner table. The tea was indeed sitting at right corner of the table. Tiyshio turned back to Kevin, expressionless, his eyes barely open.

"Oh."

Kevin Bratt, a tall, muscular African American gentleman, wanted to smack him, but held back. His skin tone was darker than Tiyshio's caramel complexion.

Tiyshio at Kevin, smiling, "Looking as professional as always, Principal Bratt."

Kevin glanced down at his neatly buttoned-up shirt and loose black pants. He shook his head and snorted. His eyes met Tiyshio's again.

"Love the outfit, but the haircut and goatee, errmm! I don't know…"

Kevin snickered, rolled his eyes, and reached for what remained of his coffee.

Tiyshio strolled over to the coffee table, noticing a few non-breakfast items there. The first thing that caught Tiyshio's attention was a badge that read, in a foreign script:

Zorian Gold Team Commander

Kino Zara

Ability: Molecular Manipulation

Next to the badge was a device shaped like a pen.

"Tiyshio!" A female voice called to him in his mind. He was drawn to the device; his hand felt pulled to it, like a magnet. When he touched

it, his surroundings changed from the living room he stood in. Now he found himself on the streets of a city where buildings were shaped like raindrops and bubbles. The sky was an orange=yellow color. Before him stood Kevin, along with a boy, and a woman.

They didn't look human. Their bright white-reddish hair blew about in the air, with flares shooting out like flames. Their skin resembled a mirror's surface, silver, and gold striped.

"Home."

Silver and black striped armored soldiers accompanied Kevin and his companions. Tiyshio focused on the boy, a younger version of himself, next to his mother. He felt connected to his younger self's thoughts.

"It's okay if you don't understand your imprint ability, Tiyshio," his mother told his younger self. "Who you are is special. The ability you have hasn't been experienced in a century. Perhaps the elders can help us understand… or maybe find out what yours might be." His mother rubbed the tears from his face.

Tiyshio looked past them, to where they had come from. It was a gigantic structure, in the middle of which stood a triangular tower, its point stretching far up into the sky.

*"**The training center on Zorin, the day I didn't find out my imprint. I still don't know**." He closed his eyes and let go of the device, proceeding to where he was actually walking. The object was the brightest thing in the room, with a thick transparent casing that didn't exactly look like glass. Inside it was a miniature sun.*

He removed the cover and reached over it. Flares reached out, traveling into the palm of his hand. As each flare came to him, his hand glowed more.

*"**Tiyshio? Are you done taking in more energy than you can spare?**" Kevin asked him telepathically.*

Tiyshio looked to him and grinned.

"No. I am just looking for another way to look different, you know, have my body adapt to its environment." Tiyshio emphasized the words.

"Well, I love the way we look; we are one of the people." Kevin pointed to himself, smiling with pure energy in his face.

Tiyshio shook his head, continuing to pull energy. He glanced toward a demographic map, which brought back a memory of his boyhood. He stared into the vast emptiness before him. In the middle, he could see our blue planet. Eyes widening, Tiyshio leaned over the console of the ship he and Kevin came in.

Kevin immediately pushed him back in his seat.

"Tiyshio, where we are going, no one will look the way we do," he grabbed the printed report from the center console. "Where we are going to land, we will look like the people that are most identifiable with us, and us with them."

"Will I be able to breathe?" Tiyshio's mouth quivered.

"Your body will know what to do. It might tickle a little bit." Kevin laughed, even tickling Tiyshio in the notation.

"Just stay beside me," Kevin added.

Tiyshio nodded. Kevin continued his phone call, as Tiyshio listened in.

"What do you mean, New York is compromised? I pushed out the Rigions years ago. They're not coming back, are they?"

Tiyshio looked away as Kevin turned around after washing the dishes.

"If it's true, where do you think they would be? Queens?"

Kevin spoke as though he didn't believe the person on the other end of the phone, but Tiyshio could see that his expression showed great concern.

"In my school! No, I cross-check everyone… What was that…? All right. Be safe. Get back to me when you have more information."

"Unless the school is compromised?" Tiyshio asked sarcastically.

Kevin walked to the table, noticeably troubled. Tiyshio kept eating his breakfast, acting as though nothing unusual had happened, but did what anyone would do in this situation.

"Rigions in New York again?" He sounded annoyed.

Kevin shook his head, implying that was indeed what Tiyshio heard, "I'm sure it's nothing we should worry about."

"Unless the school is compromised," Tiyshio repeated. "Then it is?"

"That will not happen," Kevin replied firmly.

"Kev, you have been slacking," Tiyshio whined. "In the past two years, you let two criminals teach at our school!"

"We ourselves are criminals, Tiyshio. You've killed. I've killed. Just because we killed to protect ourselves doesn't make us any better. It merely gives us an opportunity to live another day."

Tiyshio rolled his eyes, slouching further into the chair.

"Besides," Kevin added, "they turned out to be good teachers, once I found out."

"Mr. Feiz in gym class? Man, he treats battle training like we are out in the field. We barely do any sports. Makes me miss Ms. Hocha. Don't get me started on Mr. Ryan in history. I swear, he picks favorites."

"How so?" Kevin asked.

"Pass by class one of these days and you'll see. Last year Shawn and I had him for history. He gave me a B on every exam, and Shawn an A, and I had copied off of Shawn."

Kevin jolted, "First of all, you're a smart kid. You shouldn't be cheating. I taught you most of this when you were five. And why hadn't you told me this sooner? I would've had a chat with him. This is supposed to be a non-biased environment."

"I would hope so, but what about this issue with the Rigions being back?"

"Don't worry," Kevin assured him. "I'm not leaving the city to go searching for them. This time I will wait, and listen, to find out what they plan. I have over a thousand people by my side here. My goal this time around is to remain here, with you."

Tiyshio glanced toward the offed television and turned it back on with his mind, flipping through the channels until he got to the cartoons. Kevin shook his head as he placed the rest of his food on the table.

Kevin then noticed Tiyshio's eyes were so firmly glued to the television that he completely missed the wrapped gift that laid beside him in plain view. Each time Kevin moved it toward the television with his mind, Tiyshio swatted it away.

Tiyshio wasn't oblivious. He knew the item was his birthday gift, but the date on that event was nearly two months past.

Kevin could see some of his reaction in Tiyshio's mind, but never really envisioned the whole thing. It wasn't like him to offer a birthday gift so late but, being it was Tiyshio's sixteenth year, he didn't want to simply get the boy another weapon to practice with. After seeing so many options on television. and just walking around the city, he knew exactly what to get him.

"I know a *sorry* means nothing, Tiy, but I want you to know! I never forgot. It just took some time to find the right gift."

Tiyshio sat back in his chair and smiled at Kevin, almost sarcastically.

Kevin grinned back, "Don't do me like that, Tiy."

"Like what?" Tiyshio chuckled.

"I tried to outdo myself this time." Kevin adopted a fake, somber voice.

Tiyshio reached out and grabbed the box. Inside were clothes, sneakers, and, on the bottom… keys to a car. Tiyshio felt ecstatic but kept his expression stiff as a board.

"Kevin, I can fly, I can move things with my mind. I gain other abilities simply by being next to people. I don't need a car."

"Not if you don't want to *blend in,* Kevin snapped back.

"I've been *blending in* since we moved here. I learned the language. I wear the clothes," Tiyshio showed off. "I even date the women."

Kevin snickered, "I would like to see that." He knew Tiyshio's exact dating history.

"What happened yesterday?" Tiyshio snapped, "You left me alone the whole day!"

Kevin smiled as they left the apartment.

"I had to run some errands."

"Some *Kazio* errands?"

Tiyshio got slapped upside the head.

"No. I had to establish some contacts in D.C. Figured you'd have your girlfriend over." Kevin followed up his remarks in a comforting tone.

Tiyshio rubbed the back of his head. He took a deep breath to keep from showing his eyes water.

Kevin smiled.

Tiyshio's face swelled, followed by Kevin's light snickering.

"Siyshi," Tiyshio confirmed. "Nope, she didn't come back until late night, and even then, she was jet lagged. She did ask if you could pick her up, though?"

"Ahh!" Kevin responded as the elevator door closed.

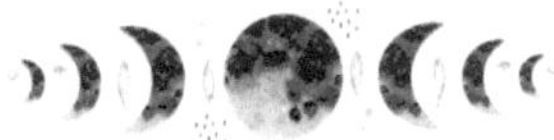

ANOTHER YOUNG MAN, NO DIFFERENT THAN TIYSHIO, ALSO RUSHED to get dressed. He had dark, faded-out hair and a light, caramel-toned body, appearing of African American descent. Big brown eyes went with his innocent-looking face. His nose was narrow, small, and rounded.

Sound of music filled every corner of the house he was in, despite it being Monday. The neighborhood was only slightly more silent than Manhattan. He had woken up late this morning, not wanting to go to school at all. What finally pushed him to do so was no less than the series of graduation pictures stuck in the frame of his wall mirror. One in particular held most of his focus, a picture of a younger version of himself, with Tiyshio and a young girl. They all appeared overjoyed, hugging each other, with him in the middle.

"Shawn! Kirk!" A voice rang out. "Breakfast is ready. I'm on my way to work,"

Shawn Damien was the boy in the pictures; Kirk Porter was his guardian, with whom he'd been living with for some time. The figure to the left was Kirk's wife, Amelia. They were Afro-Latin. Her shiny brown, curly hair added an extra radiance to her face. She was short, close to five foot three, and always dressed when going outside as if heading to work. It fit her style; she preferred elegance and fashion. Most Mondays for them were fast-paced, and they would all see each other at least once in the morning.

Shawn came from Nunta, in particular the race referred to as Hunatans. They were located in the Julius galaxy, where their race was best known for having been assassins and conquerors in their dark past. His biological parents, on the other hand, stayed away from either of those norms, instead forging their path in science and politics. Shawn possessed an ability that many Hunatans shared, turning their skin into weapons, either blunt or sharp. They did this by allowing their skin to start shedding, then pulling their creation from the tip. It began hardening as soon as it hit the air. Kirk and Amelia, on the other hand, were Zorians, being close friends of Kevin.

Shawn peered into the hallway to see if anyone else was about this early. To his surprise, all three-bedroom doors stood open, the rooms themselves empty. Below, he glimpsed Kirk climbing the stairs, saying good morning to call his full attention.

Shawn greeted him back and approached to give him a hug.

Shawn took in Kirk's appearance and his casual attire with a full smile. Kirk's own smile filled his slender face, almost mimicking Shawn's.

"I take it you're excited for school today… or… something else?" Kirk asked.

Shawn nodded, "something else!"

Kirk rubbed the back of Shawn's neck. Shawn mimicked the action by rubbing his newly shaven hair. Kirk's eyes lit up. He raised a finger to Shawn's face, then scurried downstairs. He quickly looked around as he approached a closet. Making sure Shawn hadn't followed behind.

As he pulled a folder from the filing cabinet, there came a knock on the door. The caller was a young teenage girl with straight black hair, eye features reminiscent of Asian heritage, but with exotic facial features more typical of African descent. Kirk watched her twirl her right leg back and forth, tap the floor with her left foot, and look up to the window. Kirk mouthed, "Oh my God," slowly shaking his head.

"Shawn, Sunshi is here!" he called out, letting the newcomer in. Sunshi's twin sister, Siyshi was Tiyshio's girlfriend. Their family had come from the planet Kinta, an Earth-like planet that even mimicked Earth's geography, to some extent. Even Kinta's inhabitants looked like humans, a connection Kintans, and Hunatans shared.

Their significant differences were in their hair and their abilities. Sunshi's hair remained straight, shiny, and jet black. Her sister's was curly, silky, golden brown and black at the roots, streaking to the tips. Sunshi was physically adept, highly adaptable, and possessed enough strength to stop a train, if needed. Her sister, on the other hand, could manifest into anything that came to mind. She mainly focused on molecular manipulation. Interestingly, their race shared similarities to common Zorian abilities, being able to gain more powers through contact. Not all had this capability; Sunshi's family didn't. At least so far as Sunshi knew.

"Good morning, Kirk!"

"Good morning, Sun. I don't understand. Why would you come all the way out here to Staten Island when your school is on Long Island?"

"'Cause!"

"'Cause what?"

"'Cause Shawn is here, and I never want to go to school without him." Sunshi rushed to the table, noticing a third plate already set there. She checked to make sure there was enough food for her as well, and surprisingly discovered there was. She lit up with excitement, looking at Kirk. Kirk smiled back, confused by what she might be so happy about, until she started grabbing food.

Shawn calmly rushed over to Sunshi, but only hugged her. She scoffed, kissing him in front of Kirk.

Kirk's eyes lit up, fluttering. He tilted his head, blankly staring at Sunshi.

Sunshi wiped her mouth around and snickered, but Shawn gave her a look implying he didn't want to fuss.

Kirk sighed and walked off, grabbing his own breakfast, to finish what he'd planned to earlier.

Sunshi inhaled her food; Shawn took his time. Sunshi pointed at the clock, which showed the hour as seven. Shawn merely wanted her to slow down. She didn't, instead grabbing a paper towel to bundle up his bacon, scrambled eggs, and French toast sticks together.

"Hey, Kirk," she called, "can you give us a ride on your way?"

"Eat first," he called back. "Then I can take you. Oh, I'm taking the ferry, by the way."

Shawn rushed into the other room to find Kirk sitting in his favorite chair with his reading glasses on.

"You're not gonna take the Verrazano?" he asked.

"No, because I work in Manhattan, like Amelia. Plus I'm running late."

Shawn looked at him, expressionless. "You're sitting in this chair, looking thoroughly relaxed. You don't look like you're running late."

"My next bus is in thirty minutes, and the stop is a block down. You, on the other hand, have a three-hour trip, so chop-chop."

Shawn knew he was right. Sunshi and he quickly grabbed their belongings, preparing to run for the next bus, hoping to make it in time.

Kirk made a call to Kevin so they could hitch a ride with his people.

As Sunshi and Shawn were about to leave, Kirk called out, "Go to Manhattan now. Hit Penn. Kevin will pick you up."

"Kevin is supposed to head to Brooklyn, to pick up my sister," Sunshi countered, closing the house door behind her.

"I'm sure we'll make it in time," Shawn said. He kissed his girlfriend on the lips, then gnawed on a piece of bacon.

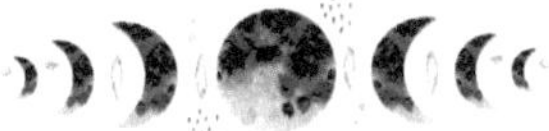

KEVIN PARKED AT THE SCHOOL, SLAMMED THE CAR DOOR SHUT, AND yelled out to his passengers as he ran, "You have twenty minutes to get to class!"

The kids raced from the car toward the main doors, passing the school's street sign.

CORENA

PRIVATE HIGH SCHOOL

Kevin followed them to the doors, admiring as usual the main hallway's mural of himself and Tiyshio's father Zorin shaking hands. The artwork boasted, in huge letters, OUR FOUNDER. The hour was eight; the homeroom bell had rung thirty minutes ago. Every one of the students looked horrified, recalling Kevin's driving like a madman while avoiding all the traffic he could. They slowly walked toward the main office, to pick up their schedules. Shawn paused read a banner: 'Good luck class of eighty-seven!'

"Come on, Shawn, let's go!" Tiyshio yelled as he and the girls began walking away.

Shawn hurried to catch up with them. "Hold up!" he cried.

"That is the craziest I've ever seen Kevin drive," Siyshi remarked.

"Well, I tell him all the time, why not just fly when we're running late?"

"You know, bruh, you should be asking him the real questions. Like, why we gotta wake up so early? Why does school gotta be so far? Why doesn't he build one in Staten Island?" Shawn sounded like a cartoon character by the time he finished.

"Or one in Brooklyn?" Sunshi followed.

"One, because no one goes to Staten Island."

Shawn felt offended.

"Two, Brooklyn is already packed," Tiyshio continued.

"Ahh, what's three?"

Siyshi cut him off. "Hope it's not. *It should be in Manhattan, so I don't have to wake up so early.*"

"YES!" Tiyshio and Shawn agreed in unison as they walked out of the main office.

"You two are just lazy!" Siyshi remarked.

"What do you mean?" Shawn snapped back. "Tiyshio and I aren't lazy!"

"You do know that Shawn was running late this morning?" Sunshi told her sister. "Had to force him to take his food to go."

"WHAT! I could've thrown it away." Tiyshio shrugged as Shawn stared at him. "I could've thrown it away," he repeated, in a lower voice, as he looked over his schedule.

The rest of the group followed his example. Their faces went blank for a fraction of a minute. Then they stared at each other in a circle.

"Who's your homeroom teacher?"

Tiyshio and Shawn yelled simultaneously, "Mr. Leggiero!"

Both darted eyes at each other, their faces filled with life.

"YES!" The shout was loud enough that the next floor up must have heard it.

Sunshi slowly scanned her paper again, rolling her eyes. Her sister tapped her shoulder and clasped her hand. "It's okay," she mouthed.

Sunshi smiled, but only with her lips, not her whole face.

Siyshi shrugged, just enough so her sister didn't see. Looking at her own schedule, yelled, "Mrs. Kazio!" Siyshi was excited to say the name of her favorite teacher.

Sunshi sank into herself, mumbling, "Mr. Ryan."

Siyshi moaned and hugged her sister.

"Hey, don't fret! I'm sure you don't have him for anything else."

"History!" Tiyshio, Shawn, and Sunshi responded in unison.

Her face brightened; as did Tiyshio's and Shawn's.

Siyshi followed up, saying, "I hope I have a class with one of you guys. I don't have time to keep looking, or I'm going to be late. See you at lunch?"

They shook their heads in agreement.

Tiyshio and Shawn wandered off, jabbing each other playfully in the chest.

"Last semester, and I'm with my boy!"

"Hell, yeah, man! This is dope!"

"Hey, when is that history class?"

"First period."

Shawn's smile fell into disarray. "Damn it!"

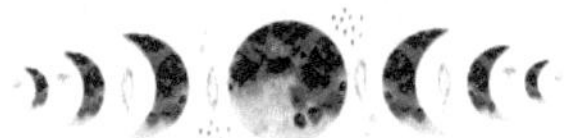

"Welcome back, students. Some of you I know. Others, I have never seen in my life." Mr. Ryan chuckled along with the class, sitting on top of the front chair desk combos.

"You know what? I could start there, have the class that I do know introduce themselves to those I don't. Perhaps you all haven't met, as well. We can help each other out. For those of you who feel you are in the wrong class and would rather be in old history with Mrs. Jensen, I'm here to say to you, my class is better. There is nothing better than Andromedan history." Mr. Ryan then turned to write on the board.

Shawn tapped Tiyshio. "Year three with this guy," he whispered. Tiyshio nodded. "In…es…capable."

Tiyshio glanced toward a girl in his class, watched her drool over their teacher's muscular figure, plainly visible from the casual business attire he wore, or maybe it was his dark chocolate skin and groomed beard, as Siyshi remarked to him when she first had him. Just the thought made him roll his eyes.

Tiyshio tapped Shawn, pointing her out to him, "Hey, she must be new?" Tiyshio whispered. Shawn snickered and nodded.

"Yes, she must be, but you two are not! Mr. Taylor, Mr. Damien. Welcome back to my class. My guess is you were hoping for a new professor by final year, correct?" Mr. Ryan's comments came across with a snarky tone. The two boys sat in their chairs, petrified.

"How the hell did he hear me?" Tiyshio mouthed.

"Your thoughts are louder than your voice, Mr. Taylor. You should expect that in this school. Especially from a telepathic race such as my own." Tiyshio nodded as his mouth dropped to the floor.

"You know what? I think you two should lead introductions."

"Ugghh! Come on, man!" Tiyshio and Shawn folded their arms into their chests as the class laughed at them.

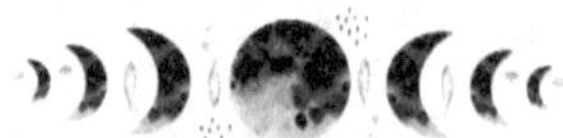

"I think most of you will like this, class," Derek addressed his students. "It's my favorite part of history. It definitely won't be boring to some of you because this is recent history. We start with the key player during this period…" Derek paused to write on the board, 'Key Players,' followed by **Zorians.**

"These guys were in a lot of wars over the past five decades. Does anyone know which ones?"

"The Hunatan war, The Avaian invasion, and the one that just ended, The Rigion devastation," called out a girl in the back of the class.

Derek's head tilted down. He stayed silent a moment before smiling and jolting back up.

Shawn whispered to Tiyshio, "Here he goes."

"I wouldn't call it… devastation," Derek replied. "More of a takeover. Not many people died. Many were turned, to become one of their enemy. Growing their army in multiple planetary systems. Why would they want to grow their army?"

"Strength in numbers?" a boy responded.

"Close, but not exactly." Derek pointed to the student, cracking a grin. "Anyone else has a response?"

"Rigions thrive on individual strength, regardless of their numbers," Tiyshio replied. "It just so happens that their numbers grow larger the more potential they find. That sucks because it makes them a greater threat. It's the reason we are here."

Tiyshio ended his sentence in a lukewarm tone.

Derek nodded in agreement as he circled the room.

"Good job, Mr. Taylor." He walked past Tiyshio, not even acknowledging his presence.

"Mr. Ryan, what about the Zorians?" another boy called out.

Derek turned around. The students behind him heard him let out a sigh equivalent to a snorting bull as he marched back to the front of the class.

"What about them?" he asked.

"You put so much focus on the Rigions, and I see you here embracing their might. What about the protectors of all those worlds that the Zorians protected too?"

Derek scanned the room. "I just want you to know, class, that not all of our focus will be on the Rigions and their bout with Zorians and their allied planets. However, I will say this." Derek approached the boy's desk and said calmly, in his ear, "The Zorians are the reason many of us are here, Mr. Ficter. Not the Rigions! The fact that the Zorians were unable to protect many of the worlds they swore they would, was what led to you, me, and everyone in this room being here. Refuge!"

Derek and Tiyshio shared a stare-down that seemed to last quite some time. The entire class looked to Mr. Ryan, with the exceptions of Tiyshio, Shawn, and Sunshi. Shawn was shaken to see how many new faces were in the room. All the students' blood rushed to their guts, and their faces paled. Derek sat on his desk, staring down at the class.

Sunshi remarked, "He seems rougher this year."

Shawn nodded slightly.

"Mr. Ryan, if I can interrupt?"

Both Sunshi and Mr. Ryan stared at Shawn.

"Many of those worlds didn't have the Zorians to rely on," Shawn continued. "They only had… themselves. Think of Piya. That world is far out in the Andromeda galaxy. They didn't stand a chance. Zorians didn't even know about them. They had to defend themselves. Now the Zorians are aware of them, and helping to get rid of the Rigions on that world."

Derek's light frown softened, then transformed into a smile. The class's expressions changed as well; each of them looked puzzled. All but Shawn.

Mr. Ryan came forward, to pat Shawn on the shoulder.

"I didn't know that Mr. Damien. It was good of you to share with the class. I like it."

Shawn let out a deep breath, and the frozen feel of the classroom came down.

"For those who have never been in my class before, you can expect debates on history like this one. I want you to know, there will be a talk on everything! Not just war. If there is anything you learn from my class, it is this: there are no heroes in war, only justice."

Derek gave Tiyshio a hard, intimidating stare.

Shawn looked at Tiyshio, who sat in place like a statue, staring deep into Mr. Ryan's eyes, and the teacher into his. Shawn nodded when Tiyshio glanced at him, but Tiyshio still held that stare as Mr. Ryan continued with class.

After school, Tiyshio went to Shawn's place to hang out and play video games. However, nothing could lighten Tiyshio up. He remained pissed off the whole day, though not showing that attitude to any of his friends.

Shawn knew. That's why he'd invited him over, of course, even asking, "Tiyshio, want to take a walk?"

"Nope, not out this late," Kirk interrupted as he passed by the living room.

Both boys smiled. Kirk stepped into the room, noticed the discomfort, and backtracked. He turned to make sure his wife wasn't following him.

"All right," he said. "It's just you boys now. What's on your mind, Tiy?"

"It's Mr. Ryan. I can never seem to get a break from this guy! First day back, and I'm already getting the business from him! He had the nerve to talk down to a student, then stared at me the whole time, like I'm the cause! He treats whoever doesn't talk trash about the Rigions with respect, and Shawn just gets pure love from him! I don't get it." Tiyshio was shouting now.

Kirk nodded. "This guy sounds like he belongs in a psych ward. Gives pure love to Shawn. Shawn, what do you do to turn this guy on?"

Shawn shivered just thinking of his smile. "What the hell, I don't do anything!"

Tiyshio and Kirk both laughed.

"Hey, I'm only joking," Kirk assured him. "Well, Tiyshio, did you at least tell Kino about this? It sounds serious."

Tiyshio nodded. "Yep. This morning, and again after class!"

"What did he tell you?"

"He'll talk with him." Tiyshio mimicked the condescending way Kevin often spoke before he laughed again.

Kirk and Shawn chuckled.

"I would say that's a start," Kirk said. "You know what's also on my mind?" He tapped them both on the shoulder.

"What?" they replied in unison.

"Your feelings about graduation.'

Both smiled excitedly.

"Man, I'm ready to leave!" Tiyshio responded.

"Yeah," Shawn agreed. "It feels like we've been in school forever."

Tiyshio agreed. "It's crazy, though. Kirk, you know that Shawn and I met almost a decade ago?"

"That's a long time you two have been friends."

"More like brothers," Shawn replied. "Tiyshio has been there for me a lot."

"As I've seen." Kirk nodded, "I like seeing you two together, though. You look out for each other. Keep doing that. In the end, all you two have are each other. I'm going back to the kitchen now to help out Amelia."

"All right!" they both yelled.

"Hey, Tiy?"

Tiyshio paused the game. "Yeah, Shawn?"

"It's been a long time, you know, for both of us since we got attacked. Life's been good. I don't feel as if I would have to fight anymore. Just live a normal life."

Tiyshio looked at him in confusion. "I don't know, Shawn. I think it's always good to be on guard. I won't lie. I would like to have a normal life. You know, chill out, feel safe, maybe later have a family."

"What, you and Siyshi?"

"I don't know if it will be with Siyshi, but I would like that."

"You and Siyshi have issues."

"What? No!"

Shawn eyed him curiously.

"I'm just saying," Tiyshio continued. "I like her a lot, but I don't know what my future holds. I mean, maybe Kevin is right, perhaps it would be better to settle down and live like a human being. It's not much different from how life was on Zorin."

"What would you do?" Shawn asked. "Why would you fight to live a normal life?"

"Shawn, look at my arm. Look where I live." Tiyshio rolled up his left sleeve, revealing the marking, 'ALAM' on his arm. "There are very few other Alam's that have lived a somewhat normal life. They shared their life with their mothers, their fathers, shit, their whole family. While, at the age of fourteen, I experienced my first near death attempt, and if it weren't for that particular person…" Tiyshio sighed, letting his head drop to his chest and putting down the controller. "Kevin has protected me for some time now. He's teaching me how to protect others, as well. I'm used to spending my life looking over my shoulder. I would protect any of my friends, no matter what. What about you?"

"Me? You know me, Tiyshio. Too much happened in my life, man! Actually, Tiy, I wanted to tell you about a dream I had the other night."

Tiyshio leaned forward. "What was it about?"

"I saw my mom. She was alive again. It made me feel really happy inside, you know. I would have loved for her to meet Kirk and Amelia. Show her how amazing they are, you know?"

"Yeah, more than you can imagine. If my own mom wasn't royalty, or even more, if her dad wasn't after me. I wish she could meet all of you guys. Back to you, though. What if she wasn't gone? Like, what if she came up to that door today and she was all good? How would everything change for you?"

"To be honest, I don't know. I would definitely want to live with her again. I'm sure Kirk and Amelia wouldn't mind. But it's been so long. I'd have so many questions. Like, why were you gone, why lie? All that jazz. You feel me? It would be an easy decision because I miss her, man. Nothing beats family. Blood family for me, but I care about my extended family just as much. You guys brought me back up when I lost hope. I still thank you for that, man."

Tiyshio nodded, looking sad but delighted. "You're welcome, man," he replied "You are my family. Coming here, meeting you all. This is my family now. I would protect you all, and you know what, if your mom was still alive, I'd be happy to see her, too."

"In any circumstance?"

"No matter the circumstance, I would be happy to see her."

"You know," said Shawn, "I would like a break. To be honest, what's going on right now only gives me a good feeling. I look forward to my future and letting my guard down. So, what do you want to do when you get out?"

"I'm considering working with computers, or at least something with technology. It reminds me of home. What about you?"

"I was thinking of finding a way to help others get off this world, give them a better opportunity than what we went through, you know. Stage it as a travel agency. Still make a bit of cash on the side."

"You want to make a front?"

Shawn laughed. "When you put it that way, it sounds worse. It's supposed to be positive, Tiyshio!"

"I didn't say it wasn't! Now you're putting words in my mouth!" Tiyshio laughed as well.

"Ha-ha no, you did that to yourself, man." Shawn sighed, then looked out the window to the stars. Tiyshio joined him, feeling from his energy something vibrant and new. "I have a feeling it's gonna be a good school year," Shawn continued.

"Same here, man." Tiyshio's vision started to blur. He rubbed his eyes, which suddenly felt covered with some substance he couldn't explain.

As he continued rubbing, the room went black. Shawn called out his name countless times. Tiyshio heard Amelia and Kirk rush back into the living room even as he felt his body grow heavier, sinking into the floor.

Once Tiyshio stopped rubbing his eyes, he found himself pinned to the wall. Kevin lay beside him. There was a lot of blood staining his shirt. He wasn't moving, and his eyes were closed. Tiyshio couldn't tell whether he was dead or alive.

In the middle of all this appeared a face he hadn't seen in a long time, a woman whose eyes shone a bright crimson red, full of rage, her hair in a ponytail. Her caramel skin tone glowed, and she offered a trusting smile that felt particularly inviting.

She was a Rigion, no doubt, holding a sword to Tiyshio's neck. She bent over and whispered, "Your grandfather is coming to get you, Tiyshio." She then pulled back slowly.

Tiyshio gazed upon her, feeling her cold kiss against his skin, goosebumps raised, his eyelids heightened so far, they touched his eyebrows.

He recognized Shawn's mother.

How was she alive, being killed so long ago, he thought.

"And I am, too!" She plunged her sword into Tiyshio's abdomen. Tiyshio screamed at the top of his lungs.

He woke in Amelia's arms. Everyone in the room was frightened.

"Tiyshio! What happened?" Shawn asked.

"I–I don't know!"

CHAPTER
TWO

PREMONITION

Amelia knew it was only the second week of school. Shawn had no business daydreaming right in front of her when he should have been doing his homework. Her lips formed a scowl as he stared up at the ceiling fan. Shawn only glanced at her twice, barely acknowledging her presence in front of him. Even now, he didn't move.

"Shawn?" she addressed him calmly.

He lowered his eyes to meet hers once more, his expression as innocent as a puppy's. She could almost forget he was only sixteen years old.

"What's holding you up?" she asked.

"Nothing!" He bent forward to write but couldn't truly answer the question in the book. Amelia approached and gently pushed his hand away. She looked into his hollow eyes and lumped lips, knowing homework wasn't going to distract him, even as she closed his book.

"You're worried about what happened to Tiyshio, aren't you?"

Shawn found it hard to admit she was right. "I don't know. He's been acting strange lately. I mean, he's okay, but he blacks out in class, and he tells me he keeps seeing the same thing."

"Did he say what it was?"

Shawn shook his head. "That's the thing. It's unlike him to not talk about what's going on with any of us. I'm worried it might have something to do with one of us, something he doesn't want us to know about?"

"Perhaps," Kirk interjected. "If Tiyshio doesn't want to tell you, maybe Kevin knows. Let him know about your concern."

Shawn shook his head in disappointment. "I tried. He told me Tiyshio would not even talk to him about it. It may be a vision that's affecting him, but it's a vision of the future. It may not happen."

"Shawn," Amelia advised, "this thing has been bothering you for over a week. You need to talk to Tiyshio, have him open up to you guys. Best case scenario, it's nothing. Zorian visions are much like human dreams. It's a view of a possible future. It isn't written in stone. For all you know, it's not going to happen."

"I hope you're right," Shawn replied, but he could not shake his concern.

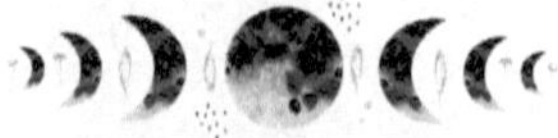

Sunshi kept tapping a distracted Shawn's shoulder. He was staring at Tiyshio, two seats across from him, looking troubled. In Shawn's head, he could barely make out the thoughts that were playing out. "*I hope it's not true. If it is, what does it mean? What should I prepare for?*" he repeatedly heard in Tiyshio's voice.

He couldn't fully understand it himself, because he wasn't telekinetic, nor did he possess any ability to read minds. "*Was Tiyshio projecting this?*"

When he finally turned his attention to his girlfriend, he bobbed his head towards Tiyshio, asking if she could tell what was going on with him. She squinted, then shrugged, lost in the mystery of whatever was going on with him. Shawn leaned in closer to ask, "Has he been like this all weekend?"

Sunshi nodded. "He was off last night, too. When he came over to hang out, he just stared up into the sky. I asked him what happened, and he just blew me off."

Shawn shrugged. "Yeah, he's not like himself."

"Why'd you ask? Has he been on your mind lately?"

Shawn looked at her as if she was crazy. "Of course he has!" He spoke softly, almost being overheard by Derek, who had been staring at him this whole time.

"If it's important, Mr. Damien," Derek snapped, "I can give you the floor to share with the whole class. Or would you prefer to take your conversation outside, and come back when you are ready to proceed with the lesson?"

Shawn and Sunshi rose and started for the door. Tiyshio watched them with twitching eyes, seeing Shawn pass Derek, mugging at him as he closed the door. Shawn continued deflecting his gaze until the two of them left the classroom.

"He's been acting weird, too," Sunshi remarked once they were outside the room.

"More so than in the past. Something doesn't feel right about him," Shawn agreed as they continued down the hall.

"Has he been on your mind lately?" She continued poking at him.

Shawn pushed her hand away.

"It isn't like Tiyshio to keep to himself. He's been open with us all the time. He knows something bad is going to happen to one of us."

"What makes you think that?"

"Why else would someone be silent, if it had nothing to do with their inner circle?"

Sunshi knew Shawn was right.

"Ever since that night," he continued, "he's been acting weird."

"The night he came over on the first day of school?"

Shawn nodded. "Yeah. I asked him what the problem was the next day, but he wouldn't talk about it."

"You know Tiyshio. He doesn't like giving out bad news."

"Well, this time I don't want to be left out. I need to be prepared, like him. I don't want to lose anyone, especially not you."

"You won't. We can protect ourselves, as much as we can protect each other. Whatever he fears may never even happen. It's a vision. The future isn't set."

"That's what Amelia said," Shawn replied, annoyed.

Sunshi halted, pressing against Shawn's chest, "What did she say?"

"Same thing as you, that it might not be the case. That I need to have a serious one-on-one with him. She knows, too! She was there! She saw how bothered he was that whole night. Had to cut the night short, after that."

"It sounds like she cares more about him than you initially thought."

Shawn smiled and nodded.

"How's living with them so far?" she asked.

"Amelia and Kirk are great, as you know. It feels like living with family again."

Sunshi's eyes widened, along with her smile.

Shawn's mouth quivered.

"I'm not saying that it didn't feel like that at all for some time," he continued. "Tiyshio is my bro, hands down, and Kevin is like a cool uncle. Just living with Kirk and Amelia feels like home again, with a twist."

"How so?"

"Kirk is like a big brother. He lets me get away with a lot, but still schools me now and then. Amelia, on the other hand, feels like the sister I never had. We fight a lot, sometimes, but we always make up. We have days where we just hang out together. Before school started, she and I took a trip to D.C. and Virginia Beach. She booked the hotel and drove all the way there. She acts like my wingman sometimes, while still being grossed out when she sees me flirt."

"You tried to cheat on me!" Sunshi punched Shawn in the arm.

Shawn laughed and pushed her away. "No! No! I would never cheat on you. I just wanted to see if you could still beat me up."

"Oh, don't play games. You know I can whup your ass, if you actually pull a stunt like that." Sunshi's hand flew toward Shawn's face.

His eyes lit up. He pulled back, seeing her fist was not going any further, and chuckled.

"No matter where I go, you are still my number one," he promised. "You are the person I most look forward to seeing every day. Except for the days when you scare me."

"No messin' around?"

Shawn smiled. "No, Cap."

She kissed him, holding him tight.

"Sun, I just really hope nothing is wrong, because you guys are all I got."

"I know, babe. I know."

"Ready to head back to class?"

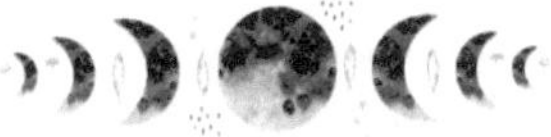

SHAWN AND TIYSHIO CAME OUT OF CLASS, GRUNTING. SUNSHI, followed behind. One look at Shawn's face told her he was so enraged, he could have shot a beam out of his mouth. Tiyshio's eyes rolled, dragging his chin down to his neck. Shawn slammed his notebooks against his own head, frustrated.

Sunshi tried to comfort them, rubbing their backs. She was noticeably unfazed by the events of today's propulsions class. Shawn and Tiyshio, noticing that, grew more annoyed.

Sunshi felt lost, looking at them, even responded, "What?"

Neither Shawn nor Tiyshio bothered answering, instead walking away from her. Their actions infected Sunshi, as she rushed to keep up.

"I take it back," Shawn admitted. "This semester is gonna suck."

"Yeah, man. If Ms. Yix continues giving us project after project like this, I don't know how I'm gonna finish my other class's homework." Tiyshio put his books in his locker.

"Yeah. I have organic chem homework due later this week, and it's already kicking my ass."

"You know, if you need help, just ask," Sunshi offered, standing behind Tiyshio's locker door as he closed it.

They both stared at her weirdly. "What do you mean?"

"Our first assignment is due Wednesday, and I don't know why you call it a project. when all of it's just review questions. Also, I got it done." Her voice took on a higher pitch.

Tiyshio's face stretched down, growing pale as she handed him her completed work.

Shawn snatched it away so fast that the paper appeared hollow. "Dibs!" he cried.

Sunshi slammed Shawn against a locker so hard it left a dent. A boy behind them cried out, "HEY, THAT'S MY LOCKER!"

Her lips puckered. Her grip slowly loosened. Shawn fell to the floor.

"My bad!" she cried. She forced the locker open to reshape it.

"Be careful with my homework, babe."

she muttered, pressing against the intruder's locker panel.

Shawn and Tiyshio looked petrified. Shawn wondered what he was so scared about.

"Hey, you wanted a strong girlfriend!" Tiyshio remarked.

"You dated her first," Shawn responded.

"Yeah, look how that worked out!"

The stare Shawn gave him came off as both satirical and cynical.

Tiyshio rolled his eyes. "I just don't get it. Why does our last year have to start so bloated? I already feel like I need a break."

"To get us ready for the world, integrate with society," Sunshi explained. "My friend Jessica said something along those lines."

"Jessica, from down the street?" Shawn asked.

"Man, I remember when I wanted to go out with her," Tiyshio recalled.

"Then imagine you two get married, and she hits eighty, and so do you?" Sunshi said. "She's gonna wonder why you haven't aged a day."

"Don't tell me you never thought of dating a human?" Shawn asked.

Sunshi shrugged. "I have, like both of you. There was a guy named Rodger who lived on the same block as us. He is so sexy! I think it was his smile. He always played on the basketball court with his boys and couple of other kids on the block."

"That black kid on Hawthorne?" Shawn asked.

Sunshi nodded erratically.

Shawn rolled his eyes.

"What happened to him?" Tiyshio asked as they began walking to their next class.

"Nothing. He still lives there. Unless you mean, what happened after him?"

"I think that's what he meant," Shawn interrupted.

"I started dating you," Sunshi said in an antsy tone. Her ears suddenly pulled to the back of her neck, picking up a conversation that, while silent to everyone else, felt as near to her as Tiyshio and Shawn were standing.

"I don't get this gym class, Rocks; I feel like Mr. Feiz is pressuring me to do more than I could do. It's not like I know my powers fully..." The young boy's voice, familiar to her, sounded from off in the corner of the hallway. She turned the corner, feeling her blood rush into her belly. Shawn and Tiyshio watched her, their eyes flickering in confusion. They then rushed after her as she sped forward.

Shawn tapped Tiyshio's shoulder, but it wasn't as though Tiyshio wasn't as much in the dark as his friend. Not until they saw the two boys down the hall did they get a hint of what was happening. Two boys they hadn't seen all summer.

"Rocks! Hayden!" They shouted the names repeatedly.

The boys in the hallway halted their conversation. The one with the short Jheri curl looked toward them. Tiyshio stared as the boy's slim, rectangular face became engulfed by a gigantic smile, reminding him of a clown. The boy next to him ran up to Tiyshio, his appearance similar to that of the Jheri curl boy. With short hair and puffy cheeks, he looked no older than twelve or thirteen.

The younger boy and Tiyshio playfully jabbed each other, before going for a hug. The Jheri curl boy stepped forward to shake Shawn's hand.

"OW!" Shawn squirmed. The boy's hand loosened, revealing red marks around his own.

"Forgot your own strength, Chris! DAMN!" Shawn continued squalling.

"Boy so skinny, you forget why we called you Rocks." Sunshi gave him a big grin, which he returned.

Shawn caught their gaze, butting himself in the middle.

"So, the Williams brothers," Tiyshio observed. "How are my favorite Nezirians?"

"Just Nez, and we're doing good. Just got back from a long vacation in Jamaica. Met some of mom's friends, who'd just arrived from Andromeda. Went to see some animals. They fell in love," Chris exaggerated.

"What caught their eye?" Shawn asked. "The fact they are cold blooded, harsh skinned, or that they could blend in?"

"The latter," Hayden intruded. "Maybe the harsh skin, too. Found it very… relatable,"

Tiyshio smiled but noticed that Chris didn't. He felt his heart stiffen into coal, as if the happiness had drained out of him.

Shawn looked up at the wall clock, seeing it was a few minutes to eleven. He looked toward Tiyshio to lead him away. Holding Sunshi by his side, he asked, "Got any training in?"

Chris scoffed. "Why would we need training when there's no war here?"

"Just because it's not affecting you now, doesn't mean it won't eventually," Tiyshio replied.

"With my muscle structure, I am already more well-built than most of those Rigion soldiers. What does it matter? It's not like they'd attack us kids."

Everyone's eyes, except for Chris' flared up, looking directly at Tiyshio. Chris's expression began to scatter as he recalled events of but a few years earlier.

It had been the middle of their first year. Chris wore a hooded sweater to cover his arms and face. Only in private would he show Tiyshio his scars. His face was red from all his crying.

"Well, that was two years ago. Nothing has happened since then."

"Don't jinx it, Rocks!" Sunshi jabbed him in the shoulder. He did not even flinch or move. Her hand stung; her face didn't show her pain, but the waving of her hand did.

"Did Hayden get some training in, at least? I know it's his first year." Tiyshio tugged on Chris's shoulder as if trying for a better view of Hayden, hidden beside him. Only to have Chris consistently hide his friend from sight.

"That's what class is for, but you know…"

Shawn glimpsed at Chris. Seeing him unphased by his own words made him shiver. Yet, he could tell something was on his brother's mind, by the way he quickly turned away from the remark.

"What's up, kid? Not even the second week, and already getting problems?"

Hayden shook his head, "It's not that. It's just… I wish I was better in gym class." All of them except for Chris looked baffled. Gym class at their high school used to be much like others around the world, with its focus on sports and fitness to blend in. However, something had occurred between Tiyshio and Shawn that made Kevin implement combat in the curriculum. This had become the main focus of the course since they started.

"I don't understand," said Sunshi, "Which part of "*gym*" are you not good at?"

Hayden watched her chuckle, but wasn't fazed by her credulity.

"Okay, okay! I will shut my mouth." Sunshi felt closed in. She turned to Shawn for rescue.

Shawn looked torn but told her to wait a moment, wanting to know why.

"It's the fighting part of the course," Chris answered. "Mr. Feiz wanted to start battle training early this semester, and he is kicking my ass, son! Like yo! I barely have a hold of my powers, and he wants us to mix them in with our combat. These other guys are walking circles around me because I don't get the practice they do."

"What do you mean, you don't get the practice?" Shawn asked, lightly tugged by Sunshi.

Chris rolled his eyes and pulled them aside, telling his brother to stay put.

"Listen, I know you may not like it, but he's my brother!" he whispered harshly to Shawn, Tiyshio, and Sunshi. "I want this to stand. Since we've moved here, I have never had to fight, run, or do any of the craziness it took to get off of Neziron. Hayden has been practically raised over here and, to be frank, I don't want him to fight." He continued huddling with them, despite their weird expressions. Chris returned their gaze with the same expression. "I don't understand. I thought you would get me. Especially you, Sunshi?"

Sunshi looked baffled. "ME?"

"Keep your voice down!" he exclaimed. "Listen, if I don't have to fight, nor does he, then I'm not teaching him. If shit does get worse, I can protect us both." His eyes reflected a serious look.

Chris felt a weight lift from his shoulders, only to have Shawn and Tiyshio bring it crashing back down with their gaze.

Sunshi calmed them both down. "Listen, Rocks…" she began, before being interrupted by the bell. "Shit, we're gonna be late for class, Shawn!"

Shawn's eyes flew up as he remembered the conversation he and his guardians had. Tiyshio nodded when Shawn yelled out, "Tiyshio, we need to talk later!"

Shawn's expression turned sad, "I know what happened earlier," he replied softly. Shawn could tell Tiyshio was still hiding how he felt, which made him more concerned when he was pulled away.

"Listen, Rocks," Tiyshio continued as they walked. Hayden had disappeared, after Tiyshio turned to see him running for his next class.

"I am only speaking from my experiences here," Tiyshio went on. "Much like you were speaking on your own. I'm just gonna say, I think you should help your brother. If you won't, I would like to step in."

Chris scoffed. "Tiyshio, we're kids. Who do you expect would come after us?"

Tiyshio's look told Chris he knew the answer. Chris rolled his eyes and began walking away quicker.

"Rocks, you know it's true."

"Nothing has happened to you in the past two years. You know Nighcos isn't coming for you anymore."

Tiyshio gave him the look again, then shrugged. "I don't expect anything less from my grandfather. He is ruthless and will do whatever he needs to get what he wants. This isn't about me! Kevin said a while ago there are Rigions in New York. You may not know this, but some of these guys don't care who I am. A group of Rigions took this family's children, had them turn against their parents, and killed them. Another one was slaughtered."

As they walked, Tiyshio frequently looked toward Chris. The latter's eyes didn't even dart in Tiyshio's direction.

Tiyshio came closer to him, just before he entered the classroom, and said softly, "Rocks, your brother needs to learn how to defend himself, sooner or later. I am not sorry! This is the life we live, until someone can find a *safer* place. You and I may be able to protect everyone, but he must also be able to protect himself."

"Teach him, then!" Chris yelled as Tiyshio walked away.

"What was that?" Tiyshio turned, looking delighted as ever. Chris was a contrast.

"Teach him, good enough that he can pass his classes. He wants to learn more. I will see how he fights."

Tiyshio clenched his fist and rocketed them to the air.

Chris stumbled back, giggling, before Tiyshio suddenly hugged him.

"I won't let you down, Rocks!"

"Please don't let him get into trouble."

Tiyshio's tone changed immediately, but he quickly hid it to avoid frightening Chris. "I promise." They took off on their separate ways. "I'll do my best to keep it," he mouthed.

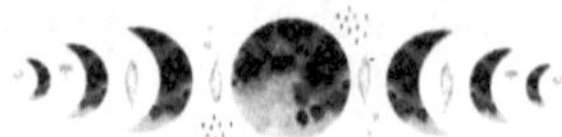

It was lunchtime. Most of the group had met up, all but the one just coming into the lunchroom. Tiyshio caught the latecomer looking as lonely as ever. His name was Jason West, a tanned Caucasian boy who looked a bit athletic, like a runner, with dirty blonde hair tied back and bangs covering his eyes, wearing a shirt and pants that looked far too big for him. His lips were medium full, and his nose was narrow. He was a Geddeon, from the planet Yade in the Heidos galaxy, the oldest race known to many outside of earth. Their evolution had spawned many races over time, even humans.

Their hierarchy had no place in the war, but Jason's family did. They traveled around the galaxy because of their science and military connections to the Zorian people. They went against the rulers of the Geddeons in their galaxy so as to be on the opposing side of a war that far outdated the one happening right now. His family had been in Andromeda at the time the destruction occurred.

Jason, on the other hand, didn't seem at all that kind of person. He made his way toward the group, who watched him sit with a bit of discomfort. All except Tiyshio, who he sat in front of, brushing his hair from his face. He then met everyone's eyes with a death stare. Suddenly:

"'Sup!" He smiled.

Shawn, next to Jason, nudged him, thinking he was serious. Yet it was Tiyshio who didn't break contact or expression. Tiyshio smiled the whole way through, offering Jason a handshake that turned into a test of strength in seconds. Their eyes became glued to each others'.

Sweat built upon Siyshi and Shawn, who sat on either side of the two. Watching their hands begin to glow a dark yellow.

Both combatants grinned, expecting the other to give up. Their grins widened as their eyes magnetized to each other.

Tiyshio broke contact for a fraction of a second, only for Jason's to follow. He observed a woman walking past, surveying her curly brown hair flow from left to right in time with her long skirt as she marched by.

Her friends called out her name, "Sade!"

Tiyshio ogled with every second as his palm became cooler.

Her movements began shifting, from Jason's point of view. He squinted, forcing his eyes to see more clearly. Watching her become transparent. As his eyes flew up, so did his hand, followed by a trail of smoke.

"SHIT!" Jason's focus darted toward Tiyshio, furious, He looked back to where the girl stood, only to find her vanished.

"Cheater," he shouted.

Tiyshio laughed victoriously. "You just couldn't handle it, could you?"

Tiyshio and Shawn both laughed.

"What did he do?" the twins asked.

"I think he made him see the love of his life." Shawn grinned, capturing Jason's obliviousness.

"Yeah," groused Jason. "It was a cheap move. He knows better than to do that."

"Oh, come on! It was only for a good laugh!" Tiyshio howled.

"Where the hell have you been, Jay?" Shawn asked.

"Yeah, skipping school for a whole week!" Tiyshio followed up.

"Traveling the world, I presume?" Chris continued.

Jason nodded at all three. He waved at the twins, and Hayden right after. "My parents decided to look for a way to get off this rock, after recent events."

Chris's eyes sprung toward Tiyshio, who shrugged. "What recent events?"

"Well, what happened to Tiyshio, not too long ago. And the attacks the other night, really showing the increased numbers of Rigions on Earth. My parents have belief they are planning something. They think it's time to get out."

The whole group, except for Jason, stared at Tiyshio. They'd all had the same feeling. Tiyshio understandably felt as if he was being backed up against a wall. When Jason looked up, after taking another bite of his lunch, he was shocked at the judgmental looks, smiling, even.

"I'm sure it all doesn't have to deal with Tiyshio being here. I think it's the increase in galactic refugees. For sure, the Rigions are up to something themselves. What about you guys? What's happened since I've been gone?"

All eyes fell on Jason as he continued munching down, but slower each bite.

"What? Did I say something wrong?"

"Just the way you talked about everything," Siyshi answered. "How are you not worried?" Her eyes scanned toward her boyfriend, who reacted much the same way. "How are both of you not worried?!"

Jason chuckled, almost choking on his food. "You guys know me. For me, this is everyday life. Home isn't a place so much as it's the people. The worst thing to experience is a fear of feeling like there is nowhere to run. The more you think it, the more you believe it."

The group's eyes, with Tiyshio's and Jason's being the exception, turned to Tiyshio himself.

"What did you do wrong, Tiyshio?" Jason asked, pacing out his words.

"Tiyshio had an episode recently," Shawn replied.

Tiyshio sucked in his lips, closing himself in, getting ready to walk away. Siyshi formed a solid plate over his shoulder to keep him down.

"Come on, Tiyshio. It can't be that bad."

Tiyshio sighed. "Fine. I saw something that challenges my way of life. When I moved here, I lost my family, and out of that tragedy I gained you all. Until now, none of you had been affected by who I am. I'm afraid it might be the case now, though, and could maybe lead to something of regret."

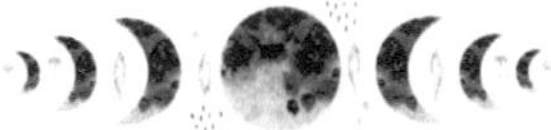

KEVIN WAS ON THE PHONE WHEN A VOICE IN HIS HEAD CALLED HIS name. The person on the other line continued speaking, but that now came as white noise to him. As he turned around in his office, the décor vanished, and the view from his window changed to a skyline of tall towers seeming to touch the sky's end, mirroring the gold atmosphere. He turned once more to find a woman standing at the other window, holding onto the back of a throne. She wore a red and silver dress, her hair braided and wrapped around her head tied. The open bun shape was similar to Tiyshio's.

As she looked on Kevin, she also gazed down on the city. Her appearance seemed melancholic. Kevin approached her, mimicking her visual watch of the peaceful people of Zorin.

"Devil's hands been busy?" he asked.

"Not if there are angels to cut them down."

"Is it true, what's happening out there?"

Zea nodded. "More worlds are being occupied. It's getting hard to balance the tide. We are trying to extend our reach before all of it gets taken over."

"I could be out there to help."

Zea heard his agitation. "You're not a one-man army, Kino!"

"That's not what this mission is."

They both paused.

"Hizen Zea?" he called out militantly.

She sighed, peering over the city.

"Have you gotten my message?"

"I have, My father is in New York. He is up to something, I'm not sure what. All I know is that he has people in place, which you have checked already. He has had them for a long time."

"I'm not sure what you mean?"

"I had a vision the other night, and I know my son has, as well."

"A vision?"

Zea came up to Kevin and placed her palm on Kevin's temple. Kevin blacked out, in much the same manner that Tiyshio had.

He woke to find himself strapped to a wall. He felt weak, barely able to move his legs or head. He scanned the room, saw Aida and three other soldiers. There was someone in the back as well. He could barely make the latter out, with his vision fading. He kept trying. At least, the figure became clear.

It was Shawn, laid on a stretcher.

Kevin struggled to force the vision to stay, but it finally went black.

"Shawn is in trouble?!"

"I don't know," Zea replied. "You need to keep him close to find out. With all that's going on, things don't feel right. Kevin, I need you to find out what Shawn is up to and protect these boys. I don't know whether it was them or us that killed that boy. All I know is that his mother is angry, and Nighcos is coming for my son again. Protect them both, no matter what."

"Yes, Hizen, as I have."

The furniture reverted, sucked back into place. Kevin lay in his chair.

His secretary tapped his hand to wake him up.

"Mr. Bratt, the head of the board from Canada is here to speak with you."

Kevin looked behind her, seeing a man smiling and waving. He waved awkwardly back, then gestured for his secretary to lean in. "Cancel the rest of my meetings for today. Something serious just happened."

"Okay," she responded, then left.

Kevin smiled at his visitor. "Come on in! Tell me, how's Toronto? I heard it looks like New York City!"

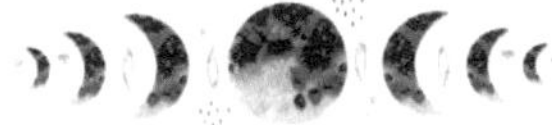

"So, that was all you saw?" Shawn asked as they walked through the hallway. "Me on a stretcher, surrounded by Rigions?"

Tiyshio kept silent, more or less confirming what he'd seen by doing nothing. He even continued to downplay the sight.

Shawn didn't. He grew more absorbed with the issue. Sunshi tried to stop him, seeing Tiyshio get more agitated.

"Look, don't worry about it," Tiyshio finally said. "I'm sure it's nothing. All I know is, you can't go to Doc Smith's lab this year, all right? I see him there, and you are dead, and Kevin's dead. I wish I'd seen more, and that's bothering me. Everything that happens there is bad!"

Tiyshio slammed his locker shut and started for his next class, but the people in front of him began to fade, and the walls turned into those of a house. He spun around to run back to his locker. Instead, he saw Kirk and Amelia, lying on the ground, bleeding out. He turned again, heading towards class. Multiple Zorian soldiers lay dead and dying in a line before him. The one closest to him called out. "Stop him. Stop Nigh–"

Kevin shook Tiyshio awake. Shawn and Sunshi surrounded him, along with a dozen other kids behind their backs.

"You guys have one more period!" he yelled. "Head to your classes!"

"Tiyshio, are you okay?" Sunshi asked.

He was too confused to answer, looked as if he didn't exactly know where he was. He grabbed Kevin's hand, and Kevin could see the same horrors Tiyshio saw.

Shawn and Sunshi watched them both in fear, unsure what was going on.

Tiyshio let go. Kevin breathed heavily in shock at the horrific sights before him. He shook his head. He now understood why Tiyshio had been so reluctant to speak on the issue.

He turned to Shawn. "Tomorrow I need to keep you, Amelia, and Kirk safe. The same goes for the rest of you."

"What's going on, Kevin?" Shawn was shaken.

Kevin could barely bring himself to speak of it, considering how long a time it had been since an attack on either of their lives.

"Nighcos has a plan for either you or Tiyshio that could lead to death, and the end of this war."

Sunshi and Shawn looked at each other, scared and lost. Tiyshio began to cry.

Shawn saw great fear well up in his friend's once fearless eyes.

Something was changing. Something not good.

CHAPTER
THREE

REVEALED

The night still dominated Manhattan's skyline, though the hour was five a.m. Tiyshio piqued his eyes, watching the sunlight slowly approach lower Manhattan. While any school day would normally see him taking his time, today would be different. He went about his daily routine and came downstairs.

Kevin followed shortly after. They grabbed leftover pizza from the fridge, sat on opposite ends of the couch, and met each other's tired eyes. In unison, they said, "Good morning."

Kevin then grabbed the phone to call Amelia and Kirk. Now was the time for them to make their move.

On the coffee table lay an assortment of pictures of men and women, all with circles around their faces and names written above. Each name was accompanied by a red eye alongside it.

Also covering the table were notes about the doctors, lawyers, and teachers that Tiyshio's panning eyes had seen, with one big question mark surrounding them all. A camera scan, dating back to the first week of school, was one photo that particularly captured Tiyshio's attention. A man stood in the corner of the frame, his face out of focus, and, on top of the photo, the eye. One year prior, seated inside a car in front of Amelia's home, was the same person who, even with the blurred view, Tiyshio knew. "*Rigion.*"

Tiyshio went back upstairs to grab their gear, should it prove necessary. He came across his sheath and what looked like a soda can. He pressed a button, and it extended into a staff. Quickly retracting it, he walked to a wall covered with photographs. Some were from the time he and Shawn went to Coney Island with Kevin, their three friends being in the Poconos for spring break. They looked more excited than a dog catching a ball. The last two he examined included a photo the backs of himself and Sunshi, their heads laid against each other as they overlooked the river, and one of Shawn and Tiyshio hugging each other with tears in their eyes. His eyes remained glued to them, even as Kevin's voice grew louder.

"Wait! Where are you right now?!" Kevin's voice carried heavily to the top floor.

Tiyshio peeked over from the mezzanine. His foot began to jitter, and his eyes went dry, seeing the pacing below.

"I told you two to call in sick today," Kevin continued, clutching the phone tighter. "This is important! Does Shawn know where the place is?"

Tiyshio and Kevin shared a look of concern.

"It doesn't matter now. You guys are already going to work. I will get him. Either way, I need you to come with me. When you finish work, come to the apartment. I will take you. I don't want you two going back there. It isn't safe. Okay, 'bye."

Kevin slammed the phone down, huffing out. Tiyshio remained silent, afraid to speak. Kevin looked his way, concerned, ready to ask a question. Tiyshio could tell from his mind that he was holding back.

"So, are we sticking to the plan?" Tiyshio asked.

Kevin shook his head and laid out a map on the coffee table. "Okay, let's do a recap!"

Tiyshio came closer, looking at all the markers Kevin had written out. He placed his finger on the marker bearing Shawn's name.

Kevin shifted their weapons and bags over to the door telekinetically.

"Shawn is still home. We need to head there fast, to have time for y'all to get to school."

"Is that a good idea?"

"Fine. Then he'll stay in the safe house until the threat is dissolved."

"Cool."

"All right. I want you to drive your new car. I left it near Shawn's, so you can drive there with me. Remember that illusion power we bumped off, first week of school?"

Tiyshio nodded, chuckling. "Yeah. I got some practice on Jason last week!" Tiyshio expelled a riotous laugh.

Kevin remained as still as a mannequin.

Tiyshio's laughter slowed. He took on an awkward, skewed visage. "Okay, not funny," he mouthed.

"Since you have practiced," Kevin continued. "I want you to hide your car while I take the bait. Across the street from him, I have reason to believe these guys don't belong." Kevin sifted through the photos he'd looked at earlier of the man standing outside Amelia's place.

"Records from the real estate office say these guys have only lived there four months. That's as long as they've been working on their plan. Maybe more."

"You are unable to point it out?"

Kevin reluctantly shook his head. "Anyway, I want them to follow my car on the way there. You should follow as close as you can. If this goes smoothly, we won't have any issues."

Tiyshio shook his head uncertainly. He wanted to speak his doubts but couldn't. He had a feeling Kevin wouldn't care, would insist on sticking to his plan.

"What is it, Tiyshio?" Kevin asked, after being tapped on the wrist.

"I'm not too confident in using illusion tactics. What if one of them are… you know?"

"What are you trying to say?"

"I might have to read their minds to create the illusion. If one of them is able to see through it… erm, I'd rather have had more practice." Tiyshio's voice was shaky.

Kevin stood there a minute while Tiyshio waited, staring at his blank, expressionless face.

Kevin sighed and stepped away, grasping his arms tightly together.

"I'm sorry, Kino," Tiyshio said, "but I don't feel comfortable making a half-assed, believable illusion if it could get us killed. What if we caused a distraction?! Something like… like a CAR CRASH!? We could be some random car on the road, create an accident so serious it would be believable you couldn't survive it?" His words came so rapidly, Kevin's face only reflected how absurd the idea sounded.

"Tiyshio? Tiyshio, I gotta get you off those movies, man! It's a BAD IDEA! At the same time, it's not, but it's risky, dangerous, and can even get me killed."

"Dude! You could teleport away, with your clothes on!"

Kevin took a deep breath, then met his gaze again. "Unfortunately, this is the only thing you can do at the moment. It's our best option. IF… we can make this run smoothly. IF I go unconscious, and they see me with no Shawn. The distraction may buy you five to ten minutes, but they will still track you down."

"I think I can manage. Remember, I am the son of Zorin. If she is there, I will simply do my best, and she will be unable to detect me. When Shawn and I were kids. I would often surprise her by doing that. If she tries to trace it back? I can make it seem as if everyone is a telepath."

Kevin laughed, "That's the spirit! Now you are speaking like your father. Ha! Let's do this." Kevin got up and grabbed the keys from the kitchen table. Tiyshio followed him.

Kevin thought more and more about the vision he had on the way down the elevator. *Envisioning the room. Seeing Shawn, Aida, and another fellow, who stood near her, focusing on the aura he felt from the vision of a few weeks ago. The shadowed man had a familiar vibration. A vibration Kevin felt at school. He allowed the vision to play out more.*

Aida walked up to him. "I didn't think I was going to see you again, Kino. I see Zorin left you with a cause that you shouldn't have to take care of. I do feel sorry for you, and it's not your fault. At least you tried to protect him. At least you did keep him safe until now. Still, you failed him, just like you failed... your lover. Best take you away from it all."

Aida used a soft, seductive voice as she slowly pierced his abdomen. Kevin, daydreaming, almost ran a red light.

Tiyshio cried out, "KEVIN!"

Kevin woke and stopped by the sidewalk, breathing heavily. "I'm sorry, kiddo!"

"Hey, Kev, were you trying to get us killed?!" Tiyshio panted heavily.

Kevin took in his surroundings. Tiyshio observed him, not understanding how such a focus came about him from before up until now.

"How the hell did we get in the tunnel this fast. We were just in the elevator!"

"You tell me! You're the one driving!" Tiyshio panted.

"Don't tell me I was caught in another one? I don't know why I looked into it, just then. There was something I couldn't explain. I felt a sudden pain.." Kevin put his hand on his abdomen.

"What kind of pain?" Tiyshio looked concerned.

Kevin patted his shoulder to calm him down.

"I felt as if I'd been stabbed in the stomach. I still feel it." Slowly raising his shirt revealed a dark bruise in the shape of blade gash.

Their faces went pale.

"You think it's her!? Let's switch places. That one was too real for you." Tiyshio shifted toward the wheel.

"No!" Kevin grasped Tiyshio's shoulder tightly. He felt his telekinetic grip release from the wheel. Tiyshio pulled away Kevin's worrisome hands as his grip lessened. Kevin's panting became less taxing as he re-took control of the car.

"I'll be fine. Let's continue with the plan. That distraction could just be in my mind."

Kevin slowed his breathing, but he knew full well Aida may have been attacking him.

"Kevin, if it's her, she may be trying to slow us down."

Kevin's silence was nerve racking as Tiyshio waited for his response. His eyes focused on the road, and he struggled to pull his mouth closed

"She won't be able to attack us again," Kevin replied. "I'll shield us, and I will heal!" Kevin slowly pulled away his hand. Tiyshio's heart ached, seeing that hand pull away. Shifting to Kevin. Grasping his side.

"Kino, please block your mind," Tiyshio said softly, keeping his eyes on him.

"*He's her son. But if she's back, why only now would she want that connection again?*" Tiyshio thought.

"We'll find out soon enough, won't we?" Kevin replied. "We're halfway there, ahead of schedule."

"That's a good thing. Where do you suspect they are?"

"Well, what time is it, like, six? Six forty-seven."

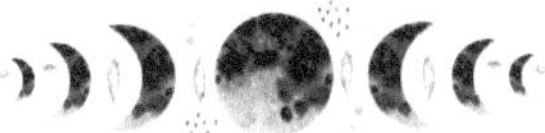

ON THEIR ARRIVAL, TIYSHIO SAW, FROM ACROSS THE STREET, SHAWN walking up to a bus stop. On the other side, two black-tinted cars followed close behind him. Kevin circled around back to the alleyway, pulling up behind Tiyshio's car. Tiyshio scurried, bent low, to the other car, while keeping the tinted cars across the way in view.

One silhouette in particular held his interest, sitting impassively in the front seat of the lead vehicle. It looked impassive, yet gave off just enough energy for Tiyshio to feel his frequency, bumped as low as headphone speaker, when he closed his eyes. Little by little, Tiyshio slowed his breath, focusing on a single sound. The lower his breath, the more he felt the wind rising up from the other person. Slowly, he clenched his fist; the twitching of hands, forcing them to close, commenced. Tiyshio stared directly at their car. From the others' point of view, they would only see an empty alleyway.

"Shawn, come around the corner. Get into my car. Got some bad guys in front of you."

Shawn heard Tiyshio's voice in his head. His eyes danced as he looked at each car. Only one felt magnetic, the black car sitting across from him. He felt as if a rope were pulling him up by the chin. Inside he made out the silhouette of a woman, frozen still, heart racing so fast it seemed audible.

"I know what you are thinking right now, Shawn, but what if it isn't her? We have got to move!"

Shawn gulped, feeling his feet move by themselves, but kept his focus glued to the car even as he began to jog.

"Hey, bro, what made you pull in here?" Shawn's focus didn't falter. He felt like he was seeing double, as if he could see inside their car as clearly as its occupants stared into the alleyway.

"Just wait." Tiyshio felt the connection strengthening between them as he pulled away.

"I guess my little trick failed." Aida looked across the street. "Where's my son?"

"He's right there, getting into that car." The driver pointed to the end of the block.

Aida looked at the driver.

Kino and Aida locked eyes.

Aida snarled.

"Follow them!" Aida demanded.

"Yes, Miss."

Kevin drove off. "They are taking the bait."

"Where's Kev going?" asked Shawn.

"He claimed there was only one way for this to work. I'm sticking close, but I know the way."

"Tiyshio! That presence?"

"I KNOW!"

"What if she's the one in trouble, Tiyshio? What if the vision you saw was one of Nighcos' games?"

"What if it's not, and you die on that table today? I won't have it!"

Shawn pulled back, feeling his heart sink to the ground. Tiyshio hadn't turned or blinked. Just determination.

Kevin continuously looked into his rearview mirror. The tinted car didn't budge. He gripped his steering wheel tighter, watching for open surroundings in which to overtake. The black car did the same. Tiyshio had trouble keeping up, with the other vehicles closing their gap.

Traffic built up as they neared the city, going through the tunnel. The black car took advantage, driving up alongside Kevin's. Kevin's grip tightened, as he saw the other vehicle from the corner of his eye. A feeling like ants, crawling into his brain, almost made his eyes roll back.

Tiyshio saw Kevin's car swerve as he got closer.

Doing a slight take, Kevin saw the silhouette of the passenger looking his way. He sped up.

So did Tiyshio and the other.

Shawn's words played among Tiyshio's thoughts. Only the fact that Shawn constantly looked his way bothered him.

The black car moved closer to Kevin, veering off to Kevin's car. Quickly he tapped into the driver's thoughts.

Or so he thought.

"Sly dog."

Aida forced her way into Tiyshio's head, scrolling through the car. Tiyshio yelped. His grip on the wheel loosened.

Shawn gripped Tiyshio's hands, pulling him out of the trance. He breathed heavily; his heart raced.

Shawn stared at him. "What happened?"

Only silence came over Tiyshio from Shawn's frightful eyes. Signaling him to hold on again. Tapping back in.

Her thoughts suddenly became loud. The voice was so clear, Aida felt as if someone was speaking directly behind her. She glanced in the rearview mirror, saw her one soldier silent but focused on the car behind them.

Tiyshio eased off, only listening to her thoughts, informing Kevin telepathically.

Kevin kept on guard, knowing Tiyshio would inform him.

"Someone might hear your thoughts." Tiyshio's warning came off sternly.

Kevin felt his energy disagree. He tuned in more aggressively.

Aida's eyes scanned from front to back. Her driver felt for her next action based on an exchange of looks.

Kevin glanced at his rearview mirror. He saw Aida and the driver as clear as day now. He was also confused, looking back on the road to see his own car in front of him.

"Hello, Kino." Aida greeted gently.

Kevin's grip tightened more, indenting the steering wheel.

"Get ready to hit them, and make sure it looks like an accident." Tiyshio heard, through Aida's mind.

Tiyshio compromised himself, yelling at the top of his lungs. "GET READY!"

Kevin sped out of the tunnel, zipping around cars that were coming up on the light. Aida's vehicle quickly followed, turning over another car.

Tiyshio shifted by.

Kevin raced down the block, avoiding most of the lights. Aida was clocking in.

Kevin spoke both out loud and in his mind. "I think she made us, Dozai. We need a distraction to get out of here quicker."

"Time to extraction point?" Tiyshio shouted, knowing Kevin could hear him.

Kevin looked at the timer he'd left in the cup holder. Twenty minutes remained. Kevin raced through the lights, heading to the Brooklyn bridge. He immediately thought of the delays.

"The traffic will put us behind another half hour."

Aida's vehicle grew larger in Kevin's rearview mirror. He sighed. "Come on, Tiyshio."

Tiyshio immediately thought a roadblock on the next street would do the trick.

The next car that followed their turn saw a crew of construction workers setting up signs and borders around one side of the road. The three cars continued toward the next block, approaching the tunnel.

Tiyshio strengthened the illusion over Shawn and himself, even as he felt his mind being penetrated by Aida.

Shawn noticed Tiyshio dozing off.

Aida suddenly saw a car appear out of nowhere, racing towards the back of their own car.

"GET OUT OF THE WAY!" Aida yelled.

Tiyshio kept dozing, veering off from his target. Shawn shook him, seeing the guard rail on their path.

Tiyshio awoke.

Colliding with them full force, Kevin saw Aida's car pushed faster, toward his own. He cried out. "Aghh."

Tiyshio whacked into his steering wheel. Shawn smacked his head on the dashboard.

The black car spun about to hit the guard rail.

Kevin swerved, regaining as much control as he could. Tires screeched. His muscles tensed from cramping. He let go of the wheel, resulting into a flip.

Tiyshio's vehicle came to a stop, colliding with the banister rail.

Kevin groaned, as his vehicle stopped rolling. In his rearview mirror, he saw Tiyshio and Shawn's car had also stopped.

So did Aida's.

"Tiyshio… Tiyshio," he called in his raspy low voice.

Tiyshio's vision cleared upon hearing Kevin.

"Tiyshio… if you can still drive, get out of here."

Kevin watched them from the mirror.

Shawn woke from his daze as Tiyshio called his name in a low tone. He watched Kevin crawl out of his car.

Tiyshio focused his attention on the black car. He tried to turn over the motor, but nothing clicked. His breathing grew rapid. He looked to Shawn, then back to the people in the black car.

"Come on, Shawn! Let's go!"

Shawn noticed Tiyshio's nose was bleeding.

"Hey, are you okay, Tiy? You don't look too good,"

"I'll be fine. Let's get Kevin and get out of here." He focused on the driver and Aida to create his illusion again as he pulled Shawn out.

Bystanders watched Aida and her people approach Kevin's and Tiyshio's cars, walking effortlessly despite their scars. One of them managed to turn Kevin over before Tiyshio could get to him. Kevin looked at Tiyshio without making a face or saying a word, to persuade him to walk away.

"It's okay. He looks fine. He knew what was coming wouldn't have made this a hot mess. I know my son is not with him. Wat about the other wreckage?"

Tiyshio turned back, seeing Aida's soldiers pull Kevin up. Shawn looked into Tiyshio's determined eyes as Kevin was carried away.

"Tiyshio."

Tiyshio reacted to Shawn's call with concern battling his troubled look. He climbed out of his car.

"Tiyshio, no."

Looking over the people who had stopped, Tiyshio came up with a plan.

"Hey, there, he don't look so good. Shouldn't we call 9-1-1?" Tiyshio asked a soldier as he walked toward the wreck.

Tiyshio moved closer to Kevin, leaning forward.

"I'm not letting them take you," Tiyshio mouthed.

Aida, seeing the weird behavior, called one of her people over to back her up.

Tiyshio turned to Aida. "Hold on. I heard him whispering. I think the young man wants to tell me something. I need to hear what he has to say."

Tiyshio lowered his head closer to Kevin as the latter whispered, "Don't you feel like you are forgetting someone?"

Tiyshio looked at him, confused, and whispered back, "Who could I be forgetting?"

Tiyshio had disguised himself, expecting Shawn to hang back reluctantly. Passing the wreckage, coming closer, teary eyed, with quivering lips and a mouth open as wide as his jaw could stretch.

Aida moved nearer, a curious look in her eyes that reflected his own.

"Mom?" Shawn called out.

Tiyshio's chest heated up as he stampeded forward. The illusion fell.

Aida yanked him down telekinetically.

"Stay with Kevin! Taylon, take Tiyshio, Brakku on me!"

Tiyshio tried pushing himself up. Taylon held him down. He fought desperately, smelling petrol leaking from Kevin's car.

"Nowhere to run."

Tiyshio struggled further, his eyes following the trail of petrol as a fire flared up from burnt tire bits. Then his struggle stopped.

Fire and petrol collided, traveling back to the car. Aida continued forward, ignoring the flames that raced passed her. Tiyshio raised his head. Eyes widened.

Boom!

"SHAWN!" Tiyshio levitated up. Aida rose to look for her son, seeing the burns he attained. She could tell he was unconscious.

Tiyshio rushed forward. Aida knocked him back telekinetically. Taylon followed up by putting him to sleep.

CHAPTER
FOUR

PAST

Aida was washing dishes, gazing out the kitchen window, taking deep breaths. Across the street, a black car was parked, its window cracked open just enough for her to see the driver watching her.

The sound of Shawn playing his video games in the next room helped bring a degree of ease to the home.

"Mom!"

Shawn's call was muffled by the game's sounds from the television. She was drifting off at the sight of her observer, leaving the water running.

"MOM!" Shawn cried out again, louder. He put down his controller and looked over his shoulder, in the kitchen.

Aida felt an unexpected pressure against her lips. Her arms felt warm, as if crossed against another body. Her heartbeat slowed, urging her to relax. Her eyelids lowered, then rose again so that she could meet the eyes of the man she was hugging.

He smiled back, holding her securely against his chest.

"I miss you, Aida." He spoke softly, embracing her forearm with a kiss. Her own lips pressed against his forehead, then her cheek, then moved to his lips.

"Mom?"

Her feet grew cold and wet from the overflowing sink water.

"Shit!" she muttered.

Shawn now stood at the kitchen door. "Mom, we've been home the whole day. I can't stay indoors anymore."

"Did you want to visit your friend, Sunshi?" she asked, wiping her feet dry.

Shawn sucked his teeth and chuckled. "No!"

"What's wrong with her?" Aida stared at her eleven-year-old son.

"Nothing is wrong with her. You, on the other hand—" Shawn turned off the faucet. "It's been a year. On my end, things are okay. It's you I worry about."

Aida sighed, turning back to the kitchen window. Shawn tried to see what she was viewing. He only saw parked cars.

"Mom, go get changed. We're going out. You're overfilling the sink. Staring at parked cars. We have to go outside; I'll finish these dishes."

Thousands of thoughts passed through Aida's mind; yet, looking at her boy, all she could do was smile. She sighed. "Okay." That was all she could say, to keep her from looking back over her shoulder.

Shawn tucked into her, making sure he felt warm.

She closed her eyes and pictured her husband again, feeling the same embrace.

Shawn finished washing the dishes. He looked out the window at the car his mother had been staring at, parked across from their own. Scattered thoughts raced in his head.

He felt a shift in his nerves, when the face pointed in his direction.

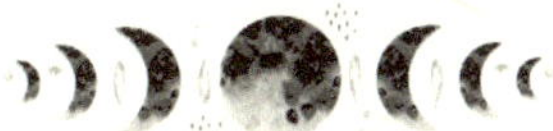

Aida's steps were slow, her focus fixed on what was immediately in front of her. Shawn slowed to match his mom's pace, keeping an eye on her puzzled stature. He shrugged, rolled his head, only catching her attention when he cupped her arm.

"What's going on in that head of yours?" He nudged his mom, making her crack a smile and break focus.

"Just work. You know how crazy it can get."

Shawn laughed. Aida laughed, too, easing up a bit more.

"Fine," she added sarcastically. "You got me."

"You miss dad, don't you?"

Aida said nothing.

"You're worried they'll come again, too?"

Still, she wouldn't budge. Shawn couldn't help but smile. The tension he shared with her began to ease up, as well. He shook his body and jumped around.

His mother, puzzled, chuckled. "Why are you jumping?"

"I really thought I was the only one that felt that way. WOOO! Feels like a breath of fresh air."

"Well, I am not surprised you miss your father. You adored that man."

"Yeah, I loved dad, but not as much as you."

Aida scoffed and pouted. "I'm your favorite?"

"Well, I won't say favorite. I don't play favorites. I know you both played your roles."

"Oh, really?"

Shawn nodded. "YEAH! You see, Dad was definitely the provider. The wise elder, the pacifist who taught me how to handle any situation with compassion."

"Okay, okay! What about me?"

"You taught me how to fight. Mentally, physically—" Shawn playfully punched his mom for calling him out in an annoyed fashion. "Ha-ha,

I'm sorry. You also taught me how to fight emotionally, spiritually, and academically."

Aida held her son's hand tight. Shawn bit his bottom lip. "If life is like a chess game," he continued. "Then, yeah, dad is definitely a king. A leader, strong, but nothing without his fighters. I might be his little knight, but you're his best queen by his side."

Aida's eyes began to water. Shawn stopped to wipe her eyes.

"You know what's the best part, mom?"

"What's that?"

"I know that, with no king, but you as the queen on the board, the game is far from over. You're a rule breaker."

Aida hugged. "I love you, son."

"I love you, too, mom."

Aida glanced over Shawn's shoulder. The black car was still parked in place. Her smile faded as she observed the same figure that had been watching all day.

Mesmerized, Aida rubbed her son's hand. Though his body had been badly burned, his skin felt smooth and natural. She even viewed it as such.

Taylon stared at her from afar, appearing anxious, from the corner of her eye.

"You're going to be okay," she whispered. "Mommy is here now,"

Tiyshio woke in the back seat of a limo, Shawn lying next to him. Kevin was in the trunk, banging the lid harder with each impact. The soldier sitting in back then put Kevin to sleep.

The soldier in the front seat turned toward Tiyshio, who was startled by his rude look.

"Why do you only come now to get your son?" Tiyshio wiped blood from his nose as he questioned Aida.

"Why did you and Kino prevent me from bringing my son back?" Her tone challenged him.

"We all believed you were dead, this whole time. He shouldn't be with someone who abandoned him, let alone one who wants to change his life now. You are one of them. You're no good. What if Shawn had died over these years?"

"You naïve little boy! You think, after he's seen me now, that my son would want to stay away from me? The only person that should've kept their distance from me is you. What does it matter to you whether I want my son back or not? He is my son!" She tugged on his throat telekinetically. Tiyshio loosened her grip, panting after she let go.

"Luckily for you, though, you were on my list."

"What list?" he asked, controlling his breathing to heal his nose.

"Don't play stupid, *ALAM*. You know what you possess. You know how important you are to all of this. The thing is, right now, you are dying. I can tell you aren't healing fast enough, are you?"

Tiyshio remained silent, feeling the blood rush down his nose. He snickered.

"Let me guess, The doc?"

Aida nodded., The grin widened on her face as she eased up. Tiyshio shifted his gaze to see what was next to Aida. She peeked to the side to share his view.

She had revealed Shawn's face. He was unconscious and burned.

Tiyshio bit his upper lip to keep from crying. Aida glanced at Tiyshio, then back to Shawn. The white noise of the drive was bathed in Shawn's taxed breathing.

"You feel it?" Aida asked. "The pain that I felt?"

"I wouldn't know how it feels to abandon someone."

"That's funny. Your mother does."

Tiyshio jolted. The soldiers held him down. He reached out to grasp her by the neck, pressing her against the seat.

"Don't you ever talk about my mother!"

She croaked. "Oh, if he could see how wholesome you are now."

"Speak for yourself! You lied!"

"Much like you are doing yourself, right now." She smirked, breaking free of his grip.

Tiyshio gave her a scorned look.

"We can keep doing this go-around, Tiyshio. This doesn't make you look any better. It already shows, literally!"

"It wouldn't have happened, for obvious reasons," he replied calmly.

"It wouldn't have happened if you didn't run!" She mimicked his tone.

Tiyshio sighed. "You betrayed your son. You choose to be with him, knowing what he brings. What does he want with me now?"

"With you, nothing, yet. With Shawn–" She pulled her son onto her lap, "you will see. I know that he would like to see you in person, but we won't have the time."

Tiyshio could felt a familiar presence. He looked toward the one she called Taylon. They stared each other down as Tiyshio focused his energy. The more he focused, the more sense things made.

Despite his Latin American appearance, from his memories, he asked, "Why do you feel so familiar?" Though he knew, he didn't want to believe. His face began changing as his skin color darkened.

"Mr. Ryan, you're one of them. Maybe I'm too dumb to know." Tiyshio laughed.

"It was a long time coming, Tiyshio," Derek said with a smile.

"Long time coming, my ass! You had better not come back to the school, because I'll kill you myself." Tiyshio smiled. "You finally got me, and him, too." Tiyshio chuckled. "Why change him, after what happened on Nunta" You surely must not care for him."

"I do. I care for my boy very much, but he won't stay with your Zorian piece of trash friends! He will be with me, as a Rigion. Now, get out of the car." She opened the door.

"When you created an illusion of your death to your son, did you even feel anything?" Tiyshio asked, as he climbed out of the car and got his hands cuffed.

"You wouldn't want to know, Tiyshio, but I have done things I regret in the past, and leaving my son was one of them."

They were brought upstairs, Shawn on a stretcher. He looked up at Tiyshio and asked, fearfully, "I feel cold. Tiyshio, what is happening to me?"

Shawn was trapped between the two other Rigion soldiers, with Kevin by his side. His head was tucked into his chest, his stare so entranced and glassy he might have been a mannequin.

Understandably, Tiyshio didn't follow his orders, which led to all of them getting captured. Tiyshio felt heavy disappointment.

Kevin closed his eyes. He did not want to see what else would happen.

"You're going into shock, and you are dying," Tiyshio told Shawn.

"Well, doesn't that suck! You knew it was her in the car. You refused to admit it." Shawn kept his voice low.

"I didn't want to believe it. I thought she had died. Then I recognized her voice when I accidentally connected to her mind. All this time, she had us under an illusion, believing she was dead."

"You heard her when we were in the car?" Shawn replied.

Tiyshio sighed and nodded. "Shawn, believe me when I say I always hoped your mother would still be alive, but not like this. Not with the people who destroyed your home. What if her plans to have you with her are malicious?"

"What if they aren't? What if she just wants to be with me again? No matter what the war has done to us! Has that ever occurred to you?" Shawn shuffled about on the stretcher, feeling chained up, "Why can't we break out of these?" he asked in frustration.

"There is a power blocker behind us," Tiyshio whispered. We are basically human right now,"

The elevator finally stopped. They progressed down the hall to a door that bore the sign:

DR. C. SMITH

DIRECTOR OF OPERATIONS

Derek opened the door.

67

Inside, Dr. Smith worked on a dark-looking liquid with a rough, thick texture.

The group followed Derek in, catching the doctor's attention when the lock clicked in place.

Aida brushed passed Tiyshio. He watched her walk up to the doctor and whispered to him as he studied Tiyshio, Shawn, and Kevin.

The doctor approached and began tending to their wounds.

Shawn looked at Tiyshio, shook his head. "Make sure your mother never sees this, Tiyshio. She would be heartbroken to see her only son hurt."

"What happened that I have to fix you both up?" Dr. Smith asked sharply.

Dr. Smith injected a needle into the black liquid, then injected it into Tiyshio and Shawn. Tiyshio started seeing his bruises heal up immediately. Shawn's burns began to disappear; his breathing improved.

Tiyshio was amazed. "Thanks, doc!" he said.

The doctor shook his head, giving Tiyshio a blank stare.

Tiyshio stared at his forearm. His veins fluctuated as if a bead were moving through them. "Doc, what did you inject into me? The thing that was black and gold, and the thing in Shawn that was red and gray. Is that safe?"

The doctor brought the plate over to Tiyshio to show him what changed its color. His device vacuumed only the liquid, separating it from what appeared microscopic shards of metal crawling over each other.

Tiyshio was horrified. The doctor found it a marvel. "You put metal bugs in me!?" he cried.

Dr. Smith chuckled, storing the containers in a secure cupboard. "Yes, but they're good bugs. They are nanobots. I must inject them in a liquid so they can flow through your bloodstream. Nighcos had me working on a new project to give better armor to his soldiers. Considering I also work for the US government, they wanted to see what I've been up to there, as well. As far as the Americans know, this substance only cures sickness. The FDA doesn't want it."

"It can do more?"

The doctor nodded. "Yes, so much more. It was created by accident. I had samples of Jason's and your blood. The idea was mainly to use nanotechnology to repair skin on its own, but with no basis to work from. I accidentally spilled Jason's blood on the plate, and the nanobots realized it to be regenerative. It used the cell structure to replicate an algorithm to create its own. I decided to mix both yours and his to create a faster regeneration. It could even solidify to form bracing or armor. Unfortunately, these are prototypes. They won't be able to save you every time."

"How long do they last?" Tiyshio asked.

"That, I don't know. As I said, Tiyshio, this is a prototype. Don't worry. It has been tested enough to work out a few kinks to prevent poisoning." Dr. Smith took a sample of Tiyshio's blood to see how his cure was working.

"How does the armor come about?" Tiyshio asked.

"I'm not sure, yet. I haven't seen any individual successfully form the armor over their bodies. It is meant to go over your clothes. I believe it reacts off the nervous system and the brain. Sensation and sight are required to initiate what it needs to do to protect its wearer. Like your bruises, for instance. The liquid runs throughout your body, so it will know what you know, see, or feel. It replicates the pattern of blood cells to rebuild your body or armor. Scorch marks on your flesh take longer to heal and may not even repair the armor. That's as much as I've seen." Dr. Smith demonstrated by putting a blow torch against one of the plates.

"Sounds like it will come in handy," Tiyshio implied.

"I hope so. It'll be my greatest breakthrough yet."

Aida was also amazed, quickly analyzing her son and Tiyshio, brushing and pressing her fingers on their skin. The flesh felt smooth and healthy.

"Doc, your science does wonders! Good job!"

Aida waved her hand up in a circular motion.

Derek and Brakku approached Tiyshio as their bodies slowly rose into the air. Tiyshio looked to Shawn, watching his body rise out of the stretcher. Aida pushed it over in front of him.

Tiyshio heard a shuffling of keys from Kevin's direction. Kevin kept struggling to break free, though he wasn't even in chains. Aida looked as if she had just given an order, with her eyes now fixated frustratingly on Kevin.

Tiyshio's head jolted softly as he heard the door unlock and more people entering. Tiyshio felt his connection to his thoughts weakening.

Two men entered.

Kevin killed the first one telepathically, seeing his eyes roll back in his head. The other nullified him before she could be killed too.

Derek entered and punched him in the stomach, to quickly raise him higher into the air.

Tiyshio heard him choking as he cackled. Tiyshio shut his eyes. He could envision his thoughts close up in a tight room that he forcibly expanded.

Kevin came into a freefall and ran toward Derek. The Rigion soldier threw him aside, pinning him against the wall. Bashing his head left a blood stain behind. Rising back up, Kevin tried breaking free from Derek's grasp. The latter only held him up tighter, copying the soldier in pinning him next to Tiyshio. Instead of being choked, Kevin felt his chest caving in.

Tiyshio saw cracks slowly form along the wall.

Kevin cried out harshly.

"You know, when this shit is over, I'm firing you!"

Mr. Ryan laughed. "I'm glad I get a great resignation present."

Kevin yelled at the top of his lungs. Derek's sinister grin faded as Kevin's arm pulled free of the wall. Kevin's ferocious stare focused on him. Derek raised his hand to press harder.

Tiyshio watched hopelessly as the wall cracks enlarged. His thoughts began caving in.

"DEREK!" Aida yelled, seeing the first drop of blood fall from Tiyshio's nose.

Aida took a deep breath to compose herself as she approached Tiyshio. "It took so long to get to this point. I can't believe this time it has finally been a great success. I must thank you, Tiyshio. I couldn't have done this without you."

Tiyshio felt a sense of ease fall over Aida. Her brown iris altered, brightening to red, like blood. The pupil formed into a tear drop shape. The sclera began bubbling, creating a triangular pattern. She formed a soundproof force field in the middle of the room, separating Shawn and herself from the others.

Tiyshio began to wrestle in an attempt to break free. The more he fought, the tighter the pull to the wall became. He looked around the room, seeing Derek in place of the blurred soldier next to Aida in his vision. Aida stood near Shawn, hovering over the stretcher.

"How are you alive?" Shawn asked in awe of her ghostly presence. "I saw your dead body when I came home from school that day!" Her appearance might be familiar, but her eyes were alien.

"I had to make a choice, a choice to protect us. I had to find out why the Zorians were attacking us. I had to make you think I died!"

"You should've brought me with you. Do you know how hard it's been for me?! To feel alone! I don't know where I'd be today if it wasn't for them."

Aida's eyes followed the direction Shawn looked. Despite both Kevin and Tiyshio being the focus, she fixated squarely on Tiyshio. Their eyes magnetized on each other's.

Tiyshio scoffed.

"Now you come back!" Shawn sneered, "Not as the person I know! No, as the person that destroyed our people, our family. Why?!"

Aida didn't appear to react to Shawn's outburst. Within, however, she felt her heart swallow itself.

"It was a decision I wasn't willing to make." She glanced at Derek. "To be honest, the situation hasn't been as bad as I thought it'd be! I am protected! I'm sorry for what I've done to you. I assure you, I will never go away again. Come with me! We can be a family again! I can protect you now, with the right people. With me, what happened before will never happen again." Aida held out her hand.

Shawn looked upon it coldly.

"Don't you still love me, Casan?" Aida asked, tears swelling up in her eyes.

"I do!" he spouted, seemed embarrassed to say as much.

Tiyshio continued staring at him, puzzled.

"How do I know I could trust you, with you being a Rigion?" Shawn asked harshly, His mother felt rightfully so.

"Because I want to protect you! I want to bring you back into my life. Trust me! The Rigions I am with are in favor of peace. Nighcos wants this war to end more than anyone. The only reason I am with them is because they saved me. The Zorians almost killed us!" She grasped the back of Shawn's head, pulling him close. His eyes nearly pierced her.

Shawn looked away from his mother, toward Tiyshio. The latter saw, in Shawn's eyes, his thoughts begin to stir.

"Don't let her use you! Don't trust her, Shawn! Anything could've happened to you. If you do this, you could be manipulated. Please!"

Shawn could only tell what Tiyshio said by reading his lips. He was torn, and his mother knew it. She raised her son's head, softly pleading. She had been gone a long time. He had been led to believe she was dead. Through her Rigion eyes appeared her natural ones.

He believed her. He couldn't even agree with it himself.

He kept looking away, but each time he did, his muscles relaxed. The only exception was his lips, which he kept biting.

"The choice is yours, son."

Shawn's eyes danced between his mother and Tiyshio. With each pass, his stare at his friend lingered longer.

He was back in the tunnel; everything moved in slow motion as he saw her. Her brows raised the look of startlement in her eyes matched his own. Her words played in his head again and again: "*I want to protect you…*"

Then he was in the car, hearing Tiyshio say, "*…I won't have it!*" He peered at his mother.

She held his hand, feeling his thoughts. "I know about his concern, Casan, but I assure you, you will be safe me. Clearly, he doesn't have your best interests in mind."

Shawn looked at Tiyshio, knowing exactly how he felt. "Maybe change is what I need now. I need my family back."

Aida was overjoyed to hear her son open up to her. Tiyshio watched his smile calm down.

Aida looked at Tiyshio, mouthing, "He's home."

"No, stop, Aida, STOP!" Tiyshio yelled at the top of his lungs.

She returned her attention to her son a long minute, then turned him to face Tiyshio, floating in the air. She forced Tiyshio to witness the change he couldn't stop. She stepped away from her son to reveal his eyes glowing red, with some elliptic lines split tangent to his pupils all around.

Shawn was slowly released down onto the stretcher, until they were eye to eye.

Staring into Tiyshio's very soul.

Tiyshio's heart pounded. *Seeing Shawn's father, through his eyes. Seeing the dead Zorians surrounding him in red.*

Shawn shared the same memory from a different perspective. Tiyshio and Sunshi walking with him to his home as kids. They had just gotten down the street when they saw the barricades. Police surrounded the area, blocking every door to every house they passed.

Shawn raced through the caution tape. Sunshi groaned, rushing after him. Tiyshio reluctantly followed.

An officer halted them, "You can't be here! Go home!"

"That is my home." Shawn told the officer calmly, pointing at the building surrounded by police. The officer sighed, turning to Shawn with a long face.

The windows had been broken on both floors. The front door was destroyed. The boy forced himself past the cops standing in front of the kitchen entryway. They tried to hold him off. The officer who finally escorted him in, told them, "Let him through".

"MOM! DAD!" he cried out.

One of the cops grabbed him as soon as he saw his father's body lying in the living room, surrounded by a pool of blood.

Tiyshio and Sunshi were held back. Sunshi kept peeking toward the living room door. Tiyshio stopped her, made her sit, while he connected Shawn and her minds.

Aida heard her son's cries coming from the kitchen. The police followed her. Seeing her boy in tears, pulling himself out of the policeman's arms, left her speechless. She grabbed her son before he fell onto the crime scene, held him in her arms, swinging him away from the sight of the four Zorian branded people that lay dead on the floor.

It was outside her control. His eyes lingered on the exposed shoulder markings. 'GALO, MIN, LAM.' Those who bore those marks led a trail from his father's severed head to his mother's feet.

Aida walked him away, holding back the tears in her own eyes, apart from the swelling in her face. "I will protect you," she told him. "I promise. I will protect you."

His mother's eyes were rolled back as her body lay on the ground. It was déjà vu. He was eleven. He couldn't keep his fingers still for one second. His tears dried. Turning to Tiyshio's worried look made his blood boil. His mother lay before him, and he was surrounded by dead Zorians and curious officers.

Shawn stepped forward to punch Tiyshio. The setting around him changed. His mother stood in front of him, giving off a nasty aura that made him feel sick. She was on one side of the room: Tiyshio on the other. They faced each other, with Shawn in the middle.

His mother turned toward him, saying just one simple word: "Remember!"

Tiyshio kept focused on Shawn, who seemed to be in a trance.

"Aida!" Derek yelled.

She walked over to him, silently calling out, "What is it!?"

He spoke softly in her ear while glancing at Tiyshio. "We have to go over the plan," he whispered.

She and Tiyshio locked eyes. Aida told the others to follow her outside, leaving the three subdued men.

Tiyshio looked at Kevin, who was distraught. "Hey, Kino, don't worry. I'm gonna get us outta here, all right."

"Why didn't you leave when I told you to?" Kevin demanded, his head dropping to his chest.

"I couldn't leave you, Kev. Not with them."

"Tiyshio, we are exactly in the spot we've been working to avoid this whole time. I could be somewhere else right now."

"Valhalla?" Tiyshio sounded annoyed, and looked that way, too, in Kevin's eyes. "I can't do this alone, Kev, even with all your connections. I can only imagine they couldn't be there to help you, as much as I didn't."

"Who's gonna help us, Tiyshio?"

Tiyshio looked away shuffling as though he could float off. "How did we not know?"

Kevin finally raised his head. "Not know what?!"

"How did we not know Mr. Ryan was one of them?"

"For starters, he shapeshifted. The rest I can't explain."

"I told you something wasn't right about him. How long have they been planning this whole thing, you think, Kino? Two years, three. He could be behind so many of the small invasions you've found in the last year. It was probably why we had to switch professors. What happened?"

"I don't know," Kevin replied, disheartened.

Tiyshio wrestled with his arms again, this time seeing his wrist move a bit. Kevin did not catch any of that.

Which was fine with Tiyshio.

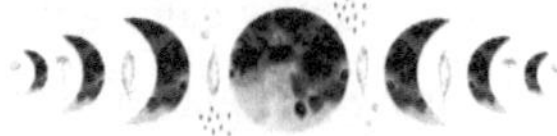

Derek watched Shawn through the crack in the door. "Is it working?"

"There is only one way to know."

"What do you suggest?" Derek asked.

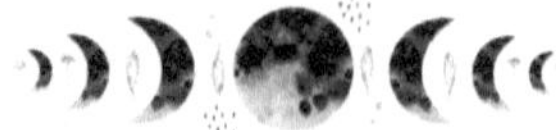

Aida walked toward Kevin, letting down the force field. She observed with great relief at his torment, as well.

Kevin's eyes never left Shawn's. He practically made the situation a blur, because he didn't want to see it.

Aida searched his mind, to see exactly what he saw, feeling extremely unsatisfied. She forced his eyes open and kept his head pointed toward Shawn, who sat motionless.

"I've been looking forward to this day, Kino, the day you get to feel what I felt when I had to decide to leave my boy behind, knowing exactly who you are," she whispered. "Defeat. Anguish. You are not turning away from it at all, just as I couldn't!"

She walked over to Tiyshio and poked him where he was originally stabbed. She pierced her nail through his restructured skin.

Tiyshio cried out, tears falling from his eyes.

"I would kill you," she told him, "if it didn't get myself killed. I just want you to have something to remember me by when this is all over." She broke off a fake fingernail in his wound and cauterized it.

Tiyshio looked down at the puncture. The burn remained. He felt her nail shifting inside his abdomen.

"I know you plan changing me next," Tiyshio sputtered in his taxed voice. "Might as well get it over with."

"You and your grandfather would like that, wouldn't you? A quick, easy win for us. No. I would rather see you tortured; see you fall. To see how you won't be able to save your friends, underneath that pride of yours. I will take them little by little, as your people took mine. Before you become one of us."

"They weren't my people!" Tiyshio yelled.

"THE HELL they weren't! You will experience so much pain, before we change you, there will be no way back to salvation, unlike your friend." She harshly pulled at his chin.

"She's gonna kill me, Tiy," Kevin called out coarsely.

"Don't say that! Don't you dare say that!" Tiyshio wrestled even more. He could feel their grip weakening.

"ENOUGH!" Aida shouted. She placed her sword against Kevin's neck, pressing it enough to cause blood to trickle down his neck. Aida glanced at Derek, exchanging looks to follow through.

Tiyshio began wrestling again, the more she pressured him.

"I trusted your people to keep my family safe. I want to see how well you can keep them safe when you can't do anything. I will give you a choice. Your grandfather doesn't want you, not yet. Give me someone you care to lose or lose your protector."

Tiyshio shook his head. "Go to hell!" he yelled.

She pierced Kevin's neck. He flinched from the blade. Aida yanked him back into it. "You want to fight, huh!" She continued pushing his neck across the blade's path. "Give me a name."

Her tone seemed calm, in contrast with the actions Tiyshio viewed. Kevin's neck bled more quickly by the centimeter. "You want him, alive, right?"

Kevin's gaze shifted to Tiyshio. Breathing heavy, he shook his head. Tears dripped down his face.

"How about your girlfriend?"

Tiyshio didn't reply.

"Christopher Williams." Kevin and Tiyshio locked eyes, pretending not to hear her.

"What, they don't matter, okay?" She pushed his neck faster along the path of her blade.

Tiyshio began pulling it away with all his mind power.

"How about your mother? You know that I have access to the temple. Come on, Tiyshio, I know you want him."

Tiyshio screamed, "NO!" His arm broke free. He slaughtered the soldier who held him, using that soldier's own weapon.

Derek swung him back up, clenching his fist.

"Aghh!" Tiyshio felt the pressure on his wrist. He'd seen it, too, the imprint of a hand.

"KEEP HOLDING HIM!" Aida yelled.

Aida stopped Kevin in his trajectory by staring at both of them. Her heart filled with joy, reading both their minds. "***What a surprise.***"

"Telsa Gond," she said softly. Kevin forced his arms down.

"GAHHHHH!"

Derek's head twitched toward Kevin. Aida turned, swiping the sword quickly towards Kevin's neck.

"KEVIN!" Tiyshio yelled.

Tiyshio reached out, extracting the sword from the wall. Derek tried to pull Tiyshio's arm down, but too late.

Aida's body flew onto the nearby table, the sword plunged deep into her skull.

CHAPTER
FIVE

RAGE

The room was still. Tiyshio felt his wrist come free of Derek's grip. Kevin healed his own neck the moment he collapsed.

Shawn's eyes filled with tears. His legs grew heavier with every step. His lips quivered as he was gazing upon Aida's lifeless eyes, hoping she would blink once more.

Blood poured from her head like a fountain. The look of shock remained frozen on her face. He reached out to close her eyes, then placed his head on her chest.

Tiyshio's heart pumped. He kept one eye on Shawn, the other on the sword that lay by Brakku's lifeless corpse.

Kevin's eyes fixed on the sword protruding from Aida's head.

Derek's hands clenched as Shawn's head slowly rose.

A gust of wind pushed against Tiyshio's body, causing the hairs on his arms to rise.

Shawn charged forward. A spike quickly engulfed his arm. He leapt backward, breathing heavily.

Air blew across Kevin's face. Shawn's eyes widened, rebounding from Kevin's piercing strike.

Tiyshio called for the sword alongside Brakku just as Shawn bolted.

Shawn tugged on his skin, forming a blade aimed at Tiyshio's heart.

Tiyshio slid forward, tripping him.

"Aghh!" Shawn's face reddened from the stomping Tiyshio gave him, cracking the blade. He reformed and twisted aside, pulling back his arm.

Tiyshio could see the skin dehydrate.

His face paled, plunging downward.

"No!" Derek swung at his face, to distract Tiyshio.

Kevin pulled him back telekinetically.

Tiyshio let out a deep breath, glancing back at Kevin.

Derek grunted, fiercely staring at Kevin. Kevin felt his brain about to burst. Derek's smile grew larger with each pulse, as his strained steps became effortless.

Kevin's heartbeat and breathing came harder the closer, and faster, Derek approached.

Tiyshio, distracted. Was kicked down by Shawn, who then formed two more blades. He looked down at his own sword to see if there was a latch, scoffing, "Wish I had my own right now."

Shawn dashed forward, aiming his newly formed blades at Tiyshio's torso. Tiyshio cut between them, spreading their path, then pushed Shawn away telekinetically and charged back. Leaping into the air, he swung at Shawn's head.

Shawn gasped, rolling out of the way, quickly breaking the skinned blades and forming new ones.

Tiyshio saw the blades coming at his rib cage, screaming out.

Kevin parried Derek's strikes, but each one rebounded closer to his collar bone. Derek laughed, crashing down with one more.

The blade slipped, slashing, down, breaking Derek's stance.

Derek smiled, only to be mirrored by his adversary. Yet, he didn't look at him. As his view transitioned to the ground, he saw the blood pouring down from his rib cage.

"Shawn! Calm down!" Tiyshio shouted.

Shawn slashed at Tiyshio, who evaded both weapons.

"I'm sorry," Tiyshio continued. "I reacted instinctively."

"Then you won't mind my doing the same." Shawn jabbed him in the face.

Tiyshio's vision blurred, only seeing Shawn's teeth. He yanked his head towards him, violently pummeling him in the face.

Kevin jolted, lunging at his opponent with his arm out. Derek jerked him back, making him snarl. Vaulting him through a window into the next room.

Shawn turned but had no time to react to Kevin pushing him out of the way. "MOVE!" he yelled.

Tiyshio and the doctor darted aside without thinking.

Kevin even dropped his blade to avoid suspicion. Shawn chased after him, pushing Kevin telekinetically without even noticing. Kevin glanced through the window, smirking, and made his exit, feeling confident with the blade as well.

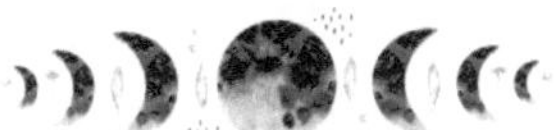

Tiyshio rushed out of the elevator, past the people in front of him, who appeared blurry and doubled. Voices echoed around him.

"What's going on with him…WATCH IT…You okay?"

They sounded as close to his ear as possible, despite barely anyone surrounding him by the time he reached the door.

Suddenly, all the sounds melded into one.

"Ding!"

He scurried through the busy Manhattan streets.

"TIYSHIO!" was all he heard in his head. He felt a hand pull on his jaw, trying to get him to look back. Shawn mustn't be far behind.

KEVIN SAW A FIGURE RUSH BY, AND QUICKLY FOLLOWED.

"Come on, kid, where are you?"

He closed his eyes, let out a deep breath. He saw himself float above the others, seeing both they and himself in continuous motion.

"There you are!"

He brushed through the crowd, passing a woman who had captured the attention of a citizen that looked familiar.

"Telsa?" he whispered; each step grew heavier as she swept pass.

"Hey, kid, you good?" asked a woman who came to his rescue as he collapsed.

Tiyshio nodded. "A migraine, that's all." He looked back to where he he'd seen *Telsa*. There was only an empty space, yet a frequent pulse played in his head.

"Kevin," he mouthed, closing his eyes to keep his focus on those around him who only appeared when his vision was cut off. Through those eyes, he was heading towards Kevin. Seeing where he walked, putting a smile on both their faces, observing the crowd that began building up near him.

Between the two was Shawn.

"*Keep going!*"

Tiyshio's and Shawn's eyes locked. He sprung up like a rocket, running like hell.

"*I trained you good, boy!*" he chuckled, speaking to Tiyshio telekinetically.

"*I am not fighting him!*"

"*Don't worry about it. Keep your toes light.*"

"*Could we make it back home for weapons?*"

"*How far are you from the house?*"

"*About six blocks and counting, maybe less. Kev, this crowd is thick for midday. I don't want to slow down.*"

"Might have to. We need to regroup, pronto! Where are you now?"

"I'm pushing two more blocks further out, to the subway."

"If you can hop a train, do it! You can use the crowd to your advantage."

"I'll do my best."

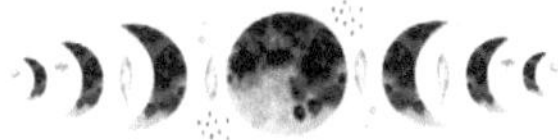

PEOPLE RUSHED PAST KEVIN IN A BLUR. HE SLID DOWNSTAIRS TO THE subway, then came to a halt, ducking behind a pillar on the entrance platform.

Tiyshio sat on bench, his head slumped down to his chest. Shawn stood across from him. Conveniently, Derek had also come down to the station, spotting Kevin from the corner of his eye.

"Hmph!" Kevin scoffed. He proceeded toward Tiyshio, his focus holding Derek's vision.

"Any reason you haven't moved?"

"Didn't feel like going anywhere without you." Tiyshio whispered.

"So, you already know they are here, waiting for your next move?"

"I know they are here, waiting for me, yes, but now, because you walked over here, they know I know it."

"I understand what you are doing. Shawn will wait here all day 'til he gets his chance."

"I know what you want me to do."

"I don't want you to do it! I want to get you out of here. Now, walk!"

Tiyshio waved his fingers.

Kevin felt as if a single large finger swept across his body. Seconds later, the same feeling came back alternatively across him.

Tiyshio started toward a tunnel near Kevin. Derek's thoughts came clearly in his head.

*"**Time to move.**"*

The person next to him was pushed back from what seemed an invisible wall. He looked back to the bench. Kevin was already long gone, down the hallway.

Shawn dashed through the crowd.

Kevin heard the commotion behind him.

Projecting more into the boy's path, Tiyshio's leisured walk turned into a brisk march.

Derek rushed through the crowd himself, attuning his sight to high dilation. He watched the next three steps Shawn took and saw a glass-like wall close shut, like a door. His fingers brushed against the air, swooping.

Shawn felt like a light shove.

From there. Shawn bolted. Kevin's heart raced, seeing him close in.

Tiyshio looked back. the strange glow from his eyes seemed to open a path for him. A woman screamed from the sight of it. The tunnel looked to continue for a while longer, yet he found a way back out onto the street.

Tiyshio squeezed through the crowd like a mouse. Shawn wasn't far behind.

Kevin pulled him back, only to be kicked in the face. A pedestrian caught him, awed by his fast-running bloody nose. Derek nudged the man off, pulling Kevin up the stairs.

Back on the street, Tiyshio rushed to the nearest alleyway. He bolted so quickly. He was heaving. He only looked back once, to confirm the coast was clear.

"Whew." He let out a deep sigh, ready to pass through a doorway. One step in, and a spike fly past his ear toward the glass-fenced door. His mouth dropped open. He slowly turned.

"You little bitch." Shawn's eerily calm tone sent chills down Tiyshio's spine.

Shawn uppercut him into the air, then pulled him back down, clenching his fist, forming a blade from his forearm.

Tiyshio pushed the weapon down with his hands and kneed Shawn in the groin.

Shawn screamed out, grabbing his legs and tackling him against the wall. Tiyshio felt as though every nerve in his back was ready to burst from the pressure.

With Tiyshio on the ground, Shawn whaled away at him. Tiyshio fought back, punching him twice in the face. Shawn screamed, whacking his hands out the way both times, bashing down at him like an ape. Tiyshio cried out again and again. He looked for something to grab.

There was nothing in sight.

Shawn slapped him in the face, to make him look at him. Huffing out, he punched him again, breaking his nose.

Tiyshio shot an energy beam at his face.

Shawn cried out in pain, blinking. The room turned white; luckily, the blinking helped. As the brightness settled

WHAM!

Tiyshio throttled his fist into Shawn's gut. "Fine! Have it your way." Tiyshio kicked him against a wall. He threw a punch, nearly breaking his hand as it struck that wall.

Shawn countered, jabbing him in the oblique to force him away. He flung his arms downward. Blades from his skin dropped like bullets.

"What? You can't fight fair?"

"She didn't get fair!" Shawn throttled toward Tiyshio's torso.

Tiyshio smiled, sliding away from the trajectory.

Shawn's arms sank into the wall. He felt the blood rush down to his feet.

Yanking at the wall, Tiyshio kicked Shawn's arm upward. He pulled his blade out of the wall and swiped at Shawn's neck.

Shawn tilted backwards, seeing Tiyshio's arms were still up high, his legs spread parallel to each other. Shawn's foot shot up toward Tiyshio's groin.

"Oww!"

Shawn lunged at Tiyshio, finally breaking free. Tiyshio's hairs shot up. His arms moved on their own, blocking the sword that came down at his head. Tiyshio headbutted Shawn in the belly.

For a moment, Shawn and Tiyshio stood still, staring eye to eye. Shawn's eyes filled with tears. He clenched his blade so tightly, his fingers bled. Tiyshio's face, filled with sweat and dried blood, appeared much the same.

"Shawn, we don't have to do this. Please?"

Shawn shook his head, Pressure built up in his lungs.

Tiyshio clenched his blade tighter. A single lonely tear crawled down his cheek.

Their blades cracked loudly in the hallway. Their hearts raced with every parry. The fury in Shawn's eyes struck Tiyshio. He felt the movement around him come to a stop.

Everything but Shawn himself.

A scowl deepened on his face with each move Tiyshio bested, putting distance between them.

"Come on! Kill me, you coward!"

Tiyshio grunted, buckling to his knees.

Shawn hammered down at him rapidly. Tiyshio peeked about, looking for an outlet.

Shawn was flung backwards as Tiyshio flicked his fingers. He appeared more animalistic as he raced back.

Tiyshio shook his head. He could barely lift his arms.

Shawn swung his blade downward.

Tiyshio flicked his fingers again, breaking free. Shawn flew down the hallway, after him, intent on nailing him to the wall.

While the boys had their bout, Derek and Kevin fought in the back alleyway. Derek smashed Kevin into the wall, blood still oozing from his nose.

"*Slink*," was the sound Kevin heard as he spat on the ground.

Derek's blade came crashing down. Kevin felt it. The setting changed around them. Kevin felt the energy shift.

So did Derek,

Twisting his stance with a swoop. Kevin slid backwards, kicking Derek in the face. Derek retaliated forcefully. Kevin followed up. His muscles relaxed; a grin began forming when Derek came at him again.

He kicked him into the hallway where Tiyshio and Shawn fought.

Tiyshio felt pulled against the wall, startled. Shawn's blade scraped the wall where Tiyshio's head had been a moment earlier. Tiyshio puffed out like a steam engine, pushing Shawn's blade up telekinetically, slicing it upward across Shawn's upper body, toward his face.

Shawn screamed, instinctively spiking Tiyshio back into the wall, bashing his head against it. He then saw his advantage. The room went dark around Tiyshio, from his angle. Tiyshio's eyes fluttered to retrieve his vision.

His heart pounded, with Shawn being right up against his face. He followed the motion of Shawn's arm pulling back, dropping the blade, and making a new one as he swung forward again.

Shawn offered a growing sneer.

Tiyshio felt his body go cold, while his face filled with heat.

The blade pierced the wall. Shawn freaked, struggling to yank himself away from Tiyshio's next attack.

Derek shoved Tiyshio away telekinetically. Kevin yanked him back to his side.

"Your fight is with me!" Kevin pulled up the blade that Shawn had dropped and swung it at Derek's neck.

Tiyshio hustled. Spikes came like bullets. He grabbed one as he got close to Shawn, stabbing him with the last one, which came for his shoulder.

Shawn stumbled.

Tiyshio pulled him back, with the spike still in him.

Shawn whacked Tiyshio's hand away and made another blade.

Tiyshio shoved-- Shawn's arm away, then quickly bent it back, injecting it into his shoulder blade.

Shawn stumbled back again.

Tiyshio kicked him to the ground.

"NO!" Derek lunged at Tiyshio; his sword aimed straight between the eyes. Frozen in fear, Tiyshio could only look up.

"Finish him!" Derek flung back to Kevin.

Tiyshio snatched the spike. Right before he plunged it down, he looked at Kevin.

Kevin could feel him.

Tiyshio's hand trembled.

Shawn cried out silently, staring at Tiyshio.

"Go on! Do it."

Tiyshio kept his hold tight. His hand continued to tremble.

"DO IT! You son of bitch!" Shawn sputtered. A vision flashed, of Shawn hugging and forgiving him. Another vision followed of their younger versions, continuing that hug.

Shawn glared at him, angry and confused. He pulled his arm free and lunged at Tiyshio.

"NO!"

The last thing Tiyshio saw was Kevin gasping, arms outstretched.

The room went black.

He saw his first day of school, here on Earth. It was already halfway through the year. When he entered the class, the teacher approached him. He remained silent, looking to everyone as though he was the one being stared at. Although she had been given his name by the principal, she stooped to his level.

"Hey, mister, what's your name?"

She appeared radiant to Tiyshio's young eyes. Her look reminded him of his mother, which made him nervous.

"Tiyshio Iori...Taylor." His reply was so soft, only she could hear. She seemed startled, a bit. To Tiyshio, however, she didn't lose her vibrant grin.

"Class. this is our new student. His name is Tiyshio. He's from the planet Zorin. Why don't you put your things under a desk and get settled in, okay?"

Tiyshio nodded excitedly, rushing to an empty desk in the middle of the classroom. He pulled out a book and began to draw a Zorian representation of the Alam.

The representation had a head of fire, a metaphor for the sun. The body was that of a human being, with skin blue and silver, in silhouette. The picture was a profile of the Alam looking up at the sun. Tiyshio drew it because it reminded him of his father and the last thing that he'd said to him, which played in his mind every day:

"When the first war of Armageddon had ended, the Alam looked up at the sun, his mind occupied. This was three days before his death. No one knows exactly what he knew or what he thought about, but many believed that, when he watched the sun, he saw his future and beyond, his own life. He chose to evolve and watch over it. To protect from beyond. One day, Tiyshio, you will have to do the same. If there is no end to this war, be who you are! You may have to decide or take on a greater role. I hope you make that decision wisely when the time is right."

Next to him, a light-skinned girl stared out the window. Outside was pouring rain. She cried throughout class, silently so as not to be bothered or noticed. This made Tiyshio uneasy.

On Tiyshio's right was a quiet boy with his head buried in his arms; from the corner of his eye, he watched Tiyshio draw. When Tiyshio finished his drawing, he marked the date, "March 10, 1978". The boy raised his head slightly and muttered, "I know who he is."

Tiyshio looked at him oddly. "I'm sorry. I don't understand?"

The boy rose his head a little more and said, more clearly, "I know who he is. He's the Alam. My father would tell stories about him. He said everyone hundred years his mark would reappear on a newborn, after the old one died. It would only be one newborn, born on Zorin. Are you a real Zorian?"

Tiyshio felt a little overwhelmed, "Ye–yeah."

"Wow! That's cool! So, you've got those tattoo marks on your arm, right?"

Tiyshio raised his right sleeve, revealing the birthmark that read, "**ALAM,** the boy's face froze in amazement as he stared at the mark.

"I'm sorry to bother you like that. It's just, you seemed pretty interesting." The boy nodded and smiled.

"Thanks, I guess," Tiyshio said awkwardly. "No one ever asked me about my Cozen before." Tiyshio slowly, turned towards the teacher. "So, what's your name?"

"Shawn, Shawn Damien. My true name is Casan Damana."

"Hi, Shawn, I'm—well, you know who I am."

"Yeah, you're Tiyshio, *right?*"

"Yep. Tiyshio Taylor. Nice to meet you!"

"Nice to meet you, too!" Shawn followed.

A girl sitting nearby added, in a groggy voice, "Same here. My name is Sunshi Guerra, since we're all announcing ourselves."

The two boys looked at each other, confused. Their only reaction was to laugh loud enough to interrupt the class once more.

CHAPTER
SIX

EYES

"**H**ey, what are you doing on Earth?"

"That's what you call this place?" Shawn responded.

"Well, I don't really know. I arrived here about a year ago, with my guardian. He never told me why. We just came… He said it would be safe. Safer as a home for me."

Tiyshio replied awkwardly, "Why do you live here? This doesn't really seem like the right place for either you or me. Everyone on this planet is so different!"

"Well, me, I had no choice. I wanted to stay on my home planet. My parents brought me here when I was five years old. I was born in Sinta Galo, in the Bolin region."

"You're Hunatan?!" Tiyshio shouted, disrupting the class, to whom he apologized immediately after. "Cool," he then continued. "I read about them in Zorian history. You were allies in the Armageddon war, but you were also enemies?"

"Actually, no. Those were the conquerors. They are outcasts from our race, with a long history. We were the allies when your people came."

"What about your family? When did everyone leave?"

"All of them, you mean?"

"Yeah!" Tiyshio exclaimed dramatically.

Shawn and Tiyshio chuckled. "My family fled when our Chancellor brought the news to our region. They begged my parents to leave with them. My mother declined their offer, however. She said Earth was safer."

"Why?"

"I never knew why. My father would say she wanted to be in a place where the war could never reach. We left when Zorigan came."

Tiyshio's eyes widened. He felt goosebumps rise along his arms. "When he was there, what did he do?" He stumbled over his words.

"Zorigan had the Zorians murdered. He killed our Chancellor, our soldiers. His people broke into homes, killing people who resisted, changing them if they complied. Dad believes the world is completely theirs now. I wish we could go back. I miss that purple sky."

"Does he really know?" Tiyshio's anger boiled. Shawn could see it. His mouth dropped, and his eyes glossed over, ready to fill with tears.

Shawn shook his head, regretful that he'd revealed the truth.

"He said our people had tried to resist, but the invaders were too much! Not just in strength, not only in numbers, but the individuals! Plus, my dad could tell certain things about them, physical things that had changed, when he dissected their bodies. One of them would be from the moon of Gensi, and they'd be missing their metal rib cage. In its place was regular bone. He said he had never seen such a thing in his life. Their strength evolved. My father told me that fights became harder, the longer they lasted. He fought them in order to get us here."

"He's okay now?"

Shawn happily shook his head. "Yeah. My dad is amazing. What is your guardian protecting you from?"

Tiyshio reminisced about a waiting area of an airport-like place. Outside, on the field, were spacecraft the size of eight cruisers, in length and height. The ship Tiyshio had been looking at bore the shape of a teardrop. *Everything around him sounded muffled. He buried his face in his chest. Alongside him stood Kevin and his mother, Zea. She was in a shouting match with his younger self.*

He wasn't dumb. He knew he would be leaving that day. Zea obviously didn't want that to happen. What choice did she have? His father Zorin and uncle Zorigan had both disappeared. That should've been the end of the whole war.

Tiyshio remembered being in his chamber in the palace, hearing his mother's screams echo down the halls. He raced to her side on his little child feet, meeting the palace aides who had arrived to check as well. He opened the door to her room, overheard the chatter,

"Lizu, are you hurt?" a female aide asked.

"No, I'm fine. It's…" She raised her head to greet her son. To Tiyshio's eyes, she looked fearful.

Kevin rushed in, to hold her reassuringly. "My queen! What's wrong?"

"I dreamt they took him."

Kevin slowly turned to Tiyshio, seeing the boy grow pale. He released Zea and moved to take Tiyshio away.

Tiyshio was back at the space gate. Zea and Kevin were in a soundproof room, surrounded by glass windows. Although Tiyshio wanted to read both their minds, Zea had blocked her son out, with no effort. Zea approached him soon after, with Kevin standing behind her. She smeared away the tears ready to fall from her golden eyes.

Tiyshio trembled, just looking at her and Kevin.

Mostly his reaction was anger towards Kevin, feeling he was the cause of Zea's upset.

Words could barely come out of her mouth. Kevin rubbed her shoulder. Zea held his hand, looked at him, and smiled. He returned the same. She tried to look at Tiyshio, keeping her emotions under control.

"Hey, Tiy, I know this hasn't been the easiest few months at home. You know Mommy has to let you go."

"But why can't I stay here with you?"

"I love you, but you can't know why. Not yet. Grandpa is a bad man now. Mommy can't protect you from him. Remember, too, your daddy is still here. You may not see him, but he sees you, and I'm still here, and I will be okay. Got it? You must do what he would want you to do. To make sure those bad guys know to never mess with you."

Zea finally began to cry.

"But Grandpa Nighcos wouldn't let them kill me, would he?"

"No, Tiyshio! Grandpa Nighcos isn't the person who we knew and loved anymore. That man now wants nothing but pain and destruction for our family."

"Is Grandpa trying to hurt you, Mommy?"

"I don't know, Tiy." Zea looked away.

"I won't let him hurt you, Mommy!"

Zea and Kevin laughed again, but with a sad undertone. Zea looked out the window, then smiled and turned her head. "No, you won't have to deal with that. I can protect myself, Tiyshio."

A man stepped forward to look at Zea. She felt his presence, barely acknowledged that he was there. She picked up Tiyshio And headed for the spacecraft.

Tiyshio gripped her robes tightly. The area he was leaving grew smaller, fainter, with each step. The moment froze before his eyes as his mother put him down.

"Will I ever see you again?" Tiyshio's eyes watered like a fountain.

She struggled to maintain her grin. Kevin couldn't even stay that stoic; he turned away. Zea wiped away his tears.

"I'll tell you what, kiddo," she advised. "If you get strong enough, when the time is right, you will be welcome to return and stay with me. You'll do that for Mommy?"

"Yes." Tiyshio drying his eyes.

"Good. Come here!" Zea stretched out her arms to embrace him tightly.

She kissed him hundreds of times as she brought him to the ship. She placed him reluctantly on the walkway, then started back. Tiyshio moved to follow her.

She pushed him back. "It's time for you to go, my son. Kino, bring Tiyshio on board the ship!"

"Come on, junior!"

Man and child, they strode up the walkway, waving goodbye.

Zea moved slowly toward the ship, covering her mouth, and bawled silently. Two men approached her as she collapsed to her knees, weeping.

Tiyshio watched her from a ship's window as they took off. He could feel his mother in him, watching her through his eyes.

Shawn saw tears fall from Tiyshio's dazed eyes.

"I'm sorry! I didn't mean to hurt your feelings!"

Tiyshio raised his head. "I think I was brought here because the Rigions were after me."

"After you? Do you know why?"

"No, man, I don't. Just that the Rigions are after me, and my mom can't protect me."

"Really! That sucks!" Shawn was stunned.

"Yeah, I don't know if she wasn't strong enough, or whatever. She had a tough time convincing my guardian to keep me home."

"My mom said that a lot of Zorians are extraordinarily strong. There's no way your mom couldn't protect you!"

Tiyshio looked at Shawn, puzzled. '*How can he be so confident, when my mom wasn't?*' he thought.

"You really think so?"

"Yeah. What's your mom's name?"

"Lizu Zea. She might be a Hizen now."

"What's Lizu and Hizen?"

"Lizu, I guess, is what you would call a queen. Hizen is an Empress."

"So you're the Zorian prince. What do they call that?"

"Yeah! They call it Dozai. My guardian said I can't tell anyone."

"*Hey,* don't worry. Your secret is safe with me."

"I know you're a prince," the girl looking out the window said mockingly.

The two boys looked at her weirdly but didn't bother with her after.

"Wow! This is so cool. This is the best day ever! I know a prince!"

"Really!" Tiyshio asked, surprised.

"Yeah, this is awesome!"

Tiyshio woke up, hearing Siyshi and Sunshi's mother, Hitomi, screaming out his name as they shook him. Hitomi, with her shiny straight black hair, looked Japanese despite her extra-terrestrial background. She had a wide bright smile that her daughters shared, and a tan, dark enough to give her skin a brownish hue. Hitomi liked to dress young, wearing tight bright blue jeans and a crop top.

Tiyshio fluttered his eyes. Hitomi called her daughter to come quickly. Her footsteps echoed as she approached.

"TIYSHIO! OH MY GOD! YOU'RE OKAY!" she cried, barging into the room, smooching him as soon as she tackled him. Her mother watched, annoyed; Siyshi could tell from the corner of her eye. She felt embarrassed, as did Tiyshio.

"I'll leave you to catch up, okay? Tiyshio, are you hungry?" She asked awkwardly.

"Yes, please!"

"Okay, I'll fix you a plate." She chuckled.

"Thank you, Mrs. Guerra!"

Siyshi's face lit up as soon as her mother left. She returned to smooching her boyfriend.

Tiyshio laughed as he rose from his seat. Siyshi quickly but gently pushed him down again, saying, "Don't get up! When you teleported here, you injured your back."

"Well, it should be healed by now."

"Healed?"

"Yeah. Zorian bodies rejuvenate quickly, remember? In a single rest period, our bodies can be back to one hundred percent health, with no sickness or scars. Not to mention the thing the doctor gave me. Hell, even our body parts can grow back in three to four days, sometimes."

"What the doc gave you?"

"Yeah. He gave me some liquid that heals instantly."

"That's weird."

"Yeah, totally, it's so disgusting!" Tiyshio said sarcastically.

Siyshi snickered, hitting him with a pillow. "Don't mock me."

"I don't. Well, not all the time. You just make it easy." They both chuckled a bit, then Tiyshio shot up.

"KEVIN!"

Siyshi yanked him back down.

"OWW!"

"CHILL! You're going to hurt yourself."

"Is he okay?"

"Yeah, he's in the house. He got here a few minutes ago. He's pretty banged up, said he had to overpower Shawn and Mr. Ryan to get away."

Tiyshio felt a sharp pain running through his rib. He gritted his teeth in response. Siyshi shoved him down with an evil stare. Tiyshio was a bit annoyed, but knew she meant well.

"I owe you a story, don't I?"

Siyshi nodded. "I gave you a report on what's happened so far…"

Tiyshio sighed, knowing exactly what she wanted. Feeling the vibrations around him, he could tell, "She's not here?"

"No. She left before I came back, went with some friends to shop in Soho."

"Okay. Good." Tiyshio sighed in relief over dramatically, making his girlfriend uncomfortable. That same energy came over the boy after feeling her thoughts flood his mind. As much as he wanted to halt time, not say what needed to be said, he knew the background would change Siyshi's and Sunshi's view on Shawn forever.

Siyshi jabbed him again. "What Happened, Tiyshio?!" The words came across as firm and aggressive.

Tiyshio took a deep breath, closing his eyes. "Today didn't go as planned."

She saw his eyes start to swell up. That happy façade for which he was known began to drop.

Siyshi looked confused. "What do you mean, not as planned, Tiyshio? What happened to Shawn?"

"Just give me a minute." Tiyshio fidgeted with his clothes, slightly rocking back and forth.

"This morning, Kev and I went to get Shawn and bring him to a safe house. The mission should have gone fine, no interruptions. However, something went wrong… Remember the dream I told you about the other day? The one about Shawn being dead?"

Siyshi nodded.

"It turned out it wasn't an illusion at all."

"WHAT HAPPENED TO HIM?"

"He's different… he's one of them! He's one of them now!"

"DIFFERENT HOW?!" she demanded.

"Everything happened so fast. S-she was going to kill Kev, so I tried to stop her, and then I–then I killed her."

Her breath slowed. Her body became petrified. She whispered, "Oh my God."

"*Now, I guess Shawn hates you for that.*"

"You figure?!" Tiyshio replied, annoyed. "I was trying to protect Kevin! She was going to kill him, Siy! I didn't know what else to do! He's been a father to me. My real father wouldn't want me to let him die," Tiyshio cried.

"That doesn't matter, Tiyshio! You could've just knocked her out. You could've even slowed down her bodily functions, make her pass out or something! Anything except for what you did to her!"

"I WAS HUNG UP!"

Siyshi fell silent, unthinkingly pushing herself away from him.

"I WAS BEING HELD BACK WHILE KINO WAS SECONDS FROM GETTING HIS HEAD CHOPPED OFF. I DID WHAT I HAD TO DO TO SAVE HIM!" Tiyshio yelled.

She leaned back, baffled, "Babe? I've heard of incidents like this a few years ago that were no different. You saved that woman and killed the assassin with your bare hands. You wanted her dead."

Tiyshio shut his eyes tight. "I'm sorry. I didn't mean to go off on you. The act was spur-of-the-moment. I didn't think of any of those things at all. I wasn't expecting to kill her."

His excuses seemed blank to her. '*How could he,*' she thought. To be real, though, she couldn't think of a plan to escape herself.

"Was it a hard decision?" Siyshi asked sadly.

"I don't understand?"

"To kill her, was it hard?" she repeated.

"Yes, Siy, it was. I begged her not to make me do it, even as I lifted the sword from the wall. I had to play it safe. She could've still killed Kevin with her bare hands."

"Why would you want to prevent Aida from reuniting with her only son? Isn't that the worst thing to do?"

"I don't know, Siy. I just didn't feel right about her being back. Nothing seemed right about her being back. What if she wanted her son dead, or to use for something other than what she told him?"

At that moment, Kevin walked in. "You know, I can hear you two arguing in the next room," he said.

Tiyshio got over excited, pulling on his muscles, trying to sit up. Siyshi pulled him down again as soon as he screeched.

Kevin laughed and gave Tiyshio a hug. "I didn't think you'd be that happy to see me, Z junior?"

Tiyshio also laughed in response. "Well, I thought you'd be dead."

"The funny thing is, I thought you would be. They tried their hardest to trace where you went. Which gave me enough time to talk to Siyshi, over here, and tell her what she needed to do to save your life. Once I did that, I teleported out. They followed my trail for a while until I knocked out Shawn. After that, Derek stopped following. Or should I say Taylon?"

"Okay. So how did you get here?"

"I had teleported away to Grand Central Terminal, in a bathroom stall, of course. I lowered my energy level, then disguised myself. I knew there would be more of them somewhere in the station. I kept my head down until I hopped on a train."

"All right. That's good that you weren't followed," Tiyshio replied.

"I know we know we've seen Rigions that were friends, family, people we don't know," Siyshi said. "They all treat us as traitors. That makes Shawn bad, as a Rigion. He was close to us. Is he just brainwashed?"

"Not exactly. Those who become Rigions need a drive of some kind. In Shawn's case, his drive was Tiyshio killing his mother. Now, based on what I've experienced, he will not stop until Tiyshio is dead, or gets his attention if he doesn't fight. Also, his anger may grow further because of what happened long ago with his father. I may be wrong. Everything could come from Derek himself. Time will tell. Shawn's eyes, when I looked at them…" Kevin looked Tiyshio sternly in his own eyes. "It's the eye of redemption."

"The eye of redemption? I thought Rigions all had the same kinds of eyes?" Siyshi sounded confused.

"They start the same," Kevin replied, "but the stages are different, during which they look different. There are supposedly four different types of eyes: Redemption, Rage, Sorrow, and Pain,"

"Also, there are two diverse types of Rigions. Born Rigions and Altered Rigions." Tiyshio added.

"What is an Altered Rigion?" Siyshi asked.

"You said it already. Those who are your family, your friends, even what Shawn is right now, that's what an Altered Rigion is." Tiyshio replied.

"Well, what are the major differences between the two?" she followed up.

"Born Rigions are born without a drive or subliminal strives. Born Rigions don't change. Altered Rigions can be a bit iffy. Sometimes they revert to who they originally were, still knowing what they did, but the effects of being a Rigion stay with them. They might even turn back into a Rigion, but in some weird way. This is only based on what I've heard. I haven't seen any such transformations myself yet."

"So, what do these different eyes do? Where does the conflict change on the person it's on?"

"First, each eye of a Rigion goes through four stages, each of which gives the individual a push thought to achieve the next stage. Every time another stage gets unlocked, it increases their strength, powers, and agility. Their bodies change. They adapt to their new abilities, and harness them, as well. Their emotions become unbalanced. Their judgment is impaired. For starters, Deska, the eye of redemption, is common in the Rigion society. These are the same eyes as Zorigan had when he fought the Zorians, and Nighcos as well. The eye's main power is to make the person redeem themselves from whatever they couldn't accomplish. That could be winning a fight, having more time, or saving their family." He looked away with a somber expression.

"The Eye of Redemption may or may not be able to change back," Tiyshio continued. "However, the three other eyes are permanent. Or so they say. Aida has the eye of sorrow, and she's at the final stage."

"What is the eye of sorrow?"

Kevin leaned forward. "Yui, the eye of sorrow, is given by a teardrop to another person. It allows a person to live out whatever pain was originally stored inside them. Including the pain that caused their change. They would hate whoever caused their sorrow, even if it were a loved one they've lost. Inij, the eye of pain, is what Derek has. He is also in the final stage. It is one of those eyes that can only be gained by the influence of a Rigion, not simply given by a stare or teardrop. To be honest, it's nearly earned."

Kevin chuckled before continuing.

"The most common reason they get this way is not from the influence of the pain given, but of failure. Nighcos had this in the beginning. When this conflict started, something happened to his sons when they fought Zorigan. He came back with these eyes. Later, they changed to Deska. The only one I know who can control them is Derek. He knows how, somehow."

"I don't understand," Siyshi said. "So anyone can become a Rigion that way?. Meaning, they just need to experience loss, pain, failure, and then… poof?"

"No, no, no!" Tiyshio quickly replied.

"Not exactly," Kevin answered. "A Rigion needs to be where the process is, like a seduction. Pheromones are given off, and the energy must match… or collide, in this case." Kevin chuckled before continuing.

"The last is Vekta, the eye of rage. This may be the second most powerful eye, third if you count Zorigan's eye now. The eye of rage is another one given to the individual from energy. In this case the energy is fed and attacked from the person wanting to give the eye to a member. The eye is a poison to the mind. Everyone it influences can become an enemy, if they are not Rigions. Most of those possessing these eyes are enforcers, assassins, and generals. They make for efficient workers."

"Back to Aida," Siyshi said. "What was her plan?"

"I don't know, exactly. For years, the Rigions wanted me. Perhaps she had a new plan to incorporate Shawn into their objectives."

"How, is what I am asking!?"

"I think I know how." Kevin began to slowly pace around the room. They watched him in great anticipation, based on the anxious look on his face.

"Jesus Christ! What is it?" Siyshi shouted.

"After the original Alam died, the people knew he would return in some other way, as the other generals did, as Cozens. The people asked, if the ability could be given to a person of unjust means, can it also be taken away? The Alam realized that could indeed happen.

And granted them a ritual ability to transfer his essence to another individual, instead of returning every hundred years or so through reincarnation. Aida knew Zorian alchemy. She may have known some way to transfer the Cozen over."

"Won't work!" Tiyshio stated firmly.

"What?" Kevin shouted.

"Cozens can only be transferred to other Zorians, and the few that knew how to do it are dead. Making that not possible."

"You would hope so, wouldn't you? Cozens can be transferred to Rigions in theory. Everything makes them like us. Who's to say Shawn couldn't be the new Alam? Despite what she told her son."

"But she's dead," Siyshi argued. "Does it matter what she had planned? What about Mr. Ryan? I am sure he has his own agenda."

"You are not wrong, Siyshi," Kevin responded, "but I cannot rule out what Aida may have had planned for him. For all I know, Derek has his own plans, too, that could lead into Aida's. Including what they may want with Telsa. Only time will tell."

"Is Telsa the woman Tiyshio saved back then?" Siyshi asked.

Kevin shook his head.

"Can I know more about her?"

Kevin and Tiyshio exchanged worried looks, Tiyshio quickly replied, "I will tell you another time."

While she sat there agreeing, it bothered to her to feel shut out.

"Whatever he wants with Telsa could just be a foolish ploy," Kevin added. "Taylon and I do have a history, but I doubt that would matter this late."

"Are you going to keep an eye on him?" Siyshi asked.

"Like a girl staring at a basketball star. I've got a bad feeling about this whole thing. I don't want Derek to know where any of you are, including Shawn. If he follows up on whatever Aida had planned for him, he will eventually be stronger than you, Tiyshio. The few places Shawn would look for you now are at school, home, or even here. I asked your parents if Tiyshio could stay with you and your sister. They know the situation, and I know now that your sister won't take the news easily, just like you. I will put you all in a safe house in Brooklyn. There are enough rooms for everyone to sleep in. NO FOOLING AROUND!"

"Not like I could, anyway. Her parents are here."

"Yeah, and you're slick, so shut up!" Siyshi laughed. Tiyshio looked embarrassed because he was right. Tiyshio had his ways.

"You will be escorted to school, and your parents escorted to work, at all times. If the threat turns out not to be so bad, I will be more lenient. Your parents will have to give my people their grocery list and arrange deliveries. Until this is over, normal life is *not* permitted."

"What about you, Kevin?" asked Siyshi. "Will you be staying with us?"

"No. I have to leave you all alone. My presence would only increase the threat level. I will be tracking this whole thing in the meantime. Clear?"

"That's all clear."

"Okay, guys, dinner's ready," Hitomi politely announced as she entered the room. "It'll be at the table."

Sunshi pulled Tiyshio aside. Seeing the trouble take him over bothered her. She brushed his hair back. "How are you feeling about all this?"

"Sun, as much as I can't do anything, I have to do something."

"Why?"

Tiyshio felt almost rushed to reply, but his calming voice brought him some ease.

"A conversation Shawn and I had a week prior... and then there's what happened today. Siy, I have to try to make things right. Right now, I don't know what to do."

"But Tiyshio, is being a Rigion what he wanted?" The room was now empty. Siyshi saw only Kevin by the door, waiting for them. Siyshi's expression begged for an answer, without saying a word.

"Let's just go eat."

They made their way downstairs as, conveniently. Sunshi came through the door. She greeted everyone by with a bow the minute she walked in.

"Dinner's ready, Sun. Go put your stuff away," Hitomi told her daughter.

"So unexpected to have you all here today, on a Monday," Sunshi noted on her return downstairs. "What's the occasion?"

Her mother looked at her, appalled. "Sunshi!" she chided.

"I'm sorry. What did I do?" She giggled.

"You don't ask that of our guests. Besides, Kevin and Tiyshio are considered family here. They are always welcome."

"Thank you, Hitomi," Kevin said awkwardly. Tiyshio's eyes widened as Kevin stared back at him, looking nervous as he sat down.

The rest of them followed his example. Tiyshio stayed with his girlfriend, Sunshi sat next to Kevin, and Hitomi settled down with her husband, Diego. Diego was a dark-skinned Black man, looking to be in his mid to late thirties. He appeared exotic and dashing. With the black sweater, he wore beige pants and white socks. His eyes were misty, and his lips set in a permanent smile. His low-cut hair was complimented by a small goatee.

Both Hitomi and Diego had been born and married on the planet Kinta. Their powers were similar, being elemental. They both possessed low-level telekinesis from Kevin's experience, but unknown to them.

"I apologize, Mrs. Guerra," said Tiyshio, "but what is this food here? I hope that wasn't rude of me to ask again."

"No, Tiyshio, it's fine. We are having sweet and sour duck. Also, I made your favorite, Siy, white rice, and sautéed vegetables. Tea, anyone?"

They all replied, "Yes, please."

"Now remember, soup first, then the main course. Tiyshio and Kevin, would you prefer a fork to chopsticks?"

"No, it's fine," both replied.

"I can eat with these now, actually," Tiyshio added enthusiastically.

"That's good!"

Sunshi couldn't help noticing the painful silence she wasn't used to during dinner, as well as the awkward stares and the food playing. The bothered look from Tiyshio particularly made her want to go ballistic. Tiyshio would never remain silent for one minute, and Kevin could talk politics all day.

"All right," she blurted out. "What's going on? No one has finished eating. It's as if you're waiting for the second coming. What's going on?!"

They all glanced at her a fraction of a second, then kept their heads down.

"Don't answer all at once, now," she continued. "It's not every day Tiyshio and Kevin show up here. It must be something serious. Just say it!"

"Sunshi, calm down!" Diego gently ordered. Hitomi quietly called out her husband's name to keep him from making things more uncomfortable. Siyshi nudged Tiyshio, who acted like he wasn't being pestered to say anything. Only Kevin's giving him a look of concern made him feel under pressure.

"SHAWN BECAME A RIGION AND I PUT US IN DANGER! HAPPY?" he shouted.

Sunshi, stunned, dropped her tough demeanor. The others stared at her. She reflected their shock right back, rising as soon as a tear began to form in her eyes.

"Sun, wait! SUN, WAIT… SUN!" Tiyshio cried. He followed her up the stairs until she slammed the door to her room in his face.

Slowly, Tiyshio returned downstairs and took his seat again, letting out a deep breath.

"See? Was that hard?" Siyshi asked.

"You know what? That went better than expected," Tiyshio replied enthusiastically.

CHAPTER
SEVEN

DIFFERENCES

Tiyshio and Shawn passed each other like ghosts in the hallway of their middle school, right in front of an unsuspecting Sunshi. She noticed Shawn hid behind the hood of his sweater, and Tiyshio had a guilty look, the same one he gave when passing Shawn every day.

This time, Tiyshio paused after passing him, his face twisted in annoyance. Sunshi thought his eagerness might be getting the better of him, and distracted him by mouthing, "Come here!"

Tiyshio was reluctant to join her, trapped, watching him prepare for next period.

"Come here!" she called again, low enough to avoid drawing attention to herself. Tiyshio glanced at her, then back to Shawn, who was leaving.

He was noticeably frustrated.

"I don't know if it's the right time to talk to him yet, Tiy," Sunshi advised. "Your body language says it all."

"Yeah? What does it say?" Tiyshio asked sarcastically.

"It's not my fault," she mocked. Tiyshio smiled as she walked alongside him, silently letting him soak in feeling unrewarded.

"You know what happened yesterday?" she asked finally.

Tiyshio stopped and shook his head.

"She's gone," she replied.

"Gone, as in dead?"

Sunshi nodded, nudging him to continue on the way to their next class.

"Kevin told my dad the news. I was sure he would tell you, too, being he's your friend and all."

"He's your friend, too, Sun."

"I know, but you two had been close up until his dad died. You two haven't even talked in a year. Pop thinks it's that radical group again. You know, the same one that killed his own dad?"

Tiyshio sighed. He didn't want to be reminded. "Disgrace to our people, that's what they are."

"Your thoughts on the whole thing?" Sunshi looked oblivious to how the news seemed not to affect him in any way.

Tiyshio walked to his locker to grab his books.

"HEY! WAIT!" Sunshi yanked Tiyshio back violently, pulling his arm out.

Tiyshio yelled in frustration. "You want to be easy on me, Sun?"

"You haven't answered my question!"

"Doesn't mean you have to yank on my arm! Shit, that hurt!" Tiyshio cooled his arm with cold pressure, to heal it faster. "You want my opinion? I don't think they were Zorian, because how could a radical person take refuge in a world where you can barely fight? They would've died before they could run. So, they must have been..."

"Rigions? Come on, Tiyshio. No matter what planet you are on, there are bad people out there! Even if they cowardly run away to survive, they gotta live, too. You have to understand that people out there, like

the ones who killed Shawn's dad, think they are doing justice for people like you."

"People like me?" Tiyshio scoffed.

"Royalty!" she explained sarcastically. "My point is, right now may not be the best time to let him know you are not the enemy. We already know Shawn feels as if Zorians are the worst, whereas you feel they are anything but. All that thought of my race are saints needs to be put aside. You'll just come off as apologetic for people you neither know nor control. Shawn is alone right now. He may be staying at my place for the time being, but he's alone. What he needs isn't someone apologetic. He needs someone that can be family to him. When the time is right, remind him why he trusted you back then, and how he can still do so now. Show him you are family."

Sunshi left Tiyshio to ponder her words. He glanced at his schedule, saw he shared the next class with her, anyway. He took a deep breath before entering the classroom.

Sunshi sat next to Shawn, greeting him with a cheerful, "Hi." Shawn smiled at her. She returned the look. Her face helped him to smile more in these darker times.

"Before you say anything," Shawn said, "I feel okay."

"How did you know I was going to ask?"

"Because, Sun, you are predictable. No matter when, you always wanna cheer someone up. You were the same way a year ago."

Sunshi laughed. "Really? I am really like that, aren't I?"

Shawn shook his head.

"Well," she continued, "it's only because I care about you, and I don't want to see you feel like you're alone, because you're not."

Shawn shook his head again, his smile fading.

"Yeah, but what if I was Tiyshio?" he asked. "Suppose what happened to me, happened to him? Would you still do the same?"

"Well, I care about him, too, but seeing how you were yesterday and all before this, I care about you more…"

His heart warmed. Without thinking, he grabbed her hand. She held on, feeling warmer herself.

On entering the classroom, Tiyshio saw Shawn and Sunshi enjoying each other's company. More so, seeing her hold his hand, making the hairs on his own arm stand up.

He calmed himself down, read her mind, and said, "That was a quick transition."

Tiyshio then took his seat behind Sunshi. "I hope you don't mind me interrupting?" he asked.

Sunshi and Shawn shook their heads.

"How's it going, bud?" Tiyshio asked.

"I'm doing better than yesterday, if that's what you mean?" Shawn replied.

The pair of them smiled.

"I'm sorry I can't bring myself to be as enthusiastic as I'm used to," added Tiyshio. "Since your dad was killed; things have been different between you and me. I can't understand what you are going through, but I do understand your mistrust and anger. I get it."

Shawn met Sunshi's trusting eyes. Her expression changed from a bright view to a comforting embrace as she gripped his hand a little tighter.

"To be honest," Shawn answered, "The first time this happened, I didn't know if I could ever trust your people anymore. I felt I couldn't trust Kevin. Worst, I couldn't trust you. This time, I feel they're all responsible. People like you; I mean. I won't ever be fully able to because I lost my grandfather to your people. My own people felt helpless that you couldn't save our planet. I felt helpless because I saw one of them change into a Rigion, who then killed my entire family. My mom and dad were killed by Zorians. As far as I know, there aren't many Zorians on this planet, except for you and Kevin, who have shown me any kindness and generosity. How do you know he wasn't the one who killed them? If I think back to a year and a half ago, that's the first time I remember that he met them. So, I don't know Tiyshio. How do I know it wasn't him?"

"Kevin's the one who brought you to Sun's place," Tiyshio replied. "He made sure you were with safe people. Kevin is not a high-profile person. I am not a high-profile person. Shawn, I know it's easy to blame *me because of what I am, but we are not all the same. Ask Sun. She knows how much I hope you are okay. Believe it or not, I've felt alone here too. It's hard to turn to someone to trust, but you are my brother, Shawn. I care about you."*

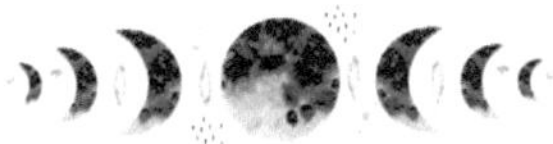

Shawn opened his eyes. He barely made out the fan spinning on the ceiling. A clenching feeling rushed through his veins as he scurried to stand up. It didn't help that everything around him appeared double.

Shawn walked into the bathroom, stared at himself in the mirror. Noticing the same torn-up clothes from the other day, and the eyes, he quickly buried his face in the water. Rubbing his eyes, he reflected on his mother's last question to him. Seeing the Rigion eyes, he felt as if his body was slowly submerging under ice. The memory of his mother being killed in front of him heightened their color. He grew even more petrified.

Then he heard a voice in his head, faint but clear.

"*It was my choice.*"

Only to be followed by the sight of Tiyshio's head at his feet. Blood splattered everywhere. His blades were drenched in it.

His eyes turned back to the mirror. He found himself smiling.

His blood ran cold. He stumbled back, toppling over the edge of this bath. Slowly, he regained his footing.

The red eyes were gone.

"Think of whatever color you want your eyes to be, and it shall be so," said a voice behind him.

Startled, Shawn twisted around, letting a blade form out of the skin he quickly shed. He was more frightened now by the fact that the weapon pulled itself out on its own.

Derek pushed aside the blade that pressed against his neck, cracking it under freezing temperature. It didn't deter Derek at all.

"Would you like some breakfast?" Derek asked, proceeding to the kitchen. Shawn slowly followed.

The rest of the apartment held the aroma of seasonings and the sound of the crackling skillet. Derek's question fell on deaf ears as he asked once more.

The skyline appeared familiar to Shawn. Midtown. Kevin's apartment was directly in the line of sight from Derek's. The view washed away his thoughts.

"I had some clothes brought in for you, as you settle in," Derek advised. "By the way, do you like spicy eggs, Mr. Damana?"

"Your home?"

"A safe house, compliments of the Rigions."

"You helped me the other day, saved me. Why not leave me alone? My mom is dead. You have no further obligation to me."

"I didn't leave you because I'm not gonna let you stay with those Zorian pigs anymore. Their job was to keep you away from people like your mother, keep you safe." Derek placed some eggs on a plate and presented them to Shawn. "Again, do you like spicy eggs?"

Shawn took the plate without saying a word.

Derek felt disrespected, but let it go. "I've never seen the amplification work so quickly. That must be from your mother's bloodline. I found out she was half Rigion, from a race of people that had split from society at the dawn of this universe. Cardogan, that's where your grandmother's from, right?"

Shawn acknowledged the statement. "I remember grandma telling me about it, back home. Teal sky, people living with the land."

"I was surprised you tried to kill me, more than startled. It was not a natural reaction from someone in a safe environment, but rather from someone in danger." Derek snickered, watching Shawn swallow.

"Don't worry," Derek continued. "It's a natural weakness of a Rigion. I will train you how to keep good control of that. That's my job now, to keep you safe and train you. To tell you the truth."

"What can I do now? I lost my mother, and my friend betrayed me."

Derek shook his head.

"First, put on some clothes. I don't know if you lounge around in your boxers all the time at home, but I will tell you now that is not allowed here. According to what you did yesterday, you have demonstrated what you wish to do."

"Yeah? What's that?"

"Simple. You want revenge. Pick out some clothes from the wardrobe in the room you were in."

Shawn returned soon after, freshly dressed, with only one goal in mind: the door. Which he quickly started for, then paused to look back at Derek.

"You're going to stop me?" he asked in a harsh voice.

"Honestly, that depends on you. After what happened, you may decide to go beyond my better judgment."

"And what is that?"

"It's that I'm not going to, I have to, and I will. You may have been half Rigion, but now you are full-fledged. You possess some abilities you do not fully understand. Going after Tiyshio now would be foolish. He's well protected and preparing for the moment you strike. Frankly, I don't know where he is right now. Apart from a place just like this. I am sure Kevin is with him, thinking we are planning our next strike in revenge, because it's crucial to what you want. I have a debt to your mother, which won't be fulfilled if you were to die. If there is any of advice I can give you, it is this: don't fight to kill, fight to survive."

"What do you mean? I held my own. I overpowered him!"

"No, you didn't! All you did was force your strikes because you wanted him dead. Tiyshio held back because he cares about you! Which you have been using his disadvantage. I'm sure by right now he realizes he can't care anymore. Because you do not."

Derek gave him a long stare, Shawn assumed because he was right. Shawn felt uncomfortable, with a divided path in his mind.

"You could've died yesterday, and it would have been on me why."

"HOW? SHE'S DEAD!" Shawn yelled.

"Just because she is dead doesn't mean I am not going to stick to what she wanted me to do when she was around! I admit, you weren't the only foolish one yesterday. I was, too, because I let you almost kill yourself! Your actions reminded me of my own when I was younger."

"Well, I'm not you! You're just doing this to keep me safe?" Shawn scoffed.

"Don't pretend you know me, Casan. All you know is my school persona. I'm just saying he's not worth it. People lose family members every day. That, I know all too well."

"What happened to you?"

"…It doesn't matter. What matters is, I can't let you waste your time on him. At least, not right now. Your mother had other plans for you. Her death puts you in line with many other Rigions who want the same thing."

"What is that supposed to mean? That I should just wait in line? For the brother who killed my family?"

"Well, if he betrayed you, broke your promise, and you want him dead *so* badly, why did you hesitate in your heart?" Derek asked, irritated.

Shawn's thoughts lingered on the sound of their blades clanking against each other, blood dripping from his palm, and the rush he got from seeing Tiyshio's fear. Yet, there was also Tiyshio pulling his friend away from his father's body so as to not get lost in hate. Tiyshio was there to make him feel he had a home when no one else was there for him, mentally.

"I–I just don't know where I would be if I took him out… Tiyshio has been family to me. I think he may not have meant to do what he did… I'm furious he did, but he and Kevin are all I have left."

"Would you be able to live with yourself if you didn't go through with killing him?"

Shawn nodded.

"Maybe walking different paths," he answered, "but if the world ended tomorrow, I'd want him around. So I wouldn't have to die alone."

Derek shook his head, squinting. He sensed a frequency not dissimilar to his own.

"Calm your mind and stay out of my head!" Derek snapped.

Shawn apologized. "I'm still learning how it all works."

"That's why I'm here. So, you can learn how to use your new abilities… What's going on? I know something still concerns you."

Shawn sighed, looking uncomfortably at a picture of his mother in the living room. "How did you *know* her?"

"Your mother?"

Shawn nodded.

"She's my wife. The first time I heard about Aida was after your father's death. I was always in company with Nighcos, while your mother was not. She came to Nighcos begging for his protection, claiming she couldn't trust the Zorians anymore. They had been watching both you and her, planning their next move. Nighcos promised to help and supply security, so, when that day came again, she would be protected. That was about a month before the day you thought you lost your mother."

"Of course, when the day came, she fought most of them."

Derek shook his head. "I intervened and killed the rest of them. She asked them what they wanted. The Zorian told her they knew her family history, just hers, and therefore wanted her whole family dead, including you. She killed him and decided it'd be safer to let you go, for two reasons. She staged her own death, to let the others know she died, as a test to see if they would then go after you. She, unfortunately, left you in the care of a man she felt she couldn't trust. Possibly he was part of the group of Zorians that killed your father—at least, that was what she thought then."

"What are the two reasons?" Shawn notched himself closer to Derek.

"First, your mother didn't know if she wanted you to live the life of a Rigion soldier. What you didn't know was a story your mother told me, which I'll save for another time. She believed exactly what Nighcos believed. When your mother came to him, you were already in the company of a Zorian. You despised Rigions for what happened to you and your family. Growing up with them around wouldn't have been the wisest idea in either's eyes. The other reason is she faked her death to draw most of them out, using you as bait."

"WHAT!"

"I knew you would not like how that sounds, but it was how she kept you safe since the day she was presumed to be dead. She observed you growing up indirectly, watched over you, even with your new guardians. Nighcos and she protected you throughout that time."

"Why?"

"She had reason to believe that the Zorians to whom you were left in the care of were also leaders of the Zorian radicals that killed your father. Even though it wouldn't seem so, since they took care of you, treated you like family. Your mother saw this as a good way to feed a farm animal."

"Feed me until it was time for slaughter."

Derek nodded, disturbed by the sound of the words. "We came today to free you from that. She had reason to believe that before you have graduated, they would have killed you. She begged Nighcos to bring you back to her so that she might fully protect you, shield you from the enemy. She even went as far to believe that they knew Kino. They were but lieutenants to that ex-war general."

"I don't believe you. If they wanted me dead, why not kill me when they first had me in their power? If Kevin were running this whole thing, killing past enemies of the Zorians, why would he train me? Why kill for patriotism? Why kill my family?"

"Zorians live by a code, not to kill a child unless their life is threatened by that particular child, and then show no mercy. There is little doubt that they could be the people we've been looking for, but there is also no doubt that they grew to love you as they cared for you. Or perhaps they were ordered not to kill you until you became of age, in Zorian terms. Meaning, once you turn eighteen, you will be considered an enemy of the Zorian Allied Planets. As for Kino being the leader–I'll be honest. We didn't know. I still don't know."

Shawn brushed the side of his head and took a deep breath. "My whole life is turning upside down."

"I know. Just take a moment. Yesterday, Aida wanted to torture him, ask questions, because of the way he was protecting you. We didn't expect him to be there with you, but I overheard the conversation between you and Tiyshio. So, I informed your mother. All she wanted was answers. Zorians are known for ending past enemies, like the Rigions. The Zorians are also known for showing no mercy. They would rather leave no one alive. Innocent or not, soldier or not, that is how it has been running for half a century now."

"That sounds more like a Rigion."

"You believe that Zorians don't operate the same way? Remember who triggered this war."

Shawn stayed silent. Derek searched his thoughts, seeing only the golden planet.

"The fact that Kino is a general in the Zorian army should tell you by now that they live by that code. It is fed or burned through their brains during their training to become soldiers. It's to demonstrate that they show no trust for their enemies."

"I can't accept them being who you told me. They've taken care of me a long time. They're family to me!"

"Yes, but they are family you cannot trust! They may have more reason to kill you now than before, if my theory is true."

"Then that leaves me with no family. No one I can trust."

"No, that's not true. You can trust me. I am your family now. I've cared about you since the day I first saw you. I took care of you during those times I could see you. This was your mother's and my mission, not only to save you, but to end them. Your mother didn't want me to include you in this for the very reason you just said. She's gone now, and you know the truth. I leave it up to you, what you wish to do. I think this is what deserves your vengeance. More than your dispute with Tiyshio."

Shawn gazed, distraught, at his mother's photo. What she must have experienced, during those times his guardians made him feel at home! How disgusted she must have been made his heart hurt. Knowing he was around an enemy ready to kill him as soon as the time was right.

Derek sat beside him, stoic, but Shawn felt he understood the weight coming down on him, bearing it just the same. His eyes began to swell.

A teardrop splashed onto his egg.

CHAPTER EIGHT

PLAN

There is nothing like a peaceful morning. Hearing birds sing, wind blowing against the leaves. Tranquility and luminance are but a contrast.

Sunshi remained under her covers. Light shone, faintly, through a small hole in the fabric. She felt comforted, surrounded by a dark abyss.

The darkness turned to windows into her past. Disembarking from their ship, which was programing to break down in an acid bath as soon as they arrived on earth. Her first days at school, with her sister. Seeing her sister make friends while she herself roamed, alone, through empty hallways. Sitting beside Tiyshio, as he curled up in her seat.

Tiyshio and Shawn were little more than fresh faces. They were heading home, walking down the block they'd continuously take until their high school years. She remembered trailing behind the boys. Seeing them occasionally take a peek at her, discomforted but shy in her presence.

"I've never seen her around others," she thought she heard Shawn say.

"Yeah, just us. I don't mind. She's cool." Tiyshio's stare somehow made her feel at ease. Shawn's look, right after, tensed her up again.

"Do you have any friends?" Tiyshio finally asked her.

"Aren't you guys?" she replied.

"Ye–" Tiyshio yelled.

"No–" Shawn yelled.

The two boys stared at each other, halting in their tracks. She could see what was going on between them. It was hilarious, actually, to watch the pair be at odds with each other, apparently for the first time. Tiyshio gave a wide smirk. Shawn had been with him since the first day they met. How could he deny their relationship?

"Sure, you're one of us," Shawn reluctantly admitted.

Sunshi couldn't get more jittery. "I knew you had it in you." She started to walk past him, only to be caught in Shawn's arms on a bench overlooking the river. She rubbed his chin, feeling warm on that cold and quiet night. He was everything, and she was exactly the words he spoke back to her.

"I knew you had it in you."

Her heart warmed as she looked at him, but then his grip on her tightened. His eyes changed. Her own eyes shot up as she pulled against him. His grip tightened further.

"How do I get out of this?"

Shawn took on a more sinister appearance. She freaked, enough to raise the hairs on her arms.

"LET GO!!"

Shawn's hands slipped off. She looked down and saw her own arm stretched out, the hand cocked into a fist. Shawn was flying, far enough away he could not be seen.

Her hands trembled enough for her to throw the covers off her face.

She marched to the bathroom, storming past Tiyshio in the hallway, not even hearing him greet her.

From his viewpoint, something odd was up.

He dressed soon after, approaching his girlfriend's door like an excited dog. She opened it before he could knock. Their communication came without words. She sighed. Tiyshio rolled his eyes, knowing exactly how she felt.

Breakfast was no different. Diego and Hitomi scanned the table with its awkward silence. Siyshi ate slowly, playing with her hair, watching her sister. Tiyshio isolated himself to concentrate on his plate, because Sunshi stared him down. Sometimes she was too distracting for him not to look back.

They continued this odd game until she finished her breakfast and headed back upstairs.

"How long is this going to last?" Diego asked.

"As long as it needs to," Hitomi replied.

Tossing herself back under the covers, Sunshi considered how much Tiyshio impacted her life. He would include her anytime he went out to play or ask her to sit with Shawn and himself when they'd first met. She fell for all of it, becoming protective of the family for what they had done for her. She'd even fallen for Tiyshio, although that didn't last long.

She could relate to Shawn better. She felt like an outcast amongst people who could not understand the abandonment she felt. Leaving her home world, coming to Earth, seeing people that looked normal but weren't exactly *normal*, felt foreign to her.

Shawn had the same sensation when he came and first arrived on Earth, surrounded by people who weren't like him. He felt he didn't belong. Whenever Tiyshio wasn't around, Sunshi and Shawn grew closer, to the point at which she fell for him, because he made her feel she was not alone anymore.

She glanced at a picture on the wall of Shawn looking delighted as ever, with Sunshi smooching him on his cheek in the photobooth.

Siyshi peered at her sister from behind the door to her room. From her vantage point, it looked as though her sister was sleeping. Yet, after that weird breakfast, how could she sleep? She had barely gotten any rest in the past few days.

The days rarely lent themselves to a quiet home, especially with Tiyshio around. Whenever he visited, the house became alive and vibrant. Now it seemed stuck in the past, like her sister staring at that photo as she lay in her bed.

"Morning!" Siyshi said timidly, in Japanese, before entering the room. The nearer she approached the bed, the more obvious it was that her sister was not asleep.

"You miss him, don't you?" Siyshi asked in Japanese.

Sunshi looked up, quickly tucking the photo under her pillow. Siyshi rolled her eyes at the absurdity of her actions.

"There's no need to hide how you feel. It's not as if I hate him or anything. He's my friend, too, you know."

Sunshi sighed, falling back onto her pillow in relief. Her sister lay next to her.

"What can I say?" she replied. "It feels wrong, wanting to be with him. Like, he could still be the same person, regardless of what happened between him and Tiyshio, you know what I mean?" Her voice grew shaky.

"We could both hope?" Siyshi smiled, holding her sister's hand yet feeling melancholy.

Sunshi nodded, rubbing the tears from her eyes.

"I wish there was something we could do," her sister offered, "but things change, and so do people. Some people are willing to be by your side. Some aren't, at least, not right now."

"You mean Tiyshio?" Sunshi asked in a hostile tone.

"Screw Tiyshio! You know who I mean! I think he's justified."

"So you also think that what Tiyshio did was wrong?"

"At first I did, but now I think what he did was an action that worked best at that very certain time. I might've done the same thing. I know you would have, too —"

"But –"

"But nothing! It's been a week, and I've thought about it every day, and I'm tired of fooling myself into thinking I would've done anything differently –"

"You are just siding with Tiyshio!"

"No, I am not. If it were mom, dad, or you in Kevin's position, I would do anything to stop her, even if that meant killing her. This isn't about my feelings for Tiyshio. I like him a lot, but you matter to me more!"

Siyshi sighed, feeling herself get heated despite being so soft toned. A sensation of ease then came over the room. Even the tension in her sister's hands released as they stared into each other's eyes.

"What would I do without you?" Sunshi asked jokingly, clearing away her tears. They both laughed.

"Sun, don't hate Tiyshio for what he did, and don't fear Shawn for what he has become. These are your two best friends, even more so than I am to them. I love you, and I hate to see you hurt like this. Tiyshio doesn't want to kill Shawn for what he is. He doesn't see him as an enemy."

"I'm sure Shawn is not, but, sis, I hope what you are saying is right, because they both need you."

"Actually, I think they need you more, Sun."

When Diego returned to the living room, he found Tiyshio sitting on the couch, watching television. He rolled his eyes and walked over to him slowly.

"Son, what do you got planned to –"

Tiyshio appeared to be sleeping. Diego groaned and left him to check on Tiyshio's room, to see if he had unpacked.

His daughter Siyshi patted him on the back. "He's gotten no sleep, dad. He's quicker than most of us." All of his boxes were folded shut and put to one side. His clothes, too, were properly placed.

"What about you, dad? Did you and Mom unpack?"

"We've been working on it since yesterday. We have a lot of stuff, you know?"

"*I'm sure you do.*" Siyshi said.

"You saw how much stuff he had?"

"Yes, I did, dad."

"It was double what me and your mom have. I wonder how he was able to fit all of it into that room. How's your sister?"

"I did what I could. It's up to her now."

"Why do you say it like that?"

"Well, look at her. She's acting like it's the end of the world. I think we may not even need the safe house but –"

"Better be safe than sorry," they said at the same time.

Diego loved how similarly he and his daughter thought, even smirking at each other after their remark.

"Yeah! Something like that. Dad, I know you feel awkward with him around."

"Who, Tiyshio?" he whispered.

Siyshi nodded.

Diego looked at Tiyshio. The way he sat made him uncomfortable because he looked as if he was awake. "I'm sure no father would be in the same predicament I am right now."

"Are you uncomfortable? I swear, I won't do anything with him."

"Siy, I wasn't worried about him before you said anything. I was a teenager once, too, you know. Though it wasn't on this planet, we still indulged in the same foolishness as you and he."

"DAD! We never did anything!"

"Mmhm!"

"I freaking swear!"

"On ya mama?"

"On mama, no doubt!" she clamored. "So, it won't be weird to you, then, that he's here?"

"Oh, no, that shit is definitely weird to me. The boy who's dated both my daughters! I'm surprised I still like him. Let alone, that I let him stay with us. It's as if Kevin messed with my mind or something. I'm glad, though, that you two chose this boy. He's a good kid, even if he's in way over his head right now. I just hope it's not like this for the whole school year."

"Because you like your privacy," Siyshi said in a snarky tone.

"Damn right, I like my privacy! Add that with not seeing the two of you kiss, either."

Siyshi laughed.

"You hear anything from your other friends?" her father continued.

"From Jason and Chris?"

Diego bobbed his head.

"They got to stay in their houses," Siyshi said, annoyed, as she started helping her father with the dishes.

"What the hell!"

"I know, right? I heard it was because they aren't in much immediate danger compared to us. That Kevin told them it's better we stay close to Tiyshio. We could protect each other, and he would know where all of us are."

"Sounds like control."

"Yeah, it does. Usually, one would keep two targets distant from each other. One doesn't know where the other is, you know? It's the easiest way for no one to get hurt."

"Yeah, but eventually someone will find out. They always do."

"Is that the only reason? I figure they would be targets, too."

"Perhaps. Chris told Kevin that Hayden wouldn't get involved. As for Jason, well, I don't know about Jason. He's always doing his own thing. I can't imagine him jumping into the conflict if he had no reason to fight."

"He's not the protecting kind?"

"Meh, kind of, but not really."

"Why is that?"

"Perhaps childhood trauma?"

"Or perhaps they won't make irrational moves," Tiyshio said, having risen from the couch.

"Hey, babe, how was your nap?" Siyshi asked.

"I was talking to Kevin," Tiyshio replied. "I wanted answers myself. Mr. Guerra, you were asking about Chris and Jason, right?"

"Yes, I was."

"I have to head over to see them soon also, to answer your earlier question, by the way."

Diego looked at his daughter in shock and horror. Siyshi just smiled as she put dishes away.

"The simple answer is that they aren't or haven't dated me."

Diego scoffed. "Okay, Casanova, calm down."

"Hey, you wanted a simple answer."

"I wanted an answer, not just a simple one."

"You're right. All jokes aside, there's less chance they would put themselves in harm's way to speak reason to Shawn, if he were to ever come close. Also, with Derek involved, Shawn probably wouldn't see them as a threat. For all we know, Derek deliberately wants me to fight Shawn, to help him achieve his full Rigion transformation."

"How would he do that with you?" Diego asked.

"Anger, hate, lust, anything that heightens his emotions, gets him in the mindset he wants, just so he becomes more like them. He could use any of you against me if he found you. As far as Kevin knows, though, neither Derek nor Shawn know of this place, or the route that Siy and Sun have been taking day-to-day."

"What about me and my wife going to work?"

"Illusionist masking your identity. You would never know who's doing it. They're good."

"Better than Aida?"

"Aida is dead," Tiyshio stated.

"No doubt," Diego stated mockingly.

"Hey, babe, why are you heading over there?" asked Siyshi.

"They want to talk about what to plan for next. To be honest, it's not a bad idea. We should all be over-prepared. I don't want anyone hurt."

Sunshi's thoughts continued to dwell on Shawn, even when she didn't want to think about him. The more she retreated, the more she felt the vibrations around her becoming vicious. Her eyes closed. All she wanted to do was rest and dwell on what her sister told her. The feelings she had were distracting.

She was in a place she had never seen before, a brightly light apartment with two bedrooms and minimal furniture. She entered one bedroom to see Shawn sitting on the bed, facing the door. He wore battle armor. The chest plate bore an "S" engraving.

She rushed back into the living room. Derek turned toward her, came at her. Panicking at his swift movements, she saw only one exit, the bedroom.

"This isn't real," she muttered, pressing her hand over her heart, begging it to slow down.

Seeing Shawn's shadow cast over her on the bedroom door didn't help.

The setting changed again to Shawn's old room. His face was shrouded in darkness.

"What is this place?" she asked.

"This is Derek's, in midtown, near Kevin's," Shawn explained. "I haven't been outside."

"I figured as much, but this is your old home. Why are we here?"

"A place you can tell represents something of me? How do I know this is real?"

"I asked the same question. I wonder if it's in your mind?"

Shawn looked behind him, then back at her. He seemed to recognize the floorboards and walls. Sunshi seeing him scan the room, was like watching him relive those memories.

"Baby, what happened yesterday?" she asked. "Is there anything I can do?"

Scanning the living room, Shawn found a VHS tape. He popped it into the VCR.

It was a tape of the first time they went to Coney Island.

"I remember this," Shawn said. "It was a fun day. What happened to me last week? What didn't happen? I found out my mom is alive. My best friend betrays me. Then it turns out Mr. Ryan is my stepdad, and he's been a Rigion all this time. Oh, and that's not the last of it. I've also been told my foster parents are the people who killed my dad and tried to kill my mom."

"Is that why the picture of them next to your bed is partly torn?"

"I don't know." He turned to look at the image. "I know they took me in. Treated me like family for the past three years. I know what Derek showed me can't be denied."

"How is that possible? What if he only showed you something you could believe? What if it was fake? Something that appears too good to be true."

"Then you tell me how images of the known murderers of my dad are in the same picture as my foster parents, walking through Central Park, talking to each other."

Sunshi stayed silent.

"You know, last week my life turned upside down, Sun. Yesterday, we were on a high-speed chase, running away from my only real relative. Someone who I haven't seen in five years came here to surprise me. Who only wanted to take me back, not to be a Rigion, no? To escape this war, find somewhere else to be! To go somewhere we could be safe, where wouldn't have to worry about who's hunting us. Who's on what side. Just pure freedom! She'd leave this planet for the same reason our parents came here, to get away from this shit. What's funny is, now I have the feeling that they knew all this time. Whether it's true or not, I just feel like they knew, and they wanted to keep me away from what she is."

"Why did you bring me here?"

"Funny you should ask. I felt you were the one who brought me here. I am not telekinetic, but something changed in me that feels like I might have been. I know you'd understand this place. We always find our ways to each other." He slowly paced around the bedroom.

"You need a way to find your truth. Shawn, I love you. I would hate to see you do something you would regret. These people are not your enemy. Nor is Tiyshio."

Shawn halted to turn back to Sunshi. She was startled by his harsh gaze. He approached her slowly, until she was pinned to the wall.

"He's not my enemy, yet you fear me now?" he calmly questioned. "Why are you afraid of me? Is it because of what I've become, or what Tiyshio told you?"

The air around her grew thin. She was too frozen to say anything else. Part of her felt he might be right.

"I do think it was you who looked for me... I'll see you next time, Sun."

The walls around her morphed back into her bedroom. Shawn began falling to the floor. As she dropped down to grab him, the door in front of her began to open. She thought the newcomer was Derek. She wasn't fast enough to close it. The door had split from the floor, too far away for her to get to, until everything merged back together. She crashed into the door to prevent it from opening, almost falling onto her mother.

"SUNSHI!"

"Oh my God! I'm sorry, Mom."

Tiyshio and Siyshi looked at her as if she had gone mad. All she could do was laugh it off.

Siyshi lightly punched Tiyshio in the shoulder for laughing himself.

Tiyshio shouted, "Hey!" and nudged her back, softly.

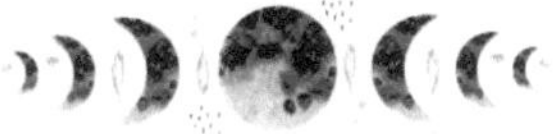

"WHAT HAPPENED?" HER SISTER ASKED, SITTING ON SUNSHI'S BED, next to Tiyshio.

"I saw Shawn in a vision. I don't know how to explain it. I saw him and the place he was in. Then it changed into his old house, when he lived with his folks." Siyshi turned to her boyfriend with a curious look.

Tiyshio shrugged, feeling just as lost as her.

"He has earned the ability to gain other gifts, I guess."

The sisters looked at him in disappointment.

"What else do you want me to say?!" he responded. "I don't have all the answers!"

"Not going to lie. I expected something else," Siyshi admitted.

"Are you sure he was responsible?" Tiyshio asked.

"Before the connection broke, he said he thought that I did it," she said, hesitantly.

Siyshi scoffed, "You did it? Did he forget your strength heightens with your emotion? What does that have to do with telepathy?"

"Telepathy is the pathway to many abilities," Tiyshio explained. "Emotions are connected to our thoughts. Our thoughts are in our minds and, by exercising the utmost control, the ability to read another's mind is possible. Tell me, were you thinking about him before you spoke to him?"

"Tiyshio, this has nothing to deal with –"

"It might come in handy later. Chill. Continue, Sun."

"I did. I tried to get him out of my head. I just couldn't stop. After what Siy and I talked about."

"What exactly did you two chat about?" Tiyshio asked Siyshi.

"Forgiveness. You three have been together for a long time. To see you break apart because of these events would be heartbreaking."

"How do you feel about it?" Tiyshio asked Sunshi.

"Just–give me time," she responded.

"Fair enough," Tiyshio replied.

"Anything else happened?" her sister asked.

"He mentioned Kirk and Amelia. He was told they had killed his father." Sunshi sounded worried.

The other two felt the same.

"No way they did that!" Tiyshio argued. "They're clean! He must know that what he heard is bullshit!"

"Is it? How well do you know Kirk and Amelia, to say that they wouldn't do anything wrong under your and Kevin's noses?"

Tiyshio said, firmly, "I know enough!"

Siyshi's eyes widened at his harsh tone. She partly moved away from him.

"Did he say how he knew?" her sister asked.

Sunshi shook her head, looking to the door. Siyshi felt discomfort and brought her sister a chair.

"Sun, it's okay. I just want to know."

Sunshi took a deep breath, pulling her hair behind her ears. "He didn't say anything. He looked confused and scared."

"He's not used to the change. Part of him wants to go back to normal," Tiyshio said.

"That sounds like good news," Siyshi replied.

"It can be, but I don't want to rule out the possibility that Derek might be messing with his mind."

"What do you want to do?" Sunshi asked with a sob.

"I want you to come with me to meet with the boys. We gotta find out where Kirk and Amelia are right now. We need answers from them."

"You want to see if they really did do it, don't you?" Siyshi asked. "If they did, what are you going to do?"

"Find out who they work for, and why they wanted him dead."

Tiyshio and Sunshi grabbed their things to head out. "I'll be back!" he yelled.

Outside the room, Tiyshio held the door open telekinetically for Sunshi to join him. "You'll be fine with me, right?" Tiyshio asked, jokingly.

Sunshi shook her head. "You want me to go with you, don't you?"

They took the subway to East Flatbush, where Chris lived. Sunshi sat across from Tiyshio, her head down so she couldn't see Tiyshio staring at her. His focused stare could go uninterrupted for minutes on end.

He was thinking of Derek's play, the one he was unable to read, hoping Sunshi wasn't a piece on the board. It looked to be the right move, but Tiyshio wondered if these new pieces were also on the board. What was Derek planning to do with them? Would it still be the same if Aida was still alive, since she just wanted to get away from all this after tying up loose ends?

Only time would tell, he thought. He hoped he didn't think wrong.

Tiyshio wrung the doorbell upon their arrival, then heard a voice call out over the intercom, "Who is it?"

The speaker was Hayden, from what Tiyshio could tell. Sunshi was annoyed by Hayden's over excited voice. Tiyshio patted her on the back.

"It's Tiyshio. Your brother knows I'm coming." Tiyshio said into the speaker.

"Tiyshio, since this morning, my whole day has been upside down. I can't believe that's why Shawn hasn't been to school in forever. And you. What was it you needed again–a person that can alter the Rigion gene?"

Tiyshio nodded

Chris scoffed. "You've got to be kidding me. And Amelia and Kirk are involved in this, how?"

"He claims they killed his dad," Sunshi replied.

"Why not go to Kevin? He's best at handling this kind of thing. Especially with Kirk and Amelia!" Chris and Tiyshio said those last words in unison, but Tiyshio muttered them, mocking him.

"Yes, I know!" Tiyshio uttered impatiently. "Look, he's doing his part to find someone! I know he knows who to talk to, but after what happened in the doc's office, what if he's reluctant?"

"Kevin?" Sunshi asked.

"I would rather not say why," Tiyshio answered.

"All right," Chris replied. "What about, umm, what about the Kirk and Amelia situation?" Chris looked at both of them. The room fell silent. Chris rolled his eyes and scoffed. "What the hell, man? You can't keep your head under the covers for a second, can you? You're supposed to keep a low profile and you're ready to do an investigation. Tiyshio, Kevin is good at this stuff. Best leave it to him."

"Kevin is too close to Amelia and Kirk. He may not make the same judgment call I would."

"Yeah? What's that? Killing them, if they did do it?"

"No! Finding out if they did. They mean a lot to him. He may have a bias, and we can't have that. It will slow us down. However, if they have a great interest in Shawn, it's worth finding out why. Don't you think so?"

"Maybe, but what if we're wrong? What if we don't find out in time?" Chris replied.

"Find out in time?" Tiyshio scoffed. "We have all the time in the world! Derek wouldn't put a timetable on this thing. Why would they rush?"

Sunshi interceded. "Tiyshio, you're being naïve. You know that we have no idea what Derek's plan is! Or if he even has a plan to begin with. Let's focus on the small part for now. Find out where Kirk and Amelia are, and what their deal with Shawn is, before Derek does."

Hayden raised his hand. "Back to Shawn. You said he wants you dead, right?".

Tiyshio nodded reluctantly. Hayden's words brought back the image of the sword piercing Aida. Then Shawn's pure rage filled him. He could feel his anger, and he could feel the fear stirring in him again for what he had done.

"Why do you want to turn him back?" Hayden continued. "It's not as if becoming a Rigion makes you bad, just to be bad. Sure, there is hate, but what you did is unforgivable in any eyes."

The images played continuously in his mind until his imagination reached a conclusion. He pictured himself and Shawn facing each other at the ends of their blades, ready for the ultimate decision. He saw their bout head to a bloody, violent conclusion.

"I'm not expecting forgiveness from him," he said after a long silence. "He can resent me just as much as the next person, and I'd rather do it to keep any of you safe if he goes after you. If he gets to the point where Derek wants him, I'm game. Are any of you willing to back me up? I won't lie. All of you are my weakness. It's something I lack as a warrior. What can I say? I grew up here. I'm not as hardened as my people. Derek, Nighcos, they can use Shawn as any means to get what they want. Including whatever this mark's power has that they fight so much for!"

Tiyshio pointed at the ALAM marking on his arm.

"Then why not take down Derek today, while Shawn is still on his first stage and not ready to trust this guy?" Chirs advised. "This is the total opportune time to do so."

Sunshi put her feet on the coffee table. "That would be smart. If we have a plan. We can't just attack him head-on today. We don't know what his situation is like, if he is protected by other soldiers, or if any traps are set up. This kind of thing needs to be scouted. Am I right?"

"Feet off the table," Chris ordered.

Sunshi lowered her feet quickly. "Sorry."

"Yeah," Chris admitted. "She's right. It's gonna take more than attacking him right now. It would take weeks of planning, knowing where he is, knowing who he's around and what kind of pull he's got. I'm sure he's not just some foot soldier."

"I'd suggest you do nothing," Kevin advised, stepping out of the kitchen into the living room. He carried a chair, which he placed next to Chris. "Tiyshio, what the hell are you doing here? I told you what you should be doing right now!"

"I know, but something happened this morning that made me want to act fast. I'd guess you already know what it is."

"Yes. Siyshi told me everything. By the way, are you okay?" he asked Sunshi.

"Yes. Thank you," she responded quietly.

"You went over there?" Tiyshio asked.

"No. Actually, I was in my safe house researching who I can consider to teach you what you want to do with Shawn. Then, all of a sudden, I felt an unusual presence, possibly someone tapping into my mind."

"Wait. You're saying Siy has telepathy?" Sunshi asked, remembering what happened to herself earlier. She reflected on the possibility she may have made that connection with Shawn.

"She might. I knew it was dormant for a while, even with reading her mind whenever we spoke. What a time for it to come about now."

Sunshi looked at Kevin, confused, then turned back to Tiyshio and Hayden. Tiyshio nodded with a look that read, 'yeah, I knew for a while.'

Chris and Hayden were as surprised as Sunshi.

"What the hell! How long?" Sunshi asked.

"Look, that's not important right now!" Kevin said. "What is important is your plan with Amelia and Kirk. Tread lightly. They're clean." Kevin chuckled a bit, pulling his chair up.

"How can you be so sure?" Tiyshio sounded unphased by Kevin's sincerity.

"I've known them longer than you have, boy. Also, I won't tell you where they are."

"WHAT!" the kids screamed.

"You have no business finding them. Where they are needed to be is best kept secret. Whatever reason you all want to find them needs to be put on the back burner."

"But, Kevin, they may be involved in the mur–"

"Leave that for another time. I also suspect Shawn wants them dead. I just hope it's not for the reason I think it is."

"What would that be?" Chris asked.

Kevin paused. He wanted to say why but, looking at Tiyshio and the rest of them, he quickly hushed himself. He passed the answer off by saying, "It's not important. What matters is that no one can know where they are. NO ONE!"

Everyone but Kevin looked disheartened. Chris offered Tiyshio a raised eyebrow. All Tiyshio could do was smirk.

"If their place of sanctuary is compromised by any of you, that information can be used against you. Derek may be reading your minds. As far as we know, he could be doing so right now."

The group looked confused, especially Tiyshio. He knew that Kevin was likely too far away, and that amount of focus on so many people from a distance couldn't be good for his brain.

"He has eyes everywhere. All his people do, and they all look like you and me. He doesn't need to interrogate any of you to get the information he needs if you are not protected."

"You are our protection, Kevin," Sunshi was quick to say.

"I am one man. I can't protect all of you. Just one at a time."

Kevin turned to the others. "Hayden, I know you asked about this before. Tiyshio's idea for saving Shawn is worth looking into. It has its benefits. No doubt, Shawn may never forgive him, but it would mean our opponents can never use or manipulate him. Right now, he's susceptible to any of their influences. Away from it, his emotions won't skew his judgment. Logic, research, and proper action will take over. I consider that a victory."

"You can't believe something as crazy as that?" Chris exclaimed.

"You're right, it's crazy, but I can believe it. Right now, there are approximately eighty million refugees on this rock. It's guessed that fifty million of them are Rigions, living among us. I strongly believe there is one person on this planet that knows how to alter the Rigion gene."

Tiyshio revealed a look of wonder as he began to smile. Sunshi was the first to notice this, then Hayden.

"Tiyshio?" Hayden asked. "What's up?"

Tiyshio shook his head.

"You're going to look for her? Even knowing they will, too?"

"Yes. If I can get to her before they do, at least she will have my protection."

"You've got to find her. She's the only person we know that's had to deal with this kind of situation."

"I will," Kevin said. He then teleported out of the apartment.

The group exchanged a defeated look. Tiyshio could tell they were thinking about what he did.

"What about the Kirk and Amelia plan?" Sunshi asked.

"Do it in your spare time. I'm not giving up on protecting them or siding with Shawn. It's worth the effort to find out the truth."

With a determined look in his eyes, Tiyshio stared at the empty space from which Kevin had just left.

CHAPTER
NINE

HIDDEN

Changing a Rigion was no simple task, let alone commonly known.

Kevin's desk was littered with pictured files, each stamped in red, as a 'POSSIBLE'. All but one. He was reluctant to go through with his decision to find the person he'd been talking about the other day. Each person he called to made it that much easier for him to make that decision, yet he was still unwilling to make that choice. He knew all too well what it took for this person to achieve what she had attained.

He didn't want to look at the file again. He took a deep breath, hoping for another way.

It was unfortunate that most of the names were crossed off, he thought. The latter part of the list were people who lived on the west coast of the United States, which was too far away.

Except for that particular one.

Aggravated, he accepted what needed to be done. He ripped the page out, crumpled it, and threw it in the trash.

He then teleported out of the apartment.

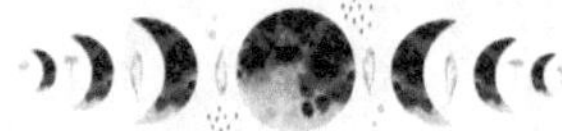

DEREK SCOUTED FROM THE HEDGES AROUND THE SCHOOL. He noticed several odd transparent objects floating in the sky. *They had to be drones, or something like it,* he thought. Dealing with them couldn't be his first move; taking them out would give him away. *If only Aida were here,* he thought. She could have shielded them both, even amongst the dozens of casually dressed soldiers he spotted. It didn't make sense for so many people to be standing in front of the school as if it was a mall.

The school actually looked like more of a government building now, with all the activity that surrounded it. "*What kind of school would be so heavily guarded, to keep it looking normal, even on the weekend?*" he wondered. Derek assumed the interior would contain three times as many figures in the hallways. He needed to make a move, but he also, more importantly, needed to be patient and vigilant. He was more concerned about the drones. He spotted an opening he could take, but the path was intersected by a pair of drones circling one of the locked entrances.

"*Anyone nearby? I need some assistance.*" Derek called out telepathically.

"*Major Taylon, I am on the other end of your location. We are ready for your call,*" a woman responded.

"*All right. I need a distraction to get these drones away from where I am. We don't need Kino knowing we were here.*"

In the distance, from behind the building, a gunshot suddenly echoed.

Derek kept his eyes on the camouflaged drones, waiting for them to move off to that area. He overheard the radio chatter, requesting the soldiers in front to move to the back to check out the disturbance. Shots were fired. The area needed to be searched.

Now was his chance. He inched forward as the drones moved away, then suddenly scurried to the door.

A moment later, he found himself airborne. He struggled to break free, then crashed onto the pavement.

"We—" Derek thrashed against his enemies. They lifted him up, then quickly cracked his skull before he could do anything more.

"Shit!" He could see Kevin tracing the bodies back to him, just for that one sloppy move.

"Someone come clean this up! I'm going inside."

He rushed into the building, spinning the camera overlooking over the door so it would not capture his image. He knew his cover was blown. It didn't matter. He figured he had survived just by getting inside, though he wasn't completely certain he was right.

The soldiers marching in the halls didn't help.

Derek tumbled to his feet, feeling his chest close in, then crawled to the nearest corner just as another set of troops passed by. Looking forward, he could see two more soldiers coming in his direction.

This is it, he thought. This is the day I die, for one misstep.

Abruptly, another figure dropped down from the overhead vent. In seconds, the newcomer then killed the troop that had just passed by Derek, as well as the two heading in his direction.

He let out a sigh of relief. It was one of his own.

"Took you long enough," Derek whispered.

"You were beginning to think I wasn't coming?"

"You had me on edge, Edami," Derek replied as they strode down the corridor.

"No need to worry At least you fulfilled your wife's wish. Might as well do one for yours."

"Thank you!"

"How many of us are outside?"

"Six."

"And those of us who can get inside?"

"Just me. That was the plan."

"What do you need me to do?"

"Take out the people in security and wipe the security tapes. The longer we can keep Kino from knowing what we're doing, the better."

"What are we doing?"

"The next part of Aida's plan."

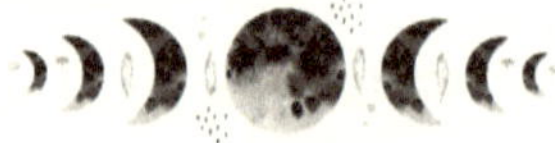

CHRIS LAY BACK IN HIS BED, COMFORTABLE AS AN INFANT, DESPITE the loud music and constant door banging that made his eyes twitch.

"Rocks, I know you're home. Open the door!"

"Hearing Kevin's voice, it must be a dream," he told himself.

The knocking continued, growing louder, as if someone was going to break down the door.

"Come on," he muttered. "Why can't this be just a dream?"

Chris and his next-door neighbor opened their doors synchronously. The neighbor stared at Kevin, her face grim, and yelled, "Can you calm that shit down?"

Kevin and Chris gave the woman a ferocious stare that intimidated her. Her eyes widened in fear. She disappeared back inside her room, muttering, "I don't understand why he got to be so loud."

Both men bore puzzled smiles as Kevin entered Chris' apartment. Chris moved to the kitchen to pour some orange juice into two glasses from the cupboard as Kevin took a seat. They looked at each other for a long moment, each waiting for the other to speak.

Kevin was the more reluctant to do so.

"She's right, you know," Chris blurted out.

Kevin looked at Chris as if he was insane. Chris turned as he finished pouring a glass. "You shouldn't be so loud, so early in the morning."

"It's twelve in the afternoon. Everyone in the building is off doing something except for you."

Chris raised his eyebrows and reluctantly said, "Touché."

"So, what brings you to my place, Kevin?" Chris continued in a more natural tone.

"Something I wish I wasn't here for."

Chris smiled at the shift in Kevin's voice. He was tempted to jump with joy from the expected news.

Instead, he merely shook his head. "I see. So that's why you seem so–irritated."

"I'm not–irritated. I'm just not keen about what I need to do. I prefer to work alone."

"Not true. You prefer working with someone on your level."

Kevin only had one response. "That's what you think."

Chris walked to the table, bobbing his head to one side as he sat across from his visitor. Kevin accidentally placed his cup on a map of Brooklyn that had, "They aren't here!!" written on it, alongside a big circle on Hawthorne and Nostrand Avenues.

"It's been three weeks," Chris observed. "There haven't been any results yet?"

Kevin shook his head, glancing at a picture on the wall of Chris and his family. Chris looked around the age of ten, Hayden closer to eight. They stood in front of their mother and father. A picture across the room looked about the same, showing Chris and his brother, but a little older. His father wasn't in that picture, or any of the other surrounding ones.

Kevin turned back to Chris. "Nope. No one wants to be a part of this effort to just help one person. Or this whole mission, in general."

"That's unfortunate."

Kevin shook his head. "Yeah, it is unfortunate. Many aliens are beginning to settle on this planet, becoming naïve to what's happening around them."

Chris gasped. "Well, are they wrong? So many fled here simply to sustain a normal life."

"Yes, and no! Everyone should be on edge when it comes to the Rigions. Look at us now, the way we've had to be since our own arrival. We are aware. We fight back. Those that aren't can be taken anytime, thinking they are safe. We all should know Earth is only a temporary sanctuary."

Chris shook his head. "You know, for some of us, our home planet is unlivable. We are planetary refugees. Earth is literally our new home. We need to settle down and start a new life, live like human beings."

"You have a solid point, young blood," Kevin admitted reluctantly.

"So, who are these people whose help you needed in order to find someone?"

"They are Telekinetic trackers. that was their task back on their home world. To find the most wanted."

"Sounds familiar. What was your exact plan?" Chris bent forward. Kevin began to slowly lean back, almost slouching.

"To track someone that I am, I was, close to. She is the key to getting Tiyshio to where he wants to go with this. I believe she's been through this before."

"You have no luck with this, how?"

"No one wants to deal with her type."

Chris looked lost. "I don't understand. Her type?"

"Sometimes, in these wars, we end up with something a little more complex. The girl I'm searching for is an interesting case. People would say, *I go too deep.* They tried looking for her, but whenever one of them gets a taste of where she might be, they also get visions of her past, how badly she was treated."

"Who is she?"

"Her name is Telsa Gond. She's a Rigion."

Chris stood. "What the actual hell?"

Kevin rolled his eyes. He knew his words didn't agree with what he stood for.

Chris began pacing.

Kevin rose from his chair, annoyed. He gave Chris a 'Hear me out' gaze.

"You know," Chris said, irritated, "you preach a lot about how much you dislike the Rigions, only to look for one for a good cause. What's so special about her?"

"She was able to break free while being attached. She's the first of them I found who was able to do so. I met her in eighty-two. She was on her own, slightly little older than you and Tiyshio are right now. Seventeen."

"You took her in?"

"I was hesitant at first, but, yes, eventually I did. After a few times meeting at a local diner where she was willing to see me."

"You treated her as your own."

Kevin shook his head. "No. I preferred to treat her as a friend. So much happened in her life. I was grateful she could pass on what she learned to Tiyshio at the time. She's a skilled fighter, caring but troubled."

"What was her task in the army?"

"She was a sleeper assassin for Nighcos. I like to believe it was one of the ways she was able to break free. She wasn't anything special in the army, but she had taken out a lot of resistant cells in London."

"U.K?" Chris asked,

Kevin nodded.

"So she's been dangerous. What makes her not so dangerous now?"

"As I said, I believe it's because of her sleeper status. It's her mind correcting itself, maybe."

"Why did she run away?"

"One weekend, while I was away from home, I left her and Tiyshio together. Tiyshio told me that one minute she had a headache; the next, dozens of soldiers came for both of them."

"Oh, shit!"

Kevin nodded. "I felt guilty for leaving them alone, severely under protected. I felt, if I had been there, none of that would've happened. Although she blames herself for the event, I'd like her to think it wasn't her. Who am I to stop her thinking that? She killed under orders of Nighcos. Word is, she was one of the best, a real hunter, inconspicuous. Like anyone in her state, it affected her mentally. I know Nighcos. If he lost one of his best, he would search for them nonstop. This one, she's the crème de la crème."

"Has he stopped looking for her?" Chris asked.

Kevin stared at him.

Chris sighed. "If you want to find her telepathically, why not use Tiyshio? He's extremely good at telepathy."

"Because his greatest strength can be used against him. It would be too risky. If Derek were to locate him, or Nighcos, our efforts would be lost."

"Hence you came here. You have no one else." Chris sat on the couch and laid back. Kevin released all his tension, nodding.

Chris laughed. "That's why? How come you couldn't just say tha–" Chris raised his eyebrows, realizing what was Derek's reason was, looking at a reflection.

"You know, Mr. Bratt, that attitude is uncalled for. Just be grateful I'm here for your help."

Chris looked disappointed. He shook his head as Kevin brought his own chair from the kitchen into the living room.

"What's the point, if you think I'm not of age?"

"I believe you're on my level, despite other aspects."

Chris shook his head, bothered, "So, what can I do?"

"If anything, I'd like to use your contacts. See if any of them are willing to help me out with this cause."

"Come on! I'm just a kid! I don't have any contacts!" Chris lied, even though he knew he couldn't hold up that lie, since he and Kevin had both looked at the map on the kitchen table. "Shit! Fine, you got me. Why do that with me if it didn't work with you?'

"I'm sure you have better pull than I do. Besides, I've heard you comment that I'm out of touch. Others may react differently to you, you know?"

"I am going to be honest with you. I don't know if they will, given what you just told me."

"Do you have any other bright ideas, smart guy?" Kevin asked mockingly.

"We need to perform a telekinetic pulse, with five to ten people."

Kevin looked confused.

Chris met his gaze. "I'm surprised that's one in a million things you don't know."

"I believe, once you explain, I might indeed know."

"Oh, I hope not, ha-ha," Chris said timidly. "A telekinetic pulse is something we learned from one of your books, funnily enough."

"Funnily enough, I didn't write many of those that have my name as the author," Kevin admitted.

"Ironic. Anyway. in one of the chapters, it speaks of a pulse wave. It's basically when a group of telekinetic people continuously think of the same thing. The technique was usually used to assassinate someone; having so many people penetrating your mind can cause you to go brain dead. There were other aspects, such as being able to use the technique to time travel or teleport. Activities that needed a lot of brainpower. Some races in the Kepler galaxy used it to track people who went out of the connection, so they're able to breach a telekinetic block."

"In all," Kevin replied, "it sounds risky without training. I don't approve."

Chris groaned. "Why not?"

"From how dangerous this sounds, I imagine, if we aren't careful, we could hurt her."

"What other choices do we have, Kevin? You already said you don't want to search for her in the traditional sense."

"It's not that I don't want to. It's too difficult to look for one person amongst millions."

"Listen, this is the only way, okay? If you don't want to hurt her, you can inhibit everybody's minds."

"You want me to be a nullifier?"

"The technique can be anything that makes you comfortable."

"Fine. I'll need you, anyway."

"Why would you need me?"

"You'll see why."

Chris shrugged the comment off and got up, finishing his drink. "Come back when the streetlights go on. I'll make sure to have a few people here for the cause."

Kevin nodded and headed for the door. "Smart man! If possible, bring a weapon with you. You never can know what might happen with this woman."

Chris gave Kevin an odd look. "I don't know, but my weapon is right here." Chris raised his arm.

Kevin shook his head, smiling as he left Chris' apartment.

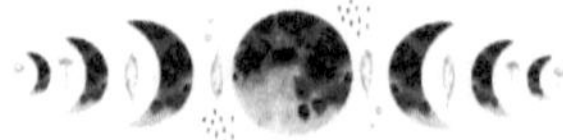

"**O**N YOUR LEFT, THREE COMING UP. **W**AIT FOR MY CALL," EDAMI SAID telepathically.

Derek checked around the corner, confirming what Edami saw from the cameras. Kevin's office was just steps away.

"Any time now," Derek said softly.

The lights shut off.

He rushed in, stabbing the first soldier in the back. The one next to him saw the blade piercing his comrade. He yelled, "INTRUDER!" even as he was thrown against the wall so hard, he died upon impact.

The third soldier attacked Derek immediately. Derek let go of his blade, blocking his attacker's weapon with his hands. He flung him to the side, his attacker still gripping his blade, and kicked him before he could get back up. Derek then pulled the sword into his hands and sliced off the man's head before it touched the ground.

"Edami, get the rest in here. I think there will be trouble."

"*No worries. I am blocking their radio chatter. I can tell someone else is blocking their powers as well. It gives us away, so whatever you need to do, do it fast.*"

"You bet ya!"

Derek cracked open the door and scanned the office beyond. He then knelt and listened. A shimmer appeared behind the desk. He peered over the top, ensuring that the soldier hadn't caught him at the last second.

The woman saw his hand charge up and swiftly rolled away. Derek vaulted toward her. She retaliated, slicing open his calf before he landed. Furious, Derek flung her violently against the wall, telekinetically. He shut her up before she could break free, then crashed her body into the large desk in the center of the office.

Her head smacked against the wall as she rolled into it. Her vision blurred. She became frightened. Pushing items around the room like a bullet, all she could see was the darkness engulfing her.

She pulled out her own sword, blocking his attacks using only her senses. Derek realized she was temporarily handicapped and used that fact to his advantage before her vision cleared again, tripping her in the process. Immediately, her vision returned. The tip of the blade came down like a raindrop. She pushed against his leg, making him stagger. Before his sword could slice her arm, she pulled it away, chucking it into the wall.

She kicked him in the face, forcing him to turn over.

"Kevin said you would come, but there is nothing here for you, Taylon."

Derek grabbed her by the neck telekinetically, then smacked her against the wall again. She tried to break free. The more she strained, the tighter his grip got. It didn't help that she was pinned right next to the sword she had just plunged into the wall. She saw it slowly work its way out as Derek got up.

"If there is nothing here, then why are you? What are you guarding, books?" Derek chuckled. "Where are the location files? I know he keeps them here!"

Derek tightened the grip tighter, pointing his blade at her throat. She made him wait by looking at the blade instead of him.

"You might as well kill me, as you did the rest of us, your people."

Derek, agitated, slowly pricked the weapon into her neck. "I will kill you once I get what I need. If it's valuable, I'll let you live to tell your lapdog."

"The file room is in the first office on the right, behind a wall."

He loosened his grip, dropping her to the floor to catch her breath.

"I'm in the office," he transmitted. "The area is cleared."

"Good. Get what you need, and we'll clear out."

Derek broke into the file room and ran through the file cabinet, searching for a specific year: 1986. He pulled out two files and smiled at the contents.

"It's been a long time since she's seen her face. Let's go. I've got what I need."

"Are you sure?"

"Yeah. This will help Shawn."

As Derek turned the corner, the soldier tried blasting him. He kicked her hand away, then shot her head clean off with an energy blast of his own. He watched her lifeless body tumble, feeling frustrated. Especially when he noticed the Cozen marking on her right arm. He felt his body sink a bit, but there was no time for that. He had to get away.

CHAPTER

TEN

CHANGES

Shawn sat in his room, concentrating. The sun's rays shone through the blinds; his long, dark shadow stretched to the door. It brightened and faded with every breath Shawn took. His eyes were closed, and his legs crossed on the floor. An odd-shaped blade beside him resembled dead skin. Throughout his breathing, his hands clutched together so tightly that ashes slowly fell with each small adjustment. These glowed faintly, as well.

Over time, he began levitating slightly off the ground.

He saw images of his father hugging him, in contrast to Kevin and Kirk, his guardians. His mother embraced him as his young eyes watched him leave his world. Amelia looked deep within his own to embrace a new one.

The emotions he felt from these visions felt similar, but part of him wanted him to see if the side he had chosen was bad.

The faint muscle memory of Sunshi's lips on his own kept him focused, away from this version of him that felt so angry and distraught. With her presence, he could let go, be free. If only his dead, impaled mother wasn't standing behind her. That frightened him.

Shawn pushed away from Sunshi, tumbling, crawling backwards to Tiyshio's feet. The latter immediately plunged his sword into his torso. He waved at Tiyshio to stop, but Kevin pulled him up. Followed by Kirk, Amelia, and his friends, surrounding him as if he was an enemy. He rose to his feet to race away from them, into the bathroom he had as a child.

He saw himself as a child in the mirror, his mother behind him. He watched himself slowly mature. His eyes changed from the brown he was born with to the Rigion eyes he had now gained. His mother, with that change happening right before him, went from a smiling, happy woman to a grudge-filled, frightening one. The eyes of regret, resentment, and rage mirrored what her own eyes had become, as a Rigion. Frightened, he turned to run away, and saw her impaled again.

"Avenge me," she whispered.

He froze, seeing her dying before his eyes again. This time, he couldn't watch. He ran away, tumbling to the ground at Derek's feet once more.

Derek looked at him, saying, "You know what you must do. You have to choose."

Derek stepped out of Shawn's path. A bright light appeared to guide him away from all this madness. As he got closer to the light, he made out a silhouette that he assumed belonged to Sunshi.

Drawing nearer, he saw a blade as long as the other's legs. A young man in battle armor stood before him, ready to fight. Derek slowed, hesitant to move closer, so the silhouette figure approached him.

It was Tiyshio again.

Shawn felt afraid. Tiyshio stood taller than him, fearless, full of anger. H reminded Shawn of a Rigion. He was obviously out for blood, ready to kill him.

Shawn felt in his heart what he needed to do to be free. It was Tiyshio, or it was him.

He only wanted to be at ease, but Tiyshio and everyone he knew would be against that. His cowardice, which prevented him from killing Tiyshio the last time they met, made him frustrated. He lifted his blade further up.

Tiyshio turned and ran away. He couldn't face the fact that he had made a bad choice. He couldn't let his prejudice be put aside, not even for his best friend's family.

Tiyshio was his family, Shawn thought. He took him in when he had no one else to alter him, change his thoughts, gain a prejudice so that, when a day such as this came, he wouldn't hesitate.

Perhaps they'd known all along. The more he dwelled on who to blame, the more it seemed to be Sunshi standing there, ready to take him away. He thought of his mother again, hoping she could bring him back to his dwelling, but the thought of her took him away instead. She showed him the best times he and Tiyshio shared, how much like family they were. Even at the beginning of the semester, playing games in a new home, officially embracing his new reality of safety.

Derek was just coming into his home. He felt the energy was off, surrounding the walls. He quickly grabbed a sage stick to burn and waved around each room to ground the energy. He wasn't sure if Shawn was responsible until he saw him in his meditative state. It brought a smile to his face, seeing his friend's body adapt to the new abilities that had sat dormant in him for so long. Tapping into his mind, Derek could see the conflict inside Shawn. Opening his eyes again, all Derek could do was take a deep breath. He slowly closed the door behind him, and leaving the sage to burn in his room, waiting for him to finish.

Shawn lifted his eyes as he gently landed on the ground. He walked to the window to look outside, watching the cars pass, but more importantly to check if his eyes looked as they had in his meditation. In his reflection, all he could see was the shimmer of his crimson red eyes, and the cloudiness moving around in his iris. The splits that formed around his pupil were as empty as the darkness of space. He continued staring at his reflection, confused by how similar he appeared to the person he saw, compared to how different he felt from him.

Knowing they were the same person.

Derek heard a knock on his door. He quickly told the visitor to enter.

Shawn gazed upon him, seeing Derek wearing glasses and looking over documents, holding a highlighter and a red pen.

"I'm sorry. I didn't know you were busy…"

"No, it's fine. What I am doing can wait. What did you get for me, son?"

"I've been thinking that I made a mistake back there. Fighting Tiyshio, I mean… at least, part of me feels like it's a mistake, and another part doesn't. He knew what she meant to me. Why would he choose to kill her? Why couldn't he just stop her doing what she was doing?"

"I can ask the same thing about you."

Shawn, confused and angry, harshly yelled, "ME!"

"Before all this happened, you cared deeply about Kevin and Tiyshio. Wouldn't you have wanted to see him die, too? I'm sure that, if you'd told your mom to stop, she would have made an exception."

"I don't think so, after what you told me."

"Why is that? Because you feel the same way she does now?"

What he said was right, Shawn thought.

"Perhaps it wasn't the right time for me to tell you, and let you go through your changes." Derek sighed.

They both had difficulty looking at each other, feeling embarrassed, Shawn more so than Derek.

"I need to apologize," Derek began. "One of the things Nighcos wants Rigions to do now is let the change be the person's choice, and make sure we refrain from giving them lust for achievement. Many Rigions now have adopted that view, so we could sleep easy."

Derek paused to let Shawn know he had seen him earlier in his room. Even Shawn recalled seeing the sage stick by his door.

"I apologize for intruding, too." Derek continued. "I noticed you've had trouble sleeping recently. Meditating, even... how good is your telepathy?"

"My telepathy? I'm not telepathic."

"Yes, you are. I'm shocked you haven't realized it yet. When I came in there, you were levitating off the ground. OFF THE GROUND!"

Shawn couldn't help but smile, as much as he wanted to keep it in.

"Your alteration has been the fastest I've ever seen," Derek continued.

"Even faster than mom's?"

"Ye–yeah, even faster than your mother's." His voice grew softer. "Three years is a long time to believe your mother was dead. I know she already apologized for all that time, but I'm sure she would have wanted to explain it all to you, right next to you, here."

"You think so?" Shawn let his guard down.

"Yeah, apart from this whole path of revenge she used to tell me about. How much she wanted to get away from all of this."

"What did you know about my mom when she was gone?"

Derek smiled. "Come with me." He threw Shawn a jacket.

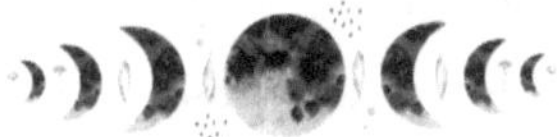

"When I first met your mother, she was timid and scared. She came with a gun in hand as well."

Shawn rolled his eyes. It was no surprise to him.

"What was she scared of?" Shawn laughed.

"Beats me!" Derek laughed as well. "Most likely, it was what happened to your dad and what you thought had happened to her. She searched out Nighcos for help and, trust me, Nighcos is not a person that wants to be found. He does a great job of avoiding that on this blue planet."

"Enemies?"

Derek shook his head. "He saw the opportunities when he came here. He needed to build an army, and here was an endless supply. Your mother saw that, once she joined, and knew –"

"That's not what she came there for."

Derek shook his head.

"How did she fall for you?"

"Your mom and I were assigned to the same team. Nighcos wanted someone with her who was seasoned, who knew how to deal with going through the motions of being a Rigion. Your mother was already vulnerable. It didn't help that she didn't want anyone listening in whenever she had her episodes. I was her partner before we married. I needed to know I was safe, and that she was, too. Most nights, she was reluctant to speak to me. When she began to fall for me, she tried to push herself far away. I'm sure she did so to stay focused and avoid getting hurt."

"How did you reassure her that you were trustworthy?"

"I didn't. I let her make that decision herself. Only then did she let go of her vulnerability and begin her new life. Of course, she never let go of her drive. That's why we are here right now, with her knowledge, fulling her promise." Derek saw this time that Shawn's reaction was far different than before. He was still in conflict, but now it was with what his mother found.

"What is wrong, Casan?"

"Nothing!" Shawn snapped.

"Hmm!" Derek remarked. "You know what? Let me take you somewhere."

Shawn gave him a curious look, wondering where. This was the most open he had ever been with one of his teachers.

Of course, none of his teachers turned out to be his stepfather, as Derek Ryan.

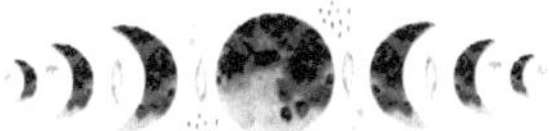

"WHILE WE STAYED IN NEW YORK, SHE MADE SURE TO SAVE everything she had with her, every file," Derek told Shawn as they passed an army of guards along the way. "While with the faction, we needed to report every place, planet, galaxy, we'd ever visited. She told Nighcos she would keep copies for herself. She somehow knew they would come in handy someday,"

"What is this place?" Shawn asked.

"What do you think? This is a sanctuary for people like us. We can be safe here, like the other refugees."

"A sanctuary?" Shawn scoffed.

"Even the Rigions fear those who can hurt them. Those who are alone. They can come here and be free from the prejudice of people like your friends." They entered the elevator.

"I never expected to replace your father," Derek went on, "not even on meeting you when you started high school. That feeling remains, but it doesn't mean that I do not care about you. I care about you as much as I care about your mother. She means everything to me, and so do you. For me, it was a great day to have found you and seen you, nonetheless. It was an honor to also be your teacher." They exited the elevator and passed a few numbered doors, finally stopping at *7546.*

"What's in here?" Shawn asked.

"Everything you needed to know about your mother. Everything she was preparing to accomplish with you once she had you. Most of these letters were written to let you know she was safe."

Derek took a long pause, just looking at Shawn. Then he looked back down at the files and unwrapped a folder, which he slid toward Shawn.

"Shawn, if you had any doubts your mother didn't love you? She loved you enough to fake her death to secure your survival. She never thought things would proceed this far, or the situation would stop her coming back to thinking of you."

Shawn opened the folder. The first report read *May 29, 1981.*

"These were all the reports she sent to me," Derek explained. "In the army, we can't tell anyone what we did telepathically. I saved all of them until now. I thought they might help you with your internal conflict."

Shawn picked out a report that caught his eye. One glimpse over that expressed her feelings towards losing her son.

"If you need me, I'll be in the other room."

Shawn nodded. Once Derek left, he sat on the floor, taking a deep breath before diving in.

> May 29th, 1981
> Report #1-5291
>
> Leaving my son was a decision I am not taking lightly. I can't believe Nighcos would even suggest such an option. However, I feel I have no other choice. I have no one to turn to except my enemy.
>
> This was my first time amongst Rigions, and becoming one, too. It feels different. I don't know if it's anger or fear. The only reason I did it was for protection. At least, this is the only protection I feel I can get. A desperate move when I can't even trust Kevin anymore. Especially with more than one group of people hanging around outside my house. How am I supposed to know which of these is friend or foe?
>
> Somehow, I know an attempt on my life, my family, is next. I am even surprised by my actions, going to the enemy for help. If Casan could read this, he would be so disappointed in me. We ran away from them. Our home and way of life were

destroyed by them. It's baffling how I could turn to them.

Livas, I just wonder what Nighcos has in mind when it comes to leaving my son. I am sure it isn't anything good. I do believe it's better than changing into a Rigion. Also, it is a risk I may have to take. I'm sure Kevin will take him in. From there, I will be able to know if he's also the one who plotted against my family, or another group.

Nighcos said to give it a month until he is ready to decide. He is honoring my decision to keep him the way he is. It is crazy, seeing how different he is, compared to what is said about him. He is welcoming, understanding, and caring. Never did I think I would be welcomed in without animosity. Perhaps this isn't all that bad.

 END OF REPORT

Shawn stared at the page, holding it up, letting the first paragraph play in his head until it became permanent. He flipped through other files, seeing details about a man named Edami, a female anti-Rigion, a race that can change moments in time, but most of the files were about him, and how much she missed her beloved son.

He closed the filing cabinet. As he did so, he felt as if the walls were caving in. He rushed outside the room to get some fresh air again, speeding to the door.

Derek heard a knock on his door and looked up at him. Shawn saw he was back, going through the files he had been looking at before.

"Hey, I'm sorry. I gotta—I'm gonna head out for a bit again. I need to take a walk. Clear my head."

Derek demonstrated his understanding with the stoic look on his face.

"Also, thank you. What you told me. It means a lot." Shawn paced his words.

"What information I gave helped you?"

"All of it… I can't tell you yes or no… it's something I gotta settle on first."

Derek nodded. "I understand. Do what you gotta do, Mr. Damana."

"Call me Shawn."

Derek smiled as Shawn walked out the door.

Strolling down the street, he noticed a family with a boy who looked exactly like him. The father and mother resembled his own, as well. The boy looked at him, laughing. He smiled back. From that faint glimpse, Shawn could tell the difference between him and the child. The changes had already begun for him, compared to the child's indulgence in delight.

His mind gravitated to those thoughts and to his own family. He felt his body moving on its own. His mind grasped his hurtling memories of the past as if his thoughts were speaking aloud to him, echoing the phrase, "remember".

The rush he got from these thoughts intoxicated him. He was embarrassed to enjoy every moment of it. He even followed that family to a nearby park, embarrassed to do so but wanting to continue, as though his mind was teaching him a lesson. He just didn't want to be seen.

He found a bench hidden under the dark shade of a tree that almost rendered the bench invisible. From there, he watched the boy playing as he used to play, the parents as his own. At ease, he slouched on the park bench, relaxing, especially since the thoughts quieted down.

"It looks great, even if it is a burden," came a faint voice. The tone pitched higher with each word. Shawn wanted to turn toward whoever had spoken to him, yet he couldn't breach his focus. He felt compelled. The sensation was too addicting.

The unknown man had a calm, low, welcoming voice, similar to Derek's. He had an idea who had approached him. He just wanted to be sure.

The speaker continued standing at the edge of Shawn's view. Apart from his face being unseen, he only saw his silhouette, since he stood between Shawn and the sun.

"I remember playing with my youngest daughter amongst the fields of Gareth. My sons, they stayed with me by my side, no matter the moment of the day."

"They meant a lot to you?" Shawn asked, still feeling compelled.

"The world! Are you having family trouble, young one?" The man took a seat.

Shawn didn't react, not even saying a word.

"How you're looking at that family tells me you miss someone, and also someone hurt you, Am I right?"

Shawn nodded.

"You've lost someone too, haven't you?" Shawn asked, feeling their thoughts combined.

"Less than fifteen years ago. It was a dark time in my life. A time I regret."

"Why?" Shawn's vision faded as he lost focus.

"I feel I was the cause of their deaths," he replied regrettably. "What about you? What happened to your family?" The man pointed to the parents with the boy at the jungle gym.

"They were killed. All I have are my guardians and my stepfather. I'm not sure I can trust them."

"Who, your guardians or your stepfather?"

"Neither of them. My stepfather tells me my guardians are the ones to not be trusted."

"Do you believe him?"

Shawn shook his head. "I don't know what to believe anymore. I am only beginning to trust him now, but how do I know he's not spitting lies like they supposedly are?"

"What if he isn't lying to you? How does he speak to you?"

"He is welcoming, non-judgmental, and seems like he wants the best for me, and to keep me out of danger."

"The danger is in your guardians. He sees something that you do not, but you have something that he doesn't."

"Experience?" Shawn asked.

"Yes, the fact that you have spent time with them, and they trust you as much as themselves. It shows the greatest amount of intel you can gather, compared to scouting. There is only one thing I ask. Because of your experience, you can always tell when someone is hiding something. People will always want to reveal all aspects of themselves because they are living a lie. Think of your own experiences and relate them to this one. Your guardians are your past, and your stepfather is your future."

Shawn could feel the man staring at him, even as he reflected on his words.

"I'll tell you something," the man continued. "I have regrets because my family died from causes that could've been avoided. Since they were not avoided, a certain chain of events happened. Something that hurt many people. Imagine that there are more like you out here. Only you can choose your own past, your own future. Make the right decision, not just one that is easy and true."

The man then stood and vanished without a trace as Shawn tried turning his head to thank him. He looked around the park to see where he had run off. He couldn't find anyone walking away.

He turned back to the family. They were gone, as well. He didn't think about it. He pushed himself erect on the bench, sighed, and looked back to the jungle gym.

He was ready for his next step.

CHAPTER
ELEVEN

ABILITY

"There is one thing you need to know about these abilities, Hayden. They are all in the mind." Tiyshio paced around Hayden.

Hayden remained still, eyes closed, meditative. Heat flowed through his mind with each breath he took in, and cold with each breath out. He felt the water circulating in his body, and the vibrations of the earth beneath him.

Tiyshio grinned vicariously through the process. They were at Jason's home, their bare feet resting on the pads laid on the hard ground.

Jason watched them both from the patio.

Tiyshio glanced through a window of the house, realizing his girlfriend was talking to someone outside his view. She constantly shook her head and toyed with her hair, which made him concerned.

Jason could not help but notice his reaction. He blocked his view as he went inside.

"What's going on?" Jason asked the newly arrived messenger.

"We haven't found Kirk and Amelia yet. We searched all around Long Island, and still nothing."

"*Obviously*, they wouldn't be in Long Island. If Kevin moved them, it wouldn't be to any place obvious." Jason turned to his other guest. "Siyshi, you found this guy?"

"I've known him since I arrived on this planet. I trust him."

"I'm sorry you think that is the only place we checked," the messenger replied. "We also looked through all of Manhattan and Queens. They are nowhere there."

Sunshi took a deep breath. "That just leaves the Bronx. They must be up there. Or Kevin doesn't want them to be found," she added gloomily.

"He doesn't even know what they did," Jason responded.

"Nor do we. At least we are willing to find out." She turned to the messenger. "Thank you. Keep checking those areas. Staten Island is off-limits. That's where they would be most expected."

The messenger agreed. They parted ways.

Siyshi started for the patio out back, deliberately not acknowledging Jason by her side as he raced next to her, waiting for her to say more. He looked bothered.

"If you want more info, Jason, you are going to have to be patient. Or bother Rocks."

"Yeah, but doesn't it seem crazy that we still haven't found anyone? It's been a week."

"In a week!" She paused, opening the door, to stare down Jason intimidatingly. "I think they've made some decent progress. Please don't stress. I'm sure we will find them before our enemy does."

They stepped outside to watch Tiyshio do his mentoring.

"Keep that rhythm. To control your abilities, you must have a clear mind. A clear mind leads to a vivid imagination, intent, emotion, and, most importantly, manifestation. These are the building blocks for handling your abilities. In time, you will become a quick thinker, a visual thinker."

Tiyshio shot a fireball from his hand, straight toward Jason. Jason rebounded it, pulling water from thin air to douse the flame.

"You need to tell it what you want, and how you want it. Hayden, you have one of the most powerful base abilities, capable of stemming to so many more. Envision your place of tranquility. In that place, you are the greatest being ever known. Whatever skills you can accomplish there, you can bring here. They will become who you are."

Hayden paced his breathing, each time holding it longer. Tiyshio slowed his own pace, feeling Hayden's energy grow. Jason and Siyshi caught his excitement and followed suit.

Tiyshio whispered into Hayden's ear. "Once you are there, I want you to imagine yourself hovering over a lake. Across that lake is something you want. To get it, you need to create a passageway. By manipulating the water, turning it to ice, you can create your bridge."

Siyshi saw steam leave Hayden's and Tiyshio's noses. She began to feel cold, which startled her. She looked to Jason to see if he felt the same. He showed no goosebumps, not even a shiver. Just looked at her in confusion about why she felt so weird.

Two pillars of ice began forming alongside Hayden's arms. The water he used to build those pillars arrived in big clumps, in a spiral formation.

"Now that you are going there, Hayden, you can see the item you want is being engulfed in that ice. The only way you can obtain what you want is to use fire."

Hayden raised his arm. A faint smell of smoke engulfed the air, and a light flame shot out of Hayden's hand.

"Now open your eyes."

For a brief moment, Hayden could see the flame. His face lit up with excitement. He danced in a circle, which made the flame dissipate.

Tiyshio chuckled. "Good, good. Now, you've got to stay focused! At least remember what you intend to achieve." Tiyshio and Hayden then walked to the table to grab a drink.

"So it is true?" Hayden asked, taking a breath. "All abilities stem from a form of telekinesis?"

"Not a form," Jason replied, following the boys to take a seat. "It is telekinesis. All powers stem from telekinesis."

Tiyshio shook his head. "Yup. This is how I was taught."

"But how are powers like strength and optic beams streamed from telekinesis?" Hayden asked.

"It is the idea of manifestation," Jason followed up. "Whatever you think, you can do. However, it does seem a bit weird when it comes to physical strength. I think it has something to do with adrenaline and focus."

"Like Sunshi?"

"Exactly like Sunshi!" Jason confirmed.

"Overall," Tiyshio added, "it is an involuntary movement that is affective at birth. It acts almost like a muscle feeder."

Jason gave Tiyshio a bizarre look. Siyshi stared at Jason's snooping.

Tiyshio felt Jason scolding him and, lightly irritated, said, "Look, man, I'm not the greatest with descriptions. Stop scolding me."

Jason and Siyshi laughed. "As long as you know," Jason replied.

Tiyshio rolled his eyes, then shook the feeling off. Hayden seemed clueless but joined their laughter just to be part of the fun. When Tiyshio turned his attention to his girlfriend, Siyshi's smile faded, and Tiyshio grew stern. He noticed Jason change up as well, from the corner of his eye.

"Hayden?" Tiyshio called.

Hayden tapped Tiyshio's shoulder to get his attention.

"Keep practicing what I told you."

"Okay!" Hayden responded nervously.

Tiyshio entered the house. Siyshi reluctantly followed. Jason stepped onto the mat with Hayden to help him practice, as far as Siyshi could see behind her.

"You looked worried earlier," Tiyshio asked his girlfriend. "What's wrong?"

Siyshi sighed and began to slowly move away from Tiyshio. Tiyshio lightly pulled her back.

"Hey, don't shut me out. I just want to understand."

"Heit wasn't able to find anything."

Tiyshio looked puzzled. Why would that bother her? It was too early for proper news.

"Okay!" he responded.

"Ugh! Nor did Rocks. Sun told me she'd found out as much this morning when she went to his place."

"What are they doing? We should all be here, searching for our own."

"I don't know what they are doing, but the two of them have been getting… close."

"Close?"

"Yeah, close. Ever since the change, things have been different between those two."

"Have you seen them together at school?"

Siyshi shook her head.

"Anything like her and Shawn?"

"I don't know. It's too early to say."

"I hope it's nothing like that."

"Me, too. I've been thinking, Tiy. What if they didn't do it? What if Kevin knows and, somehow, is aware we would want to find them, and so would Shawn?"

"I'm sure he's banking on it. More so than us. Why ask that, though? Because Heit didn't find anyone today?"

Siyshi shook her head, looking about to buckle.

Tiyshio came to her side to sit her down.

"Something Jason said earlier got to me," she said. "I didn't want to admit I felt the same. I wanted to feel what I said."

"What did you say?"

"Be patient. The truth is, I'm not. I feel, if someone can get him out of this, it wouldn't be you, it would be them. I feel time is really not on our side. Like it's true that Kevin doesn't want us to find them. Like he's afraid that, if we do, he does."

"You really feel that?"

"I have a hunch, Tiyshio. The city isn't that big. There is no way they couldn't find someone who has been going through the same pattern."

"Pattern?"

"Come on, Tiyshio! Going to work, going home, riding the subway. Rocks and my contacts are only good here. If they aren't here in New York, or hidden, we are kind of useless."

"Listen, Siyshi. Now is not the time to get distraught. What you said was right: be patient. The more negative thoughts there are on this, the more chances this can happen. It's okay if we didn't get the news right away. If it was, say, a month from now, I would be throwing a fit, too."

Tiyshio chuckled. Siyshi did as well.

"Let's get back out there," he continued, standing up. He smiled to calm Siyshi down, feeling as if she could see through him. As though his smile looked much like frail grass.

Hayden met them on the patio. "Hey, Tiy, I'm really happy with what we accomplished here, but I was wondering if we could mix in what I've learned today with a bit of… you know!" Hayden punched his fist in the air.

"You want a bit of combat training mixed in?" Tiyshio asked enthusiastically.

Hayden nodded.

Tiyshio sighed in anticipation.

Jason looked at Hayden, concerned.

Hayden's excitement diminished, along with Tiyshio's, as Jason took on the aspect of a wise older brother.

"Today is only day one of your controlling your elemental powers," Jason explained. "Moving on to combat today is just… too fast. Are you sure this is the approach you want to go for?"

"Why not?! Given the way things are going currently, I want to be prepared to defend myself when the time is right."

Siyshi sat back down. The look she gave Tiyshio made him feel he was acting immature. He didn't like that.

Tiyshio chipped in. "I know you can hold your own in a normal fight. Remember that kid that used to bother you on the subway? That was a good way to hold back against a human. However, what we're dealing with now is someone like us. Is there any ability you can say you felt comfortable with during our session today?"

Hayden shrugged. "I don't think so. That's why I asked you to help me out. I don't feel I have control over any of my powers."

"Well, don't tell me we didn't make any progress! We've been at this for four hours!".

"No–no, we have, it's just–I, I don't feel as if I personally made any real progress."

Jason tapped Hayden on the shoulder. "Not true," he said, in a drawn-out voice. "One thing I learned from Tiyshio, Hayden, is sometimes you have to be under pressure to understand what you are capable of." He then backed away.

Jason suddenly darted toward Hayden again, kicking him, giving him barely time to react. Jason then followed up. Hayden blocked his next attack, pushed his leg down, and punched Jason hard enough to knock him backwards.

A barrage of punches came at Hayden with blinding speed. Hayden ducked, dodged, and swept them away, with barely a moment to breathe. A spike of ice flew toward his eye. He thrust his head back. The piercing spike grazed his chin.

"That injury could have been avoided if you trusted your abilities." Jason shot three more spikes out of thin air.

Hayden's eyes widened. He pushed the first two spikes away.

Aggravated, Jason shot another two. This time, Hayden grabbed them. He lunged at Jason, one spike aimed at his neck, the other at his torso.

"Yield?!" Hayden read the horror in Jason's face, even the raised goosebumps, from the sensation of the spike poking deeply into him.

"Nice recovery, but we need to work on your other elements," Jason said as he landed. "Now, Tiy, you know what to do to help this young blood out?"

Tiyshio lightly nodded, sighing. "Indeed. It will take some time. On another note, his using those elements mainly reminds me that we never truly found my own ID power."

"You're sure?!" Jason teased.

"Yeah, man! I feel like I'm the only Zorian who doesn't know his ID ability." Tiyshio's tone was excited but upset.

"ID power? What's that?" asked Hayden.

"It's a basic ability all Zorians are born with," Tiyshio explained. "Another way to look at it is as the most dominant ability. It shows up after puberty."

"How do you know you have this new ability?"

"Hmm. It feels like an epiphany, or an involuntary movement. My mother's ability is atom bonding. When she developed it, she claimed she could feel particles all around her. She felt them move about in the air, become part of her, then fade away. Over time, she advanced to further control her ability, which led it to do bigger things. She could create moons and restore life on worlds, including vegetation. The only downside is, it takes a lot out of her. I'm sure she's gotten better at it."

"You never got that feeling?"

"Not really. I felt the same way I did after I hit puberty," he answered regretfully.

"Not even mentally? Nothing changed?"

"Well… I had dreams where I lived the lives of my predecessors. As well as people I'd never seen before. It's probably nothing, just dreams and premonitions. Kevin has those a lot, too. I can't say my power is to see into the future." Tiyshio chuckled.

"Tiy, you said that my powers stem from the mind. What do you mean by that?"

Tiyshio's grin grew so big it spanned from ear to ear. "My grandfather used to tell me that all abilities spawned from telekinesis, telepathy, and imagination. Anything you can think of, you can make. That means your abilities as well. Although you are born with elemental abilities, they are still limitless. You saw how Jason used his body as a defense mechanism when he heated up to stop my fireball?"

Hayden shook his head.

"That was your ability of fire and heat. Living beings can combust into flames. It's an unnatural phenomenon, but it can be controlled here." Tiyshio pointed at his head.

"At the moment," he continued, "we can say your dominant ability is fire or water, but we will find out for certain over the course of your training. You can learn to mix your abilities with your combat skills. That is only after we practice with that ability, along with others. There are more than a hundred elements on the periodic table. Mastering a mere four is only the beginning. There is also fighting under pressure."

"Why is that important? Why would I need to be under pressure that I didn't understand?"

"To be under pressure is to fight for survival. Often, in pressure situations, we are not calm, not in control. We just want out. The light at the end of the submerging tunnel only pushes us to go beyond for mere moments, because we know we will be safe soon. In combat, that light you imagine is a mirage. It has to be earned, and to earn it requires focus and awareness. Instincts will point you in the right direction, but knowledge, skill, will keep you alive. Also, in these types of situations, a weapon would be viable."

Hayden's expression was quickly swallowed by confusion. "I'm sorry. A weapon?"

Tiyshio stopped pacing around the backyard and slowly marched back to Hayden. "Yes, a weapon. You'll need it in defense against those who attack you."

"I have elemental abilities. If they tried to stab me with a sword, or shoot me with a gun, I could melt it down or blow the bullets away. I don't need a weapon. Nor do you."

"For me, I may be able to stop a sword strike inches away, but I won't be focused on their leg suddenly sweeping me under." He performed the motion on Hayden.

"Weapons, for us, can be used as a distraction, defense, and offensive strategy. It is one of the best ways we can focus on a quick end, as well as keeping our opponent's eyes elsewhere. We are magicians, Hayden. Our powers are for defense, but they are not our only source of protection and attack. Remember that."

"That's fine, but does it matter right now? I mean, with everything going on?"

The three older kids gave each other grave looks. Each knew what the others thought, but refused to say anything.

Jason sighed. "The school prepares us for what lies ahead, but not really, when it comes to protection versus integration. Considering our current situation, it's best we are prepared for whatever may happen."

Hayden turned away, although he knew the importance from Jason's point of view.

Jason looked at Tiyshio, making sure he knew where to pick up from. Besides, he had agreed to train him, even though mentioning Shawn had turned his thoughts elsewhere.

Jason went inside to grab two Bo staffs for Tiyshio and Hayden.

"Hayden," he remarked on his return, "don't feel pressured that this is a necessity. These aren't our worse days. Remember, you are the one who asked for this. Why? Because your brother wanted you to live like others from this world, as well as those who only sought refuge and solidarity. They were ignorant to think the fight wouldn't come to them. We all were. It's good that you want to be ready."

Jason sat, sighing, feeling all that he had to deal with. Siyshi assured him it was his burden alone. Yet, Jason felt as much responsibility as Tiyshio did. Especially for helping Tiyshio train him during an unprecedented time.

Siyshi grinned at how serious he looked.

Jason snickered with embarrassment. He didn't want to seem bothered.

"What's got you riled up?" he asked Siyshi.

"Tiyshio. These past few weeks, he hasn't been on edge! He's just been on kind of a binge!"

"What do you mean, a binge?" Jason asked.

"He's put traps around the house. He's been training Sunshi like a dog."

"Did she choose to be trained that way?" Jason asked, shocked.

"She did, but –"

"She didn't choose it to be *that* vicious?"

"They are normally at it for four hours. Mainly weapons training, and teaching her how to overpower him, should things get to that. He is certain something will happen involving both."

"How forceful?"

"Forceful enough that he had to quit it for a while. He's worried nothing has happened yet. I've never seen him so eager. Nor have I seen you this eager, either!"

"I understand why he's eager, but me? Mine is all on him." Jason pointed at Hayden. "I'm afraid of anything happening to him. He looks up to us. Especially your boyfriend, who's like another older brother to him. He would follow him to hell and back, just to make sure he's safe. All because his teacher would do the same." He pointing at Tiyshio again. "I would like to teach him discipline. Knowing when to fight, and when not to. That's the most important aspect for me."

CHAPTER
TWELVE

PULSE

It was nearing sundown when Kevin climbed onto the rooftop to meet with Chris. Several other individuals there were talking amongst themselves. Kevin scanned around them, searching for Chris. He finally found him chatting with another man near the corner of the rooftop, hidden amongst the groups.

"Why does it feel like I'm in an Alcoholics Anonymous get-together?" Kevin joked.

"Mr. Bratt, this was your idea!" Chris laughed. "Remember to tell them what made you want to clean up your act." They laughed and hugged. Chris excused himself from his previous conversation.

"I know what you want to say. You're impressed, right?" Chris smirked. "Mmhm! Come on, let me know."

"I won't lie. I'm—I'm impressed! How the hell did you pull this off?"

"My man, I got that connection, son! You just gotta learn to accept that I'm getting to be in your shoes now."

Kevin rolled his eyes, smiling, barely able to hold back his amusement.

"You know I'm just fooling around?" Chris said, laughing.

"So am I. Good work, kid!" Kevin sounded pleased, which delighted Chris.

"So, where did you find these guys? A sewer or something?" Kevin observed one individual in particular, who looked decidedly out of place.

"Some of them are co-workers of my mom. Others I've seen on the way, whenever I sneak out the house. As you can tell." Chris scanned the people he had brought in.

Kevin couldn't help but see a strong level of confusion on Chris' face.

"If you weren't able to tell already, some of these guys are homeless," he remarked. "I didn't have much to work with, given what little bit of time you gave me."

"I understand what you mean, Mr. Williams, but what matters most is being able to find Telsa."

"I'm sure we'll find Telsa, no matter how difficult you think it might be."

Kevin walked to the edge of the roof to observe Manhattan's skyline, in particular, the Empire State building.

Chris was curious what exactly he was looking for. He figured Kevin must be staring at someone from a great distance, which made him feel he was intruding on a private moment.

Kevin finally broke his silence. "You know, for as long as I've lived here, I've never been."

"Been where?"

"There." Kevin pointed to the Empire State Building. "The girl we are searching for once told me, that first day she moved into my apartment, how much she loved the view. She said the skyline, and the clouds made her feel safe. She called the Empire State, the space elevator. She would stare at that tower until the sun rose."

Chris slapped him on the chest. "I understand how you feel about this one. Soon, she'll be able to go inside. Perhaps World Trade, too. Let's get this thing started, shall we?"

"After you get these people some new clothes and a shower."

They both laughed.

A couple of hours later, Chris called the group to gather around. They formed a semi-circle around the two. Kevin stood beside Chris at ease, like a soldier.

"What's good, everyone? I'm glad so many of you could make it. Let me refresh you on what we are about to do. We are looking for a young lady in her early twenties. Kevin here will show you pictures of the girl we are looking for."

Most of the photographs were of her at the time Kevin took her in. Some were of her and Tiyshio when he was a little younger. The last few were taken when he first found her.

"Most of these photos are two years old," Kevin stated. "Some a little older. I would guess she hasn't changed much in her appearance. She may have gotten a little bigger, or a little skinnier. She may not even appear to your mind, because she is blocking you out. Or she is dead,"

"Any particular idea where she might be in the city, or if she is even in the city?" asked one of the girls.

Chris shook his head and looked to Kevin, who replied, "We'll start the pulse search here, and amplify it if we're not able to find her in New York."

"How far are you willing to take it?" asked a man in a trench coat.

"Ohio to the west, Tennessee heading southwest, South Carolina, Toronto heading North."

"And how long do you plan to keep this pulse going?" queried a person standing to his left.

"An hour, tops. Any longer, and we'd cause a city-wide blackout. We don't need that, the way we live. You dig?"

"Yeah!" shouted everyone except Chris and Kevin.

They all joined hands and closed their eyes. Chris stood outside the circle, slipping on his headphones to keep himself occupied. He sat on a crate he'd brought with him, resting his back against the rooftop railing.

The entire group began to breathe in slowly, the sound growing deeper with every breath they let out.

Kevin visualized Telsa in his mind. She stood about five foot four, with hair reaching to her shoulders, shiny, jet black. Her small eyes were a little sharp at the ends, tending to squint. She appeared to be of African American descent, despite that being her disguise on Earth. In his visualization, she wore black dress pants, shiny black slip-on dress shoes, a white button-up shirt, and a black suit jacket. He figured she would look like that now and projected his vision to everyone.

The effect amplified, flinging Chris's head back. He felt as if a freight train had hit him. "That was something," he mouthed.

Chris rose from the crate and approached the group, feeling the vibrations of the continuous pulse hitting him. The closer he stepped, the more pain he felt. Chris smiled, in too much pain to laugh, shook his head and returned to the crate, pushing it further back so the pulses wouldn't hurt his mind so much.

"Looks like some weird-ass spiritual cult now," he remarked under his breath.

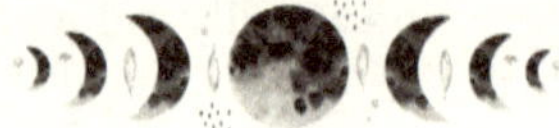

KEVIN FLOATED OVER BROOKLYN. HE COULD SEE THE ENTIRE CITY'S skyline, but all the lights were dimmed. Even the sky looked completely black, without a single star in view. Below him, he saw moving yellow lights, also a little dim but bright enough to appear as a sunset color. He looked around at the others that joined him in the pulse, watching them as they, too, stared down.

"I know many of you have never seen anything like this before," he explained. "This isn't your astral projection. In fact, you are merely connected to the millions of minds living in this city. I provided a more familiar way to make this search easier. Time moves much slower here than in real life. One hour out there will feel like a week here. However, I believe we'll find her quicker than that. Remember, in a pulse, people who are blocking their minds may not appear to us, but if we focus harder, we can blur out the open minds and search for the closed ones. Some won't appear, some will appear black as night, and some will appear red. Let's begin."

The people glowing yellow faded until only a few red moving lights remained. The ground seemed darker. So did a few of the buildings. Kevin closed his eyes to visualize only the subject of their search within his own mental space. The rest of the group followed suit.

Thinking of Telsa caused his mind to fade. He was no longer in the city, but in a white space.

Then he was on the streets of Brooklyn, but it didn't look the same. The people stood out. He needed to focus more to see her. Although mentally on a street in Brooklyn, he had thousands of people around him. A few hundred of them he had met before. He severed his link to those people, freeing his mind.

"Remember to unlink your minds from those you know," Kevin told the group. "That will make our search quicker."

They all agreed. Kevin saw a few hundred more people disappear. He exited his deeper telekinetic state, seeing fewer red lights and more buildings with a light inside of them.

"That's almost half of New York. You sure she is here?" asked the man with the trench coat, returning to his connected telekinetic state.

"We'll find out soon enough. The others haven't returned yet."

"*How are you guys doing in there so far?*" Chris called out.

"That must have been five minutes already," Kevin replied. "We haven't found anything yet. Almost half of New York is dark. My guess is we may not find her here." Kevin projected his reply directly into Chris's head.

"*Then where might you think we can find her*?" Chris asked.

"As I said, Chris, I don't know!" Kevin snapped.

The others started to reappear, two minutes after each other. Most of the red lights went out. The dark shadows faded away, leaving only a few.

Kevin and the rest spotted about twenty lights around the entire city.

"There are enough lights here. We don't need to go into a deeper pulse. Search the grounds."

They flew toward the streets of New York, each one looking amongst the people, unable to notice any faces. Some of those they observed were homeless; others were in families. Most could feel themselves watched by the group. They grew violent, searching for ways to remove the plague from their minds. Kevin saw this happening and shielded his group.

He ordered them to remain in the skies while he thought of another approach. After all their efforts, they still couldn't find the woman.

The group looked anxiously at Kevin as he figured out what to do next.

Chris heard them scream as their minds were suddenly attacked. He was confused about how that could happen. He looked toward Kevin.

"Hey, man, you good? Sounds like they were about to die."

"Don't be melodramatic! We were having a bit of a complication. I think we're fine now."

"Yeah, fine!" one of the girls said, frustrated. "We need another plan. A plan that only includes her."

Another guy said, "I might know a trick, but I thought, and still think, it might be dangerous."

"What is it you want to do that you think would work?" the girl asked.

"The fishing trick. It's something I would normally only do when it's just me. It could literally drive someone insane. I mean, like, they start seeing shit that isn't there."

Everyone but Kevin looked bothered by this idea.

One of the girls gave Kevin a crazy look. She floated over to him. "Why aren't you disturbed by this plan?"

"I know it's dangerous. Even finding her is dangerous in her current state. We'd need to see her mind and find her location to get to her. Fishing her out, not the way we are doing right now, but the way he's talking about, just might work."

"You know exactly what this trick is?" the girl asked.

"Unfortunately, yes. Before Earth, I was a soldier, much like these black ops agents. Whenever we were looking for a target, we would use the fishing trick to take the enemy leader out first, followed by his squadron in person. The technique can be used, but I'd need to be fast."

"What do you need to do?" the man in the trench coat asked.

"I need to stir up a memory of hers. One that would catch her mind. If I think of her, the mind will know. The mind always knows. It would be attracted to the memory, no matter how strong her block is."

"I hope it's a good one," the short-haired girl said, frustrated.

"Luckily, everyone loves memories. Connect to me when my eyes close."

Kevin shut his eyes.

Everyone in the group grabbed on to him.

Back in the real world, Chris grabbed on to him as well, closing his own eyes. He felt he was being sucked in; he felt like collapsing, mostly because he could still feel the effect on his brain. He stepped back, then asked, "Hey, Kevin, is there a way you can protect my mind?"

"Yeah. Stay away from me, and you'll be safe. I'll need full focus on this."

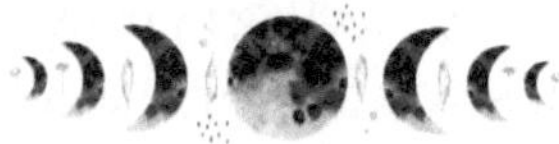

KEVIN APPROACHED HIS APARTMENT DOOR AND PULLED OUT HIS KEYS. HE put them away on hearing someone walk up to the other side of the door, ready to unlock it. Once he heard the last lock click open, he reached for the knob.

He could feel the resistance of someone pushing against the door.

"Really?" Groaning about the actions on the other side, he turned the knob and pulled the door open. He nearly stumbled on entering.

Tiyshio was the one holding the door. Then a girl ran up, looking annoyed, yelling, "Tiyshio, you can't just unlock the door for anyone!"

"Don't worry, Telsa," Kevin reassured her. "He's just fooling around. Where's Shawn?"

"He's doing his homework. This little guy already did his. He just wants to fool around, as you said."

Kevin shook his head and placed his bag on the counter. Telsa followed him into the kitchen, heading straight to the stove. Kevin opened the fridge and grabbed a beer. Telsa rushed over and grabbed a case of fruit, which she then opened and started eating quickly.

Tiyshio, meanwhile, returned to his room, where Kevin was looking.

Kevin couldn't see Shawn from his vantage point, but he heard him, since Tiyshio was bothering him. Telsa got a little annoyed herself, but she didn't care much, as she was watching the pasta cook.

"Tiyshio, come out here! Don't bother Shawn while he's doing his homework. Got it?"

Tiyshio rushed into the kitchen area, taking a seat near the table. Kevin nodded as he plucked the cap off his bottle.

Kevin walked to the couch. He saw that his sword, which he remembered placing under the couch, had been taken out. The rest of the living room was a mess. Tiyshio's game console sat in the middle of the floor. Kevin's quilts, unfolded, had been thrown to the side.

Little by little, patience was wearing thin.

"How was school?" Kevin asked, settled down.

"Cool," Tiyshio said, staring into Kevin's eyes.

"Anyone messed with you today?"

"Nope."

"Are you and Shawn being nice to Ms. Gond?"

"Yeah, she's cool. She doesn't make the house feel crowded."

"I thought as much. Clean up the living room and get ready for tomorrow. I'll tell you when dinner is ready. That goes for you, too, Shawn!"

"Got it!" Shawn yelled back.

Tiyshio walked to the living room and changed the channel on the television.

"What was all that about?" Telsa asked, grabbing the pot.

"Tiyshio has a hard time adapting to new things," Kevin explained. "Even new people. You should've seen him when Shawn moved in."

"I'm sure he was quite happy."

"On the contrary. He already knew he was losing his room."

"Any reason why he felt that way?"

"It stems from the time we left Zorin. Coming to Earth was a big change, having new people around, a small apartment, four strangers… you get the gist. What about you? Are you settling in well? The boys treating you nice?"

Telsa laughed. "Yes, they are well behaved. Shawn more so than Tiyshio. I feel Tiy is going to be an attention seeker when he gets a little older. The question is, does he have a lot of friends?"

Kevin nodded.

"Figured as much. Yeah, I am happy with being off the streets, in a home, staying indoors with nothing to do but look outside. I love the view, by the way."

Kevin looked out the window at his own favorite spot. "Many do."

"But! One thing bothers me. Why is there no food in the fridge?"

Telsa posed her complaint just as Kevin opened the fridge door.

"Umm… I'm just not used to eating a lot. None of us are. Sometimes we eat for pleasure, but mostly we eat maybe or twice a month."

Telsa looked at him in shock. "Is Shawn like one of your kind?"

"Shawn? No, he's part Hunatan."

"Then how does his metabolism never hit him? How does he eat as little as you and Tiyshio if he's not like you?"

"I really don't know. He told me everything about his race. Taking him in was a blessing when it came to food. So, when I do buy food for the house, I buy big. Enough to kill someone."

Telsa nodded, stirring the sauce. "Interesting."

Kevin peered over her shoulder at the spaghetti sauce. Telsa turned to him, and Kevin quickly met her gaze.

"Who taught you how to cook?" he asked. "And how is it you still have an appetite, knowing the change in your anatomy?"

"A Rigion named Edami was my teacher. He was one of the generals watching over me whenever I had to report to Nighcos. When I first changed, I'd have hunger issues. Edami knew how to cook so I wouldn't complain."

Kevin grabbed the saucepan and put it aside. "I can tell you are bothered by this. I won't talk about it."

"No, it's not that. It's just, I don't want to see you guys hurt. I'm glad you are taking me in. This is great! You don't have to be a part of my problem."

"I took you in because I can protect you. Give all this a few months. Hell, give it a year. If you are so much as thought of by our enemy then, let me know. I'll do something about it."

Telsa shook her head and began dishing out pasta for the boys.

"Boys, come and eat!" Kevin yelled.

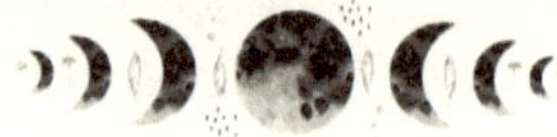

"Hey, listen, it's just another day in hell. Don't let it bother you." Telsa addressed a woman who was part of a small crowd leaving an office building.

"Tanya," she responded, "if I'd known you were this cool, we could've been hanging out since the day you started. Why do you never speak to anyone until today?"

The woman smiled at Telsa. Telsa shrugged, laughing off her question.

"Well, anyway, listen," the woman continued. "A few of us were going to the bar to get drinks. Do you want to join us?"

Telsa shook her head, keeping the smile on her face, "No, I'm gonna pass. I'm just gonna head home."

"Come on, girl, don't be like that. Don't tell me you have a man waiting at home with a nice cooked meal?"

"Man… no. Nice, cooked meal, and TV, those I do have, ha-ha. Listen, I'll join you another time, trust me. We'll catch up. Okay?"

The girl shook her head and began walking away with the group. Telsa watched them leave. Her smile faded.

She grasped her purse against her side and began walking in the opposite direction. She reached her subway station and move to the turnstiles. She glanced over the platform to determine which side had the fewest people for space.

When the train came, she did the same on boarding. She settled on a lone seat, next to no one. Her eyes danced around the train car, one hand gripping her bag and the other by her side. Also at her side was a small knife the size of her palm. Nothing too lethal.

On the train, she forced herself not to nod off, despite her long-distance commute. She kept herself awake by staring at a shadow beneath her feet. She occasionally looked out the window at her reflection, which almost seemed unrecognizable, as she'd blurred her view.

Now, flashes of Kevin's face showed in place of her own. She assumed she was dozing off because she had begun to dream of him. Specifically, of an exact moment they had shared, that made her feel again. The sensation did not feel right. It had to be a play. She stood, looking at the map to plan an exit strategy. She had a few more stops to go.

With the rising in her gut feeling, she couldn't wait that long.

Her eyes swayed toward the other passengers. Her mind began to feel crowded. It was confusing. She knew she had cut herself off. Even those other passengers on the train looked unfamiliar.

Her anxiety spiked. The stares she got on the train were ones back at herself. Except for one guy walking through the outside car door, a well-dressed man in a nice black suit, with a straight black tie. At the next stop, she quickly got off. She didn't run, but she did move swiftly, keeping her head down. Things couldn't feel any worse.

More odd people, she thought.

She bumped into a guy wearing a long trench coat. She looked up, sensing something familiar, despite having never seeing him before in her life.

"Miss, are you okay?"

She said nothing, speeding up alongside the track. Her heart raced. Tears slowly formed in her eyes. She didn't want to break down. She wanted to remain focused.

The trench coat guy stared after her, looking confused when she went up the subway stairs, past another guy standing at a hot dog stand. This new guy turned to get a good look at her. She ignored him, darting around the corner.

There, she took off her high-heeled shoes, holding one with the heel pointed out. The man from the hot dog stand followed her, though not too close. Telsa felt him approach and continued walking quickly away.

Then a man in a white shirt stepped out at the end of the street. She turned into an alleyway. The two men looked at each other, then walked toward the alleyway together.

Telsa dropped her shoes and pulled out the knife. With a flick, and the blade extended into a sword the size of her forearm.

From behind, another man came toward her. Hesitant to turn, she shot an energy beam from her hand at the first two. They jumped out of the way. She turned then, holding her sword, ready to swing.

Then she identified him. "Kevin!"

The other guy faded away, and only one more remained. Chris.

"Wanna go somewhere more discreet?" Kevin asked.

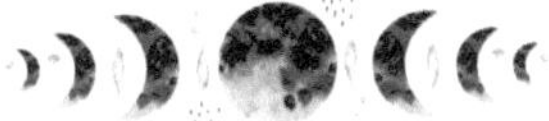

CHRIS PERCHED ON THE EDGE OF A KITCHEN COUNTERTOP IN TELSA'S home, while Kevin walked around. She lived in a small townhouse in Cambridge, near Boston. What Kevin saw all looked familiar.

The first floor didn't hold much furniture, not even a dinner table. What she did have was a small couch and a television. Upstairs, he saw three bedrooms. Only one was used for resting; the other two were used as rec rooms. One was for exercise, with a weightlifting set, a bench, and a punching bag. The other room held a wooden fighting dummy, alongside a hard foam fighting dummy. There were even a few weapons on the wall, mostly blades, though some were guns, primarily assault weapons and handguns. All were suppressed.

Downstairs, Chris rose to circle the living room. Telsa had framed photos covering the back wall. They weren't of her family, but someone else. The framed photos were stacked up like a Christmas tree. The top photo showed a man with short black hair, small brown eyes, and a sharp facial structure. Below him was a picture of another man, with a stylized haircut, like a small low top, and big brown eyes. The photograph resembled the kind used for a business; a forty-five-degree angle shot. Below him were three more pictures: a woman, a man, and a boy.

He moved in closer. Something about the woman seemed familiar, yet it wasn't clicking. She had caramel skin and a long dark brown hair ponytail and wore a dress shirt and suit jacket. This image also appeared as a company photograph.

The picture of the boy was more in the style of an elementary school photo. He leaned toward to get a better look but was interrupted by Telsa.

"Having fun looking at the photos, kid?"

Chris stepped away from the wall, toward Telsa. Telsa and Kevin had been coming downstairs, pausing on the last few steps.

"No," Chris said. "I was just curious about your wall."

"Well, do me a favor?"

Chris nodded.

"Don't be," Telsa said.

Kevin laughed.

"Well," she continued, "I hope you like the place, Kevin, because this will be the last time you see it."

"I don't think there's any need for that attitude, Telsa."

"Unfortunately, there is the way you pulled that number on me a couple of hours ago. If you can find me, what makes you think they won't be able to?!" Frustrated, Telsa marched to the kitchen to pull out a teapot. "Tea, anyone?"

The two men replied, "No, thanks."

"Then what brings you to find me? Whatever the reason, it must be desperate."

"I need to know how you were able to beat the virus, or at least how were you able to suppress it?"

"I honestly can't tell you. When you're a sleeper, there are back doors to suppressing key thoughts."

"Then, how do you keep your eyes looking like any humans'?" Kevin asked.

Telsa touched the bottom of her eye. "This? Hmm, well, this wasn't me. Before I tell you, what does all this mean to you, anyway?"

"Tiyshio's friend is one of them. I need your help to find a way to turn him back."

"Someone he loves?" Telsa took teacups from the cupboard.

"He's like a brother to him. He is family."

"It's Shawn," Telsa said.

Kevin and Chris shook their heads.

"What's your name?" Telsa asked, looking directly at Chris. Chris pointed at himself. Telsa nodded.

"Umm, my name is Christopher, but everyone calls me Rocks. You're Telsa, right?"

Telsa smiled, nodding again.

"You want me to save Shawn. How did he turn, anyway?"

Kevin glanced at the wall Chris had been standing in front of a few minutes ago. He pointed to the photo of the woman with the long ponytail. Telsa stepped out of the kitchen to see what Kevin was pointing at.

"Aida Ryan. I should've put two and two together." Telsa sounded unsurprised.

"That's Shawn's mother?" Chris asked.

"By birth and blood," Kevin said, "They look almost the same. I never paid close attention."

"Why do you want to save the boy?" asked Telsa. "He should be with his mother. It's a necessary loss."

"I would think so, but there is more at stake here, and Tiyshio killed his mother."

Telsa chuckled as she poured hot water into the mugs. "Looks like he found one thing he can't do right."

"We all know that," Chris remarked. "Do you think you can help Tiy?"

"I'm sorry. I can't."

Kevin looked annoyed. "What do you mean, you can't help us, T? Are you still afraid to join the fight?"

"What is with you and this fight!? No, that's not why I can't help you. I can't help you because someone helped me escape the conflict." She pointed back at her eye. "The reason my eyes are like this isn't that I am trying to blend in with the humans. It's because someone took the virus out of me!"

Chris looked at Kevin, confused. Kevin turned back to Telsa.

"What do you mean, someone took it out of you? I thought only creators could do that!"

"As I mentioned, there's always a back door. This one found it. Her name is Azuka. Azuka Fawzi. She is an anarchist, yet she would call herself more like you. Except for the whole building up an army thing. She likes to work for the money with her group."

"Did you seek her out?"

Telsa moved to the couch, signaling the men to join her. They took seats next to her. She grabbed the television remote to put on a program.

"I didn't really seek her out, not completely," she said. "About a year ago, I was tasked to find them. I lost control. They got into my head. I had been given a mission to find and kill her. When we met, she knew I was resisting the urges given to me. She released me from them, searched for me after a while, wanted me to fight them, too. Of course, I refused. She stays connected to them, but the way she separates someone from the virus is dirty."

"What do you mean, dirty?" Kevin asked.

"I mean that I am separated, but my body is still one of them. I have their anatomy. I can never go back to who I was. Yet it does come with perks. It took a while for some of them to settle in. I eat less, I'm stronger, that whole thing. Not to say I didn't possess all these abilities already. It's just that a lot of the old me isn't there anymore."

"Did you stay connected with her?" Chris asked.

"She's connected with me. I, not so much with her. I'll give you her address. She's in New York, somewhere in the Bronx. However, she moves around a lot. She's like your cause. She might even join you. What would you need her to do?" Telsa handed him a piece of paper with Azuka's address on it.

"Perhaps that's why Aida wanted you," Kevin surmised. "She figured you were still alive and could find her."

"If she did find her, what would happen to Telsa?" Chris asked.

"They would torture her to learn Azuka's whereabouts, then kill her for not submitting, as well as many of *her own*." Kevin bore a deeply worried look.

"They want Azuka because she could weaken their numbers. She already had gotten their attention. It was only a matter of time before someone went after her."

"Suukai chose you?" Kevin asked.

"He chose well for the last time. I moved here after that. I still feel safe if you are somewhere nearby. Teach Tiyshio how to get rid of the virus.".

The men prepared to leave. Telsa quickly followed.

"Hey, Kino?"

Kevin turned. Chris noticed how his look softened.

"I'm glad you found me," she said. "Just don't try so hard again, okay?"

Kevin smiled as he and Chris left.

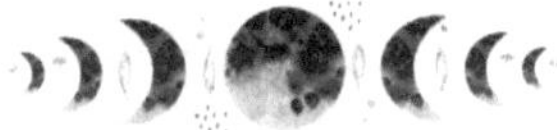

It must have been six in the morning when Tiyshio heard knocking on the door from outside his window. The sun was barely up, and the house otherwise quiet. The dawn was like a spell to his slumber.

Though the knocking continued. He made his way to the door, reluctantly. Everyone was asleep except his cat-like self.

"In what world can I become a drifter in the dawn, awaiting a sunrise and sunset that is never-ending?" His voice issued as softly as a whisper, with his mouth near shut.

"In a place that has a divine space, where youth is never-ending, and peace is on the horizon." Kevin's low but firm tone issued through the door.

"Another time, I live in another place, where harmony and peace have not been erased," they said in unison.

He was annoyed to see not only Kevin, but Chris, standing so early in the doorway. Their appearance was more than he could function for.

"For a secret code, that was pretty long." Chris bore a big smile as Tiyshio stepped outside, shutting the door behind him.

"It's safer than a simple password like strawberry sherbet. Rocks, where were you yesterday? Hayden stayed home alone. Not really alone, but, you know, with mom?"

"We were in Boston. It was quite a wild ride."

"Ahh. Did you guys finally find a lead?" He put on a smile that set the two off.

"Yeah," Kevin confirmed. "Get dressed. We're going to the Bronx."

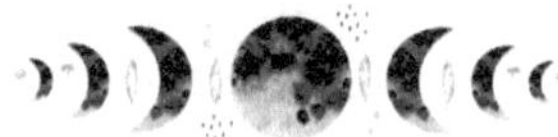

"Who the hell is Azuka Fawzi, and what kind of last name is Fawzi?" Tiyshio growled as they walked the streets of the Bronx.

"What kind of person has last and first names which both start with T?" Chris asked.

"Cool it, you two. What we do know is that she's some radical, and she can definitely help you."

"How do you know that?" Tiyshio queried. "Because Telsa told you she could?" They slowed down in front of an apartment building.

"I don't have anything else to go on but what I got," Kevin replied. Frankly, Tiyshio, I don't feel we have time, even if this boy is here. I've no idea what Nighcos or Derek have planned for him. If Azuka can teach you how to get rid of the Rigion gene without killing someone, she can be a big help. If not now, at least later."

Chris looked at an upper window and spotted someone peeking through the curtains. He felt odd, which caught the attention of Tiyshio. Kevin entered the lobby, searching for the number of the apartment number that had been given him, to ring the bell.

"You have ten seconds," came the voice on the speaker.

"I've come with the prince of Zorin. We need your assistance to change a Rigion back to his original state."

The door buzzed. They stepped inside, heading for the elevator.

"That was easy," Chris told him.

"Too easy. We are not out of the heat yet. Eyes sharp! Keep on your guard."

They exited the elevator and approached the apartment door. Tiyshio and Chris stood to one side, Kevin on the other. "Ready up," Kevin said quietly.

Chris raised his fist, Tiyshio unsheathed the sword he held, and Kevin pulled out a gun that looked anything but normal. His weapon was black, shaped like a teardrop, with an opening in the back. He nodded, signaling Tiyshio and Chris.

As he prepared to knock on the door, It suddenly opened. Surprised, Tiyshio and Kevin stared inside the apartment, then at each other, confused.

"What's going on?" Chris asked.

"Quiet!" Kevin whispered.

"How about you guys stop being a bunch of pansies and come inside?"

Kevin, bothered and confused, complied with the woman's request. He put his gun away. Tiyshio and Chris looked at him weirdly as Kevin signaled them to follow.

What they could see was nothing more than a small apartment. One could see the far end from the door. On the wall next to the kitchen was a bunch of pictures of people taken from different vantage points. On top of the wall, a label, **Tree of Rigions,** caught Chris's attention.

"This is some weird shit," Tiyshio said.

"Some weird shit for the son of Zorin, it might be," the woman's voice continued, "but I'm sure it will come in handy one day."

The speaker stepped out of the kitchen. The men watched her walk toward them, clad in short shorts and a tank top. She was a Caucasian female, with long straight black hair and brown eyes that occasionally glowed red. She had long legs and a small upper body, stood about five foot six, and carried a sword and an assault rifle on her back.

"Kevin Bratt. I never expected to see you on the same side. You're a wanted man."

"Many people already have that information."

"Yes, and not many people want you, either. Definitely not for the faint of heart." Azuka stared down at Chris.

"Hey! I know I look tall and strong to you, but I'm not the prince of all Zorians."

"I know you're not Lementan. I just admire your strength, compared to how you look. For your information, I'm Azuka, and, yes, I can help save to your friend, Tiyshio."

She focused her attention on him.

CHAPTER THIRTEEN

WEAK

The tree grew visibly larger as Tiyshio soared toward it. Then: Wham! His head rebounded off the trunk. His vision blurred momentarily. When his sight cleared, the glare of metal grew increasingly blinding.

He ducked the incoming blade, which then stuck in the tree. Surprised the weapon didn't sink in fully, he reached for it, only to have it elude his grasp.

Azuka had yanked the weapon back toward herself.

Tiyshio rushed after it.

With a sour look, Azuka yanked it faster into her grip.

Tiyshio stumbled from the force she used. His quick steps were silent against the leaves as he raced toward her. He wailed as if fighting air.

She didn't even flinch.

He snarled at her like an animal, ultimately whacking his own blade on the ground with his next strike. His wrist pulsed with pain. Distracted, he suddenly found himself shoved against the tree telepathically.

Tiyshio nudged Azuka back, before she could do any more.

That got her adrenaline pumping. Tiyshio witnessed her determination turn vicious. Their blades clashed, echoing through the forest.

The pressure she exerted against him increased.

"How can this petite woman have so much strength?" His blade crept down to his shoulder blade. He was losing footing. Joy filled her eyes, startling him. If he could look around her. Or he could follow the blade's motion with his body. Either way, he needed to act fast.

He slid down, protecting his back, diving between her legs as he kicked them apart. This action exposed her chest to be slit open.

She yelped.

He rolled over as her boot sped toward his face. He felt Azuka closing in he flipped away. She tugged against his wrist. The skin then reddened the harder she grasped. Tiyshio felt as though his fingers were being sprung open.

Headbutting her forced her to drop her swords. He kicked her away before she could get back up, then pulled roots from the trees to hold her down. From the crackling he heard, he didn't have enough time. Vibrations of her mind helped her keep up with the tightening.

Her arms rose quicker than he could fasten them back down. Invoking more force, he tied her to a tree, pulling her arms far enough apart for a chance of leverage. His heart slowed to a momentary silence.

The sound of a twig snapping let him know there was more to be done.

Tiyshio pressed his forearm against her neck, telekinetically turning her head toward him. Her eyes were tightly closed from the pain. That didn't matter. With a flick of his energy, he forced her eyes open, staring deep into them.

She screamed. Little chunks of red liquid oozed from her eyes like gelatin.

He heard a shuffling, no doubt some animal in the distance. It was enough to distract him. Enough for her to take a chance.

He tightened his grip, pulled harder on her eyes. Her screams heightened. He was halfway to defeating her.

Then he felt something come his way. He ducked, continuing to hold Azuka against the tree telepathically.

Tiyshio saw Azuka's sword frozen in the air, pointed at her temple. Shaken, he let out a sigh of relief. Azuka grabbed her sword, pulling back a bothered Tiyshio as he was about to leave.

Azuka smiled, patting him on the back.

"Are you serious?" he exclaimed. "I thought you said no cheap tricks?!"

Azuka shook her head. "That wasn't a cheap trick."

Tiyshio scoffed. "That–that wasn't? Get the hell out of here!" He was baffled by how calm she appeared, after all their commotion.

"What do you think?" she replied. "They're gonna play fair out there?"

"So, you admit it!"

"You didn't answer my question."

"No!"

"Then why do you seem so beat?"

"Because you're making it damn near impossible to succeed. Why can't we just do this in your apartment? Sit down and just focus on taking things out, you know. Like the first week you taught me. Finding a way to do this quickly?"

"It's only as impossible as you make it, and you are making it a fricking mountain climb! It doesn't have to be."

"A mountain climb! You threw a sword at my head! You damn near took off my head! TWICE!"

"From the looks of it, you're still alive." Azuka smiled.

"Oh, so this is just a joke to you?" Tiyshio scoffed.

Her laugh was obnoxiously loud, enough to embarrass Tiyshio. "No, this is not," she replied. "What is, is the fact that you don't want to take this seriously. You want to be taught how to take the drive away from the enemy, but you don't want the consequences."

"I don't want the consequences!? Who would want consequences?"

"Clearly you don't! If it was me, I'd give myself two choices."

"What would they be?!"

"Find a way to save the others, knowing I may lose my life, or simply kill the son of a bitch. Either option sucks, but it's a necessary loss."

Tiyshio took the time to breathe out. He gazed over the sea of trees.

"Keep up! I don't want to miss the bus!" Azuka yelled back.

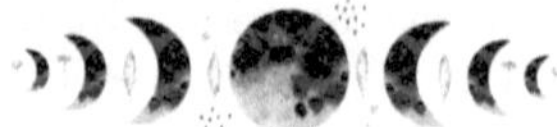

BACK AT AZUKA'S APARTMENT, SHE TOOK A SHOWER WHILE TIYSHIO flipped through the pictures lying next to her sofa. These showed her, among a few other people, holding guns, swords, staffs, and maces. In every picture, the people appeared militant. Especially their gear. Only a few of subjects were in casual wear.

What was she? Tiyshio wondered. He had two possibilities in mind. He knew she was a mercenary, but these photos looked like her life before her present one. Inhabitants from other worlds didn't keep pictures. They preferred visual memories, captured on crystals. The process of capture was a jolting sensation that imprinted the memory image into the stone. Touching that stone let the person relive that memory. She only had one of those. He wanted to touch it, but was afraid Azuka would catch him.

The image next to the stone showed a woman and a young girl. He presumed the latter was Azuka. It had to be. Still, he wasn't sure. He was curious, but his best choice for the present was to leave it alone.

He continued looking around the apartment to see what else he could find.

The rooms were dark, mostly shielded from the outside light. What little light there was overshadowed parts of the interior by only hitting the wall of weapons covering the bedroom. His attention focused on something he could barely see, but he hesitated, approaching it, knowing to do so would be wrong.

His gut feeling churned.

"*The shower is still running,*" he then realized. What better time than now to take a peek? A few more photos lay by her bed. One was of the Rigion eye, but a different variation, one Tiyshio had never seen.

The cornea had a honeycomb pattern, making it look infected. The iris itself was similar to that of the eye of Redemption's first stage, although the lines were not black, but white. The next few photos showed other Rigion eyes, with the one Tiyshio knew faced the bed: the eye of Redemption. It was the largest.

In the closet lay a chest without a lock. Tiyshio opened it. Inside were combat clothes. At the bottom was a picture of a much younger Azuka, around her early teens. Standing beside her was Nighcos, looking no older than the last time Tiyshio saw him, at the age of nine.

Tiyshio glanced toward the bathroom. Curious, he reached out to Azuka.

She blocked all his attempts.

Something wasn't right.

Tiyshio heard the water turn off in the bathroom. He rushed to put the chest away.

"Having fun looking at my past?" she asked.

"Yeah. I like a good soldier." He sounded sarcastic but shaky in tone.

"I know you saw something that bothered you. You don't have to hide it."

Tiyshio quickly put down the last photo.

"Umm…yeah! You're right. I did see something odd. I know you're a merc. I know you were one of them. I just didn't know you were close to Nighcos. How did you manage that?"

"The same way you're close to your uncle."

"Kevin's not my uncle. Sometimes he feels like it, but he's not."

"Then what is he to you?"

"He's my guardian. He's been that way since I was five. Actually, he's been around my entire life, as much as my real father was, before I left Zorin."

"Where's your real dad?"

"I don't know. I feel like I made him disappear. If he was here, I could be stronger."

"He trained you?"

"Not as much as Kevin did. Kevin has been training me day in and day out. He's taught me right from wrong. Raised me like I was his own son."

"I sense that you resent Kevin right now."

"How did you get that?"

"I can read minds, you know. I know this is something he is doing for you. When I met all of you for the first time, I saw it on his face. You know what else I saw?"

"What?"

"He'd feel guilty if he didn't save someone he took care of. So, my question holds: do you resent him?"

"I don't. I just have my moments. There are days in which I don't respect him as I should. Especially right now, with all that's going on."

"He's helping you now. Take, for example, what happened to us at the park. That attitude won't get you far. Our lives are cutthroat, not made for the weak. We arrived here because we wanted to survive. The others came to keep us in fear, to remind us we have nowhere to go. This is no place for the weak. You must work harder, play their game. They are forcing others to have a drive they don't want. At least, some of them. I assume you can do the same if you want to save your friend. You cannot be weak. Got it?"

Tiyshio nodded. "But I must know what you did for him?"

Azuka stared at Tiyshio. "I did things that were out of my control. Now I help those people find a way to get control again." Azuka pulled a chair out of the kitchen with her mind. "I'll have it your way."

Tiyshio looked at her weirdly.

"Take a seat!"

He obeyed without thinking.

"Let's go back to lesson one. You know what a Rigion is, what they are capable of. What you don't seem to understand is the drive they have."

"I do get their drive. They want to kill my people."

"It's more than that, and you know it. For instance, what is the drive of your best friend?"

"He wants me dead, in revenge for his mother's death."

"He… wants you dead… for the death… of… his… mother." Her smile made Tiyshio feel both warm and cold, even as she agreed. Her delivery was mesmerizing.

"Now, I know what you are thinking," she continued. "No matter what had become of him, he couldn't forgive you."

Tiyshio shook his head. "You're wrong, at least partially."

"Oh, really?" she replied, shocked but sarcastic. "Let's run through the list. His choice to be with his mother, him. The resentment toward you, him. The idea that your killing his mother justifies his killing you. However, I believe there's another reason he shouldn't kill you. Shawn had already been in a vulnerable place, seeing his mother again. I would be, too. He would have done anything to be with her. He's not wrong in that."

"I can see that you know more about this than you are telling me."

Azuka's expression stayed blank. "Have you ever seen a person become a Rigion, before Shawn?"

Tiyshio shook his head.

"When you become a Rigion, you also become very susceptible to choice. You have a hard time deciphering what's the right choice. It doesn't help when someone is with you in these moments. You are already your own worst enemy. It's as if you were fighting amnesia every morning when you wake up, and the only thing keeping you from going crazy is this." Azuka pointed to her head.

"Your mind?"

"Helps you remember who you are, and what you need to accomplish."

"Is there any particular reason a Rigion would undergo so much stress?"

"They are weak in their mind, as I said. The actual way of their past life is to fight against the way of life that the Rigion gene wants them to accept. I realize that isn't the best explanation. Rigions are still a mystery, and a relatively young race."

"What does this have to do with what we're trying to accomplish here?"

"You must be able to play mind games with them. When you are caught in a battle with your friend, you need to get inside his head. They work best off memories; it's the first course of judgments for any Rigion. If there is anyone he'd hurt before you, it'd be your friends. His guardians. You need to watch out for that. Watch his mind. It will tell you his intentions. When pulling out the virus quickly, it's best to use these tactics, since it's a way to get to their head. I want you to try it on me."

"Try it on you? But I know nothing about you."

"If you focus, you will know as much as you need to use it against me."

"But you aren't someone who was recently changed into a Rigion?"

"Then what is the point of my helping you?" she snapped. "Why do you want to save him so bad?"

"BECAUSE I CAN'T LIVE WITH MY MISTAKE! I wake up every morning scared to see if anyone is in danger, apart from myself. I spend every GODDAMN night reliving the moment I killed his mom, wishing I had done something different. MY ACTIONS MAKE ME FEEL LIKE I LOST…EVERYTHING!! I am theoretically able to do anything. The least I can do is correct my own consequences from fear of the unknown."

"In that case, do you think I wouldn't have chosen to help save your friend?"

His eyes swelled with tears, She could see him transform smaller.

"I know how you feel, but you are already maturing as a result of these reflections. Understand your grief. Get to know your actions. Now, let's begin."

His heart calmed under the influence of her soothing voice. He moved closer to her, taking a deep breath. Her eyes shifted to those of a Rigion.

"Like when I first taught you this trick, I want you to remember to focus. I also want you to multitask. I know you can do it."

Tiyshio looked at her as if she was fooling.

"Just get started, you joker. I'm proud of your efforts today."

"Thanks. That means a lot." He shook his head.

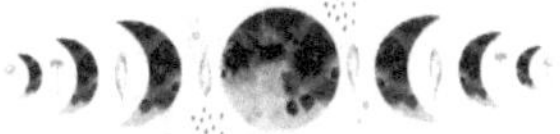

WHILE TIYSHIO SPENT TIME WITH AZUKA, KEVIN, AND TELSA WERE running errands, boring the life out of Kevin. Telsa smiled, knowing he wished to do something important. She believed that something could wait. Now, in a grocery store, Kevin slowly followed Telsa down each aisle, practically dragging his feet, clenching and rolling his teeth every second. Yet, in each store they visited, he tended to let go of something on his mind.

He looked on Telsa as a walking memory in front of him. Everything around her moved slowly; she alone, moved in real time.

Telsa guessed something was up with Kevin, yet she just kept letting out sighs.

When they later went for a jog, Kevin stayed far behind Telsa. He wanted to keep watching her, but differently, remembering the events of the week before. Her head would cock from left to right, studying everyone she passed by, and those who passed by her as well. The action felt infectious; he couldn't help copying it.

He understood why she lived in fear, as much as the reason they had parted before. He finally understood why he had so much trouble. He felt the same even now, with her right in front of him. He had needed time to understand.

Telsa continued running around the park. She failed to notice Kevin was no longer behind her, though he had been half an hour earlier. She began breathing heavily, not from exhaustion, but because of him. Her eyes danced around the park, searching for him, feeling everyone around her. She scurried back to where they had first entered the park. She could not find him there, either.

"This is no time to play games, Kino!" she muttered under her breath.

She continued down the running course, finally discovering him sitting on the grass, meditating. She sighed, shook her head, and walked up to him.

"Had trouble keeping up?" she asked.

"Not at all. You were bothering me."

Telsa's eyes flew open. "WHAT! Then what was the point of your being here?"

"To spend time with you, make sure you're safe. I owe you that much."

"First off, I was doing fine without you here, thank you very much! Also… you know I don't mind your company, but if I'm a burden to you, I think you'd be better off staying in New York."

"There's the girl that left New York! Yet you still haven't left that city, have you?"

Silence hung in the air for a long moment.

"Mentally I am still there, most days," she admitted. "I left you because I believed it'd be safer if you and Tiyshio weren't with someone who once was a sleeper. Remember what happened last time? I figured you'd be fine on your own. That seemed to work out for the best. Until now."

She sighed, sitting next to him. "I'm sorry. I know I can be on edge at times."

Kevin opened his eyes to look at her. "Yeah, I can feel the vibrations from a few miles away," he joked.

She nudged him in the shoulder, smiling.

"It's sad, what happened to that boy. I really liked him. So well-mannered and innocent."

"Innocent? Boy, you have been gone too long."

Telsa's eyes widened. "What did he do?"

Kevin realized then he should have kept his mouth shut.

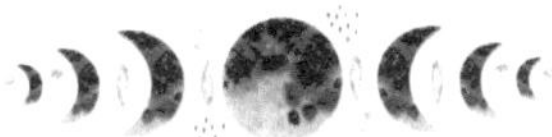

"Azuka, can I ask you a question?" Tiyshio posed. "How did you track down someone like Telsa?"

"Oh, that simple beauty? She had been in my sights for three to four years before these recent events. You know what she was worth to Lord Nighcos. She was worth a lot to me, as well. To get her meant getting to his favorite. I never wanted to kill her I needed her as my way to him. What I did not know was that she was never loyal. I could see it in her mind, so I took it out of her. She became my message, in a different way. I was pretty satisfied that it worked damn well."

"Why do you think so? Aren't you afraid they'll come after you, eventually?"

"Because I've never seen someone send so many squads to scavenge for just one woman. I know she holds secrets, lots of them. Since Nighcos wants her, he will find ways. I am not afraid. After what I did, I am sure he would want to know me, too. I'm grateful he forgot about me."

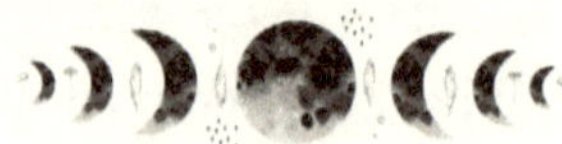

"You heard what I said a year ago. He just wanted me back."

"And he still wants you back, or is it all in your head?" Kevin asked.

"NO! I saw one of his pawns. Kevin, he sent squads after me. One day, as I was heading home from work, like the day that you found me, they were close to succeeding in their goal. They locked me down in a mall not far from here. I had passed out for…I don't know. I don't know how many hours I was gone. Next thing you know, I'm in a room with him. If it weren't for her help, I'd still be his."

"The day Azuka took out the eyes." Telsa nodded. "How did you guys get away from Nighcos?"

"I don't know, exactly. She made it easy, but she has a group of mercs, strong soldiers, all ex-Rigions. Also, she could teleport. Not like you do with the particle thing, it's more like using a portal or wormhole. The only similarity is that it's just as disorienting."

They both laughed. Kevin got up off the grass, then helped pick her up so they could head back to her townhouse to get changed.

"So, how are you enjoying Boston so far?"

"You found her in one of your raid attempts?" Tiyshio asked.

"Yes," Azuka confirmed. "It wasn't planned. She just happened to be right where I didn't expect her to be. Look, you're losing focus. You said you wanted to practice doing nothing. I'm not going to tell you her whole life story here, okay?!"

"Then who should I ask, other than the source?"

"The other source. Telsa. Got it?"

Tiyshio looked annoyed, "Yeah, yeah, I got it. Sheesh."

"Good. Now, take out the virus before the timer goes out."

Tiyshio saw the timer was set to twenty seconds. He looked back at Azuka, bewildered.

"You're mad!" she argued. She appeared to be filled with joy. "You complain too much!"

"It's impossible to take it out within that time frame!"

"What was that you said earlier? Things are only as impossible as you make them?"

"Good point."

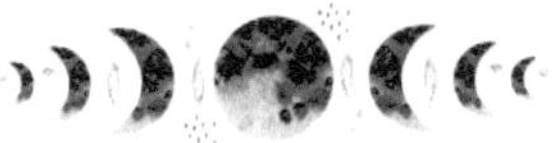

"You were not wrong. These hoagies are great. Now I can't hate on your decision to leave of New York."

"Beats that bagel shop you used to take me to. Do you still go?"

"Every weekend now, before Tiyshio wakes up."

"You started making breakfast, I'm guessing? It looks good on you. You have a lady, then?"

"I need to have a lady to cook?"

"No, but you didn't cook much when I was there. Come on, Kino. You're always so serious. You know I'm busting your balls."

"Yeah, I know. Just watch yourself. How'd you take such a wild guess? You know about Mrs. Kazio?"

"Not too much, just that she's Tiyshio's old teacher! Doesn't that break the rules of conduct?"

"It does' but it's mutual. We keep it professional on school grounds. Anywhere else, it's free rein."

"Does she have a first name?"

Kevin smiled. "It's only been a few months. I don't want to give anything away until I can call it solid."

"I respect that." Telsa nodded. "But you're still messed up for ruining a marriage."

"Who said I was ruining a marriage?"

Telsa's eyes widened. She almost looked like a wind-up doll from her minor snickering.

"I want to get back to Azuka. How long have you two been around each other since you first met?"

"Us two? Last year, I stayed with her for six months. She trained me, prepared me for the next encounter. She tried to make me less afraid, and even how to do the thing that she's doing with Tiy."

"If you knew how to do it, why didn't you take on the task?"

"Because the way I do it is crude. These people may no longer be connected to the network, but they still carry symptoms of a Rigion. They'd be a stray. Or, a better term, an outcast."

"But they are still themselves, are they not?" Kevin asked, slightly annoyed.

"Not necessarily. Most of them still have the craving. Some revert to being Rigion because those tendencies in them begin to fight back. Soon after, the network will find its way back to them. I prefer not to help. You can see why."

"How long have you trained with her, doing that?"

"Since I met her. A long time."

"A long time could mean either you didn't get it, or you had a bad teacher."

"I know what you're getting at, Kino. You should know I'm a slow learner."

"Not with me, you weren't. You were able to knock me on my ass plenty of times before."

"That was because Tiyshio was young, and you were barely trying. I've seen you fighting those foot soldiers. You don't hesitate to kill every single one of them. It's like you're angry at something. I think that rubbed off on Tiyshio, as well."

"Well, that was him then. You should see him now."

"See him now? What's the boy fighting for this time?" she asked.

Kevin shook his head. "You got a point."

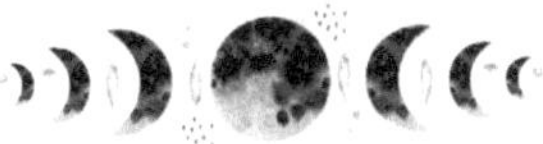

Tɪʏsнɪо continued staring deep into Azuka's eyes, noticing the defect in her iris, a split that ran horizontally across it. Tiyshio commented on it.

Azuka slapped him across the face. "Stay focused!"

"You're so physical!"

"You think I don't know what you're doing?"

"What am I doing, exactly?"

"You're looking at me like you want me."

"And that question was rhetorical," he stated under his breath.

"Tiyshio, do you want to take a break? You're starting to fool around, and you were doing good this morning."

"Yes, I would like to. I haven't eaten since this morning."

"I'll make some steak and eggs. You're lucky I had seasoned two the other day. It's crazy to know a Zorin who eats constantly like you."

"I learned to blend in with humanity. Eating is one of the assimilations. On the plus side, I gained a taste for it. It's pretty amazing, actually."

Azuka smiled at him, grabbing the steak and eggs from the fridge. "I feel the same."

Tiyshio finished his food, then looked at Azuka. A big smile crossed his face. "You may be mean, but you sure can cook."

Azuka laughed. "Next time you're over, you cook."

"I never cook. Correction: I don't know how."

Azuka looked at him in shock. "Does Kevin know how to –"

"He does. He wouldn't teach me until I left the house, and even then, based on whoever I decided to stay with for the rest of my unnatural life."

"Whom would that be?"

"My guess would be my girlfriend. She looks like a mix of Black and Japanese, but like most of the people I have associated with so far…"

"Is not from Earth," Azuka finished.

Tiyshio nodded.

"I guess you like staying close to home?"

Tiyshio smiled. Azuka grabbed a photo of her and Telsa off the wall.

"She really matters to you, doesn't she?"

"She's family. She protected me when I was in danger. I just want to know, if you worked together then, why not now? You seem good at your job. Why is she still fearful?"

"That, you already know the answer to. We separated because she said she was done fighting. I can't hold her back from that decision. Most of us came here for a normal life, away from invasion and war. She's had a life of hardship; she's a runaway. Even from you. I reminded her of a life she didn't want to be a part of. Do you know how she became a Rigion?"

Tiyshio shook his head.

"Like your friend, she was changed because of the death of her father, by a friend. The person who changed her was Nighcos. He raised her, trained her, got her to kill the person that killed her father. That friend was going to be her protector."

Tiyshio gave a look that seemed justified.

"But you know what you and she do have in common?"

Tiyshio nodded.

"You are both strong, but not mentally strong."

Tiyshio, confused, blurted, "What the hell is that supposed to mean?!"

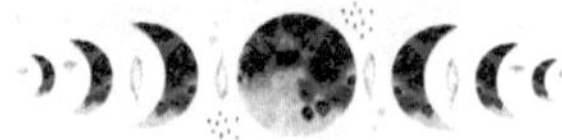

HEADING BACK TO THE APARTMENT, TELSA AND KEVIN SHARED A BOX of donuts. Telsa couldn't keep her eyes off Kevin after the previous revelation.

"You know, to some, this is considered cheating?"

"Well, not for us, at least." Telsa smiled.

"I just got to know. Are you sure I can trust Azuka? She seems radical and unhinged. For one, you left her side."

"I left her side because I am done fighting. I have a life I can try to live, and my abilities are the only thing getting me this far. If I wanted to fight, I'd do it with her. I know she is a planner and gets things done."

"What is that supposed to mean? Are you trying to say I'm not a good planner?"

Telsa laughed. "On the contrary. I believe you're a great leader. You can plan an attack like there's no tomorrow."

"There is no tomorrow."

Telsa looked annoyed. "You get my point, Kino. Also, you trust Azuka, She may have not been able to teach me. She used to say I'm not *mentally strong*. She wasn't wrong, at the time, I'm sure now I'd be a big help to her. I know Tiyshio would be good with her. His hard-headedness and her lack of patience would work out very well."

"You're sure?"

"Yeah!"

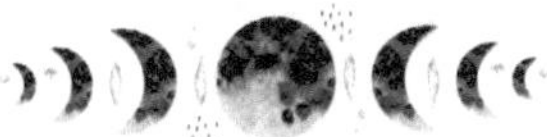

A young man, in his mid-twenties, overlooked the Manhattan skyline. He stood tall and slim, gazing upon the view, blank-faced but calm. For this man, it was a tranquil experience. With each gust of wind, he took a deep breath. His hands were stuffed into his jacket pocket. A woman stood by his side. He couldn't help but smile, with a literal feeling of being on top of the world. He looked around the rooftop, searching the other people there. The woman tapped him on his shoulder.

"What's up?" she asked.

"I'm just gonna look for Shawn."

The woman mouthed, 'okay.'

Shawn stood on the opposite side of the rooftop, looking at Staten Island. From behind approached the man looking for him. The latter nudged his side, then stood right next to him. He copied what the other was doing, noticing him looking at a particular house as if it were right in front of his eyes.

"I'm guessing you want to go home?" Kirk asked, a little disappointed.

"No. I'm right where I want to be." Shawn looked at Kirk.

"But, the house?"

Shawn stopped him before he could continue. "That home was just a look at the past. God, Sun would love it up here."

"I've got my lady. You could've had yours. What happened?"

"She traveled to Japan to visit family for the break."

"What about your brother?"

"Tiyshio is out with Kevin, traveling the world on business."

"Business!? That's what he calls it." Kirk scoffed. "Does Tiyshio ever get to have fun?"

"I don't think so," Shawn replied. They both laughed.

"It sucks, going to all these new cities and never really getting to enjoy them. Unlike me, stuck here, living life quietly."

"You sure that'd be the right thing to do? I mean, with Kevin, I've learned that here isn't safe. Hearing about people being taken from their homes. Sometimes they make it out; if they do, they're probably a Rigion already. To live out here, like there isn't a threat, is too naïve."

"Not necessarily. I know it sounds idiotic. Think about it! The world was at war not too long ago. Still, now, people travel around this globe without any fear of being killed or questioned. They're safe. The only focus they have is practically nothing. They call it a vacation." Kirk flaunted his hands in a rainbow.

"So, would this be a vacation?" Shawn mimicked.

"By my guess, yeah! I feel relaxed! Do you feel relaxed?"

Shawn nodded.

"I believed you would. Up here, there are no worries."

Shawn nodded again, looking up to the sky. He wanted to see the stars shine through.

"I've been meaning to ask sometimes I feel that you treat me like someone you know. You never talk of your own family, but I feel you once had a brother. Maybe you still do?"

"Back on Zorin, yeah! A sister, actually, two years older than me. **Mad soldier***! Never taking any shit. Her name was Mita. As much of a pain in the ass as she was to me, she's always been a great person to learn from. More so when I was older, and willing to listen. You'd know. Amelia's always on my ass."*

Shawn shouted, "Yeah!" then laughed.

"I came to Earth in '74 with her. She knew something was off here. She came to protect the people, as I said. **Mad soldier.** *Our parents went one way, we went another. We learned to survive until she became one of them, and I had to get rid of her. Add that to not hearing from Mom or Dad, because they're protecting themselves. It wasn't until I met Amelia that I no longer felt alone."*

"How long were you alone?"

"Two and a half years. I felt lost. You know what? I wish I hadn't killed her."

"Why?"

"Because at least, even if she was my enemy, I knew she'd always be there. I'd want to find a way to help her get rid of her drive. When you're alone, you grow desperate to find a family. In any form, you and Amelia are just that. I'd do anything to protect you two. I love you two."

Shawn smiled, getting a little choked up.

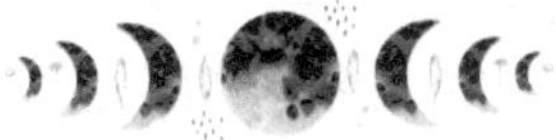

SHAWN AWOKE FROM HIS MEMORY, SLOWLY ADJUSTING OUT FROM HIS meditative state. Gathering up his surroundings, he saw below reports riddled with Kirk and Amelia's names. Something looked different. Notes were written in the margins of the report, some of which read as though he were writing back to his mother. He had them circled in his space, as if keeping him captive. On one report, it read, *'I don't know why she would keep me out of this, if she knew they weren't best to be with. Why leave me in danger? I can't live in the past, because at least now I know my enemies.'*

Derek sat in his room, talking on the phone, removing photos and a report from a thick envelope. He sorted the pictures on his desk, focusing on one: a picture of Kevin, shaking hands with Shawn's parental guardian, Kirk. Behind Kirk stood a group of armed men and women. One thing gave them away: a 'Z' outline, prominent on the arms of the group in gold.

"Was this taken recently?" Derek asked, adopting a slightly vulgar tone. His eyes rose once he heard the answer. He got up and levitated the items he needed towards him as he left the room.

Shawn and Derek met in the living room, facing each other. Shawn had his sword wrapped around his back. A mess levitated behind Derek.

"Where are you off to?" Shawn asked.

"I could ask you the same thing." Derek arranged the items he was levitating inside a bag.

"I'm sorry. It's been taking me some time to decide. Perhaps Nighcos made me a believer. I'd still rather see for myself. I'm hoping to find somebody who could help me find all of our enemies, teach me how to infiltrate their location, and get rid of them."

"There's no need. That envelope I got in the mail this morning? It contains the location of some of those Zorians, the ones that harmed your mother and killed your father. I've gotten word that they plan to make a move on another family of Rigion sympathizers. Whether that family is a friend or not, they have one of our own whom we should protect, and that includes the entire family. It doesn't matter where they're from. Casan, I want you to join me. I see in your mind you'd rather get your answers from the source. I know you are still unsure. This raid may help you get the answers you are looking for. Possibly even assist you in the search for your guardians, which you have been doing for the past few weeks. What do you say?"

"I'm game. What's your plan?"

Derek strapped the rest of the bag's contents to Shawn's back.

"What made you change your mind?"

"Nighcos told me his story. I don't want to wait around, not knowing theirs. I've been alone for a while, but I don't mind having you with me."

Shawn fastened the bag more tightly to his back, while Derek laid out a map and a blueprint on the dinner table over which they stood.

With a worried expression, he said, "Let's get started."

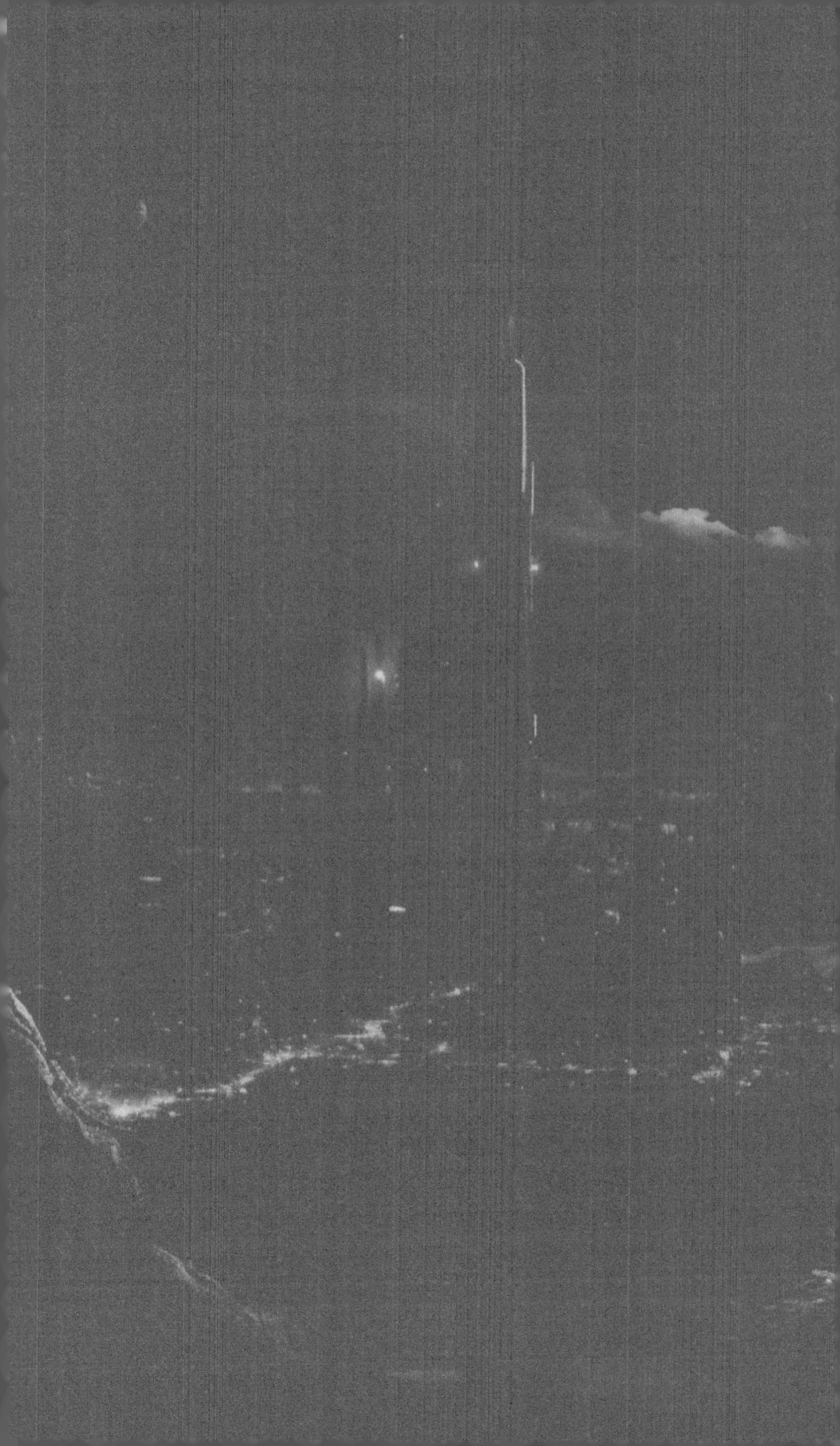

CHAPTER

FOURTEEN

FALLEN

Swords clashed. Shawn was up in the face of the Zorian soldier. Sweat and fear coated that soldier's face; rage filled Shawn's. The soldier pushed Shawn away with all his might. Shawn shrugged the attack off, retaliating maliciously. Each hit he made was harder than the last.

Derek could see the ferociousness fueling him.

The soldier's back pressed against the wall. His eyes rose upward as Shawn swung at his head. He could feel the heated chars scrape off the wall and flinched.

Shawn wore the armor that had been given to him by the doctor who'd protected him. His opponent raised an arm to push Shawn away with his mind. Shawn made quick work of him, slicing off his arm, letting the soldier plead for his life before beheading him. He then blasted the soldier's body until nothing remained but ash.

A sword swung over Shawn's head. He quickly blasted the wielder's arm upwards and shoved him, too, against the wall. Before his attacker could recover, Shawn shot a spike straight through the wielder's heart, pinning him to that wall. He ran up close to the soldier's face, offering a sinister smile before severing his limbs, letting him bleed out.

A woman then ran up to punch Shawn as he turned away from his latest victim. He felt his jaw almost jolt out of place.

He sneered, reading her mind, feeling her nerves tingle with fear before her last moments.

He turned to Derek, who looked back sternly. They scanned the room to look for any more threats before continuing.

Shawn and Derek both felt the room was now too quiet, and unnaturally empty. Derek raised his left hand, then signaled with his right hand for Shawn to stay silent. Derek then clutched his hand into a fist.

The soldiers that had been hiding launched into view.

"Cool, right?" Derek rhetorically asked. Shawn shook his head, prepared to toy with the oncoming crowd.

The lead soldier had trouble getting back to his feet, with his vision blurred. He had originally launched toward Shawn and Derek headfirst. That he could still stand was amazing.

Derek strolled toward him.

The soldier let out a deep, worried breath, pulling a sword from the far wall to his side.

Derek stared deep into the soldier's eyes. His enemy was surely in fear.

"If you're gonna stab me, just do it!" the Zorian soldier yelled.

"You're eager for death? I can help you with that." Derek thrust his sword against the man's torso.

The man raised his own blade to Derek's neck. He then grasped Derek's sword, not caring that his hand bled as long as he pierced Derek's neck.

Shawn closed in, swinging his arm as he stripped off the skin to form a spike. He launched at the man's skull.

"You okay?"

Derek wiped the blood from his neck. "Now I am." He grabbed his sword.

The soldier stared at them both, while holding his own sword in a defensive position. Shawn and Derek stared at him as the soldier breathed heavier with each passing moment. Shawn stripped off one more layer of dead skin, with which to make another blade.

The two of them slowly closed in on the soldier. He wasted no time swinging his sword toward Derek's head while blasting at Shawn's legs. Derek reacted quickly, striking down at the man's arm. Shawn flicked a finger, launching a spike toward the man's leg. He cried out, limping.

The soldier scanned his two attackers, then snarled, "You're making this difficult."

"No, I think you're handling this just fine," Derek replied sarcastically. Shawn swung his sword toward the man's head, only to be parried and responded to in kind. For a few minutes, they had their back and forth.

Derek tried to join them, but then felt push him to the side.

"I thought you killed everybody else?" Derek snapped as he rushed toward the woman who had knocked him down.

"Well, actually, I knocked some of them out mentally. You know, to make surviving easier." Shawn tried to tap into the soldier's mind.

"That's not going to work!" his opponent exclaimed.

"It was worth a shot!" Shawn replied, pushing him off his blade.

"Next time we do this, just kill them!" Derek screamed, shooting his sword around the room to take out whoever remained. He ran toward the woman who'd attacked him and pulled out the support bracket in the wall. He sprung the bracket up as a spear to run her through and began pushing her toward the bracket.

She shielded herself to prevent Derek doing anything too drastic.

Around the room, the soldiers tried their hardest to dodge the sword that kept coming at them relentlessly. Blood flowed around the room as if from a broken faucet.

Derek looked to Shawn to see if he needed help. Despite a long gash across his head, and blood dripping down his wrist, he seemed to be doing fine.

He encased the woman in a bubble, which he then began shrinking. She dropped her weapon. Both her blade and his came to him.

Shawn noticed this as he finally stabbed his own attacker in the stomach. He grabbed the sword from Derek's hand, then approached the suffocating woman. He stared directly into her eyes, watching them change from brown to their natural gold color. The sclera quickly turned red, tearing up. Her eyes rolled. Shawn tossed the sword back to Derek, then sprung a spike and slit her throat, watching her bleed out.

Derek took in the sight with a bit of fear, but the situation seemed familiar.

Shawn turned to him. "That trick you pulled. You could've done it earlier."

"I'm not that good at multitasking… Come on. We have one more room to go."

Shawn and Derek moved forward, easily killing the remaining soldiers, leaving just their leader—the man they were looking for. The leader's leg was broken, and his arm scarred. Half his face was burnt; the other half was covered in blood. Breathing heavily as he tried crawling toward an odd-looking gun. Shawn and Derek, behind him, pulled him away from the gun and raised him into the air. Shawn formed another blade out of his arm. Derek pressed his sword against the man's neck.

"You have some information I want to know," Derek said.

The man started searching Derek's and Shawn's minds. "I don't have what you want! You came to the wrong place! AGHHHH!"

The man screamed as Derek began to pull him by the limbs.

"You're lying. You know I can search your mind, and I feel you hiding it. Now tell me. Please." Derek raised the man's other arm and began stretching them apart.

The man cried out again.

"You can continue doing what you do, Loctai. You're the piece of shit that's got this boy all wrapped up in this mess." Shawn started moving closer.

Derek held him back.

"Don't bring him into this. Amelia and Kirk Parker, Kevin hid them. Where are they?!"

"Why don't you ask him?" Shawn said, pointing at the soldier. "He knows exactly where they are."

The man laughed, coughing up blood. Shawn pierced him slowly in his stomach.

The man groaned. "You think I know where they are? If I knew, they'd already be dead!"

Then he laughed. "You'd like that, wouldn't you? What has he told you, Casan?"

Shawn glared at him fiercely.

"You aren't allowed to say that name!"

"That is your name, right? Casan! I don't have to be in your head to know. You think we killed your father? Attacked your mother? Broke your family? I'd say we did, and you know what? You can kill me. At least I know my job has been fulfilled." The man chuckled.

Shawn sprung a spike from his hand. Derek tried holding him back, but Shawn brushed him off, pressing his blade against the soldier's neck.

"How about I take something from you, hmm? You got family? From my mind, it appears you haven't any, but you do have a girlfriend. She lives in the Bronx, has a son. If I get into her mind, SHE'S DONE!"

"Don't you dare invade her mind!"

"Then give me what I want, Loctai! No more games, because I won't torture you. I will take!"

"Hahaha, like you could! Go ahead, kill them. I want to see you take innocent lives," the man mocked.

"It's your lucky day." Shawn placed his hand on the soldier's head. He saw, through the eyes, an image of his loved one feeding her five-year-old son. Her son suddenly collapsed onto the plate he was eating from. His girlfriend screamed out her son's name. "TENSAE! TENSAE!"

The soldier stared into the distance, tears slowly sliding down his cheeks. The woman did the same, wiping her face as she said, "Rico, I love you."

"You still think I'm playing games? That was my final warning. Give me what I want." Shawn repointing the blade toward the soldier's neck.

"You want answers? They're in Newark, New Jersey, in a two-story house about half an hour from the city. You should be able to sense them from there. They'll tell you exactly what we did when we killed your fat –"

Shawn chopped off the soldier's head.

Derek released his arms and looked at his companion, a little troubled. He knew the next move.

"Let's head home." Derek then left the warehouse.

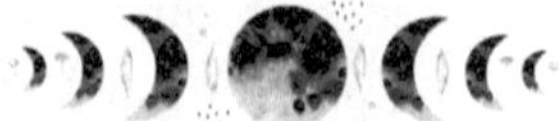

DEREK RESTED WITH HIS BACK AGAINST THE WALL, NEXT TO A window. Shawn sat at the table; their swords lay on top of it. Shawn looked uneasy to Derek. His head was down, hands and legs shaking sporadically. *Why hesitate now, when you know the truth?* Truth was, he knew exactly why. The answer had been there since they first met: family. It was the only thing on his mind.

Derek saw the decision was made. It was written all over Shawn's face. He was simply dancing in silence.

"Shawn, you don't have to do this. No one asked you to."

"Then why bring me? You knew I'd want the answers!"

"Now you've got them. At first, I wanted you to help me get rid of them, but you care about them. If you go over there, you'll hesitate, and they will kill you!"

"How do you know I'll hesitate, huh? How do you know they'll kill me? How do you know if I care about them still?"

"Because if you didn't care about them, you would have ordered that cab to leave already. On top of that, you wouldn't have mentioned it."

Shawn looked down again. Derek walked to the door and gestured for his sword to come to him.

"I'll return when it's done. For now, rest and meditate on what we should do tomorrow."

Derek opened the door, then suddenly collapsed to the ground. Shawn rose from his chair and levitated Derek to lay on the couch.

"It's okay, Derek. This will always be something I have to do."

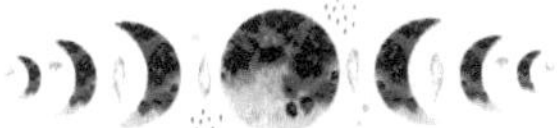

AMELIA SLAVED OVER THE BATHROOM, CLAWING AT A BLACK SPOT that seemed almost engraved on the frame of the tub. Her face was red as fire; her hair tied back. Annoyed as she was, she just wanted to finish setting up the place. Only three weeks ago, Kevin gave them the space, a dusty, cluttered mess. There were boxes everywhere. Some furniture had never been set up. The sink and bathrooms hadn't been cleaned since probably the place was first set up.

When they first moved in, Amelia claimed, "This place is just like Kevin." Kirk believed she meant he was disorganized, but she actually meant cluttered. Considering Kevin had so many connections that seemed so close, it'd be a long time before he contacted them again.

Much like how Shawn came into their care.

Kirk was in the kitchen, grooving to Eric B and Rakim. On one end, he was grilling chicken on the stovetop; on the other, he was cleaning countertops. It all seemed unsanitary. In fact, he was cleaning so close to the stove that Amelia kept stopping him mentally. To the point at which he yelled, "Okay, okay! I got your message. Damn it!"

Kirk could hear her laughing from his place in the kitchen.

"You can't cook food next to your cleaning area," she chided. "That's mixing it with poison, you know?"

"I'm sorry. We're just so close to getting this space finished. I don't know if we should pack up all our old stuff and move in. What do you think?"

Kirk put the food aside and traveled upstairs, during which time Amelia replied, "Why would I want to move from Staten Island? I like it there. We're not too far from the ferry. Only thirty minutes to downtown. Why would you want to move?"

"I mean, this place is big!" Kirk explained. "We fixed it up, even did a little DIY! I feel Kevin owes us for this place."

"Kevin doesn't owe us jack shit!" Amelia grinned, putting away the cleaning products. "In fact, I think he would consider all of this an even trade. I just don't understand what's wrong with our apartment?"

"Who wants to stay in an apartment in New York? You smell your neighbor's cooking, which never goes away. There's a weird piss smell at the end of the hall. The rats. The roaches. The rats!"

"Okay, I get it, but I'm okay with it! Think about it. We don't need a lot. We don't plan on having any kids anytime soon!"

"But we do have a kid?" Amelia stopped smiling, instead looking down and rushing out of the bathroom.

"You're still thinking about Shawn?"

"You already know the deal."

Kirk followed her premise. "Amelia, I understand how you feel. I miss him, too, but you know why we're here." Kirk heard a faint rattling in the background as he marched down the steps.

"But how much of that do you believe is the truth?"

"Kevin hasn't lied to us for the longest time."

"Doesn't mean he won't start today. He is getting older."

"Older for a human. Don't judge him. Why do you want him to slip up so bad?"

"I don't, but Shawn's a good kid. Keeping us safe from him? He knows we aren't the enemy."

"He's a Rigion, with another Rigion. He could be spoon-fed all kinds of crap right now. How would he be able to tell?"

"From what I know, it's a choice, right?"

Amelia nodded. She heard a faint crash but dismissed it as belonging to the neighbor.

"Yes, but from what we were told, he's in a state that's hard to persuade. Kirk, I just hope he's safe, that he's okay, and no one is toying with him."

"Nor do I!"

The back door creaked open. Amelia slowly walked toward it, bringing a battle ax. Kirk did the same, wrapping a chain around his wrist.

At the entrance stood Shawn.

His body was covered in dirt and blood, his shirt and pants ripped, and his knee injured. Amelia and Kirk froze. Their hands barely clutched their weapons. They breathed slowly but heavily, watching Shawn.

Shawn entered the house as if nothing was wrong. He even greeted them, leaving them standing where they were. Shawn got something to drink, then sat down and suggested they do the same. Amelia took the lead, despite the anxious rush she felt through her veins. Kirk just couldn't bring himself to do it.

"There's nothing wrong, Kirk," Shawn explained. "You have nothing to be afraid of. I came here to visit my family."

Kirk slowly sat next to Shawn.

"Can I say that I have had a crazy-ass month?" Shawn began. "I did something I never thought I would. I found my mom. I take it you know that already. She was killed right before my eyes by Tiy. I never thought he would do that. I wanted to kill him for what he did, yet a bit of me just couldn't."

"Why is that?" Amelia asked.

"I just couldn't. He's the last family I got. I even considered living with what happened, just leaving it alone, you know. Probably just leave town."

"And leave us?" Kirk asked. "What about us, Shawn?"

"That's why I'm here. I forgot to mention that my mom married again, to one of them, actually. You've seen her new husband before. He's one of my professors at school."

"Derek?" Amelia asked.

"How did you know?"

"Your thoughts scream it," Amelia replied.

"He told me something about you guys I'm having trouble believing. He said you killed my dad, and you tried to kill my mom."

Amelia and Kirk clutched their weapons tighter, but calmed their minds.

"Even now, I still don't want to believe it. Despite the pictures, and all the evidence on the scene. Even the people I've killed today. They all point to you two."

Amelia's face turned cold. Kirk moved to comfort her.

"This is what he has you believing?"

"At this point, it's hard not to. I just want an honest answer. You don't have to be so uptight if you haven't done it. This whole thing can end now."

Neither of them was quick to answer. Amelia stared straight at Shawn. Kirk could barely look at him.

Shawn dropped his blade and approached Amelia with open arms. "I want you both to prove me wrong. I love you two." Shawn's voice shook.

Amelia looked at him, after she felt moisture drop in her hands, to see him tearing up. Shawn knelt, grabbing her hands. Both Kirk and Amelia looked timid. Amelia's palms were sweaty.

"Why aren't you guys saying anything? I know you didn't do anything, right? Right?"

Kirk dropped the chains in his hands. Amelia raised her head, eyes full of tears, meeting Shawn's bright red eyes. Shawn slowly let go of her hand.

"Please, Amelia! Say something!" he cried.

Amelia let out a long sigh. "Before we took responsibility for you, we did some horrible things that Kirk and I regret. Not even Kevin knows about them. We kept that secret as long as we could. We didn't want anyone finding out. Especially once we took you in. We initially had a plan which now we can no longer continue. We care about you now, Casan. I'm sorry."

Shawn shot up angrily, tried to slam Amelia against the wall. Instead, Shawn found himself slammed into the wall.

Kirk flung his chain around Shawn's neck, attached the chain to a hook on the wall, and slowly pulled Shawn up. Amelia threw Shawn's dropped sword at his head. Shawn grabbed it, cutting off the part of the chain wrapped around his neck. The action caught Kirk off guard. He let go.

Amelia swung at the boy's neck. Shawn intercepted, pushing her telepathically to the ground, holding her there. The more she struggled, the closer Shawn pushed her to the wall.

Kirk dashed toward Shawn, plunging a knife into Shawn's back. Shawn pulled the knife out, stuck his sword in the floorboard, and turned his attention to Kirk. Shawn snarled as the two approached each other with extreme intensity.

Kirk kicked Shawn in the groin. He recovered quickly, pulling Kirk toward him with one hand. Kirk resisted, struggling, but Shawn didn't even flinch at whatever Kirk threw at him. His grasp tightened around Kirk's neck. He raised him in the air and began choking him, pinning him to a wall. Kirk's eyes turned red as he tugged on the chains.

He then watched Shawn stride back to Amelia. Gasping for air, he yelled, "DON'T TOUCH HER!"

Shawn formed a blade from his hand and met Amelia's eyes. He fixed on her fear as she was trapped against the wall, paralyzed, helpless, knowing these would be her final moments. She took one last look at her husband.

Kirk stopped shuffling around. He knew what was coming next.

Shawn shut Amelia's eyes and plunged the blade into her skull.

CHAPTER

FIFTEEN

CHASE

"Sun, wanna just ride the cyclone, then? Sun?!" Chris asked an oblivious Sunshi as she stared into his eyes. They sat inside a hot dog parlor. The two of them made for a jarring contrast.

Chris appeared radiant in her eyes, internally a flow of constant thoughts. Sunshi just showed a blank face, behind which were all sorts of weird feelings.

Unbearably flustered, he said. "Sun, are you sure you don't want to get out of here?".

"No," she responded. "I'm fine. I'm sorry! I wasn't paying attention. What did you want to do?"

Chris sighed and flew off his seat.

Sunshi took his wrist with her tightest grip. "Wait! I'm sorry! I'm sorry! Just stop!"

Their bodies froze like static as the restaurant's owner approached to address their commotion. Chris pulled his hand away, scolding her with a look as he walked away. Sunshi quietly apologized again.

"Chris? Where are you going?"

"I'm going home. Today was a waste."

"It's not a waste. I'm happy I'm out here. We can go do whatever you wanted to."

"No, Sun. I didn't come out here for me. I came out here for you. You called me, wanting to hang out, but for most of the day you've been distant."

"I know. I'm sorry. I want to be here."

"Then be here. I feel like you're off somewhere else. What's going on?"

"I am here, mentally," she claimed, despite feeling as if she were somewhere else. Somewhere she could smell blood, feel colder than the autumn wind that brushed her face right now, and shiver from fears that gave her goosebumps. "It's just, these last few days, I've felt like I'm somewhere I'm not."

She wanted to give in. Chris could tell. Her gaze ran right through him. Touching her, he sensed how she felt. Shaking her. Begging for her attention.

Nothing seemed to work. He watched as the flow of blood faded from her visage. Her visions became tangible. She could hear glass crunch beneath her feet, even though there wasn't any.

Chris halted.

Sunshi stumbled with every step.

"Is everything all right?!"

The ground began feeling like water beneath her feet. The building started turning like the hands of a clock.

Chris saw her nose begin to bleed. She stumbled into a fall. Chris caught her before she hit the ground. Bystanders came to his aid. He shivered, seeing her glare so lifeless.

"You're not doing so hot, Sun. I ought to take you home."

Sunshi began tearing up. "I don't want to go home. I want to find him." She felt Chris pull her back to reality with his touch. She could see the effect her episode had.

"Find who? I don't understand."

"I don't know how I know, but I feel Amelia and Kirk are in trouble."

"How do you know?"

"I felt their essence, their energy, but Amelia's–I don't know, it was fading."

"So, you want to see…Shawn? You think it's him?"

Sunshi shook her head. "I don't know, but I have to find him. I have to let him know."

"But what if…?"

"What if what?!"

"What if it was him?"

Sunshi thought to herself, *come on babe, find me. I want you to find me.* The smell of blood and sweat grew stronger. Her surroundings turned into a torn-up living room. To one side, she saw Amelia pinned against the wall; on the other, Kirk was held up by a chain wrapped around his neck. She traced the smell to what she wore. A suit with an *S* logo on her chest, her left arm drenched in blood. She felt her face, noticing a scar. She got goosebumps as someone approached alongside her.

It was Shawn, his face bearing the same scar as hers. Her body turned cold. Fear and surprise swept through her. She saw Shawn stick a spike through Amelia's head, then start for Kirk, who broke free of the chain.

Chris continued shaking her. Her pupils were extremely dilated, even appearing red, along with the iris.

"SUN, SUN!" Chris called, until she squeezed his hand, returning fully.

"Shawn is there! He killed Amelia!"

Chris stared at her, wide-eyed.

"Where do they live?" she demanded. "Did you find out?"

"I don't –"

"Don't give me that shit. I know you've been buddy-buddy with Kevin recently. You must know where they live by now!"

"They're in Newark on south 12th street. A three-story white house."

"How long have you known?" she yelled.

"I–I just found out today." Chris stumbled over his words.

"That should've been the first thing you mentioned, Rocks. You know how long we've been searching!"

Sunshi raced toward the subway station. Chris started to follow. She turned to him.

"Don't follow me. I'm putting myself in danger for a reason. I don't want to involve you in this!"

"But. Sun?"

"DON'T! I won't say this again. Follow me, and I will give you a reason never to follow me again."

Chris dropped his head against his chest as the space between them widened. He finally looked up again to see a train passing overhead.

"What the hell are you up to, Sun?"

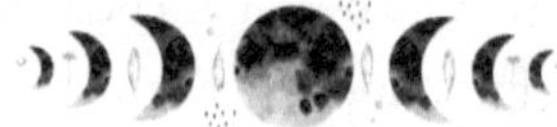

KIRK WHIPPED THE CHAIN AROUND SHAWN'S SWORD, PULLING HIM closer. He pummeled his face and chest before knocking him to the ground. He bonded metal in thin air to form a blade, then plunged it down Shawn's chest.

Shawn spat in Kirk's face, then flung him into the kitchen. He turned on the stove, where Kirk's hand landed. The burner ignited.

Kirk cried out as he tried to pull away. Shawn pressured him, pushing his face toward the flame as he got closer.

Shawn glared at Kirk with pure hatred. His heart raced when he saw the knives flying toward him. Shawn dodged as many as he could, screeching from the cuts he had garnered. He yanked out one knife that had impaled him and thrust it toward Kirk's heart. Instead, he only got his shoulder.

Shawn flung Kirk's chain over his neck again. Kirk grabbed it, twirling it around, taunting Shawn. Kirk then whipped the chain at the back of Shawn's head as he charged forward. Shawn snarled, rushing at him, only to be whipped again. He tried a third time, and the chain wrapped around his neck.

Kirk yanked Shawn to the ground, pulled him to a place where he could get some leverage. He blasted open the ceiling to reveal a water pipe, which he hooked him to.

Kicking his legs back and forth, Shawn reached out to the pipe, which Kirk then yanked him away from. His head dropped.

The struggles ended. All that remained was a gaze. The last sound was of the two weapons dropping to the ground.

A feeling built in Shawn, as if a mob were charging at him, pushing with all their might. He crashed into the corner of the countertop, back first.

Shawn slowly sank to the ground.

Shawn could taste the salty sweat trickling from his forehead. He looked at Kirk, now moving slower than earlier. He yanked at his leg telepathically, then slid forward and swung the blade he had just formed toward Kirk's neck.

Kirk parried, launching Shawn to the ceiling, crushing his ribs.

Shawn broke free, but Kirk then gripped him tighter.

Kirk glanced at Amelia's lifeless body. Her eyes remained open, staring directly at the blade stuck inside her. Kirk slowly pulled it out, letting her body gently fall back.

Shawn struggled to break free, gasping for air. His eyes glistened. He looked around the spinning room for anything he could throw.

Kirk flung his blade at Shawn. It collapsed. He was too slow. He didn't even see the shard of glass stuck in his torso.

Shawn dashed forward with a final insertion.

Kirk's eyes widened. He grabbed Amelia's body and started for the door. Though he couldn't move his feet any faster, he feared *what it was.* He used all his willpower to move, grasping Amelia in his arms, his tears falling into her mouth. He used his mind to close her eyes, which had been staring at him one last time. Dragging his feet, one slow movement at a time, he focused on getting closer to the door.

Then time seemed to speed up.

He flung open the door. On the other side, stood the silhouette of a young girl with long, flowing hair past her shoulders and bangs that hid her eyebrows.

He recognized Sunshi.

Sunshi watched a spike shoot through his chest like a bullet. Behind Kirk staggered Shawn, leaning against the wall, blade in hand, looking exactly as he had in her vision.

Shawn stared at the silhouette in the door frame. "Who's there?"

Sunshi looked down at Kirk, still clutching Amelia. Kirk met her gaze, smiling, seeing at least someone he could trust one last time.

"RUN!" he yelled.

"WHO'S THERE!" Shawn shouted as his vision cleared.

Sunshi's heart raced. She scanned the area. Everything seemed to be moving quicker. Kirk, trying not to swallow his own blood. Shawn, getting closer by the second. The destroyed living room behind them. She looked at Shawn, felt him peering into her mind.

"Sun!" he cried.

Sunshi choked up. Shawn was the only one standing. Amelia lay dead at her feet. Kirk was dying, struggling to hold on to Amelia.

Sunshi's legs began moving back, almost on their own.

Shawn looked at her, smiling, then confused, not understanding why she fell back.

"Sun. What's wrong?"

Of course, he only had to look at his surroundings to see what was wrong. He rushed toward her.

Sunshi began to scurry away, then couldn't move. She muttered fearfully.

Shawn yelled, "No!" as he grew nearer.

She punched him in the face as hard as she could.

"Stay the hell away from me!"

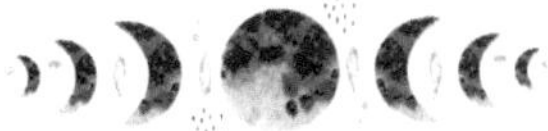

"See? You're already starting to get it! H-time, proud of you, man!"

The flame steamed, then formed rapidly into ice. Hayden, too, could jump with joy. Tiyshio felt the same, nearly rushing up to hug him like a proud parent.

Jason admired their attention towards one another.

"What do you want?" Jason asked.

"He's good at the small stuff, but it's time to work on the more complex."

Hayden hesitated. "I don't know if I'm ready for…"

"Don't worry kiddo, Mr. Hoguy isn't gonna teach us self-defense on this level, because we aren't allowed to get–aggressive."

Tiyshio smiled. Hayden looked at both of them oddly,

"Man, I remember freshman year," Tiyshio joked. "He didn't like me putting the knife at your neck. Ha!"

"Yeah, that man has no backbone. Could be because of Kevin."

"Nah. When Kevin got control of the school a few years ago, he got a long letter from angry parents about fighting, only one semester in."

"Oof, that's cold! Didn't know that was behind it," Jason responded.

"You know Kevin," Tiyshio replied.

Jason and Hayden shook their heads. "He likes to keep things below the table." They said in unison.

"Still, I don't get it. Why is it so important for me to fight? I know I've asked this before."

Jason looked to Tiyshio, who shrugged and walked away.

"I used to ask the same thing," Jason explained, before I met Tiy and Kevin. Kevin showed me the invaded homes, the destroyed families, the scars Tiyshio used to have. Those families couldn't protect themselves well enough to stay alive. Tiyshio was like those destroyed families. If he or Kevin couldn't fight, Kevin would be dead, and Tiyshio gone. Tiyshio has been sought after countless times; he's an important target. Knowing him could make us important targets as well. Being able to fight means you can protect your family. It means you can fend your attackers off. Got it? Now put your guns up. We're going for another round."

Hayden raised his fists. One arm turned to solid rock. The other was engulfed by a flame.

"Hmm, reminds me of a certain comic-book villain," Tiyshio wittily remarked.

"I know who you're talking about," Hayden said, starting for Jason.

"Same rules as always," Jason advised.

Jason began shooting beams at Hayden. The ground rumbled beneath them. He saw pieces of earth rapidly fly toward Hayden, creating a shield, before the beams struck him.

Jason backed off, seeing the shield thrown toward him. He grabbed it, slamming it to the ground.

For sure, the next-door neighbors knew what was going on. Luckily, they were like the combatants.

Hayden halted him, the reason the shield was slammed. Hayden had him on his toes, a fireball here, a hard gut punch there. Jason could only block a few of the attacks; he could barely keep up.

Jason smiled. So did Tiyshio.

Jason grabbed Hayden's arm and slammed him into the mat. Hayden ignited a flame in Jason's face. Jason cried out, feeling his face to check for deformities. He grinned sinisterly. "Getting dirty there, H-time! I like that."

Jason jump-kicked toward him, attacking him until his back came against the fence. He ducked when the rock shield he had made came flying at him.

Hayden kicked down Jason, took the rock shield, and slammed it on his back. Jason tried getting up, but was too winded. Hayden ignited a stronger flame, shooting it violently from the ends of his hand.

"I think you're beat this time, Jay."

Tiyshio applauded. "Good stuff, man!"

Hayden laughed. "I think I just got lucky."

"Perhaps, but you did well. Next time we train, we should start perfecting your martial arts skills."

"I think so, too."

Chris continuously knocked on the door, so hard and loud the group in the back heard it as if they were right next to it.

"Hi, Mrs. West! Is the group back there?" Chris asked between each breath.

"Yes, Christopher. They're out there, destroying my backyard. Remind Tiyshio to fix it when they're done."

"I always do!" Tiyshio called from around the corridor. "What seems to be the issue?"

"Sunshi is in trouble, Chris replied." She went to Amelia and Kirk's safehouse. She suspected Shawn went to kill them." Chris gulped down two glasses of water.

"Who else knows?" Tiyshio demanded.

Jason and Hayden stared at Tiyshio.

"No one. Only those in this room."

"I know you've been hanging with Kev. Did he tell you where they live?"

Reluctant to answer once more, he spoke disheartened, "they're in Newark on south 12th. It's a white house, three stories high."

Tiyshio figured she wasn't there anymore She had to be five or six blocks away by now. He shut his eyes to track Sunshi.

In his mind, he hovered in the sky above Manhattan. Tiyshio faded out the structures to only see the people, whom he then sorted into those not from earth. Finally, he isolated his viewing to Sunshi.

She was running like lightning. He lifted his focus to see who she ran from. As he approached her at ground level, he saw she was crying, frightened. Behind, Shawn was chasing her, blade in hand.

Chris looked at Tiyshio, lightly called out, "Tiyshio?"

Tiyshio raised his eyes. He stormed outside, hurriedly making repairs.

"Mrs. West, I'm sorry about our mess, like always, but I gotta go a little early."

"That's fine with me!" Mrs. West yelled out in joy.

Tiyshio headed for the bathroom. The boys quickly followed.

"Tiyshio, what are you doing?" Jason asked.

"I'm heading over there! I don't want anyone else to know about this."

"Why not?" they cried.

Tiyshio looked at all of them. They knew he was hiding something.

"I'll tell you once she's safe." Tiyshio began stripping, shutting the door before he got to his pants.

Jason asked, "Why are you taking off your clothes?"

"I'm not the best at teleporting. Sometimes I get clothing in my stomach or somewhere worse. I'll use what the doc gave me for clothing. Besides, he's armored, too."

"He has armor like yours?" Hayden asked.

"Yeah! It makes it harder to hurt him, and the armor heals him whenever he's injured. I think it's the nanobots."

"Wouldn't the armor get stuck in your stomach?" Jason asked.

"No. It's attached to my blood." Facing the mirror, Tiyshio formed the armor around himself. Before teleporting, he glanced at the 'A' on his chest. "I guess I'll be a superhero real quick."

He reformed in place in the air, landing on his side. He looked around the area, searching his mind for Sunshi, checking if she was in an alleyway. He listened for her cry, to show which street she might be on.

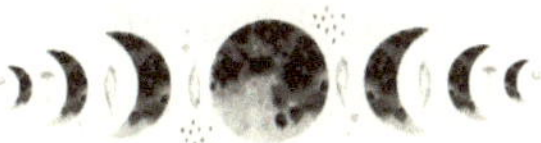

SSUNSHI PAUSED A MOMENT BEHIND A CORNER TO CATCH HER BREATH. She sank slowly to her feet, hands wiping her eyes. *I came too late! Why did I come here? Why did I come here?* Her chest felt unusually warm. She knew it was him. She looked around, planning her next move. If she went to her right, she could continue toward the street, but risked bringing attention to herself. If she went left, she could continue down what looked like a not-so-populated street. She decided to take the risk of going left. It didn't matter. She knew Shawn wouldn't bring risk to her. He'd just get himself caught.

She took her time once she was in the street. The hairs on the back of her neck let her know Shawn was not far from her. She looked at some of the shops around her. One of the stores had a rack of hooded sweaters on display out front. She quickly snatched one. Despite the store owner's thinking, he noticed her action from the corner of his eye.

Each time Sun looked behind her, her chest grew ever-so-slightly hotter.

This time, she could not explain why. She knew Shawn was telepathic, but didn't understand why it linked to her mind. She wiped her face every time she sweated. As she prepared to cross the street, she looked to her side. Shawn spotted and dashed for her. She still didn't want to bring attention to herself. Crossing in a rush was all she could think.

Luckily, it brought her to Tiyshio.

"We need to go now!" Tiyshio pulled her by the wrist, moving to the next block to find the next alleyway. Shawn was close behind them. "I'm gonna get you to Jason's, but you're gonna have to get naked."

"WHAT! Tiyshio, you better have a better option."

"I'm not the one who got myself in a mess! It's Kevin's ability, it's particle based, and I am not good with particles."

"I'm sorry! I wanted to help! You can't just particle my clothes?" She yanked her arm back. "You've should've brought Jason. He has portal teleportation."

"I thought I could handle it!"

"Up until I saw my boyfriend just kill his guardians."

Then it was too late.

"Mmhm!" Sunshi said.

Shawn formed a blade from his hand. Tiyshio sensed his intent. "SUNSHI!?"

Sunshi slowly turned. Her eyes widened.

"Run!"

Shawn struck at Tiyshio, who blocked him from striking Sunshi. Sunshi screamed, staring at both.

"RUN, DAMNIT!"

Sunshi blitzed to the end of the alleyway.

Tiyshio forced Shawn off his arm and teleported his blade into his own hand. "Glad I can still do that."

Tiyshio blasted Shawn away, swinging his sword continuously as he chased him.

Shawn dodged and clashed back with double the force.

Tiyshio saw his exposed arm appeared scorched. When Shawn came at him with a punch, he knocked his arm up. He shot an energy beam, but it only grazed the limb.

Tiyshio hammered on Shawn's weapon until it bent backward.

"Hell, yeah!"

Tiyshio yanked at Shawn telekinetically, only to be countered. Tiyshio then struck back and lunged his head against the wall, knocking Shawn unconscious.

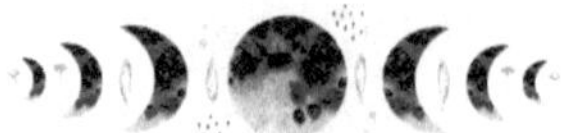

TIYSHIO PACED QUICKLY THROUGH THE CROWDS ON THE SIDEWALK, searching for anyone wearing a hooded sweater. No one matched Sunshi who, meanwhile, kept looking back for Tiyshio. "Where is he?" she mouthed. Tiyshio felt he had to move quicker; getting a warm feeling. His movements grew more rapid. He flung down the hoods of anyone, with a gust of wind, one by one.

Sunshi looked behind her again. Seeing Tiyshio at last, she started for him.

Tiyshio spotted her rummaging through the distant crowd. He moved in to meet up with her.

She felt the same, seeing a person who dressed funny.

"Thank God, it's you!" she exclaimed. "You're gonna have to hide if we're gonna be in this crowd."

"Yeah. I stick out, don't I?"

Sunshi looked at his sword. "Yup!"

Tiyshio shrugged. "You're right." He sheathed his sword. "So. You got money to buy a sweater or something?"

"No. I spent it all."

"Where?"

"At Coney Island, with Chris."

"I don't remember your leaving the house with that sweater you're wearing. I don't even think it's your style."

Sunshi stopped Tiyshio tugging on it as they walked.

"I found it."

"Oh, really? A homeless guy gave it to you?"

"Shut up, Tiyshio! I stole it."

"That was my second guess. Still gotta get you out of here."

"Does that still involve my taking my clothes off?"

"Maybe. I was thinking about teleporting you."

"When Kevin teleports, he keeps his clothes on."

"It's his identity power. He had more time to perfect it. I only got it at twelve."

"So?"

"I'm still getting better at it."

"What about you? You're gonna leave on your armor?"

"It's a part of me."

"*Of course it is!*"

"I'm serious. It is. I teleported here, naked, from Jason's."

Sunshi saw how embarrassed he was to say that. She laughed. "I'm sorry that had to happen."

"Be sorry later. Go through that alleyway." Tiyshio hurried her through the gap. He looked to see if Shawn was following, but saw no one.

Within the crowd, however, someone was keeping their head down as they followed Tiyshio and Sunshi's movements. The shadow saw Tiyshio dart into the alleyway, and followed.

Tiyshio kept glancing behind as he and Sunshi approached the next sidewalk.

"If we can't teleport, let's try to make it to the next subway. Do you know where it is?"

Sunshi shrugged.

"Shit, then we'll just keep going until we find one. It can't be far. Right?"

"Yeah, nor can he?"

Tiyshio glanced at Sunshi, confused, before turning around. He heard something pierce the wind, and his eyes shot up.

"DUCK!"

As Tiyshio rose, he saw the shadow dash toward him, blade in hand. Tiyshio prepared to defend himself. Their blades clashed. Their gazes were fierce. Tiyshio met the shadow's bright red eyes shining through the lenses of their goggles. Tiyshio ignited a flame in his hand and shot it at the shadow.

"Leave her alone, Shawn! She did nothing to you!"

Shawn flipped away, then leapt to Tiyshio, securing his arms telekinetically. Shawn yanked Sunshi toward him.

As she was drawn closer, she kicked him in the head.

Shawn staggered back, recovered, then saw her run toward him again.

Sunshi kicked and punched Shawn countless times until he managed to grasp her wrist. She yanked him closer, clubbing him in the face. Shawn wiped the blood from his mouth. He felt a tooth fall out, then grew back just as quickly.

Tiyshio teleported, then shot a beam at Shawn. Shawn countered. In the ensuing smoke cloud, he came at Tiyshio, shooting a spike at him with one hand while readying to strike with the other.

Tiyshio evaded the attack, pushing Sunshi out of the way. Sunshi knew to leave but, before doing so, she stomped on the ground, cracking it.

Shawn stumbled.

Tiyshio took advantage of the opportunity, grabbing him and throwing him upward.

Shawn shot spikes at him.

Tiyshio launched himself up and shot his sword at Shawn.

Shawn deflected the weapon, grabbing Tiyshio and flinging him onto the roof of a nearby building. He then dashed forward to kick him in the neck.

Tiyshio gasped for air before the blow was relieved by his armor.

Tiyshio then went for Shawn's neck, but his metallic neck covering formed over him, continuing to the rest of his body. *This had to be the armor made by Dr. Smith,* Tiyshio thought.

Shawn pushed him back, grabbed his blade, and rushed at him, blasting Tiyshio and launching spikes.

Tiyshio knocked the projectiles aside.

"ENOUGH WITH THESE OLD TRICKS!"

They were now blinding him. He felt an opening near his elbow and kicked. Just the sight of the half-inserted spike sent pain throughout his body.

Shawn grappled onto his leg, flinging him to the ground like a ragdoll. Tiyshio tried getting up, but lost his footing. Shawn pinned him down. Tiyshio pushed against the floor. Shawn flung Tiyshio's arm under his chest feeling a connection to his abilities that would allow him to blast his opponent directly in the heart.

Shawn wasn't quick enough. The beam connected with a portion of his head before he could pull away.

Tiyshio lunged back up. His right leg wanted to give out, which was odd. He looked down to check the wound was already healed, again, noticing the same metallic armor forming around his body.

Tiyshio lifted rubble from the rooftop, Heating and clumping it together.

While Tiyshio and Shawn did their back-and-forth, Tiyshio chucked the heated rock. Shawn shielded his face. When he let down his guard, Tiyshio charged at him, screaming at the top of his lungs. When he struck, Shawn parried him. The strike landed so hard, his injured arm lost feeling.

His guard came free. Relieved, Shawn shoved his arm back while he lay on the ground, releasing his blade. Shawn struggled against the unknown force.

Tiyshio walked over to him, slowly raising a hand. Blood rushed through the arms up to his shoulder before it burst.

Shawn screamed.

Tiyshio wasted no time. He plunged his sword into Shawn's stomach, then duplicated his weapon and stuck it into both of Shawn's arms.

Shawn screamed once more.

Tiyshio stared t at him as he cried out.

"She fought me–because of you, didn't she?" His words came out with effort.

Tiyshio could barely face him, as he knelt on Shawn's chest.

"She fought you because she's scared." Seeing him struggling to get up, so full of anger. Tiyshio plunged his swords deeper into Shawn. "She went to the safe house to save Amelia and Kirk."

Shawn quivered.

Tiyshio forced Shawn's eyes open and began extracting the Rigion bacteria from his body through his eyes. He didn't expect that with the bacteria would also come blood, and roaring screams from Shawn. There was so much pain, Shawn yanked the swords from his hands with his mind, chucking one at Tiyshio. Tiyshio knocked it away and continued the extraction process.

The screams sounded even more painful. The further he went into the process, the more faded became his iris' color.

Something didn't seem right. Tiyshio realized what he was doing came from a feeling of desperation. The fight was to get what he wanted. He pushed further, telling himself, "*I could do this, I could do this.*"

Yet his eyes faded more as Shawn resisted him.

He rose up hesitantly and thrust the sword into Shawn's hand. Tiyshio was shocked at what he had become.

"Shawn, how–how could things get this bad? How did you drop this far? How could you kill those people?"

"I found out who they are, Tiyshio. The same way I found out who I thought my girlfriend was, who my best friend was, and my guardian himself. Did you know, Tiyshio? Did you know that this was all Kevin's fault? Did you know, because of him, my parents are dead?"

"Shawn, we've been through this. He didn't know!"

"Cut the shit!" Shawn interrupted. "Did you not know he was behind the plot of my father's death? The plot against my mother's death? So many years later, you fulfill his deed. You serve as a good soldier, Tiy. You follow orders, and you follow hate. I used to consider you family. As it turns out, you are worse than what I've become."

Tiyshio could barely look at Shawn. Goosebumps covered his arms.

"Shawn, how do you know he's telling the truth? They cared about you, regardless of what they did or didn't do. You must know that."

"They told me. Don't believe me? Go visit them. I'm sure you will find the truth."

Before Tiyshio jumped off the roof, Shawn stared at him, confused by what had just happened. Tiyshio bore a lifeless expression. He shook his head at the slight gray in Shawn's eyes. Something needed to be done. "**Sun, he's down. I'm on my way.**"

CHAPTER

SIXTEEN

SIDES

Tiyshio sat motionless in the subway car. A kid no older than five tried getting a good look at him, convinced the stranger had no face. Tiyshio stared at the boy with the coldest of eyes, the only facial component visible beneath his deep hood. He wore the latter to conceal the slowly healing wounds he had not allowed to instantly recover.

The moments that had just occurred played back in his head, over and over. He needed that pain to understand what was happening. Things weren't easy this time around. He didn't want to show his face, because he would look as if he had lost someone, and that would increase the concerns of the citizens of New York City. He knew his training. He also knew his body felt squeezed, despite there being no one immediately beside him except for the young boy.

Once he was off the train, roaming the streets, he kept tabs on Sunshi's location in the Upper East Side of Manhattan. That was not far from where he now was, in Central Park, walking along a shaded path, still keeping his head down.

He felt someone approach.

"What happened, kid? I felt you try your first go at the trick."

He recognized Azuka, despite not seeing her face.

"It didn't work," Tiyshio said, deadpan.

Azuka sighed. *"If I'm reading your mind right, he was in pain, wasn't he?"*

Tiyshio agreed.

"Okay, that's good. Blood was coming out?"

Tiyshio nodded.

"Hmm, curious?"

"Curious how!?"

"Curious that maybe he was holding onto the genes. Or, in more accurate terms, that thing is becoming more of him."

"What does that mean?"

"It means my trick may not work on him. Also, what you did might have accelerated the process, body and mind acting like white blood cells, to protect itself."

"So, you're saying this could be a race against time thing. If I don't perform my trick in time, I won't be able to change him?"

"Not necessarily. Remember, I changed Telsa, who had been a Rigion a long time, like me. The trick still works. You just need a willing mind, like Telsa's. Subconsciously, her right mind knew to get out. Shawn's mind and his Rigion urges now are working together. What's weird is, as I said, it is happening at an accelerated rate. Which could mean someone is in his ear, feeding him information that, in turn, feeds his drive and sets his right mind up for the same road. What else happened while you were extracting the virus?"

"I think I was making him go blind."

"Yep. That has to be the resistance I was thinking of. Your thoughts show me he killed some people close to him. A woman

named Amelia and Kirk. His guardians, right? Did he have any grievances with them beforehand, like with yourself?"

"He loved them both. Kirk was like a big brother to him. That is what makes this confusing. Wouldn't Shawn, at this point in the change, still have a sense of choice, not simply some voice in his head by which to follow the deed?"

"Rigions don't have a voice in their head. Like the fight or flight that we have on living, it is the same as the hate for anyone that is Zorian, and who pledges with them. 'They must die, or they will slaughter us.' Which feeds on him already. He has that exact hate deep down in his head. However, you are right. He does still have a choice, should still be able to tell right from wrong, even with his heightened sense. However, manipulation is still king to playing with that loophole. Remember, Tiyshio: mess with the mind, mess with the crime. Go to their place, like he said. You may find your answers there."

"All right. And if I find nothing?"

"Truth reveals itself eventually. Keep that in mind. Oh, and you're gonna miss your stop."

Azuka smacked him across his head, waking him up. He was still on the subway, though he'd sworn he left it. Still, he was exactly at the stop he needed to be, despite having to walk a few blocks down.

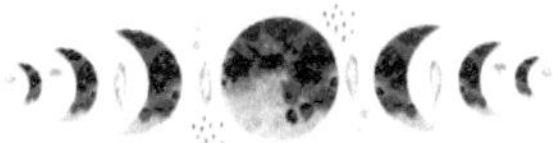

SHAWN STRUGGLED TO PULL THE SWORDS FROM HIS HAND AND ARM. He tried shedding his skin to lean the blade out. He even tried using telekinesis to remove them, but he couldn't focus on taking them out; he was too focused on the pain.

He could barely raise his head to look at the sword protruding from his stomach. The item appeared as two, but the pain from his wound felt like one. His breath grew heavier, as did his body. He tried again to pull his hand out. It was too painful. Thoughts of his mother and father passed through his mind, seeing them more prominent.

Derek felt every part of his body weakening in himself. For a moment, he saw what Shawn could, blurry. His essence began fading.

A person appeared out of nowhere, teleporting Derek from his apartment to that rooftop. Derek raced over to Shawn, removing the swords. He brought Shawn's body upright and met his fading eyes as they began to turn gray. His body had been soaking in a pool of blood. Derek was shaken but surprised to find Shawn still alive.

He rushed him back to his apartment.

Shawn woke a few hours later. He saw his arm, hand, and abdomen bandaged up. He had to rise slowly. Removing the wrappings, he discovered the wounds and inflictions were gone.

Derek was in the living room with another person, who then teleported away. Shawn entered and sat down across from him, sucking in his pain, putting on a pensive face.

"You lost. You lost badly." Derek focused on Shawn's eyes.

"I'm alive, aren't I?" Shawn replied.

"Barely. If I hadn't felt what you felt, seen what you had seen, you would be dead. I'm sorry. I don't think it's time to joke around. What happened out there?"

"Don't worry about it!"

"Don't tell me *NOT* to worry about it! If you didn't want me to be concerned, why are you here?"

It made sense for Derek to ask that. Shawn never felt at home with Derek. He only had Derek go with him originally because he felt Derek would have him followed, anyway. He wanted to be at Amelia and Kirk's side before he knew what they did. He didn't know if they would accept him the way he was.

It was the stigma that burnt into his head, the ignorance of knowing who he was. He needed Derek; he needed his trust, above all he needed that sense of care. More than ever now.

"Perhaps I'm a fool for following so blindly," Derek said, brushing his hair down with a hand. "It was retribution, wasn't it?"

Shawn shook his head. "It was Tiyshio."

Derek stared, then took a deep breath. "Tiyshio," Derek repeated.

Shawn nodded again.

"How did he know you would be there?"

"Sunshi saw me kill Kirk and Amelia. She called for help."

Derek sat back down, taking another deep breath.

"Why would she want to do that? Doesn't she care about you?"

"Because I chased her." Shawn paced his words. "I wanted to stop her. I wanted to–I didn't know I had this rage in me. Like, I didn't want her to know I wanted her to keep quiet, even if that meant killing her. I don't know, man. Look at me. She punched me." He seemed ready to break down. "I felt like she betrayed me, and I don't understand why."

"That's the exact reason why, Casan–because she betrayed you. Who you're becoming now. You can pick up that vibe. She's unfaithful, untrustworthy. She doesn't love you! Perhaps she did at one point, but that was before you chose to become a Rigion."

"She was afraid?"

"Of someone she loved? Don't play me for a fool, Casan! She knows people die every day. She could've easily said '*Shawn, this isn't you*'. Or she could've talked some sense into you. She's afraid of who you are! She doesn't even know what they did to your father. Did you even have time to say *hear me out*?"

"No, I was too busy–"

Derek interrupted him. "No excuses. Truth is, she wouldn't have given you the chance. Looking through your memory right now proves it. She knows what Tiyshio did to you and me. There were plenty of people she could have called upon. She chose the boy that betrayed you. Your *so-called brother*. He left you for dead, Casan. He even let you go blind. Can you see?"

Shawn focused on the sign above the kitchen entry, which read, 'Only God knows.'

"Everything looks blurry…he did something to me."

"How did it feel?"

"I felt my guts being pulled out or–or something else I can't explain. I just felt it was all gonna be over, then and there."

"Yet he spared you, as you spared him. Consider it even."

"He didn't hold back. I wouldn't consider it even. He let me lay there, in pain, bleeding out."

"This should prove something to you. He's willing to let you die."

"Not necessarily. He did something that felt like he was pulling me out of my body."

Derek rushed to his room. Shawn followed.

He flung his file cabinet open and surfed through the files until he reached one with Telsa's name on it. It contained information the time before she no longer connected to the minds of all the Rigions. Derek connected this file to Azuka, whose file he also pulled up.

"Four years ago, Nighcos lost his greatest assassin, Telsa Gond. Because of her, we knew when and how to attack and obtain Tiyshio. As you know, we failed. We've been tracking her until a year ago, when we lost her, because of this woman. You may remember your mother asking about her."

He handed Shawn Azuka's file.

Shawn nodded. "Telsa Gond. I remember her. She stayed with Kevin, Tiyshio and I. When I thought my mom died."

"At least you've had experience with her."

"She's a good person."

"She will kill you, too, since she knows what you are."

Shawn sighed, finding that hard to believe. "Azuka–Fawzi. She was one of the Rigions, then somehow was no longer connected to the collective minds. Whenever she came across others like us, she disconnected them from the Rigion people. We've only approached one that was a part of us. They were no longer Rigion. What happened? Weren't you tracking them down?"

"We were for a while," Derek admitted, "but the trail ran cold for both of them. Still, if Kevin found them, we could, too. If Tiyshio held back, it's because he wasn't successful. Whatever skill these ladies taught him, we must stop him from perfecting it. If you two come across each other again, I want him to not be prepared."

"He'll know you are going after them. Kevin, as well."

"Then I will get what you want all in one place."

"No!" Shawn shouted.

Derek looked at him, angered, ready to counter him.

Shawn continued.

"I can still fight. Tiyshio will kill me either way, impaired or not. I will help you search for her. It's time to even the ground."

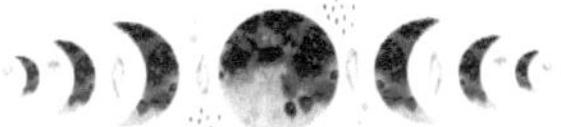

Tiyshio kept walking, feeling the wounds in his arm and rib beginning to close. The armor relieved him of pain, as he was no longer in battle. He had felt air brushing against his open wound earlier. Now, it merely braised his skin. He needed to make a stop before visiting Amelia and Kirk's house.

It was the end of the day for Doctor Smith. He closed his lab, making certain that everyone was gone. The time was several minutes past six on a Friday evening. There was no one he wanted to be with more than his family.

The first face he saw was Tiyshio's, in the main downstairs lobby. No one noticed him, aside from Clinton himself.

After months of not seeing him, a Rigion, or being caught up in their quarrel, all he could think was, *when can I be free of this?* As Tiyshio got closer, he noticed his ripped clothes, and the confusion on his face.

The worried look he initially had faded into concern.

He rushed to Tiyshio's side and brought him back upstairs. Removing his shirt, he saw exactly what Tiyshio had seen earlier. No wounds, scars, or other inflictions. When he looked up at Tiyshio again, he finally understood why. Tiyshio was confused.

"It was the armor, wasn't it?"

Tiyshio nodded.

"What saved Shawn last month can create armor," Tiyshio replied. "Crazy that I missed that detail. It would've come in handy when I first fought him."

"I did say it will protect you," Doctor Smith said. "What happened?" Doctor Smith asked.

"Another unfortunate altercation, that's all." Tiyshio looked around Dr. Smith's lab. "This isn't the same room. What did you tell them?"

"There was not much I could tell them. Rigions took control of everything before Kevin could."

"Kevin came here!?" Tiyshio shouted.

"He did, but too late. Rigions run the whole place now. Essentially, I work for them. I can't play both sides anymore." He took a sample of Tiyshio's blood using a special needle.

"What kind of needle is that?"

"You can call it a smart needle. It lets me bypass the defense mechanism in the nano tech I'd injected in both of you."

"What about now? Am I in danger, being here?"

"No Rigion ever comes here. They own the company and the security. They only want my reports and extra-planetary research. They particularly don't come on Fridays. It's the weekend for them, too, you know. They can have fun."

Tiyshio scoffed. "That's hard to believe."

"Mmhm!" the doctor muttered, checking the nanotech through a microscope. "No damage at all. Remarkable."

"What does that mean? Will it make it harder for me to kill Shawn?"

Dr. Smith looked at Tiyshio, confused. "Why would you want to kill your best friend?"

"Things have gotten much worse between us since I killed his mother. I just left him on a rooftop to bleed out. I'm sure Derek will be on his way to find him through their network. However, based on how I healed, or how any Rigion heals, he should be fine. This happened a little under two hours ago. Sometimes recovery takes a half-day, two days, depending on the injury."

Doctor Smith nodded. "I was told you had lost your arm, then grew it back. According to Kevin, that only took five hours, rather than the normal full Earth day. The tech increases the rate of repairability of your genes. You should now be able to fight better, with less pain and less time of disability."

"It protected Shawn's neck when I fought him. How am I to defeat him if I might not be able to stab him in his heart, let alone cut off his head?"

"Tiyshio, what you and he have is a prototype. I have an issue with the nano tech getting to the head. It poisons the bloodstream and the mind. I only have it go, to a certain extent, up to your neck. The remainder is a breathing apparatus and eye shield glasses, leaving the cranium exposed. Go ahead. Try it. Let the armor cover you completely."

"How?"

"Just think of releasing it. It will tell by your nervous system."

The armor fully formed around him. On his chest appeared what looked like an '**A**,' from the Zorian characters, which matched the one on his arm, spelling out Alam. That had been noticed by a bystander earlier. The entire armor is black, with gold accents, stretching from his shoulders to his feet. A mask covered his mouth, nose, and chin, from the arm to the eye shields he wore, the ones that look more like sunglasses.

Tiyshio gazed at his reflection in the window, loving how the armor looked, surprised by its flexibility and comfort. The inner material was compressive and stitched. Tiyshio thought again of making the armor come off his body and it did so, liquifying quickly, injecting itself through each pore in his body.

It looked gross, but interesting.

"Are you sure you want to kill Shawn? He is your friend, Tiyshio. You two practically grew up together. into fine men,"

"No, doc, I don't want to, but even fine men can be tainted."

The doctor looked saddened.

Tiyshio pointed to his forehead. "This is the weakest spot I can attack?"

The doctor nodded reluctantly. Tiyshio grabbed his shirt and sweater, ready to head back out. Before doing so, he asked, "These armors you made for Shawn and myself, they're for the Rigion army, right?"

The doctor looked down in disappointment.

"It's unfortunate you can't keep this war even, Doc. Couldn't say I trusted you, either. Thanks for the news."

Tiyshio left for Amelia's place.

SUNSHI SAT IN A DINER BOOTH, HOLDING THE ONLY THING THAT gave her comfort: a chocolate chip milkshake. She also had a plate of bacon cheese fries in front of her. The irony, while she always ordered those fries, she wouldn't touch them until they got cold.

Tiyshio entered and rushed over to her. The waitress wasn't far behind, ready to bring him something to drink.

Sunshi saw the water in his zoned out, twitching eyes. All she could say was, "That much of a loss, huh!"

Tiyshio remained a statue.

"It's been a month since the last time we fought," He said at last

Sunshi stayed static.

"He almost killed me then, after I held back. So did he. This time I did some major damage. I was killing him."

"Obviously, you didn't want to."

"*Obviously!*" Tiyshio mocked.

Sunshi rolled her eyes. "I know you're thinking I'm about to ask. *Why did you even go?* Well, I'm long past that. You believed you could help. You arrived too late. Oh, well."

"*I see you are taking it well.*"

"Save it, Sun."

Sunshi smiled, meeting Tiyshio's face. Then her smile began to fade, as she remembered that she felt no different.

"Okay. Something more serious happened up there. What was it?"

"It's nothing. I don't want to talk about it."

Sunshi rolled her eyes again. "Of course you don't!"

Tiyshio pulled the plate of loaded fries toward him and began to quickly but calmly ravage them.

"I thought you weren't hungry?"

"I never said I wasn't." Tiyshio paused to look where Sunshi was sitting, and their surroundings. "No matter what, you always saved him a spot."

Sunshi looked confused. She indeed sat in the corner of the booth, leaving enough space next to her for another person. She never gave herself a comfortable amount of space. The diner they were in held memories. They came here every day after school. The exact spot. The exact placement.

"Perhaps I'm not ready to get rid of an old habit yet."

"Perhaps not... I told the rest of our friends to meet us."

"Why?"

"I thought Shawn would be training, preparing to fight me. I think Derek had other plans for him. We're trying to figure out why Shawn would kill his guardians? What led him to such an act? He claimed he found out the truth."

"Maybe because they're Zorian, and nothing else?"

"That would be Derek's reason. He doesn't give a damn about prejudice, who's innocent or guilty."

"So what! You think Shawn, in the past month, hasn't gotten that in his head himself?".

"No, I don't. Otherwise, we would have been fighting all this time. He wouldn't care about not hurting you."

"NOT HURTING ME!"

"Hey! Keep your voice down!" Tiyshio exclaimed.

Sunshi looked around, then continued, in a softer, whispered tone. "Not hurting me? You saw how he rushed at me, then followed me through the streets!"

"I'm sure you provoked him."

"Well, I might have punched him…"

"*Of course you did.*"

Sunshi rolled her eyes.

"Can you stop with the eye-rolling? Jeez!"

"Sorry. you're just being kind of *smart*. Do you have any idea of what this deeper plan might be? What if there isn't any, and he's just doing it himself? There's got to be an easier way to find out, without going to a crime scene."

"I know there's a deeper plan because Rigions don't just kill for no good reason. I'll get the scrubbers to clean up the house after we leave."

"How do you expect to do that when –"

"I just did." Tiyshio tapped his temple.

Tiyshio walked up to the bar of the diner and signaled the waitress over to pay for Sunshi as they prepared to exit.

As they continued down the street, Sunshi said, "I don't know what you expect to find there, Tiyshio."

"Answers, Sun! That's what I expect to find. Amongst the dead, you can find many things."

"That sounds like something an important person would say."

"Yeah. That would have been my dad."

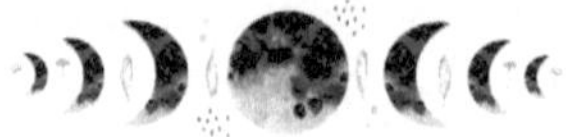

Tiyshio went straight to the back of the house, heading for the basement. Sunshi looked at him nervously. "How good are your illusion abilities?" she asked.

"Good enough that no one should hear anything."

"You're sure?"

"Not really, because I'm never on the inside of these things I create. You're coming with me, or not?"

"I'm gonna head upstairs to see if I can find anything there."

Tiyshio nodded.

The basement didn't look at all the way Tiyshio had envisioned it, with cobwebs and dust everywhere. Instead, it was well kept and in order matching any other room of the house. Mostly, it contained remnants from Zorin. One significant item was Amelia's casual gown from Zorin, which resembled a kanzu dress. Checking the two other rooms in the basement wasn't any help.

He kept wondering what, if anything, he might find.

Sunshi hadn't even moved to other rooms yet. She stared at Kirk's lifeless body, his hand clutching Amelia's. She still heard his voice yell, "Run!" in the back of her head.

Just as she leaned forward to shut his eyes, Sunshi heard a knock on the door. She grabbed the sword that lay beneath Kirk's torso, then moved to the family room for a glimpse of who might be calling.

There were four people at the door, one girl and three boys. She couldn't make them out clearly.

She said, in her head, "*I think that's them, Tiyshio. Can you see?*"

Tiyshio closed his eyes, connecting to Siyshi's mind, recognizing the group at the door. He gave Sunshi the go-ahead to let them in.

"Hey! Get inside quick!" Sunshi ordered.

"I don't see the point in coming here," Siyshi responded.

"But you know the reason you are here?" Sunshi asked.

Siyshi nodded as she went upstairs.

"I'm guessing this is where I come in?" Jason added, sounding down.

"Hopefully not, Jason. Whatever is going on won't need you to do that thing," Sunshi reassured him.

"Yeah, Jason. Kirk and Amelia were the most *human* of anyone we know. Just look around, see what we can find."

Hayden quickly went upstairs with Jason, while Siyshi tracked the blood, manipulating the fresh blood to point her in the direction of where it all started.

Chris turned over Kirk's body. Sunshi tried to stop him.

"Hey! Don't you ever *not* touch a dead body?"

"Does it matter? Anyway, cleaners will be here soon."

"Doesn't matter. You should respect the dead."

"I do. Where is Tiyshio?"

"He's downstairs."

Chris hurried to meet him. Sunshi quickly followed.

Tiyshio searched through a stack of tiles in one cabinet, written in the Rina dialect of the Zorian languages. They told of their last escape from the planet Wita, in the Andromeda galaxy. Kirk had worked there as a scientist, from what Tiyshio could remember. That planet was the beginning of the invasion.

He found nothing relating to what he was looking for.

Chris entered the basement. "Tiyshio, where you at, man?"

Tiyshio began returning the tiles to the cabinet in which he found them. He told the scrubbers at the same time to save the tiles and bring them to Kevin. He held on to them tight, reluctant to let them go, almost second-guessing his decision, but it was the right thing to do.

"I'm in the backroom," he called out

"Hey, man, this is stupid. You know Kirk and Amelia are clean."

"Everyone has their skeletons. Even the good ones."

Chris sighed. "You found anything?" he asked Sunshi.

"Not yet."

"And the others?"

"They've just started."

"If shit gets worse, we're gonna have to do Jason's thing," Tiyshio said, starting for the door.

"He won't be looking forward to that."

"At this point, it doesn't matter what he's looking forward to. There's got to be a reason Shawn killed them."

"What if the reason was that they were Rigions?" Chris asked. "That seems to be the number one reason in any Rigion's head.".

"You may be right, but his mind hasn't succumbed to that burning thought yet. I always suspected manipulation. Now I think I will get some clarity."

Siyshi came downstairs, looking irritated. "Tiyshio, there's nothing in Shawn's room or the guest room."

"Where's Jason?"

"He's in their room."

Tiyshio rushed upstairs to find Jason going through more tiles. He looked up, hopeless, as Tiyshio entered the room.

"I'm sorry, Tiyshio. They're –"

"I know they're clean. Something doesn't add up. He wouldn't kill them for no reason." Tiyshio sat down.

Siyshi entered and hugged him as she sat beside him.

"Tiyshio, we can't just stay here playing detective. Why did you come up with such an idea?"

"Because I know Derek is in his ear, telling him bullshit. I don't care if he hates me, he wants me dead. I care about you guys. I want to make sure you are safe. If he killed these two, what makes you think he won't kill you, protecting me? He could have killed your sister, Siy!"

Jason looked at them, then started for the door.

"Did he hurt you?" Chris asked.

"No, he just... chased after me–" Sunshi replied. She heard someone rush down the stairs.

It was Jason, heading towards the bodies of Amelia and Kirk. The blood on Amelia was already very dry. He rolled up his sleeves before touching her temples with a disgusted look on his face. He stared into her eye, watching as life began filling back into it. Her body trembled; the hair on her forearm began to rise.

His eyes started matching hers.

His vision faded for a second. Once it returned, the house appeared back to normal. He still knelt on the ground. He heard chopping and music in the kitchen, coming from Kirk. Once he saw him, he knew Amelia was upstairs. He heard running water from the bathroom.

Sunshi lightly grabbed his leg up to place a pillow under it. Chris was right beside him in case he fell. Siyshi and Tiyshio came downstairs, wondering why Jason stormed down so quickly.

"He just did the thing, didn't he?" Siyshi asked her sister.

Sunshi nodded.

"Here we go," Tiyshio said as he sat down, trying to read her mind.

Jason watched Shawn ask them about their connection to the group that killed Shawn's parents. He felt in his soul that he wanted to yell out, 'Tell him the truth!'. He couldn't. He was a ghost in the mind of the dead. He could only replay what they went through.

Amelia began to breathe, but her eyes still did not move. Things got weird once she said, "Before we got you, we did horrible things that Kirk and I regret. Not even Kevin knows. We kept it that way as long as we could. We didn't want anyone to find out. Including when we took you in. We initially had a plan that, now, we can no longer continue. We care about you now, Casan. I'm sorry."

The sisters looked at each other, baffled.

"What the hell?" Chris uttered.

Shawn dashed toward them, attacking. Jason stood like a statue as he watched Shawn run the blade he had made through Amelia's head.

Jason let go of her head. At the same time, Tiyshio's connection was severed.

Jason looked toward Tiyshio, seeing Amelia sitting next to him, consoling him. All he could think was, "Great! Another spirit to follow me."

"So, what I just heard is it true?" Sunshi asked.

"That's what it sounds like. They killed Shawn's dad."

"It doesn't add up," Tiyshio commented. "Even when I spoke to her, that's what she said.".

"It must be the truth," Chris continued. "Shawn got his retribution. Killed the people that killed his family."

"I'm sorry, but I feel they were tampered with," Tiyshio said. "Made to say something they weren't meant to. Even in her voice, there was no sincerity,".

"Either way, it all could've been averted if Chris had only said something," Sunshi blurted out.

"What did he need to say?" her sister asked.

"Chris knew where they were. If we could've gotten to them a day earlier, all of this could have been avoided. We could've even saved Shawn!"

"Is this true?" Tiyshio asked.

Chris looked embarrassed. "It wasn't until last night that I found out. Kevin stayed up a long time while I was over. It was hard to find out where he kept everyone. He had documents for where everyone stayed. Probably for security."

"What are you thinking about, with this situation?" Sunshi asked.

"I think Derek had something to do with this. Even then, I'm not sure. If it's not true, you guys may be next, if he has his way."

"Let's say it is a worst-case scenario," Hayden said. "Shawn's doing the right thing for himself. Wouldn't it be worse to not intervene?"

"Eventually, Shawn will come for me, remember?" Tiyshio advised. "I did kill his mother. He's on a revenge path. What happened today just got in the way. I can't ask you guys to stay away. All I can ask is for you to be ready."

"Tiyshio, my brother is not fighting in this!" Chris shouted.

"It's not going to be your choice, Rocks, or any of you, for that manner, Tiyshio exclaimed. "Be ready! All of you."

Chris looked at his brother sternly, "Not when I'm around, not with this going on," Chris whispered.

Hayden's eyes followed his brother as he turned to speak to Tiyshio. His head almost fell into his chest for a fraction of a second. Turning his attitude from helpless to determined, he continued watching his brother, then decided to leave.

Sunshi followed him out, grabbing his shoulder. "I know what Chris is doing, and I don't fully agree with it. Hayden, please, just make the right decision when it comes down to it, okay?"

Hayden answered, "Okay," as he brushed her hand off.

Siyshi stepped outside. "I think we should do the same."

Sunshi grabbed her sister around her waist and laid her head on her shoulder as they watched Hayden walk away.

CHAPTER SEVENTEEN

HELP

The fresh scent of cleaning solution traveled through Kevin's body. The corridors appeared empty as he roamed past them, their lights bright enough to extinguish every shadow. Even the welcoming, "Good morning, Kevin!" offered the greatest ease he felt upon entering the main office. "It's been a while. How's Tiyshio?"

"I don't know. He's still staying at his girlfriend's. The hallways are silent today. What's happening out there?"

"Beats me," one receptionist remarked. "But I can tell you Ms. Kazio put in some work as your replacement. It's time to take that woman on a date,"

"I'm surprised you still keep contact to a minimum," another said. "How long will this altercation between the two of them be? It's almost two months now."

"She's divorced?" Kevin asked. "Wow. I didn't know she had something going on at home." Kevin walked into his office, laid his briefcase down, let out a sigh of relief. He had an empty feeling inside.

"Is Kevin here?" came a voice from outside his office.

He stopped what he was doing.

The newcomer's voice was deep, heavy with each breath. He watched the silhouette approach his office door with a package in hand. '*Why couldn't it be a student?*'

As Kevin glanced at the package's contents, his feeling of emptiness was filled. The room felt colder. Alongside his desk, he could barely make out a woman's high-heeled shoes. He looked up to see the scrubber in front of him.

After what he had gone through, and the effort it took to keep everyone safe, his arms felt like rubber.

BOOM!

The receptionist ran over, thinking a gun had gone off, to see the tile in Kevin's hand broken.

"How long ago did he tell you to get this?" Kevin asked, calming himself.

"We just grabbed it last night. We finished cleaning everything this morning. The house is already listed."

"Where are they?"

"They are in our vacancy, Kevin."

"I assume Tiyshio is still at home with Siyshi's family?"

The woman nodded.

Barely settled, Kevin was now on his way out again with the newcomer. He advised the secretaries to let his replacement take over for one more day.

Outside, the man glanced at Kevin as they walked to his car.

Kevin shouted, "Use all our scouts in this northeast sector! I want Derek found and, if you defeat him, bring him to me!"

The man nodded before they both drove off.

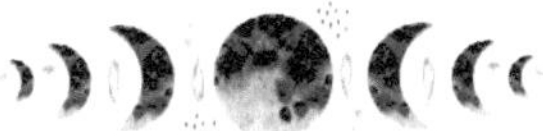

Azuka was positioned in an empty apartment, accompanied by six others r, all wearing civilian clothing. The one next to her watched the windows of the building across the street through binoculars. Another, at her side, held a sniper's gun, with a silencer attachment, at the ready. The rest waited behind her, ready and emotion filled.

"Alpha is ready," Azuka said. "Beta taking position to lock the room. They won't risk compromising their existence."

"That's a lot of faith to go by, Azuka."

"That's all I need. You, me, and Daz will be the eyes from above. Call out wherever you feel you are being attacked."

The men in the back began moving out of the room. As they approached the door, Kevin appeared there, about to knock. Azuka, curious, came to meet him, gently asking him to work with her.

Kevin followed the other squad; they readied their positions. The floor they secured was gassed up; most occupants, civilians. The meeting room was the only place sealed off from the gas.

One of the people in the conference room looked at every window across from them, waiting each time for clouds to cover the sun, to allow a better look at whatever might seem odd.

Two others stood by the door, advising Azuka to keep her people ten feet from the openings. Something wasn't right. Those inside could tell, all twenty of them.

Kevin asked, "How special are these Rigs?"

"They are not, just some soldiers, that's for sure," the man in front of him said.

"*They are an elite squad, handled by Nighcos himself,*" Azuka said directly to Kevin telepathically. "*They pushed me, so I am pushing back. This time I don't give a damn that it's daytime.*"

"Amazing!" Kevin replied.

"On the count of three, I want you to disintegrate that door, neutralize anyone that attacks you," Azuka ordered. "Try to keep most of them alive. I have questions."

"What type of questions, exactly?" Kevin asked.

"You can find out later. Consider this payment."

Both squads moved in closer. From inside the conference room came a light shuffling.

Azuka started the countdown. The two snipers at her side watched one of the people in the room walk closer to the window, waiting for the next cloud to shadow over the view. Her countdown matched the timing of the cloud.

One sniper realized they were about to get made. He felt someone enter the room, yet no doors had opened.

Azuka's count down reached two when she heard a light breath.

When she reached one, the sniper fired at the man, looking directly at him. Azuka slit the throat of a copy of that same man appearing behind them.

The two squads converged in the room. Gunfire and energy blasts flew around. One person in the room approached behind Kevin as he hid beside the door. Kevin struck him with the butt of his gun, shot him once in the head and a second time in the heart.

"Once a soldier, always a soldier, huh?" Azuka teased.

"Never leaves and never goes away!"

"I love it. You know what else I love? Why you are here? Why didn't you see him instead?"

"Because you are teaching, and I have a hunch you know what happened the other day."

Azuka sighed. She looked toward Kevin, still in the midst of a fight. Yet his presence was just behind her.

Kevin noticed Azuka seemed far more curious than on their walk.

"You have a hunch?" she asked. "That's hard to believe, Kino… He spoke to me yesterday. However, I didn't tell him to fight his friend. He did that on his own."

"Are you saying you saw everything?"

"No, not everything. I only heard the boy's cry. His friend. He left him up there to die."

"Why?!" Kevin asked firmly.

"Kino – I'm sure you already know why. That's why I don't see any reason to come here. You need to talk to him."

"He left his friend there to die because he couldn't kill him, or because he couldn't change him back?"

"What do you think?"

Kevin looked down. "He wasn't able to finish the change."

Azuka smiled. "Two things could be happening. Shawn's resistant because of his drive, or time is running out. I told this to Tiyshio already. We both know there's no doubt Derek is in his head. However, those actions he just did, that could be all on him."

"Time–I thought this could work, no matter how long the change."

"You don't listen, do you, Kino? Remember what Telsa said? The way I do this isn't the cleanest. Not everything is going away. If he likes being the way he is, he will resist. Tiyshio was killing him when trying to change him back. He made the right move. Go to him. He needs you right now!"

Azuka saw Kevin grow more reclusive with each step he took. Her body trembled. She snatched his arm to pull him back.

"There is something else, Kino. I know the couple that died were close to you. Perhaps something else is at work here. Derek may have other plans for the boy, beyond what the boy wants." Azuka looked down in pain.

"Are you okay?" Kevin asked.

She brushed him off. "Find Derek. Find out what he wants with Shawn, and protect Telsa. What happened has caused a shift."

As Kevin started walking away, Azuka added, "Also, I'm sorry for your loss, Kino. Don't be hard on the boy. He's been making good progress."

Kevin went to visit the safe house, telling Tiyshio to meet him there.

The entire house was barren. Every bit of furniture had been removed. He scoffed at how all the objects that filled this home gave the house life, but what made it living for him were Kirk and Amelia, for the short time they were there.

Tiyshio flew through the door. He stuffed his hands in his pockets, shoulders tucking into his chest. Kevin looked at him like a disappointed father.

Tiyshio could barely speak, mumbling when greeting him.

"Speak up!" Kevin said firmly.

Tiyshio let loose a bit, muttering, "'Sup?"

Kevin chuckled. "Why are you acting like you did something bad? Stop cowering. I taught you better than that."

"You know why. I failed."

"Yes, and I know you are going to try again."

"Not unless I have to."

"You're giving up?"

"It feels like it, but I want to try harder."

"Tiyshio, why do you want to try harder?"

"You know why he killed them doesn't make sense. They loved him! He loved them! If there was any family he could trust, that wasn't me or you, it was them. They had been nothing but accepting of him. This had to be Derek, messing with his head! At least, that's what I want to believe."

"What are you trying to say?" The hairs on Kevin's arms stood tall, while his whole chest sucked in.

"When I left him there, he claimed Amelia and Kirk were the ones who killed his dad. They did it because you ordered it. You were also behind the plot for her death."

Kevin had no words for Tiyshio, just a look of discomfort and confusion.

"You believe him?"

Tiyshio shook his head. "Not all of it, because you've been open with me. However, I know there are things you don't tell me. When we first arrived on Earth, I thought we were the only Zorians on this planet. Then Shawn's dad was killed by one, his mom supposedly also killed by one until she later returned. We never took the time to ask why she came back now, and how come you didn't know of the others that day?"

Kevin let go of his claustrophobic feeling. "You are right. I did know there were others. When Amelia and Kirk came here, they were visited by the group that killed Shawn's dad. I didn't know that at the time, nor did they. They told me how nice and welcoming they were. They wanted me to meet them. Then Shawn's dad died. We didn't know they would continuously visit until Shawn's mom was also supposedly dead. That was the last time I'd heard from them. What Amelia and Kirk did with them, I can't say. I do know it wasn't part of their schemes."

After a pause, he added, "So, you do know it's all Derek?"

"Do I!?" Tiyshio looked down in shame, knowing Kevin was right.

"I saw Chris and his family earlier today, too," Kevin continued. "He told me you had talked to him this morning about keeping his brother close and training him. Are you sure this is the right time to take on an apprentice?"

"He needs to be prepared, if you saw what I saw yesterday. The way he went after Sun, that had to be Derek getting into his head, making him think we are his enemy."

"TIYSHIO, THINK! WE ARE HIS ENEMY!"

Tiyshio froze, then dropped to the ground.

"Chris doesn't want you to train his brother," Kevin went on, "but you already knew that. What happened with Sunshi scared him, and rightfully so. Hayden isn't a fighter! He was born and bred here. He's from Earth and needs to be treated as such."

"Which is?"

"A civilian. The more we talk about this, Tiyshio, I don't know, I'm beginning to believe there are many more things we don't know about the Rigions than we initially experienced." Kevin sat on the ground, to be on the same level as Tiyshio.

"Tiyshio, we never experienced a Rigion so close to home since… you know. After so many weeks of nothing, this happens. We don't even know what's happening on the other side. Azuka says he probably fought you off when you were taking this thing out of him. It got me thinking, Shawn may be happier the way he is now. Also, you may have to consider that he wants you dead, either way. I also won't rule that Derek is, indeed, manipulating him. So here's what's up. I know you want to try again, but leave Hayden out of it. I'm already looking for them, regardless of whether it's all Derek or Shawn. If you find him before I do, change him. He lives, and we will see the aftereffects. Otherwise, he dies. You will not stop me."

Kevin teleported Tiyshio back to the Guerra's safe house, distraught but determined to see what was to come.

CHAPTER
EIGHTEEN

POWER

Hayden's arm felt heavy as he left his house, despite all the shuffling and preparation he caused earlier. It was five in the morning. Hayden had nothing to worry about. Despite feeling like a rebel in a household, he behaved like a boy scout. Not as much as his brother. He knew why his brother acted the way he did. Hayden also knew something had to give after the recent events. There was only one place they could go.

Tiyshio answered the door when Hayden arrived at the safe house, already dressed in gear, with weapons on his back and surrounding him.

"Are you sure about this?" Tiyshio asked.

Hayden nodded.

"From this point forward, you must tell your family. This is for you."

Traffic was not bad as they took the car to an uninhabited stretch of land in New Jersey. Azuka met them on arrival.

She wasn't happy to see Hayden. "I am only required to train you, Tiyshio. You shouldn't be with this person. Who is he? Why is he here?"

"His name is Hayden. He is one of my friend's brothers. He is family to me."

"The one that Kino told me about."

She looked even more disapproving. Hayden saw Tiyshio simmering down to his shoes.

"After what had happened to Sunshi, I couldn't imagine anything happening to him, Azuka. He needs to be prepared, despite what his family thinks."

The look on her face was like talking to a wall.

"Is his brother a fighter?" she asked, breaking the silence after nearly two minutes.

Tiyshio nodded.

"His mother is a fighter, too?"

He nodded again.

"Then he doesn't need me. He needs his family."

"His family refuses to train him. They want him to stay a civilian!"

"Tiyshio, I am training you on how to remove the Rigion gene from someone's body. How to make that work. Not how to fight or harness your – something tells me you were originally training him to harness his powers. Why hasn't he?"

"My mom told me I'd have an easier time fitting in compared to my brother," Hayden explained. "Plus, I had no reason to know how best to make use of their living here. Our family was never hunted. We were civilians on Tal. We wanted to be civilians here. Earth became a place of refuge for us. I used to know how to balance between all this before, but I forgot."

"Was it your choice to bring the boy here?"

"That was all on me, Miss!" interrupted Hayden. "He said you were good with special abilities and dealing with situations under pressure. I felt I could learn from that."

"You can call me Azuka."

"It was my choice, Azuka."

"What are you afraid of?" she paused, unsure of his name.

"Hayden! I'm afraid that any of my family could be threatened. Maybe not by Shawn, but by someone. My brother Chris thinks he can protect us all by himself, but he's not invincible. He will need help eventually. Even under his thick skin."

"Your brother, Chris, is a proud protector. I like that. I want you to know something, Hayden. Most people don't die in wars or battles because they are proud, or more skilled, on the battlefield. That is very rare. They die because they made a mistake. They weren't vigilant or agile. I've seen people die blaming the last thing they'd done. In most cases, you will do anything to live, even if you don't know how to fight. That is how they learn. We call those survivors. They soon become teachers. I am that teacher. Tiyshio is something of a teacher. Your brother is not that person. He can fight to run, not fight to survive. Pride can only get you so far. Humility will help get you further. Even a tyrant like Nighcos knows that help goes a long way. I will teach you how to fight to survive through him." She pointed at Tiyshio.

Tiyshio was confused. "I am in no position to train him. That's why I brought him to you! We don't have time. Azuka!"

Azuka pulled Tiyshio to the side. "That was a foolish move, Tiyshio. I don't teach you how to fight here. I teach you to survive and resist the enemy. In this case, I will teach you how to change the enemy into a *friend*. Hayden wants to learn how to defend himself. His family and you should teach him this, not me. Today, and maybe, *MAYBE,* at the next meeting I will teach him. The rest is up to you. The boy wants to defend himself. I am afraid that, if I teach him, his overconfidence will be his downfall, and you will be blamed for it. I've seen this happen, Tiyshio. He's young. I don't want that to happen to him."

"Think about it," Azuka finished, starting towards Hayden.

In the distance, Tiyshio heard her asking Hayden about his powers, and what he wanted to focus on. Tiyshio sat on a patch of the grass, relaxed and upright, legs crossed, taking deep breaths as he realized the choice he had just made.

Azuka grasped Hayden's hands, pressing her thumbs into his palms. He felt her searching through the subconscious of his mind, saw her mimic his elemental-like abilities. Her eyes closed. She asked him to do the same.

"Can you feel what I am doing?" he heard in his head.

"Yes!" he cried out.

Azuka told him to search for her.

Hayden opened his eyes. His surroundings were now of his home world, Tal. Buildings were on fire. Starships filled the skyline. He was inside a home, seeing a calendar that told the date.

The day they left Tal.

He raced to a window to look at his surroundings once more, taking his time, getting a feel for the area. His own home had to be close by.

Two guards approached, blocking the front. More moved in to surround the back. Visible from the window, Azuka was inside, being interrogated by them.

Hayden blasted the ones in front with ice shards at their torsos. Azuka saw the commotion, warned the soldiers to stay with them.

Hayden saw himself fall behind his brother. He looked at the remaining soldiers, knowing more were coming. The first one charged at him. He ducked, stabbing his attacker.

Two more came at him, uncoordinated. The one on the left prepared to knee him. The other pulled his body away, preparing to stab him.

With a quick motion, Hayden cupped his attacker's body within a rock wall. The soldier plunged unknowingly, getting stuck in the process, Hayden engulfed him in earth, then shoved the rock formation toward his oppressors,

Azuka, meanwhile, escorted his family out of their home.

Hayden rushed toward his opponent, only to be pulled in multiple directions. He felt his eyelids being yanked up. With a mere twitch of a finger, a storm of dust arose, pushing everyone away, giving him a clear path. He remembered a young woman that had attacked his family. He remembered blacking out, then waking up to find only his brother and mother left, under his father's protection.

Hayden rushed at Azuka, picturing his father protecting the family. Azuka pulled out her sword, oblivious to Hayden, who was creating an ice blade to shoot towards Azuka.

Azuka deflected the blade toward Hayden. Surprised, he didn't react quickly enough to prevent the blade going straight to his heart. He bled out, his vision blurring

Azuka continued toward his father, who called out, "Help! Help!" She gutted him like a fish.

Chris had the younger version of himself in a sleeper hold, knowing it was better for him not to see his plea.

On waking, Hayden pulled away from Azuka's hand. Confused, in tears, he asked again, "Why there?"

"You know why! Think! What was the most crucial thing that happened on Tal?"

"My father dying… by your hand?"

"No. Since this person had no face, she was easy to pick. I put you under pressure so that you would fight. You mostly ran away. Why?"

"I was scared. Back then, I wasn't allowed to do anything. I felt the same now. With the numbers surrounding me, I felt overwhelmed. I am certain I would never be overwhelmed by so many Rigions like that in real life."

"You keep hanging around him, you will," she said, pointing to Tiyshio.

Tiyshio looked at them, confused. He didn't do anything wrong.

"Hayden, you need to prepare yourself for the worst. What I showed you wasn't close to that. It was a window. I want you to think: why did I choose that memory? Why are you here with

Tiyshio? Keep in mind what happened to your father. What were your thoughts that night?"

Flashes of that night played in Hayden's head, reflecting how much it was like what he had just experienced. "I felt powerless."

"You felt powerless? And what are you and Tiyshio here for?"

"More power," Hayden said, saddened by his defeat.

"Right. You are here for more power. Which is no different than what Shawn is going through right now. You were young and wished you had more power to save your father. The way this training played out was not my doing, I was just an actor in your play. Your training, your subconscious, excuse me, told you that you feel more powerful now than when you were a child. If there is a lesson to be taken here for both of you, it is to stop doubting yourself." She looked at Tiyshio. "Especially you, considering what happened earlier."

She continued. "You both can survive with the special abilities that lay within you. Your entire body is a weapon. That goes for you, mostly, Hayden. I love your elemental powers and your quick thinking to break free. Survival requires everything. Confidence is everything, knowing you can accomplish it. Cool!"

They both agreed.

"Great. Tiyshio, you and I will now continue where we left off. Hayden, you will train with my clone. She will teach you how to best use your abilities."

Hayden looked confused. There was no clone present. Then a leg popped out of Azuka's body.

Hayden mouthed, "Okay," his eyes widening in surprise.

"Have you changed your mind about training him?" Tiyshio asked.

"Wishful thinking. He's still your priority. I'm just holding up my end of the deal. My reason still stands. I don't know if that boy will be able to handle these situations so soon. If Shawn comes back, and he's with you, he will bravely protect you, but he isn't good at defending himself. You must protect him as best you can, Tiyshio.

I fear for his life, as he feared for his father's. Something doesn't feel right about recent movements. Including Kevin's. Please, be careful."

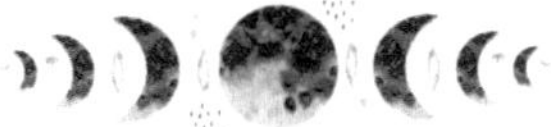

May 29th, 1986

Report #1549-5296

It's been five years since my first report. I look back now and wonder about all the decisions, the choices I made to protect my son. I can say I regret some of them.

At least my boy was safe through it all. Those Zorians didn't go after him, nor did Kevin kill him, despite his allegiance to those fiends. They have no understanding of those who just want to live. That war against other Hunatans ended such a long time ago, and yet it hadn't, for them.

At least I can say that Kevin trained him well. My boy can fight, was taken care of, even given a family that made him feel at home. Too bad those who took him in are no good. They plotted against us. When he finds out, it won't be so pleasant.

Nighcos wants us to do one last thing for him before we separate from the faction. He wants us to take Casan in, saying it's time he knows that I am alive, to make the choice on his own. I can only imagine the look on his face when he sees me.

He may resent me for the choice I made, but that is a risk I am willing to take. As long as he knows I am still alive. Also, whether he hears it from me or not, he will know I did all this to protect him, and to find out who was truly behind all our torment.

I want him to read all of this because something tells me that events may not play out as they seem. Derek may be someone he cannot trust, and I understand. However, he loves me, has taken care of me, shows how much he wants to be a part of my life. Including the fact that he didn't listen to Nighcos when taking that position at Kevin's school.

He did that to retrieve Casan beyond Nighcos' plan. He should've trusted him now that he's in the belly of the beast. Surprisingly, Kevin never once suspected him. Whatever happens in the following months, I have already given specific instructions to follow if I am gone. One of those instructions is to read every report I wrote.

Casan, when you read this, I want you to know I wrote it with you in mind all the time. I know you probably won't forgive me for the decisions I made. I was reckless and afraid, with no other way of knowing how to protect us. I know that turning to Nighcos seemed wrong at the time, but he has protected us all. Yes, that includes you.

Countless times he sent Rigions to your side, to protect you from others that wanted you dead. I know you would wonder why anyone might want us dead. Just know, there are cruel people in this universe. Including those that killed your father. Just for the person you are.

Right now, you are a Rigion, and things may not make any sense. Trust me. In time, things will. If you are reading this, and I am dead, remember that I always loved you.

Your Mom,
Aida

END OF REPORT

That report was made earlier this year, Shawn noticed. It seemed surreal to him that Aida was dead, how fast everything occurred. He stepped out of his bedroom and, with ease, asked, "Derek, mind if we go somewhere?"

Derek agreed.

They took a boat ride to Liberty Island. Derek kept his distance, watching Shawn, eyes wide open, face expressionless, staring across the Hudson River toward the Atlantic Ocean. It was a cold day. A passing breeze made Derek tighten his coat.

Shawn seemed unbothered, calling over to Derek, looking at him in wonder, then back to Lady Liberty.

"Have you ever been there?"

"The statue? I never had the time."

"It was the first thing I saw when I came to New York. We arrived in nineteen seventy-five in New Jersey, moved here a year later. The insane thing was, living on a spaceship for a whole year. We had this ship with twenty-four living quarters and three escape rafts. You know who it was meant for?"

Derek shook his head.

"It was for my family; grandparents on both my mom and dad's side, my Mom's brother, and his family and four kids, my dad's sister, and her daughter, since my uncle was turned. Then there was us. The trip should've taken us three years, but we planned to complete it in eight months. We made stops in nearby worlds to see if we could live there. How close were the Rigion troops to us? That was the plan for months, because my dad saw it coming. The Avaian war seemed to have no end until Zorigan came in. Dad always felt wrong about him, especially when the war almost came to our world. He knew, somehow, he was going to betray the Zorians. When we left, we got separated, because soldiers stormed our hangar bay. We boarded the ship. The rest were caught between two other ships that could only get them to the outer rim. While I like to think they are okay, we couldn't contact them. No one could know we were fleeing the planet. We were mere workers until we got here." Shawn scoffed. "Not even the ride to this planet was as lively as it could've been. Every day, quiet, serious…depressing. When we arrived, it seemed unlikely we would be spared by the butcher. We waited for our turn to come. The first time I came here, I was told by a tour guide this statue was the first thing many immigrants saw, coming to this country, to know they were safe. For us, we wanted it to mean the same thing."

"Why doesn't it now? Is it that you are a Rigion, or because you lost your family to the war?"

"War caught up to us. It didn't matter which side, anymore. Think about the first time you were here. What happened to your family before my mother?"

"My family." Derek remembered the sword in his hands, Kevin towering over him, with blood dripping from his own sword. "We lived on Kaisa. That's not where I'm originally from, but where we moved to. We enjoyed going from planet to planet, keeping ourselves moving. Arriving on Kaisa was different. It was the first planet we ran to for safety. My family turned on the previous world we had been on. It was the choice we were given: die or become one of them. I defended my family as best as I could. We ran away because we didn't want to fight for them. We just wanted peace. It was weird, going to worlds we've already been to, under new regimes. Kaisa was one of them. The Zorians tried to take it back. Nighcos at the time led the mission. His general, Kino Zara, was the one who killed my family, all because we were Rigions."

They stayed silent as the ferry docked. Shawn could not stop looking at Derek. Derek would force himself to look away and walk ahead of Shawn anytime he got caught up. Shawn knew his loss couldn't undercut what this place meant to him.

Derek could feel that Shawn couldn't tell.

"Anything positive you can take away from living on Earth?"

"Hmm… I admire the diversity. The encouragement for ease of access. The architecture reminds me of home, sometimes. To be surrounded by those that worry about smaller things, like bills, or what to eat that night. They never have to look up."

"Perhaps because we are already down here with them."

Derek agreed. "How about you? What have you enjoyed about being here?"

"Seeing other races of people, including those from Earth. When I lived in Jersey, I used to play basketball with my next-door neighbor. His name was Adonis. He has a sister named Monique, and she'd play with us, too. He couldn't leave the house without her. One day we went to the amusement park. He found it crazy that I had never been to one. Mom and Dad joined in to get to know them and human life a bit. I remember looking at the rollercoasters and other rides and thinking, '*these look like torture devices.*' At first, it was scary, but it got more fun over time. I guess it was the sensation. That's why I took Sun every summer. I felt like one of the people."

"Did you ever speak to Adonis again?"

Shawn shook his head. "He and his family moved to D.C. A month later, we moved to New York."

"I remember that the time I felt the most alive again was meeting your mother. She told me how much she enjoyed New York. The city staying so busy reminded her of the Hunatan capital."

"I could barely remember that." They fell silent for a moment. Derek figured he didn't have to share the experience he had undergone.

"Do you find this city beautiful?"

Shawn looked at the Manhattan skyline. "Without the ready-to-fight walks home, and from afar. Yeah, it's beautiful. Makes me wonder how they fit so many tall buildings on such a tiny island."

"Mom used to say the same thing. She said the towers in Vez were spread out, filling the skyline. From afar, the buildings looked like a massive, crystal-like fortress. Here, she pictured the view more like multicolored trees."

"I guess that's why they call it the concrete jungle." They both chuckled. "You ever miss being a dad, Mr. Ryan?"

"It had its perks. It was fun raising three girls. Tried to have a boy for the longest. Just wasn't working. Waking up early, the energy you needed to have, kept me feeling alive. Especially at the beginning of the war."

"How does it feel, being a guardian?"

"Feels no different than being a father. I just missed how to raise you as best I can, I would say." He chuckled. "Overall, it's a different experience. I had to come to terms with a lot of things. The first was to let you be you, and allow you to make your own choices." Derek patted Shawn on the shoulder, turning away from the skyline to look directly at him.

"My father taught me that actions have consequences you have to live with. Your job, as you grow older, is to learn whether certain actions were the right thing to do, or easy. Right is a difficult choice. Easy is just a means to an out. Both have consequences. Making that choice will lead you to want to know whether those consequences have positive or negative repercussions. I stood by your choices, no matter what, as your guardian. I think I did a fine job, no matter how long it took getting used to."

"Yes, you did. I know I apologized before for not playing ball with you. Seriously, though, thank you for having my back, Mr. Ryan. You were unexpected in my life."

"Ready to go back?"

Shawn told him, "Yes!"

Shawn gathered the rest of the reports and placed them in a binder. Derek sat next to him, watching for dilation in his eyes when the light reflected off them. It's been a month, he thought. The pupils were still as gray as they were then. "How easy was it for you to read?"

"Still a little blurry, but I could manage."

Derek sighed in relief. "Hopefully, you can fight?"

Shawn looked at him weirdly. "Of course I can fight. I was trained blindfolded."

Derek smiled. "I guess Kino taught you well."

"He did, but it appears Mom wanted that." Shawn stared at Derek in a statue-like pose. "Is there something on your mind, Mr. Ryan?"

"Yeah. I never agreed with your mom about leaving you with Kevin, knowing what he is. Nighcos trusted you would be in good hands, and you would've despised her. You've read through everything. How do you feel about it all?"

"To be honest, she was right. At that time, everything was so fresh. She was right to leave me with them. If I'd found out at that time that's what she chose to do, I would have considered her a traitor and a coward. Only now do I realize the choice she had to make was desperate, like she said."

"I'm surprised. I honestly thought you wouldn't care, as long as you were with your family. Being somewhere you don't know, with no family around, it's hard to be left alone. You need someone until proven otherwise."

"That's why I lived my life as I did. I understand how it feels to be alone. To have no one. To compromise. That's what I did, to be with Mom."

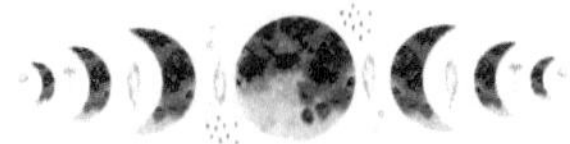

A KNOCK ON THE DOOR INTERRUPTED THEIR CONVERSATION. DEREK got up to bring the guest in.

"What update do you have for us?" Shawn asked the newcomer. Derek, surprised at his tone of authority, smiled.

"Our scouts are not one hundred percent sure, but they say it's a match." The man spread out photos of Telsa on the table. "She's in Boston. We couldn't track exactly where she lived. Her daily commute pattern is erratic, to say the least."

"Sounds like she knows she's being followed," Shawn replied.

"More like she expects to be. Find out where she works, where she lives, who her friends are. Her life is our life now," Derek ordered.

"Why do you say that?" asked the man.

"She knows Nighcos has been after her a long time. Since we can't see her, and she can't see us, it's safe to assume she's been looking over her shoulder for some time. What of the other one?"

"We have nothing on Azuka. We suspect she was behind the attack over a month ago."

"The one in Queens?" Derek asked.

The man confirmed.

"That one is close to home. There were no survivors, right?" Shawn asked.

"No. In fact, Kino Zara was associated with the attack." Derek and Shawn looked at each other. "No one followed Kino?"

"Whoever did was killed by his group. He stays protected, since you've turned."

"I've never seen him with others before," Shawn said. "He always travels alone."

"Kino is a high-value target; he will never travel alone. His confidants will protect him without his orders," Derek advised Shawn.

Derek turned to his agent. "Thank you. Should you learn anything else about Azuka's team, to help us find her, let me know. We will do the same when we locate Telsa. Got it?"

The man shook his head, then left.

Derek stared into space.

"What's up?" Shawn asked, confused.

"I just thought you may have never faced an assassin before."

"It's only an assassin. She can't kill both of us."

"Rigion assassins are different. Especially the ones trained by Nighcos. When he was a Zorian, he had them in his army, and they were highly efficient in taking down entire civilizations."

Shawn showed no change in attitude. "Remember, Mr. Ryan hurt him where he hurt me. I can handle this. Let me. I want him to come after me."

The nameless agent returned, looking at Derek, ready for his next instructions. Derek exchanged information with the man using only a look with worried eyes, shielded with a confident smile. The man knew to leave the situation alone.

"I will give you the power to defeat them. Next time you see Tiyshio, you will be able to kill him?"

"Yes!" Shawn strongly replied.

CHAPTER
NINETEEN

FAILED

Back in Boston, Telsa and a young African American man left a restaurant. Laughing, clearly enjoying each other's company. From afar, Kevin could tell how relaxed she was, her eyes never veering off her companion. She wore a short gold dress that hugged her body, with gold chandelier-like earrings to match.

Kevin followed the pair from across the street, making sure he wasn't seen. He knew how much this evening meant to her. He was not used to seeing her this way.

In his head, he heard a message: "Chicago is clear. All personnel have infiltrated all known Rigion members."

"Were they neutralized or captured?" Kevin asked.

"By your orders, sir," the voice in his head replied.

"Good. How are D.C., Virginia, and Maryland?"

"No sightings of Shawn or Derek." Another voice intruded. "Commander, what if they never left New York? Do we have scouts in that city looking for him?"

"I have them tearing down the whole state. I swear the son of a bitch hasn't left his house, nor does he have a tunnel network not to be seen."

"I can confirm that, sir," came a New York voice. "No sign of him in New York, but we did see one of Derek's scouts a week prior,"

"Have you tracked them down?"

"We have, but we haven't infiltrated them yet. We are planning our breach as we speak."

"Let me know the aftermath. Make sure they sing. I want to know everything."

"How's Boston so far, sir?"

"Boston is secure. All soldiers here are protecting Telsa with great care." Kevin took another gander at Telsa.

"I don't know about you," Telsa's date offered, "but I would like a drink, and there's a great bar by the riverside I think you may like."

Telsa smiled, ready to agree. Then she spotted, from the corner of her eye, one of Kevin's militia soldiers disguised as a civilian. Her smile faded, catching her date off guard.

"What's on your mind?" he asked.

Before glancing back at the woman now staring at her, she smiled and said, "Oh, I'm sorry. I was distracted. Let's go!"

Kevin overheard the conversation and turned to look at the woman Telsa had spotted. She looked back, seeing his disbelief. He ordered the entire group to fall back as the two subjects walked to the subway.

Telsa returned home later, throwing her keys aside. She knew Kevin was sitting outside on the fire escape with the window open to let him in. Telsa changed into more comfortable clothes, then approached Kevin, offering him a mug of black coffee.

"Freshly ground?" he asked.

"Just the way you taught me," she replied, taking a seat on the window ledge.

"Hope you don't mind me opening the window. I saw it wasn't locked. Figured you'd like company for your new place."

Telsa reluctantly smiled. "What are you trying to say, Kino?"

"Perhaps you are getting sloppy. I thought it was just the date, but it looks like it's at home, too."

Telsa turned away with a sigh.

"He's a good-looking guy, though. Where did you meet him?"

"My route in the park. I met him not long after you first showed up. Figured I should live a little."

Kevin slid the window up and down a couple times. "I think you're living a lot! Did you forget that you are a wanted woman? What if he's one of them?"

"No, I didn't forget, but I also figured you wouldn't come here again. Interrupting my date with your people! For the record, I'm sure he's not one of them."

"I didn't interrupt your date!" Kevin replied sternly. "As soon as Ula was compromised, I pulled us out. I didn't want to ruin your night. Also, how do you know he's not?".

"Thank you, Kino. You are so thoughtful," she replied sarcastically. "I know he's not, because a Rigion wouldn't take a month to infiltrate my livelihood. Just a little under three weeks. Remember, I was one of them." She smiled.

"I remember. Haven't forgotten at all. Does he treat you all right, at least?" Kevin raised his fist as if ready to fight.

"You don't have to fight anyone, Kino. He's a good guy. He's a data analyst for a bank. Makes 60K, is very smart, quite nerdy. Always stern, like you."

Kevin's eyes shot up. "Like me!"

"Yeah! Like you. I know you aren't always serious, but most of the time, I see you focused on the safety of others. Living that double life."

Telsa decided to change the subject. "How's that married woman you've been messing with? What's her name again?"

"Kazio," Kevin said.

"That's right. Kazio. How's she doing at the moment?"

"She is, apparently, divorced."

"Oh, really. Thinking of making the move?" she asked jokingly.

"I don't know." Kevin played it off.

"Not from what I've heard."

"*What you've heard?*" he responded, baffled. "I thought you were cooped up living the human life out here. I didn't know you had ears!"

"How do you think I've stayed safe for so long, Kino? Even I need friends on the inside. My inside is just smaller than yours. I'm surprised the Rigions haven't knocked at your door yet."

"They're not ready for this," He emphasized himself. They both laughed.

"Listen," he said. "*Mrs. Kazio* is a nice woman. Getting caught a little too close, that one time, in the school hallway, just led to rumors ready to spread."

"Possibly. It would be good to see you happy, at least. You always look as if someone just stole your juice box. The last time I saw you happy was with Amelia and Kirk."

Kevin turned from Telsa. It didn't take long for her to put the pieces together.

"What happened?" she asked softly.

"That situation between Tiyshio and his friend, it's gotten worse. Shawn killed Amelia and Kirk. Tiyshio almost killed him. I think Derek's next move will be to come after the one person no longer connected to them."

Telsa looked at him with a frozen expression of worry.

"I don't know, Telsa. Something tells me there's more to these deaths than just revenge."

"What are your thoughts?"

"Okay. Before I go any further… I think, before he went to kill Amelia and Kirk, Shawn paid a visit to my team from Zorin. I helped get them here safely when I discovered there were Rigions here. He slaughtered them, Telsa. Nothing remained of some of them but shreds of clothing. My team helped Amelia and Kirk get here. They had nothing else to do with them. Derek got Shawn to kill them all. Even tortured one of them to find out where they lived now."

"Hadn't you kept them secret this whole time? How was he able to find them?"

"I don't know, Telsa. What I do know is that Derek's preparing the boy for something much worse. I don't want to leave Shawn in a situation like that. Unlike Tiyshio, I'm willing to make difficult choices."

"What makes you think he's not going to be able to?"

"What other family does Tiyshio have outside of me? He's on a planet where all he has is his friends, and I take that away. Tiyshio is a broken man. Shawn means the world to him. He's, his brother. I know that based on how they acted with each other. If it came down to it, I have no faith in him. I'm sorry."

"Don't be." Telsa shook the weight off her shoulders. "So, I have to move again. Shit, Kino!" she said softly. "I haven't been here that long. I am running out of places to go! You know how difficult it is to get off this planet now? The enemy waits as far off as Venus and Mars's orbit lines. to make you think you can get out, leave, ready to take any ship. How long have you been in Boston?"

"A month, watching over you."

"A month!" Telsa shot up from her seat.

"A mon– " she started to repeat, then paused. "You know what? That's not so bad. Perhaps you are overreacting." Telsa started her normal night ritual, finishing up the dishes, turning on the television to watch the late news.

"A month is still a short time, Telsa. I'm here to protect you, in case he finds you."

"The only way he could find me is by following one of your rookie soldiers, who doesn't know how to blend in with the crowd. What was up with that?!"

"I talked to Ula. You know she knows better than that."

"Apparently, she does not!" Telsa looked stressed, staring toward her sword on the wall, which was hidden within a painting. "Why did he kill that couple?"

"He suspected they were behind his father's death and his mother's attempted murder."

Telsa uncomfortably pushed her hair behind her ear. "They don't just want me," she muttered.

"What?"

"Azuka. If they want me, they'll want her just as bad."

"They will still kill you!"

"Oh, yeah, well, they've been trying for so long I wonder if they are any good at finding me at all, but you are scared. Shit, it makes me think, you know, they may find me. Why is that?"

Kevin sat beside her, turning off the television. He met Telsa's eyes and smiled, offering a sad look. "They may go to the same lengths as I did to find you. If they do, I want to be right here, protecting you."

"When you guys did that, I felt I was connected again. It reminded me of being on the run. Remember those first couple of nights?"

Kevin nodded.

"Yeah," he said. "You couldn't sleep. I taught you how to block them out. Until I couldn't, and then I got you and Tiyshio in trouble."

He added, "If you came back, at least now you would be in two protective hands."

"Yeah? When was the last time you fought, Kino?"

"Two months ago, against Derek. This whole time, I've been searching for him. I know he isn't in New York. That's what brought me to you. Tiyshio has Azuka, and a bunch of other soldiers have many of my closest confidantes by their side."

"So, you want me to go back to New York and stay with you? You think I'll be safe there?"

In truth, Kevin didn't know. He only knew having her within eyesight meant he could do more than if he wasn't there. He would rather lose himself than lose a dozen other people volunteering to fight for him. Even with his loss for words, he could tell he wasn't justified.

"What are you going to do if he comes, Tel? You said it yourself. You have nowhere else to go."

"What can I do? Does he want me dead, for giving him access to their first-ever weakness, which they didn't even know someone other than Zorin could do? I am not putting your life in danger for me, Kevin. Not again. Your best bet is to find him before he finds me. You've been wasting time keeping eyes on me when you should be looking for him personally."

"Tel, just stay with me! Please! He doesn't know where I live or how protected I am now! He'd be a fool to try."

"I will tell you my decision tomorrow. For now, I think you should go, Kev."

Kevin shut and locked the window before approaching the door. "First sign of anything that's off, you let me know, Telsa. Okay?"

Telsa's answer was to open the door telekinetically and shove Kevin out. That was something she hadn't done in years. Kevin understood, but left, discouraged.

Across the street, a man had been listening in on their whole conversation, in his own apartment. Once outside, Kevin glanced straight at him, not noticing who it was, since the room was dark.

Derek sat with binoculars on his lap, looking down at Kevin, murmuring, "*Sure, Kevin looks alone, but I know he has protection nearby. Her, on the other hand, she'll bring out everyone we are looking for.*"

CHAPTER
TWENTY

SECRETS

Something seemed off when Telsa began to wake. Sunlight blaring through her eyelids felt like it was already noon. She remembered closing the blinds. She turned toward the shaded side of the bed, felt her hand hanging off the side. She stretched her legs out to the other end and ended up pushing herself more off the bed. She jolted fully awake. '*No blinds,*' she noted. She looked around the barren room, with its one small bedside table and light blue colored walls. *Something definitely wasn't right.* She looked out the window as she rose, to see a mile and half of long plains stretching out to a wooded area. Telsa made her way to the door. Before she could open it, she suddenly found herself pinned against the wall.

Three unknown men entered the room, followed by Derek. Smiling, he looked straight into Telsa's eyes. He suddenly looked confused, seeing that her eyes were brown.

She grew annoyed at his knowingly mocking her.

He smiled again. Two men with him held her up, while the third attempted to block her powers.

Derek noticed his efforts.

"Having a hard time?" he asked. "It's all right, boys. We don't need you here. She knows she can't get out of here easily." He turned to Telsa. "You know where you are?"

Telsa nodded. "Nighcos' pad. I found this place years ago."

"Yes. It is still one of his favorites. Gosh, you know how difficult it was to find you! I missed you, Telsa. So many empires we took down during the middle part of the war. It only took one slip up, and no, it wasn't your boyfriend. To be honest, I wish I had thought of that. Repetition gave away the city you were in. One of our scouts found you using the same route every day. Unluckily, that was all we had gotten, but Kino, shit, he practically gave me the keys to your apartment! Nice place, by the way! Is the rent good?"

"Why would it matter to you? I heard you like living with *daddy*."

"You're the one to talk, *sis*. You basically slept in the same room as him. I wonder, how did you know that you could slip through his fingers on an away mission, hmm? How did you lose your loyalty? He gave you everything you need—home, family, training, and your payback was separating yourself from us."

He slowly let her sink to the floor. She could walk again, but only because he had full power over her motor control.

"Like you, with your people," Telsa snapped. "I heard you have a new pet."

"Shawn is my son. He means the world to me."

"I'm sure he does. What does he *truly* mean to you, Derek?"

"What does he truly mean? He is a promise I made to his mother, if she were to perish. I promised to keep him safe."

"Bullshit. You're doing more than keeping him safe."

"It won't matter once I get what I am looking for. For the record, I'm doing it for him."

"You are wasting your time with me, Derek. Might as well kill me now."

"Why do you say that?"

"I know you want Azuka Fawzi. I know you want Tiyshio Taylor. You can't find Azuka, she finds you, and I have made it my mission to never know where Tiyshio Taylor is, ever again. By the way, my eyes, they're natural. I know you're wondering how I'm no longer connected."

"You *really* think that is what I want?" he asked slowly. "I want to know how she changed you. I know you haven't seen her. You've been living a *normal* life. Tell me, how does it feel, waking up every day in the dark hours of the morning, doing the same thing day after day, commuting home in hours-long traffic, repeating the same actions over and over?"

Telsa looked away. "It's a simple life. You wouldn't understand."

"I wouldn't!? I taught in a high school for three years. At least I still had a chance to leave this world, knowing I wouldn't be captured. I'm sure you miss not having to look over your shoulder, Telsa. I'm sure you miss being able to use the abilities you were born with." Derek saw the denial on Telsa's face and basked in it. "I can have him bring you back, as long as you give me what I want."

"You're such a horrible liar, Derek."

"You do want back in. In that case, I am not a liar, and I will give you what you want. As long as you give me what I want."

"I am never going back there. Nighcos took everything from me. Like you are doing to this boy."

Without realizing, she fought him off, seeing his calm face transform, growing more sinister, angrier, as he tightened his grip on her arm. He kept her mouth shut, even as tears rolled down her cheeks and her face reddened.

"I know Azuka changed you, Telsa. I tried the easy way to get what I want. Now I will get it by force. You will show me how she did it, and you will show me how I can stop Tiyshio."

Telsa pushed him away telekinetically, trying to break Derek's arm.

Derek cut her connection to her powers, then began bashing her ribs.

She cried out in pain.

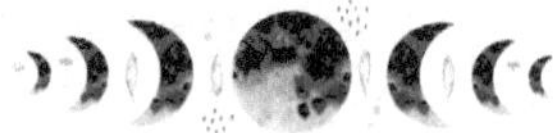

Kevin arrived at Telsa's apartment, knocked on the door, and yelled out her name. Ula was with him, as confused as he was. "Check if anyone is inside as I unlock the door," Kevin ordered.

Ula saw the room was empty but felt someone observing from afar.

"There isn't anyone inside, but stay low. Someone is watching. I told our people to check out the buildings across the street. They have a vantage point to the living room and bedroom."

Kevin nodded and teleported in, crouching. He peeked back at the other building to see who might be out there, but saw nothing. He ordered Ula to get to the roof telepathically, then looked around the apartment from the kitchen. The lock on the window was open.

He leaned out.

A sniper bullet rushed past his face. He breathed out a sigh of relief. Where the bullet made its impact, he saw only scorch marks,

"Enemy is using a light energy pulse rifle. Almost invisible in direct sunlight."

The soldiers acknowledged his warning.

Kevin peeked out once more, searching for a blind spot the rifleman couldn't see. The further he leaned out, the more confidence he gained to move forward.

Another shot grazed past his arm.

Kevin shoved himself against the wall. He then followed the trajectory of the sniper's first shot. It came from an apartment across the street, four to five stories higher than the one he was in. He told his people to check the seventh and eighth floor of that building, exactly where to look.

At this point, Kevin was certain Telsa wasn't in her apartment, that she had been taken by Derek, but he needed to see for himself. He wanted to be wrong.

As long as he stayed low to the ground and moved slowly, he shouldn't be noticed. When he reached the dark-shaded bedroom, he confirmed that it was empty.

"***She's not here! I want that shooter alive!***" he demanded.

"***Yes, commander!***" one of his soldiers replied.

Kevin returned to the center of the living room, exposing himself just enough to be seen. Kevin closed his eyes, listening through the sounds of the crowd outside and the cars passing by for the next shot, or the next crackle of electrical energy blasting past his ears to give his opponent's spot away to his people.

One second after firing that shot, the sniper realized Kevin was using himself as bait.

Soldiers swarmed around the sniper, dragging him away, knocking him out.

The man woke to find himself surrounded by a trio of soldiers. In their midst stood Kevin. The light placed in front of the sniper's face blinded him, so he could not see Kevin's reactions.

Kevin appeared as a shadowy figure in the room, a ghost amongst ghosts. The sniper scanned the room. It was so dark, from his vantage point, it seemed endless.

"I know why you got me," the sniper admitted.

"I'm amazed at how you led her to us."

"How long have Derek and Shawn been in Boston?" Kevin asked.

"Just as long as you have. One of our scouts was surprised at how similar your operation was to ours. Rather than taking you, we followed your trail. It was a big mistake going to her place. You were compromised before knowing you were."

"Shit!" Ula shouted.

"Calm down, Ula," Kevin ordered. He turned back to their captive. "So, where did he take her?"

"You'd like to know, wouldn't you?"

Kevin shot an energy blast at the man, scarring his face. "I have no time for games, and I'm sure you have no time for death. Don't think I know who you are, Niro. You have a family of four waiting at home. I've got people waiting outside the location of each."

"Getting your hands dirty? I thought you were a boy scout, Kino," Niro replied.

"Not when Telsa's involved. Now." Kevin grasped Niro's hand with both of his and began to heat them. "If you want to be able to feel your kids again, you will tell me where she is."

Niro grinned. The heat around his hands felt like nothing. He assumed Kevin was bluffing.

Then, as Kevin's face grew more serious, his hands became hotter.

Niro's smile faded. He shifted around, trying to pull away.

Kevin's grip tightened.

Sweat dripping from Niro's palm splattered on the ground, steam rising from it. Still, he didn't budge, even as his hand grew hotter. Even the others in the room began to feel it.

Niro's skin began melting, dripping to the ground. Ula stared. Niro cried out in pain, but still didn't budge.

Kevin called on one of his crew to start burning their captive's face. Niro tried biting the man's fingers, and got punched in the face. The soldier's hands were already heated; the punch left a burn mark on his face.

The soldier held Niro's head back and continued punching him in the face with his heated hand. He broke Niro's nose; blood dripping from it dried quickly with each punch. He began heating up Niro's face while he was dazed.

When Niro looked ready to pass out, Kevin stopped his comrade and shared a small bit of energy to the Rigion.

"That was fun, right?" Kevin smiled, holding up Niro's head.

Their captive looked lost and dazed.

"So, we are going to do this again. Where is Telsa Gond?" Kevin heated his hands once more.

"Nighcos's ranch, in upstate New York," Niro answered, slurring.

"Shawn is with him?" Kevin asked calmly.

"Yes!" Niro replied in a low voice.

"Good!"

Kevin shot a high-energy blast from his hand, killing Niro.

Kevin strode out of the room and instructed Ula, who followed him, "Get everything else from his mind before it goes cold. When you're done, burn him. I want his family to know they'll have a better life without this piece of shit."

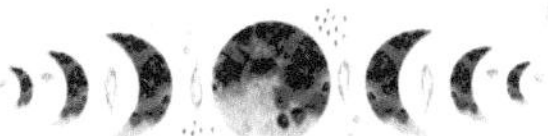

DEREK HELD TELSA UP BY THE CROWN OF HER HEAD. SHE TRIED TO pull him off. She felt him racing through her every single memory. The force moved so quickly through her mind; even mere events arose, like silhouettes in her eyes. She looked down the hallway, saw her mother staring back, but couldn't make out her expression. All she could hear was, "Telsa?"

She kept fighting Derek as he continued plunging deeper into her mind. She struggled to use her powers to block him.

She saw a memory of herself and Tiyshio, together. Tiyshio must have been thirteen years old.

"Telsa, can you teach me how to fight with your staff?" he begged her. "I hate this wooden one. Kevin thinks I can't handle the real thing."

Telsa laughed, "Sure, Tiyshio, but it isn't about fighting with the real thing or a fake. It's about knowing the weight of what can be done with the weapon in your hand. Are you ready to take a life?"

Tiyshio nervously said, "No. I think I'll be scared, too."

"Good. You should be. Taking a life can change you. Kevin teaches you with this *wooden* thing because it will help you survive. If you can best someone in battle, then you have the choice, either take a life, or show mercy and let your opponent live to fight another day. Got it?"

Tiyshio nodded.

Derek focused on memories that might have Azuka in them, seeing her with Azuka and her crew.

Azuka introduced them: "These were each one of them. Now they are one of us. Ram, Herris, Yevin, Nuit, and Daz."

Telsa greeted them all. Yevin caught her eye. Everything about him looked human, except for his yellowish eyes. He resembled a middle eastern man of around five foot nine, dressed in blue jeans and a spotted dress shirt. Telsa held his hand a little too long, making him feel awkward.

Derek backed away from that memory, knowing the event took place after she got changed. The deeper he entered her mind, the more it felt like walking through deep mud, increasingly difficult to trek through.

Some memories felt fake. There were awkward pauses, like her memory with Yevin. He deduced she was making those up on the spot.

Opening his eyes, he saw his thumb practically digging into her temple. He put her to sleep and laid her on the bed, no matter how much she fought him off. Her mind became wilder, more aggressive. Derek shielded himself with only his fingers, holding her head. He released most of the tension in his grip and tried again, this time just slightly pressing on her temple, closing his eyes, and taking a deep breath.

He was in a parking garage filled with cars. The corners were dark; Most of the light filled the middle of the garage. Sounds of clashing swords echoed through the walls. He ran toward the noise, saw Azuka and Telsa fighting. Azuka moved fast, aggressively, while Telsa fought much more defensively, her strikes not connecting with Azuka's swipes or plunges. When Telsa struck at her in retaliation, using her staff, she aimed for her hands and legs.

Azuka vaulted over Telsa's weapons. Both fighters' eyes glowed as red as a Rigion's. Azuka's had a honeycomb look, with a circuit-looking pattern on her pupil leading to her iris. Derek recognized that as the eye of rage. Telsa's cornea looked like snakeskin, the iris forming a four-pointed star shape.

Derek moved closer to the bout.

"This must be it," he commented.

He returned to the beginning of the memory. Telsa was getting into her car, but did not notice someone sitting inside. At the last moment, she always checked her rearview mirror for safety.

Azuka sat there, looking at her in the mirror.

"Nighcos's lapdog!" Azuka exclaimed from the back seat. "Tell me, are normally liars and ghosts on earth protected?" A sinister smile crossed Azuka's face.

Telsa froze, her key in the ignition. "How did he find me?" she asked quietly.

"I have ways of finding people that aren't through our connected minds."

Telsa looked at the middle compartment of her car. Azuka saw her eyes rise suddenly. Telsa flung the door open as a spear emerged from the middle compartment toward her head.

Telsa grabbed her gun from the glove compartment. At the same time, she yanked out the spear and extended it into a staff, with another cone on the opposite end. Azuka rushed at her, breaking off her car door and knocking her to the ground. Telsa had already let go of the staff, throwing it aside, but quickly had it coming for Azuka's head.

Azuka swung the door to knock the weapon back. Telsa took a couple of shots at Azuka, missing her head but hitting her chest, knocking her back. She letting the door go.

Telsa took the opportunity to run.

Azuka wasn't far behind. She pulled out a gun and started shooting.

Telsa ducked and charged away faster, looking for a place to hide. She even shot back at Azuka, making her duck.

Then Telsa saw an opening to the lower level.

Azuka waited for only a few minutes before realizing she hadn't heard any further sounds. She took off her shoes and snuck forward, peering between each car.

Telsa hid where she could see the gap between the cars. She slipped through, her gun ready.

Azuka paused when she made out light coming from the ground. Squatting a little further, she saw Telsa.

Telsa began shooting, with only three bullets left in her clip. Azuka could tell when she ran out. She jumped down, rushed at her, pulling out her sword.

Telsa dodged and rolled away from her, then took any opening she could to attack Azuka.

Azuka kicked her the next time she tried attacking, then lifted her telekinetically.

Telsa took that moment to grab her sword, distracting her.

Azuka made another sword appear when Telsa struck her head, retaliating with a vicious swing. Telsa hopped back, furiously swung again for her head with the full momentum of her body. This time, she buckled Azuka.

Telsa pushed Azuka's knees down telekinetically. then plunged her sword toward her chest to finish the battle.

Azuka rolled away, launching her sword as she fell toward Telsa's torso, piercing straight through, immobilizing her. Azuka pressed her against a car, keeping Telsa's head up.

Her thoughts exposed how tired she was growing.

She saw the first time her drive began fading. She was on a spaceship with a crew of thirteen. The president of one planet wouldn't surrender to the Rigions and had been taken onto her ship. He wasn't innocent; he had been head of a smaller alliance before the Zorians could come to ally with their world.

He was President Contro, of Dendas. Riza, Telsa's home world, was part of their solar system. Instead of putting in place a proper army to protect their world, he gave it up as a truce to the Rigion army, a plea for protection. He never trusted the ruler of her world, which led to her planet's suffering. This time, she did the same.

Her assignment: assassinate the people of Dendas.

First by having them turn against each other. Then by having them claim it uninhabitable. Making Contro watch each day as years passed. As he had done to the ruler of Riza, all this before she could kill him herself. The mission was to let go of the Dendans for their treason.

What made no sense to her was how little joy she took in the task. She thought she would've been happy, admired her work. This was the man responsible for her mother's death. The only person to have rescued her, even from other Rigions, was Nighcos.

She returned to the Rigions, confused and fearing others would notice she was different. She went on missions that she tasked others to do for her until she couldn't take it anymore. She found a way to focus on blocking her mind from connecting to them. She secluded herself in abandoned Rigion strongholds to survive. Walking away from altercations, she removed herself whenever she came across any Zorian, or affiliate of the race.

Until Kevin found her.

*What got Azuka's attention most was seeing a boy in her memories with the '***Alam***' mark on his arm. She saw herself as happy and relaxed. It made no sense to her that there would be someone out there so much like herself.*

"You aren't linked to them?"

Telsa shook her head.

"How do you know him?" Azuka asked, backing away.

"He found me. At my worst, I was ready to fully let go. I didn't want to run anymore. Kino Zara took me in, trained me, cared for me, befriended me. If I didn't know there couldn't be prejudice from a Zorian before, it was he who gave me hope."

"How did you let go so easily?"

"I became my enemy, only to kill one of my own. You saw what happened to my family. Nothing would've helped, had I stayed. I gave myself free will."

"How are you killing our own?" Telsa questioned.

"My purpose was fulfilled a long time ago. I had the same effects as you, but one above you." The color of Azuka's eyes swallowed inward, revealing her natural silver eyes.

Telsa's own eyes slowly widened.

"Are those natural?"

Azuka nodded.

"You are Menti?"

"Many races have my eyes. That doesn't mean that I am one of them. However, I can bring you back to who you are."

Telsa looked at her, puzzled. Azuka pressed her hand against one side of her torso, removing her sword with the other. "How would you like to never be on the run again?"

Telsa, not following quickly, said, "What!"

Azuka held Telsa's eyes wide open telekinetically, shut her mouth knowing she would scream, removing every piece of the Rigion gene from her.

Derek marveled, seeing the strands spill out as bacteria. He felt her pain and her mind being severed from the Rigions by force, as if her brain was being ripped from her head.

In the distance, Derek heard gunfire and shouts ordering an attack.

Derek opened his eyes, looking out the window to see Kevin. He raced out of the room, told his guards to remain at their post.

Shawn rushed toward him. "Did you find out where she was?"

"No. I found out our weakness, and will make sure Kevin doesn't exploit it."

"Kevin knows how to do it, too?"

Derek nodded. "Stay here. I will call if I need you. Stay by that room. Make sure she doesn't leave."

Shawn agreed.

Kevin had a spear in one hand, his other charged with energy. Bullets flew over his head as he peered from his cover. He saw three soldiers blocking his intended route. On the other path, there were only two.

He chose the side with less.

The soldiers didn't see him coming. Both were blasted in their heads for their obliviousness. The sound of the energy shot attracted others in the courtyard, who started shooting at Kevin.

He got thrown into the bushes after being shot in the shoulder twice. He grasped at his wounds, healed them as much as he could, knowing the action would make him weaker, briefly.

Another soldier tried to intercept him. Kevin heard his light footsteps, threw the spear through his head, and quickly called it back. Kevin looked toward a narrow pathway with barely any cover as his best way to get around.

The next soldier tried converging to his left. Kevin made a run for it, getting shot at a bit more. Kevin dove toward the ground, then twisted in the air, blasting the next soldier to come at him twice.

The impact only knocked his opponent down. At least that was enough to let him see the last soldier in the courtyard, who had not moved from his position.

Derek glanced out the window, sword in hand, surrounded by a dozen more soldiers. "Prepare for breach," he ordered. "He will come through these walls. I need six of you here in the foyer, and another six hiding in the corridor of this first floor. He must not be allowed upstairs. I will be in here with you."

Kevin looked at the windows, barely seeing any movement in the house. The door was unguarded. That seemed too easy. He shot a blast at the door, blowing it open, as Derek watched from his point of view.

Shawn looked out from the room where Telsa stayed, while grasping his sword tightly.

Kevin launched his spear at a soldier in the distance. He missed, but used that moment the soldier dodged to kill the other one, whom he knocked to the ground just as he was getting up.

One of the inside soldiers was about to make a run the outside, seeing Kevin's back towards them, to shoot him. Another stopped him, stating quietly, "We don't know if he's shielded or with others."

Derek showed displeasure.

Kevin approached the soldier. He simply threw the spear after getting shot a few times, barely flinching, to blast him in the head. The soldier pushed Kevin's hand away and tried to stab him. Kevin jolted back, immediately knocking him on the head. Kevin then tripped him and called his spear back. The soldier tried grabbing it off the ground.

Kevin blasted it away, stabbed him in the heart, and made his way toward the door.

Derek called for the soldiers to open fire. Kevin put up an energy field around himself as he ran. Two soldiers intercepted him at the door; he quickly killed them. Another four fired at him until he came closer. Six more disobeyed Derek's order, starting for him.

Kevin felt them coming and launched three of them up into the air, telekinetically.

Another two took down his energy field by blocking his powers. The men then stopped firing. His movements were too quick; they risked hitting one of their own.

Kevin was quickly grabbed. That was when Derek came out.

Kevin, infuriated, used all his mind power to bring his abilities back to their useful status.

The blockers collapsed from the stress. The two men holding him were blasted through the window and against a wall. Kevin breathed heavily, feeling the toll this action took on him.

Shawn heard the loud crash downstairs. He left the room, leaving the door slightly open.

Telsa awoke up and, noticing that, slowly started for the door.

Two men tried to stab Kevin. He quickly dodged, making them stab each other.

Kevin scanned around the room. He was down to eleven soldiers. He shot two energy blasts to the blockers' heads and launched his spear through the head of another, who fell outside, without looking.

The last eight soldiers stood beside Derek.

"Might as well stop now, Kino," Derek advised. "You're getting tired."

"Not until you're dead. Not until you tell me why you killed my daughter."

Derek smiled. "Me? Kill your daughter? Who might that be, Kino? Was it–Amelia?"

Kevin grasped his hands tight, calling back the spear.

Derek was shocked. "Holy shit! It was!"

"Cut the shit, Nyra. I know you did it in revenge for what I did to you, years back. Is that why you chose to take the boy now? Use one of my own against me? Have him turn against the people that took care of him? Loved him?" Kevin's voice rose to a yell.

"See, that's the thing you don't get, Kevin. They never loved him. They were always out to kill the boy. I just showed him the truth. I took him away from your lies, not mine!"

"All you had to do was leave. They were innocent."

"Just as much as you are, isn't that right, Kino?"

Kevin attacked Derek, but his soldiers grappled him once more. Derek moved in to stab Kevin.

Kevin shoved one of the soldiers in the way.

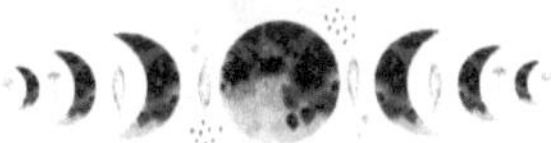

SHAWN WATCHED THE WHOLE BATTLE FROM ATOP THE STEPS. HE started down to join in, but Telsa stopped him, pulling him back. Shawn then saw the two guards by her room door had been killed, along with the others in the hallway.

"You told Tiyshio and Kevin a way to kill me," he chided. "How long have you wanted me dead?"

"I never wanted you dead, Shawn. I wanted you safe."

"Liar!" Shawn clashed his sword against Telsa's to throw her off balance. He followed up, jump-kicking her to the ground.

Kevin pulled a soldier in front of himself as a shield when a dagger came flying at his head. The soldier he held tried using the opportunity to attack Kevin, as well, but, as soon as the soldier was stabbed, Kevin blasted a hole in his chest.

Kevin was getting tired. He could barely hold up his hands, but he could still move his body. Derek took a few blasts at him. Kevin canceled them out by shooting a few himself. One soldier swung his sword down at Kevin's arm. He would have made it through if Kevin hadn't hardened his muscle structure solid. The man stared up at Kevin in fear. Kevin headbutted him a few times before the man dropped to the ground and had his chest crushed by Kevin's foot.

Derek went after Kevin, swinging his sword towards his neck.

Kevin used the sword in his arm to block Derek, then kicked Derek to the other room. Four soldiers surrounded him, preventing him from moving forward. Holding out their arms, they synchronously pushed Kevin to the ground, making the sword in his arm slide further in.

Derek stood up and raised Kevin at the same time, yanking him closer, his sword ready to plunge through his heart. Kevin blasted Derek in the face, burning his left eye and the left side of his head. Kevin then turned around to face two soldiers rushing at him.

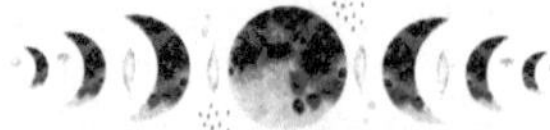

Shawn violently struck down Telsa, stumbling. She used the action to her advantage, knocking him off balance telekinetically. She kicked his sword away as he fell, then plunged her own sword down toward his head.

Shawn knocked her off balance and pulled her towards him. Telsa held onto her sword as she fell, pointing it at Shawn's head.

Shawn let go of her, rolling away, picking up his blade and taking a moment to recover before his next attack.

Telsa shook off the attack, then pulled the other sword out of the dead soldier next to her.

Shawn attacked fiercely.

Telsa defended with ease.

Shawn grew fiercer with every blow. Telsa's wrist weakened more every time she wasn't holding a good form.

Telsa pushed Shawn back telekinetically. He rebounded, sliding her against the wall. Shawn shot a series of spikes at Telsa as he raced toward her.

Telsa cut them away, then vaulted over him.

Shawn swung at her, slashing her back, and quickly moved in to stab her.

Telsa cried out in pain, swiftly covering herself in an energy field which blew Shawn back when he struck it. Once she saw he was down, she raced downstairs and killed the soldier who was about to chop off Kevin's neck.

Kevin looked at Telsa with a smile. There were only three soldiers remaining. Two were ready to attack them; one lay unconscious on the ground.

Derek was still collecting himself.

One Rigion soldier fired two energy blasts at Telsa. These, Telsa deflected, as she raced forward and stabbed the soldier. Kevin killed the one on the ground with the sword stuck in his arm.

The last soldier swung his sword at Kevin's arm as he threw it. Telsa blocked him, then kicked him aside.

The soldier then attacked both of them, consecutively. Each defended the other, striking each time he let his attention go off one of them.

Derek saw Telsa about to chop off the soldier's arm. He shot an energy blast that blew her weapon clean away.

Kevin caught sight of this and killed the soldier to prevent his finishing her.

Derek shot another energy blast, hitting Kevin in the back of his left shoulder.

Kevin couldn't lift his arm. The soldier noticed as he dropped his spear. Kevin dodged the soldier's first three strikes, but couldn't avoid the last two blasts to the chest that Derek fired, knocking him down.

The soldier took that opportunity to make his final strike.

Telsa moved in to kill the soldier before being shot by Derek once again, in the stomach, knocking her to the ground.

The next time Derek fired, Kevin leapt in the way, firing an energy blast back at him, blowing off his arm.

Kevin pulled Derek toward him. Bringing his spear in the trajectory of Derek as the latter prepared to shoot one more energy blast at Kevin.

. Kevin was only grazed on his shoulder, leaving his wound exposed. Derek pierced his stomach.

Derek's body then landed on top of Kevin's, Derek's head on his shoulder. He felt heavy. Kevin was barely able to hold him, letting him tumble to the ground.

Kevin struggled to pull himself up after his injuries. Still, it wasn't over. Derek also pulled himself up, just enough to look toward the stairs.

They all heard someone coming down just as the last soldier dropped. Grinning, with blood spilling from his mouth, Derek whispered in Kevin's ear, "Only now have I truly won."

Kevin pulled out his spear and cut off Derek's head. There was nothing more he could do now. Derek's head rolled to the ground, staring straight at Shawn, fully enraged.

Kevin and Telsa also looked at him, battered, tired, and afraid. Knowing what he had become capable of.

In a low, faint voice, Kevin whispered, "Telsa… go!"

CHAPTER
TWENTY-ONE

DEATH

Shawn shot an energy beam at Telsa.

Kevin countered it with one of his own.

Telsa looked to him, distraught,. Kevin assured her he would be okay. He quickly distracted Shawn from attacking her as she took off.

Shawn let go of the beam, vaulting over the railing onto the staircase, Kevin quickly pulled the spear out of Derek's body, then pressed a button to mechanically transform it into a staff.

Suddenly, Shawn struck Kevin, bringing him to his knees. '*Damn, he's gotten* stronger.' Shawn swiped at his victim's torso, cutting him. Kevin broke his nose with the shaft and pushed him back telekinetically.

Shawn gripped his nose in pain, then attacked Kevin again. Kevin easily dodged his move, stabbing him where he had an opening.

Shawn stumbled back, gripping his torso, pushing Kevin back telekinetically to give himself time to recover. The nanobots inside Shawn flocked toward his wound to repair it.

Kevin started to get that hopeless feeling again. "Son of a bitch."

Shawn lunged at Kevin. Kevin knocked his blade away, retaliating harder. Shawn never broke eye contact. With every swing of his blade, the impact vibrated through his arms, causing them to buckle even more. If one more strike impacted, his arm would give out.

Kevin reached forward to push Shawn out of his way. Shawn nudged his hand off, pushing back harder.

Kevin flew through the wall, cratering into the next in the hallway.

Kevin stared at the floor, dazed. He raised his head in time to see Shawn shoot another spike from his fingertips. Kevin jumped, dashing away. Spikes flew at him like bullets from a machine gun. He ducked behind a counter.

Shawn slowly approached his hiding place.

Kevin slowed his breathing to ease the pain. He tried raising his burned arm, but it wouldn't budge as much as he wanted.

He tried to heal it as fast as he could. Then he heard a spike pierce the counter, protruding inches from his neck. Two more followed rapidly as Kevin shifted over.

He bumped into Shawn, who raised him up.

Kevin's face was in shock. He kicked Shawn in the shin, getting him to drop him.

Shawn stumbled, continuing forward to brutally slash at this victim. Kevin scanned the room, saw a rack of knives, and shot them toward Shawn.

Shawn didn't see them coming. Four of them pierced his back. Shawn froze in pain, pulled out the one nearest his shoulder, and threw it at Kevin. It caught him right in the chest.

Shawn threw another, which Kevin deflected with the knife he just pulled out of his chest.

In a split second, Kevin rushed at his attacker, barraging him with kicks and punches. None of them landed; Shawn was too quick. Kevin then launched the spear he had dropped earlier at Shawn. Shawn grabbed it and, using its momentum, plunged it toward Kevin's head. Kevin rolled away, kicking the weapon out of Shawn's grasp. He then grabbed his opponent, slamming him to the ground as he slid toward the wall.

Shawn swung his blade at Kevin's torso, meeting him eye to eye with an ominous smile. Kevin could tell Shawn was planning to stab him. Kevin let go, bringing himself erect to kick Shawn in the groin, hard enough to make Shawn slide to the other end of the house.

Kevin felt on the open wound in his torso where Shawn had stabbed him. "Shit!"

Shawn groaned, writhing on the floor, barely able to get up. The knives in his back were slowly easing their way out, rather than pushing back in each time Shawn rolled around. Kevin needed another plan. The fight was becoming one-sided, and he himself could barely stand. Kevin called his staff back into his hand and raised a gun from the main foyer.

Kevin wiped sweat off his face. He slowly approached Shawn, leaning on his staff.

Shawn couldn't stay down. He glanced toward Derek's body in the main foyer. His long face turned sour. He used the corner of the wall to pull himself erect, watching as Kevin slowly neared him.

Kevin heard the weapons scattered on the ground, shifting past the bodies, coming for him. He repelled them back, this time launching them outside.

Shawn searched Kevin's thoughts, feeling the same anger he did. He felt satisfied, knowing they were on the same page. Shawn felt for his wounds, but found nothing. The pain in his groin had almost gone away.

Kevin watched Shawn start toward him, shedding his skin to create two blades for each hand.

"All this time," Shawn accused him, "you taught me Zorians were different from Rigions. Now I see you act like one."

"Yet you were manipulated by one. How could you let him lie to you? Amelia and Kirk cared about you! I care about you!"

"Lie to me!? Kevin, you're the one who lied to me, not him! I found a family in my enemy. What have you found?"

Kevin stood silent, meditating briefly over his life. All he knew was his mission to protect, at whatever cost. Rigions were the enemy, the cause of what had happened to his family.

"It took him a long time to pull out the shit that you put in my head," Shawn continued. "You had me believing you would find my father's killers, all of them, when you were the kingpin. What's wrong with me, my people? You can't stand that we invaded your planet, killed millions, just to take it over? Or is it simply that some of us are different, and we aren't all like those savages?"

"Shawn, I had nothing to do with that!"

"Shut up! You lying piece of shit!" Shawn smiled with sorrow in his eyes.

Shawn pointed to Derek's body. "I trusted you and, believe it or not, at one time, he trusted you, too."

Kevin looked at Derek, then back to Shawn. "Taylon-Nyra never trusted me! He blames me for the death of his family! He never trusted Zorian people. You trusted us, Casan, you can again."

"I won't fall for that again." Shawn's body was now engulfed by the armor he had been given by Dr. Smith, crimson red with silver accents.

Kevin sighed. He knew exactly what this meant for him. He aimed the gun at Shawn, waiting for his next strike.

Telsa had gotten far enough away to find a gas station. She found the outside bathroom. Locked. She could barely focus, given the wound to her stomach hurting so much, but she had to try. She searched the bathroom in her mind to make sure it was free before she mentally undid the lock and entered.

In the mirror, the wound looked worse than she suspected. She felt herself fading. She thought back to when Kevin found her again, focusing on his face and their energy.

In seconds, she landed on Chris's wooden dinner table.

Chris and his mother quickly helped her up. Chris's mom saw the seriousness of her wound. She turned to her son.

"We can't take her to the hospital, Mom," he insisted. "Call Kevin!"

Telsa grabbed his hand, smearing his arm with her blood.

"No," she said faintly. "Kino is in trouble. Help me get Tiyshio."

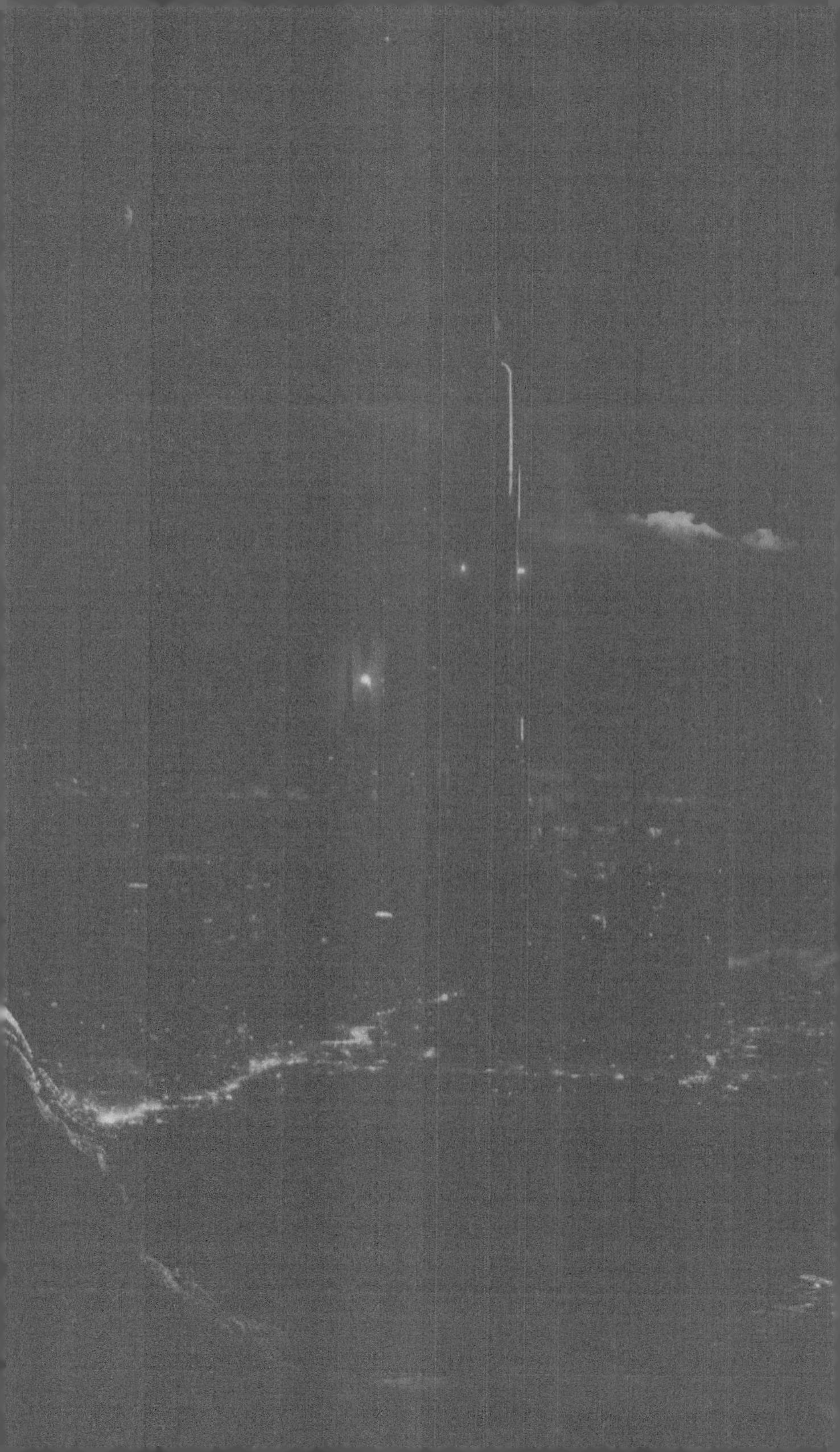

CHAPTER
TWENTY-TWO

HOUSE

Hayden felt air flowing through his lungs, his body merging with the ground, as he listening to Tiyshio gently guided him toward becoming an element himself. Although he did not understand all that meant, he knew one important step was to stay calm and breathe naturally.

Azuka sat on a box, eating toast, about four feet from the two of them. Tiyshio looked to her for assistance. She didn't even glance his way, annoying Tiyshio. Fortunately, Hayden was extremely focused. It also helped that the field was so quiet.

Hayden saw the field as empty in his mind. He rubbed his hands together, feeling their warmth, despite not physically doing so. Excited as he was to feel that connection, he never broke focus.

Tiyshio sensed the freedom Hayden gave himself in his mind and offered a thumbs up to Azuka. She half-heartedly gave one back, while chowing down another chunk of bread in one bite. Tiyshio slowly lowered his hand.

Hayden began rising into the air, due to the whirlwind that formed under him. The dust blurred their vision. Azuka crunched down on dirt accidentally, then threw away her last piece of toast.

Tiyshio looked into Hayden's mind again, saw him encouraging himself, repeating, "Good. Keep balance. Remember, it's all in the mind."

Tiyshio smiled. Those were the exact words he told Hayden during their earlier training sessions.

From the circling dirt, small glands of water swirled toward Hayden, orbiting him. There was a problem, however. Most of the glands didn't make it to him. Those that did reach only made one rotation, moving aggressively. Hayden's eyes focused on each strand of water as it neared him.

Tiyshio saw the problem. He entered Hayden's mind to advise him, "Let go. Your focus shouldn't be on individual glands, but on all of them. Use your imagination."

Hayden took a deep breath. Little by little his eyes went from following each strand to not following any. At that point, the water circled him calmly.

"Good!" Tiyshio encouraged. "Now, like we practiced, use that imagination to build that water shield around you."

A wind above them began to pick up, pushing down on them. With that wind came water from the sky, wrapping around Hayden like a bubble until he was fully immersed. Hayden opened his eyes, confident that he was now in control.

Azuka rose. With a hint of excitement in her voice, she told him to move around.

Tiyshio felt his confidence break a bit.

"Hey," he advised, "don't fret. Just think of yourself as inside a ball. In the ball, you would shift your weight forward to move. Think of the wind shifting the water ball forward."

Hayden shook his head uncomfortably, gazing into the distance, concerned that the session was taking longer than it initially seemed. He mouthed, "Just like we practiced." This was his fourth time this month doing this activity. To date, he had been proud of his progress. However, every time he gained control, he always had a distraction set him off balance.

Hayden looked at the ground, this time focusing on the whirlwind he had created below. He thought it should move forward. Slowly, it did so, but then he started losing the integrity of the water ball he was in. He knew he had to keep the ball strong enough to repel any objects that came at him. He used his thoughts to keep moving, and to keep the ball strong as he gained speed. He grew more satisfied that he managed not to lose focus.

Tiyshio found himself in great awe, considering how many times Hayden had previously fallen, feeling the accomplishments he was witnessing.

"That's two elements so far," Azuka said to Tiyshio. "Let's see if he can produce another."

"What did you have in mind?"

"Hmm?" Azuka shot a beam straight at Hayden, bright enough for him to see. Once again, Hayden almost lost concentration.

Tiyshio felt him losing that, and yelled, "Don't let go! Improvise."

Hayden almost dropped down before he thought to raise the ground, lessening the blast. He switched direction.

Another beam came at him immediately. He repeated his action, this time pushing the shielded ground toward Azuka.

Azuka's face lit up. She jumped toward him, sucking the water away from his body.

Hayden looked upwards, then formed the water shield again as she struck at it. He nearly froze in panic at the sight of her blade barely piercing the water, as well as her not falling because she held onto her sword. Hayden froze the water surrounding him, to break Azuka's blade. Instead, it crawled up to her heels.

She vaulted off as the bubble exploded. Hayden still managed to keep himself in the air.

Azuka was indeed impressed. She told Hayden to come down and rest.

Tiyshio rushed to his side to celebrate. Azuka even threw him a sword.

"Keep it!" she said. "You've earned it. You're not out of the woodwork yet, but at least now you can defend yourself."

"Yeah, but, as you see, I'm still not fully confident about my abilities."

"That's a lie!" she snapped.

Tiyshio looked at her, perplexed.

"Sorry," she continued, "but that's a lie you are telling yourself. Hayden, you've made more progress this month than most kids your age do by living here. It's good that you want to take a stand. That is confidence. That is wanting not to go down without a fight."

"Like you?!" he asked.

"Uhh, not exactly. I am ready to die, after living the life that I have with no recollection of the past before becoming a Rigion. I feel I have no real identity. My attack on them is more of a martyr's job."

"Is that what you wish to be?" Tiyshio asked.

"I was going to say yes, but I am not sure yet. Maybe I do want to go down in a blaze of glory. For now, it's enough to know I've hurt the people that took everything away from me."

"Azuka, you were able to stop being a Rigion here." Hayden observed. "Why not rebuild your life, and who you are, while on this planet, the way I did…or my brother?"

"It would feel artificial. I want to know my people. I only have fragmented memories of who they are and what they fought for. I do what I do now because it makes me feel alive. As you are doing with this training."

"Your regular eyes look like a Menti's."

"I've been told that, you know. I've looked for signs before. Too bad that none of my ships can travel as far as the outer rim planets of the Andromeda galaxy. I once had a vision that I went there, though. I arrived there and liberated the whole place. I even confirmed whether I was from there. Heck, I even built a family. What's crazy is, I can't see myself doing any of that right now. I have so much else to do."

"You're allowed to take a break, Azuka," Tiyshio advised her. "These guys ain't going anywhere. Not as long as I'm here."

"Yeah. As long as you're here, I think you might make more frenemies." Azuka laughed. "Which reminds me, it's your turn now. No combat training this time."

Tiyshio looked at her, confused, "What'd you mean? We've been practicing that for weeks. We've got to keep up the pace if I'm to best Shawn in battle."

"That's if there ever is a fight between you two. Listen, Tiy, I want this to be the last time I train you for a while."

"WHAT!?"

"You aren't going to need me soon. You nearly perfected the transfer, and fighting me isn't fighting him. I don't even know how the boy fights. Right now, I want you to remind me of everything that happened. Exactly how did the transfer play out? What did you see? What did you feel? How did you feel in your head during the whole transfer? Were you confident that you could save him?"

"Why are you asking me this now?"

"There are factors that go into making this transfer a success. I remember telling you that. He can't fight if he doesn't want to be in it. Now, tell me."

Thinking back to that afternoon, Tiyshio remembered forcing his eyes open and pulling out quickly. "I...knew I just wanted it out. I felt it was a way to end the problem, then and there. I didn't know if it would work. I remember the room in which this whole thing started. Shawn's pain. His determination to see it through. He kept replaying the day his father died, and Amelia and Kirk somehow seeing it as well. I saw myself killing Aida, without hesitation."

"Is Aida his mother?"

Tiyshio said yes.

"His subconscious is reminding him why he believes being a Rigion is better," Azuka explained. "He is focused and determined, doing things he's never done, or even thought he could do, before he fully became one of them. His mind is telling him that, without this power, he will never achieve his vengeance. Searching through your mind, Tiyshio, only tells me that he is very deep. Killing Amelia and Kirk amplified that. Your job is to defeat his amplifier by nullifying it."

"How would I do that?"

"What's one thing we must do when we live?"

"Move on... Let go."

"The opposite of that is to hold on. Never let go! Rigions thrive on that grudge behavior: remember what hurt you!" Azuka moved a rock into position for Tiyshio to sit on, then did the same for herself. "Shawn and I are alike in many ways," she continued, quieter. "I don't know what caused my drive, but I do know I never want to kill anyone who fails to protect those they promised they would help. That was my drive."

"Then how are you no longer feeding off your drive?" Hayden asked.

"Because I know who my real enemy is, Hayden. It took for me and my squad at the time to do the same thing, to realize the cycle would only continue. I remembered, and I broke out of it." Azuka's eyes changed to her Rigion ones. Tears flowed from them as they reached their full form. "Tiyshio, while my eyes are like this, they can track me. I want you to take them out completely."

"But... wait... don't you want..."

"Don't worry. I can pull them back. Follow my directions to counter my subconscious and you can accomplish it in the easiest way possible. The same way I did it with Telsa."

Tiyshio focused on Azuka's eyes. He felt his mind connect to hers, feeling the anguish and remorse.

Tiyshio discovered version of herself in her mind, repeating a phrase on a constant loop, picking her up from the ground, and telling her, "You don't have to fight anymore. You did exactly what you didn't get. You served your purpose."

Tiyshio began to pull strands of gene out of Azuka, still connected to her mind, hugging her, his weapon in hand. Azuka took a moment to hug him back. Hayden watched her eyes turn slowly from the crimson red of Rigion eyes to a bright silver.

Tiyshio stopped pulling the strands out once she began putting them back inside herself again.

"You did it wonderfully. You saw the free will I was gaining and gave me a purpose to let go."

"You had nothing left," Tiyshio replied. "I understand why you are the way you are now."

Azuka shook her head in agreement. "Even while you were in there, you are privileged to see something I cannot." She gazed out into the distance. Somehow, she pictured Telsa, hurt and weak, calling her name. She closed her eyes, and was able to see Kevin slowly walking back to Nighcos's mansion, nearly about to fall.

Tiyshio noticed. "What's up?"

"Training is over," she said in a critical tone.

Tiyshio and Hayden both responded, "What!"

"Go home. Someone is waiting there to see you. Get there fast!" Her voice heightened.

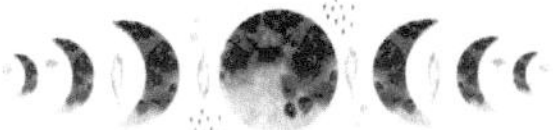

Tiyshio and Hayden raced back to the safe house, barging through the door.

Telsa laid on the couch, towels under her, with two doctors there to treat her wounds. Her face lit up on seeing Tiyshio.

So did his.

Tiyshio rushed over to kiss her on her forehead, getting in the way of the doctors who were working to heal her.

She stopped him. "Let them do their job, Tiyshio."

Tiyshio looked angry. "No. I gotta help you."

Telsa smiled. "No! Help Kino. He's the one in trouble. We got our asses kicked, and Shawn is the only one left. He's going to kill him, Tiyshio! Help him!"

Tiyshio turned to Hayden and shook his head, looking very concerned.

"I know what you're going to say. Might as well say it." Hayden could not keep the disappointment from his voice.

"I can't ask you to not go there," Tiyshio said, "because I know you will. All I ask is that you get Kevin out of there as fast as you can. I will prevent Shawn from getting to him. Got it?"

Hayden agreed.

Tiyshio turned to Telsa. "Where is he?"

As they teleported onto the premises, Tiyshio kept his eyes closed, hoping his month of training had paid off. Looking up slowly, he noticed Hayden was fully clothed. So was he. Hayden was not sure why Tiyshio's face suddenly seemed to light up with excitement.

Tiyshio shrugged off his reaction. "Just be happy you aren't naked."

Hayden followed Tiyshio, puzzled. They were nearly crawling on the ground, taking in the trail of bodies Kevin had left behind.

Hayden's heartbeat faster as his stride behind Tiyshio slowed. This felt no different than when he was at Amelia and Kirk's house. The area surrounding them was dead silent. Given everything around him, Hayden could not help feeling anxious.

Tiyshio was too focused on the surroundings to observe his reaction. He was nearly at the door when he finally noticed that Hayden was no longer behind him.

Tiyshio rushed back, silently. While trying to understand what was stopping Hayden, he had to look down on the ground himself.

"Hey," he reassured him, "if it makes you feel any better, they weren't on our side. This means we may have little to worry about, except for whatever is inside here. Stay behind me, until I tell you to break."

Tiyshio began walking toward the house.

It only took a few seconds for Hayden to join him. The ambiance unsettled them both.

As they entered the house, the sensation grew worse. Tiyshio felt a small bit of relief once he spotted Derek's dead body among the others in the main foyer. Hayden looked to Tiyshio, then followed a trail of blood leading from the hallway to the kitchen, where it merged with a larger puddle.

Tiyshio noticed the corner window leading to the woods was now broken. He almost took flight, but he couldn't leave Hayden. Something was very wrong here.

Hayden continued through the kitchen, toward the living room in the back. Unlike the main two rooms, it was clean. Hayden continued on into the family room.

He missed the open door that led to the back porch.

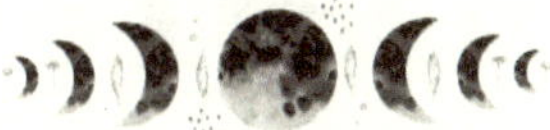

Tiyshio went upstairs, where he found the two dead guards outside the bedroom in which Telsa had been held. The door stood wide open. Tiyshio saw no one inside there. He continued further along the upstairs foyer toward the right wing of the mansion and the other bedrooms, slowly checking each one.

Kevin was still nowhere to be found.

Tiyshio turned to check the left wing.

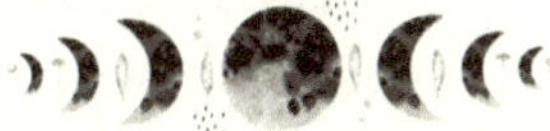

Hayden saw the family room was pretty much the same as the living room, with furniture untouched and generally clean. He even checked the closet, avoiding the basement. He was certain this house would prove a typical place to find trouble.

He forced himself to remember Azuka's advice: "Stop doubting yourself. You have the power."

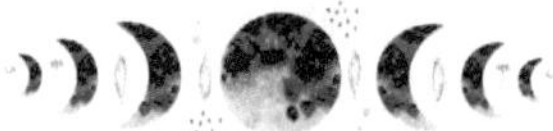

TIYSHIO HEARD A RUMBLE COMING FROM A ROOM HIDDEN AT THE end of the hallway. He closed his eyes, calling out Kevin's name in his mind with each step he took. His arm filled with goosebumps as he opened the door.

There was Kevin, letting himself down, using his staff to bear his weight. He was still badly bruised, from what Tiyshio could tell, as he raised his arm with the burnt shoulder.

"Kevin! Why didn't you teleport out of here?"

"Too tired……too tired……he's…he's coming…he's coming." He paced his words with each breath. Tiyshio was leery of analyzing Kevin once more.

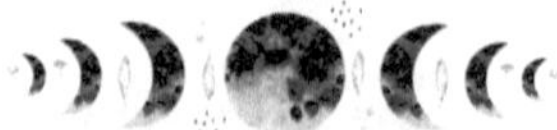

HAYDEN FOUND NOTHING DOWNSTAIRS EXCEPT VACANT BEDROOMS, cobwebs, and a lot of natural light. At least that took the weight off of Hayden's shoulders as he made his way back upstairs. Shawn wasn't there, so he wanted to regroup with Tiyshio and get out of this house as fast as he could.

Until he opened the door.

Shawn, looking around the room, immediately locked eyes with him. Hayden, shaken, put a handout as a signal to Shawn to back off, despite his already being eight feet away.

Shawn wasn't looking at anything but Hayden holding the handle of his sword. Hayden froze for a second, following Shawn's eyes.

"Oh, no!" he mouthed.

Shawn flung his arms down, shedding his skin into blades to cover his hands. He darted at Hayden, attacking him relentlessly.

Shawn might well have been a ghost, in Hayden's eyes. The only thing he felt was the chomping down of those newly created blades at his sword. Hayden rebounded him into the air, then swung at him before Shawn reached the ground.

Shawn ducked so quickly Hayden was certain he had gotten him.

Then Shawn tried to knock away his sword.

Hayden didn't let go, but he was hardly ready for Shawn's hard-hitting blow. Hayden buckled, lashing out at his opponent. Shawn recovered quickly and struck back at him, blow after blow, wearing him down.

Hayden's elbows began giving in. He got frustrated, barely able to lift his arms. Seeing Shawn's next move, he ducked at lightning speed.

Pushing Hayden back once more, Shawn plunged his sword into the ground to lessen the impact. He viciously pulled Hayden towards himself to finish him off.

Hayden swung as hard as he could to break the blade coming at him. He then made sure Shawn couldn't attack again. He raised Shawn's last bladed arm into the air to stab him.

Shawn pulled his arm out of Hayden's grasp, nearly spraining his wrist, then yanked Hayden forward once more.

Hayden blasted a jolt of fire. He then held Shawn down on the wooden floors to stab him once again.

Shawn broke free with ease. He deflected Hayden's blade, ferociously pinning Hayden to the ceiling, and began to crush him telekinetically.

"TIYSHIO!" Hayden cried.

Shawn threw Hayden to the ground. He began searching the house to find his other opponent.

Tiyshio paused in his healing of Kevin, finally realizing what all the shifting was about. He teleported Kevin back to Siyshi's safe house, then rushed downstairs.

He found Hayden, but Shawn was nowhere in sight.

"Hayden, are you okay? Where did he go?"

Hayden pointed behind Tiyshio, fearfully.

Tiyshio twisted around to see Shawn's blade flying toward his eyes. He blocked the weapon and pushed Shawn back, wailing continuously.

Shawn blocked him effortlessly, only to get more frustrated with each strike. Finally, he threw Tiyshio across the living room and swung at his stomach.

Hayden knocked Shawn away, using the air around him. He leaped, blasting a fireball at him before striking at his shoulder.

Shawn spread the fire around himself and rebounded at Hayden, causing him to stumble. Shawn then attacked him until Tiyshio stepped in, pushing Hayden to safety and shattering Shawn's blades.

Hayden regained his footing. His breathing felt pressured. The pain from his ribs made him want to drop.

Tiyshio was bothered by his movements. He read Hayden's mind to determine exactly what was wrong.

Hayden looked back at him. "I'm not leaving you here alone."

Shawn abruptly tricked Hayden into thinking he was going for him. Hayden swung at his opponent's head. Shawn bent backward, kicking him out of the way just before Tiyshio attacked him again. He shed two more blades over his hands and pointed one each at Tiyshio and Hayden. He glared at both of them aggressively.

"You afraid, Tiy? You had to bring help to kill me?"

"I just wanted Kevin, Shawn. I want to save you."

"Either way, Tiyshio, I will kill you for what you've done. Kevin, too."

Shawn thrashed Hayden over to the sink as he swung at him.

Tiyshio circled Shawn, baiting him with his sword at his neck. Shawn whacked it down and followed up with his next blade to Tiyshio's neck, cutting him.

Tiyshio felt the open wound but knew he would be okay as soon as the armor healed him. Shawn noticed this, vigorously striking at him again. Tiyshio dodged, swept, and deflected the attacks quicker each time. He got cut at least twice. He knew he had more injuries, but they quickly healed, to Shawn's dismay.

Shawn snarled, shooting an energy beam at close quarters toward Tiyshio's face, and breaking his blade. Tiyshio knocked his arm away, burning a hole in the wall and floor.

Shawn swiped at his head again.

Tiyshio swiftly knocked his blade aside, following up by plunging him to the ground telekinetically.

Shawn then pinned him to the ceiling and shot spikes at Tiyshio's stomach. The latter deflected them telekinetically.

Tiyshio dragged across the room to release himself, then dropped to the ground as Shawn recovered and shot more spikes at him. Tiyshio whacked each spike down until he got to cover in the next room.

Hayden pulled at Shawn to prevent his continuing after Tiyshio.

Shawn quickly turned, using the momentum to stab at Hayden. The latter quickly moved out of the way, blocking each attack Shawn subsequently struck at him, though not without effort.

Shawn's swings were so powerful, they brought Hayden's arms down almost to the point where he dropped them completely.

Tiyshio blasted Shawn out the window just before Shawn chopped Hayden down.

"Hayden! I'm getting you out of here! You can't stay!"

"Tiyshio!" Hayden called back. "Look out!"

Shawn smashed Tiyshio to the ground, then slowly started toward for Hayden. Tiyshio cracked his back when he crashed to the ground, crying out.

Hayden crawled backwards; his sword ready to defend himself.

Shawn thrashed at him continuously.

Hayden breathed heavily. His arms buckled in with each attack. Finally, he gave out.

Tiyshio tossed him back to the living room.

"GO!" Tiyshio yelled as he was yanked toward Shawn, standing ready to impale him.

"NO!"

Hayden yanked Shawn to the wall, using the wooden floor to pull him back and the foundation of the wall to hold him down.

Tiyshio rushed in as soon as he broke free.

Shawn yanked Hayden's arm backward as Hayden at his head, breaking it. He moved in closer to stab him.

Hayden wouldn't let the pain of his injury stop him. He acted quickly, burning off most of Shawn's armor.

Shawn walked through the flames, choking Hayden.

Tiyshio spread open Shawn's fingers before his grasp grew any tighter, then pushed Hayden away. Shawn turned to Tiyshio, kicking him in the face while he was still on the ground. He then picked him up by a leg and pierced his armor by shooting spikes into it.

Tiyshio screamed as he was thrown back down to the ground.

Hayden rushed in, barraging Shawn to let go.

Shawn grabbed Hayden's leg and crushed it. He then lifted Hayden and rushed him against a wall. Hayden tried using the wood in the ceiling to pierce Shawn's skull, but kept missing. All but one went directly into his shoulder.

Shawn locked him into the wall as Hayden blew fire in his face with his good arm. Shawn then broke that arm telekinetically. With all his frustration, he continued to shoot spikes into Hayden's stomach until the boy stopped moving.

"HAYDEN!" Tiyshio cried.

Tiyshio flew at Shawn, breaking into the main foyer. Shawn twisted him around, smashing into the wall, nearly going through it to the other side. Shawn then sucker punched him into the wall.

Tiyshio dodged, breaking the armor inward to his hand. Tiyshio saw Shawn come at him again with another punch. He caught it, crushing his opponent's hand.

Shawn cried out, smashing his head into Tiyshio's. Both their skulls bled. The floor caved in on them as they dropped into the basement.

Tiyshio got up as fast as Shawn did, dodging a flurry of kicks. Tiyshio blocked all of them, and grabbed his leg at the last one, throwing him to the other side of the basement.

Shawn recovered quickly, flying into Tiyshio, knocking him into the wall again. Tiyshio pushed back, heating his hand to shoot an energy beam in his face.

Shawn released Tiyshio, making him fly into the stairs. He then flung his arms downward to create more blades from his hands, then swung at every part of his opponent's body.

Tiyshio dodged and dipped, searching for his sword, in his mind, to launch it through the ground.

Shawn dodged as the weapon broke through the ground, coming at his head.

Tiyshio used that distraction to break Shawn's arm, and his blade to pin him to the wall.

Shawn tried to pull free by attacking Tiyshio's mind. It didn't faze him. Tiyshio instead flung his other arm against the wall, shattering the other blade. He molded cement from under the ground onto Shawn's armored feet.

Shawn began creating another blade from his fingertips.

Tiyshio began to break the weapon as it grew closer to his neck. He forced Shawn's head up to keep it from dancing around, then forced his eyes open.

Shawn looked terrified, making the blade form faster. Tiyshio could barely keep up. He retrieved his own sword with his mind and pointed it straight at Shawn's head.

All Tiyshio could think was, "*This is all I have left.*"

He dove into Shawn's mind, looking for the best memory.

Shawn felt Tiyshio searching his mind. He struggled to push him out.

Tiyshio tried forcing his eyes open. Strands of the Rigion gene began coming out.

Shawn quickly formed a new blade, piercing Tiyshio's neck.

Tiyshio cried out in pain.

Tiyshio found Shawn in his head, himself, and his parents. His father hugged him, but the vision faded. Shawn's blade dug deeper into Tiyshio's neck.

"Shawn, no!" he cried. "Let me do it!"

Shawn continued thrusting the sword as the gene started returning inside him. Shawn managed to break his head free from Tiyshio's grip.

Tiyshio was losing concentration.

Inside Shawn's mind, he smiled at Tiyshio. Tiyshio looked confused, thinking he was looking at someone else, but, truthfully, it was him.

Shawn pulled his arm free, causing Tiyshio to break away from seeing his thoughts. Tiyshio needed to save himself.

He launched his sword into Shawn's head, killing him instantly.

Still connected to his mind, Tiyshio approached a young Shawn. He hugged him, saying, "I'm sorry. I'm sorry for everything I did." He kept hugging Shawn until all he could see was Shawn pinned to the wall with the sword stuck in his head.

Tiyshio rushed upstairs, feeling Hayden's faint energy still beating within him. He found Hayden, barely moving, and, through his eyes, saw his vision fading. Tiyshio tried to heal him, but Hayden wasn't fighting. He began to cry, yelling to Hayden, "Stay with me, Hayden! Stay with me! Not you too!"

Hayden was too tired and weak. Tiyshio cut himself to allow some of his blood to drop into the wound. Regardless of whether it worked or not, he wanted the nanobots to save him.

The act did nothing. Hayden lay lifeless in Tiyshio's arms.

He looked out the window, scared and shaken. He didn't want to leave, knowing his world was beginning to turn around for the first time.

CHAPTER
TWENTY-THREE

TRUTH

Jason brandished a huge smile as he stood alongside Siyshi and Sunshi, outside their school. They wore black regalia on that bright summer's day. Siyshi looked as if waiting for something. Sunshi also kept scanning the horizon.

Their mother asked them to bunch up while she prepared to take a picture.

"Not everyone is here, Mom!" Siyshi yelled.

Hitomi didn't bother telling them that. "You guys are supposed to be inside already. I have to take the picture now!"

"No, you don't!" Siyshi yelled again, as her mom started counting down.

When Hitomi reached one, all of them smiled in the picture. After Hitomi showed them the polaroid, Jason was surprised to see Sunshi still smiling as he looked back at her, her expression unchanged. He called her out on it. She didn't flinch or even say a word.

Hitomi and Jason looked at her, confused. Hitomi was more bothered by how rude she was with him.

"Siy, can you tell your sister to get her head out of the clouds and ask her where her boyfriend is?"

Siyshi went and did that. Jason followed.

"It's been six months! She's like this every day! What's up with her?"

"She's caught in between. I mean, she's moved on, as you know. She's happy with her new boyfriend, but even he gets annoyed at how torn she gets."

"She misses him that much, doesn't she?"

"I don't blame her, I do too."

Siyshi tapped her sister's shoulder. Sunshi continued standing like a statue. Siyshi then slapped her atop the head to get her attention.

Sunshi hit her back twice as hard. This got the attention of her mother as Siyshi was about to slap her again.

"HEY!" her mom yelled.

Both apologized to Hitomi, who looked ready to bring the fury down on them.

Jason felt shaken, just looking at her. "I don't want to piss her off."

"You never want to. The beatings were the worst." Sunshi exaggerated. "What is it?"

"Where is Chris? He said he was coming."

"He is! He went to the cemetery to see his brother. Where is Tiyshio?"

"He did the same…" Siyshi appeared a little bothered.

Her sister looked at her, pissed off. "He isn't coming, is he? He said he'd be here for every graduation. What the hell!"

"Things changed."

"OH YEAH! SO DID HE!"

Hitomi looked back at them with fury in her eyes.

"Sorry, Mom!" Sunshi said in a frightened tone.

"Does she always have to be like that?"

Siyshi shrugged. "If you keep being a pain in the ass."

Tiyshio wore a gray suit with a red tie. He held the jacket over his shoulder, so he wouldn't sweat too much from the heat. He stood over Shawn's grave, tears streaming down his face. The grave was next to that of his father and mother, his headstone between theirs. It read:

A MAN FINALLY FREE FROM HIS PAIN AND WITH HIS
FAMILY AGAIN
SHAWN MITCHELL DAMIEN
AUGUST 19, 1970– NOVEMBER 10, 1986

"Hey, bro, it's graduation day. I know on a day like this you would like to say we made it. I know you would hate for me to say your girl was taken by your best friend. Don't worry. I trust Rocks with my life. Better than I did facing you. Not a day goes by that I don't live with that regret. Kevin would tell me all the time now, *'don't regret, remember.'* Not sure what that means. I guess it's that I have to live with the choices I made, and to be honest, if it happened again, I would do it all the same. I'm not sorry. Nor should you be. All this time, I had to come to grips with what you said back then. That, no matter what happened that day, you were going to kill me. Now, I believe you. I just wonder, if you were here today, if we reconciled and you heard me out, would you say the same, too?"

Tiyshio lost his train of thought. He felt someone staring at him. In the distance, he spotted another young man, wearing a black and white suit with a red tie. When he focused, he recognized Chris.

Chris immediately looked away, but not for long, since Tiyshio approached him. He was standing at Hayden's grave.

Tiyshio looked down at the rectangular headstone marker, which laid recessed in the ground. The engraving showed just his name and birthdate.

He couldn't stand having it look like that, so he added something more.

A BRAVE WARRIOR UNTIL THE END

HAYDEN WILLIAMS

APRIL 9, 1972-NOVEMBER 10, 1986

Smoke drifted off Tiyshio's eyes, from what Chris could see. He didn't show a hint of emotion to let Tiyshio know he was happy for what he'd just done. All he could think about was that his brother would have been one year older now.

Tiyshio looked at him. "It's the least I can do now."

Chris continued staring at the words, letting them sink in.

"Perhaps," Tiyshio continued, "it's better than the silent treatment we've been giving each other for months now. Chris, I want to settle this. Anything is better than what happened between Shawn and I. He didn't want to be held back. He wanted to protect you, not fight with you. Not have you take on everything."

"What did it cost?" Chris interrupted.

"I'm sorry?"

"What did it cost?" he repeated, slower.

"Don't do that to me. We both know what it cost. I didn't want Hayden to go, but I wasn't going to fight him on it. He wanted to fight, because he was afraid of seeing you get hurt. If not with Shawn, then someone else."

"But I didn't want him out there! He had no business in your quarrel! You know that! Teleport him out! Go alone! What happened to that?"

"I did all of that, but I was not going to fight him. Remember, Rocks. No one, NO ONE stopped you from training, from learning how to fight, to do what's best to protect yourself and others around you. Azuka told him something I'd like to remember every day. We don't fight to be better; we fight to survive. If not Shawn, then

340

another, greater threat. You can only protect so much until you can't anymore. An apology won't bring him back, but I hope to explain to you what happened that day. This might make you see things another way."

Chris looked at Tiyshio, his face sour. "What do you expect from me, Tiyshio? My brother is dead."

"I don't expect anything from you. I'm living with that failure. Every day. It hurts me more than you. I'm just hoping you understand."

Chris's eyes began to water, but his expression remained stoic.

"I'm not looking for you to forgive me, Chris. He saved me that day countless times. I wish I could have gotten him out of there sooner. So, please understand, not just me, but what your brother was trying to achieve!" Tiyshio patted him on the shoulder, uncomfortably, before he eased up.

Tiyshio started walking away, then looked back. "Come on, Chris. We have a graduation to go to."

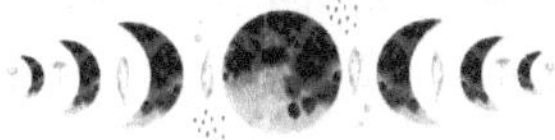

"Hush up," Siyshi replied in annoyance. "I'm sure he's only running late. Besides, he would be sitting two rows behind."

"Oh yeah? Take a look!" Sunshi snapped.

Siyshi turned to see two empty spots. She glanced at Jason. He seemed oblivious.

"*I guess he's not coming,*" he responded.

"*Don't tell me that, Jason. She's been looking forward to this.*"

Their row got called up. Sunshi and Siyshi grew worried. Jason began fidgeting.

"Oh, shit!" he remarked silently.

"I wish she looked happier, Diego. I haven't seen her this down since Shawn died."

Diego turned to his wife, confused. "Have you seen her at all in the last six months?"

"I have. What are you getting at?"

At that moment, Hitomi saw two figures pass by on the main floor. It was two young boys, with their caps and gowns barely in place and about to fly off. Hitomi smiled. She knew exactly who they were.

Kevin, on stage, giggled as he saw Tiyshio rush up to the podium alongside Kevin. "Where do I sit?" he queried, panting.

"Same row as Jason," he replied, covering the microphone.

Sunshi spotted Chris, who blew a kiss at her. Tiyshio and Chris started to bump fists before racing each other to the ceremony, but stopped doing so. Kevin shook his head, continuing the ceremony.

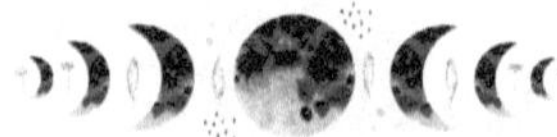

THE GROUP GATHERED WHEN THE CEREMONY ENDED, MEETING outside the stadium to get another picture from Siyshi and Sunshi's Mom. She remarked how wonderful they looked, which made them awkwardly smile.

Sunshi laid a big smooch on Chris's lips. He was completely unprepared.

"HEY! Can I get one with you guys not kissing? I'm still here!"

"Sorry, Mom!" Sunshi yelled.

Tiyshio looked toward Kevin, who applauded them from afar. He stood next to Ms. Kazio, who hugged him. Tiyshio smiled back at them, seeing how proud he was.

Jason then ruined the moment by vaulting over him.

"How do you feel, man? We did it!" Jason sounded like it was the biggest accomplishment ever.

Tiyshio, on the other hand, had only this to say: "It's just high school, Jay. We have one more to go."

"So, you plan on going to college?"

"I don't know. I've been thinking about going into computers. Seems pretty cool."

"Sounds good. Why?"

"To find a way off Earth." Tiyshio then walked toward Siyshi, who was calling him over.

"I am so proud of all of you! To all of you grown-ups, oh!" Hitomi shouted, hugging her children and Tiyshio. Suddenly, her look changed. She realized they were missing one more person.

"I know, Miss Guerra. I miss him too," Tiyshio remarked somberly.

"It's okay. I'm sure, if things didn't pan out the way they had, he'd have been happy to be here with you guys."

"Yeah!" they all agreed.

"Hey, Mom, I am going to talk to Tiyshio for a bit, okay?"

"Sure, go ahead. You're coming over tonight?"

"Yes, Miss Guerra. I'll let Jason know to come as well."

"Oh, don't worry about that. I just did!"

"I thought you weren't coming?" Siyshi asked, pulling Tiyshio to the side to walk.

"I changed my mind."

"You went to see him?"

Tiyshio nodded.

Siyshi slowly shook her head. "Why do you do that to yourself?"

"Why ask questions you know the answers to?"

"Because I know you are hurting yourself, going there. I feel you go there for answers."

"Like what?" Tiyshio quietly snapped.

"Like, if you can be forgiven. Remember what you did, the last thing you saw, when you tried to take that thing away from him?"

"His happiest moment. He didn't want to leave it. I don't blame him, but that's not what stopped me."

"Then what does?" Kevin asked, as they reflected on what Siyshi, and he were talking about.

They were back home, at Kevin's and Tiyshio's apartment, sitting on the balcony, watching the sunset, which had almost gone down. The lights of passing cars were the stars they followed.

"He was about to kill me. I knew I would have to kill him, but I didn't want to."

"Even though he said…"

"No matter what you do, I will kill you," they both replied.

Kevin shook his head. "You think he was lying?"

"No, but, to be honest, I hoped he was. I didn't want to believe what he said or what Azuka told me. I told something to Chris that I can't yet agree on, myself."

"What's that?"

"Needing help, he went to see his brother while I was there. Chris is still understandably angry with me. I don't blame him. I know you told me the same thing."

"You thought you could go around me, and have him be trained by Azuka?"

"No!" Tiyshio said in frustration. "I honestly let him make his own choices. I spoke against them, but he didn't listen."

"Yet, you still let it happen," Kevin remarked, sternly.

"I DID EXACTLY WHAT YOU DID! What Mom and Dad did! What their parents did. I gave him the means to protect himself. Unlike Chris, Jason, Siy, Sun, or Shawn, he wanted this. I'm sorry. I wasn't going to take that away from him." Tiyshio grew more defensive with each word.

"Tiyshio, Hayden trusted you more than his brother, at times. In this instance…back then, I didn't want you to put another life on your head. Not the way things were going. Now, I feel different about it."

"What changed your mind?"

"Nothing, really. It was just another moment. I can tell you the same thing."

Tiyshio agreed. "Don't regret. Remember."

Kevin nodded. "Yes, the choices you made, you know why you made them. The next step is, are you choosing to learn from them?"

Tiyshio nodded. "Hey, any word from the cleaners? It seems to be the longest process."

"Still nothing. It's good that you brought Shawn and Hayden back at the same time. Finding the others is still a drag. The house was cleared not long after you left. It's not like the Rigions to clean up after themselves. Not all Rigions, more so."

"Are you going to follow up?"

"Maybe later! I got a date tonight." Kevin stood up to stretch. "You got any plans?"

"Before I answer, you're going with who I think it is?"

"Just as friends. She is a divorced woman. She needs to heal."

"Sounds like something she would say. Are you becoming agreeable, Kino?"

"Cut it, Tiyshio," Kevin said, joking but stern.

"All right. I'll stop playing around. If you're going out, I'd like to do tradition."

"Tradition, huh? When is she coming?"

Tiyshio pointed at his head. "Just now." His face had a cheesy look.

"All right. Keep the place to yourself tonight. Don't do anything wild."

"I won't!" he promised as Kevin entered his bedroom.

Tiyshio looked out at the city once more, taking a deep breath.

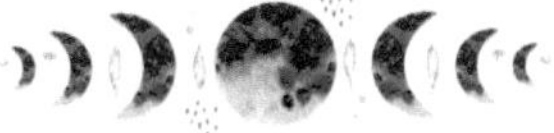

SUNSHI HUNG OFF THE ROOF LEDGE OF TIYSHIO'S APARTMENT. BOTH looked disappointed. Tiyshio watched Sunshi, who held a bottle of wine only three-quarters drunk. Sunshi looked down at the cars passing by, continuously brushing her hair to the side.

"You know what? Let's head back to your place. I know this didn't end up the way you hoped, Sun." Tiyshio stood, holding his arm out to Sunshi.

She looked at him, concerned and disappointed.

"I'm sorry, Tiyshio. I…I know it's a tradition. We go up here. We chill. We watch you fly. Just the three of us."

"I know. It doesn't feel the same without our third amigo. I was hoping we could still keep it fun, you know? For his sake."

"Yeah, but, Tiyshio, shit wasn't the same since the school year started. You know, the weirdest thing was, when he was alive, I could read his thoughts once in a while."

Tiyshio had an intrigued look on his face.

"How?" remarked Tiyshio. "I thought you were just really strong. Funny enough, that does make you and Chris a legit power couple."

Sunshi shook her head, snickering. "Tiyshio, you are so stupid. I'm being serious right now. I did."

"So am I right now? Can you explain it?"

"Not exactly. I used to think it was him. Now, not so much."

"What gave it away?"

"You know Cara, from Mrs. Aurora's class?"

Tiyshio nodded.

"Well, I caught her fantasizing about Rocks one day. You know the rest."

Tiyshio's face lit up. "That's why you fought her! You gotta control your anger."

"You can't tell me what to do!"

Tiyshio gave her an 'I told you so' look. They both sighed and looked back down to the streets.

Then Tiyshio offered, "How would you like to fly back?"

"Tiyshio, I get scared when I fly with you!" she protested.

"No. You're gonna fly yourself."

She looked at Tiyshio, confused.

"Look. I will hold you for a bit, but just follow my directions."

Sunshi grabbed onto him with a bear grip as he stepped off the ledge.

Tiyshio chuckled, "Step one. I need you to close your eyes and loosen up."

"WHAT!" she yelled.

"Just trust me."

So she did.

Tiyshio breathed out dramatically.

"Shut up, Tiyshio!"

Tiyshio chuckled harder.

"You are doing good. Now I'm going to lay you on your stomach."

"TIYSHIO!" she yelled frustratingly.

"Come on, just listen. Think of yourself right now. Can you see you and me?"

Sunshi nodded.

"Good. Now, I want you to imagine you're on a comfortable bed, and that bed is moving with you in the air. Once you have that image in your head, believe in it. Let it manifest." Tiyshio kept his hold until the tip of his fingers felt like the pressure of bed padding pressed against them. With each passing moment, he slowly loosened his grip on Sunshi, without her noticing.

"Tiyshio, are you still here?" she called, opening her eyes.

"Right beside you."

She gazed at Tiyshio, flying next to her.

"Tiyshio! You let go?!"

Sunshi started to dip.

"Hey, stay focused. You're doing good so far. Don't let go."

Sunshi grinned. Her speed began increasing, as she imagined it.

"Looks like you are getting the hang of it. Follow me to the moon?"

"What?" she asked, barely hearing him.

Tiyshio sped up to a blitz speed, straight to the sky.

"Hey, wait!" Sunshi yelled out, excited.

Tiyshio pushed faster, closing his eyes.

Sunshi saw a cloud stream from behind him.

He imagined the last thing he'd seen when he fought Shawn. The image of hugging him. All the memories he had. His speed was so great, he broke the sound barrier.

Sunshi had a hard time following him, because of the thin air. The sonic boom made her cover her ears.

Tiyshio kept pushing until the stars in the sky distinguished themselves, and the moon appeared larger. As he felt weightlessness, he opened his eyes to reveal their natural gold color, looking out to space for what was to come.

HISTORICAL EVENTS

THE DAWN OF TIME

- 0: Shakana, an interdimensional being, creates the universe. The Geddeons, her first creations, were to be the protectors of the universe and her connection to the other creations she made. She comes to them in physical form every thousand years.

- 1510 (After Dawn of Time): Zorin creates a planet as his namesake. He places it in a galaxy called Andromeda. He went on to create life and vegetation on the light absorbent planet from the dirt and the sun, to fuel them with abilities remarkably close to his own. They were bred to oppose the tyrants of Gidos, beginning the first universal war.

- 1601 - 1626 ADOT: A Zorian known as the Alam is born. At age twenty-five, he fought amongst seven other Zorian generals; Galo, Lam, Aia, Qito, Oma, Min, Gion.

- 1689 - 1800 ADOT: Alam, with the help of many other worlds, had defeated the Geddeons and become the savior. By the end of the war, many of them became the Cozen for next generation of Zorians as their evolution.

THE SECOND ANDROMEDAN WAR

- 1960: Zorigan is awakened and joined in the Avaian war.
- 1961: Azuka Fawzi is born on an unknown world believed to be the planet Mentis.

- 1963: Hitomi Kobashi and Diego Guerra are married.
  - Jason's parents are married.
- 1964: Zorin Returns to the planet that shares his namesake.
  - Aida Yokin and Fohas Damana from Hunata are married.
- 1965: Zea and Zorin get married.
  - Telsa Gond is born on the planet Riza.
- 1969: The Avaian invasion comes closer to an end as Zorigan helps defeat them with Nighcos.
  - Zorigan betrays Nighcos and shows how he has eliminated the current Zorian army by his control.
  - The second Andromedian war begins.
- 1970: Tiyshio Taylor is born, June 10, 1970. Jason Vincent (Jaisones Demga) is born January 20, 1970. Siyshi and Sunshi Guerra are born May 4, 1970. Christopher Williams (Chi-tan Wesa) is born August 19, 1970. Shawn Damien (Casan Damana) is born June 6, 1970.
  - Azuka Fawzi becomes a Rigion.
- 1972: Hayden Williams (Hai-din Wesa) is born April 9.
  - Zorin goes to Earth to establish a base of operations out of a vision he sees of what can happen soon.
- 1974: Suukai (Akil) Nighcos becomes a Rigion.
- Rigion army becomes a planetary force, with over 10 billion people taken over.
  - 500 worlds had already been taken over within the Zorian controlled space, mostly on the outskirts of the system, away from some of the Zorians allied planets.
  - Telsa Gond is saved by Suukai Nighcos during one of the raids on the planet Riza. He kills the squad that invaded her home and killed her mother and brother. He raises her after finding out most Rigions do this to less than desirable families.
  - Siyshi, Sunshi, Jason, and Shawn are all forced off their home worlds due to Rigion occupation.

- 1975: Siyshi, Sunshi, Jason, and Shawn all arrive on Earth.
- 1976: The war against the Rigions becomes unwinnable, so Zorin states he wants to end the war with an exhibition against his brother.
    - Zorin and Zorigan are presumed dead after vanishing.
    - A cease fire is put in place from Zea and Nighcos. Out of fear, she decides to separate from her son.
- 1977: Tiyshio and Kevin arrive to Earth.
    - Chris and Hayden leave their world during invasion.
    - Kevin becomes the new leader of all of Zorin's operations.
- 1978: Tiyshio begins his first year of elementary school.
    - March 10, 1978, Tiyshio befriends Sunshi Guerra and Shawn Damien.
    - Azuka finds a way to break free from the Rigion army and change back to her race.
- 1979: Suukai finds out Tiyshio is on Earth and makes plans to have him kidnapped.
    - Chris and Hayden arrive on Earth.
- 1980: Zorian extremist kills Shawn's father.
    - Kevin begins investigating the murder of Shawn's father.
    - A raid on Kevin's home goes horribly wrong for the Rigions. They believe they had killed the Alam. Suukai tries for an alternative plan to win this war.
- 1981: Shawn's mother is killed by new band of Zorian extremist, presumed to be the same group.
    - Shawn and Tiyshio begin living with each other.
    - Shawn's resentment begins.
    - Telsa's connection to the Rigion gene begins to fade at age 16.
    - Aida turned out not to be dead; her death was staged.
- 1982: Tiyshio begins to date Sunshi, and meets her twin sister, Siyshi.
    - Telsa becomes a girl on the street who looks more like a runaway. Kevin takes her in to train and take care of her.

- ○ Suukai learns that Tiyshio still lives on Earth, from Telsa's eyes.
- 1983: Shawn is given legal guardians to live with, in Amelia and Kirk Porter.
- Suukai begins his first raid against Kevin and Tiyshio, which he continuously constructs throughout the years.
- 1984: Telsa finishes her training with Kevin and Tiyshio and leaves them due to feeling like she is endangering.
- 1985: Derek Ryan and Aida get married.
- Azuka and Telsa have an encounter that leads to her losing the Rigion eyes.

ACKNOWLEDGMENTS

I will be myself here as this is one of the greatest accomplishments of my life. So this will go in order of how Alam was made. I want to first start off by thanking my Mom. If it weren't for her, this story would have never been written and sold. Every train ride and car ride of me speaking about the weirdest dream, is now on paper. I want to thank my father and sister as they helped encourage me with their enthusiasm, wisdom, and aide to the success of this novel.

I want to return to my mother, being the geek that she is. If it weren't for those Saturday morning cartoons, I watched as a kid. If weren't for my cousins and I being engaged in anime and one of the greatest sci-fi films of all time. This book what not be what it is today. So, also thank you to the late Stan Lee, Akira Toriyama, Haim Saban, Masashi Kishimoto and most importantly George Lucas. As all of you have inspired a generation of authors and creators like me into what we are today. I only look forward to being as inspirational as you.

I want to thank Jon Kim, who gave me a great author photo found at the end of this novel. Although, now it is an old photo I was not going to let it go to waste. Thank you for it wholeheartedly.

I want to thank my friends who became my family over the duration of this novel coming to life. They have inspired, themes, trials, characteristics of this story becoming what it is today. Including my friend I call my brother Sean.

We spoke of this novel every hangout, brainstormed stories and ideas. I would love to flesh them out now becoming the author that I am. Those days helped shape the character of Tiyshio and his friends.

I want to thank my high school English professor Ms. Sipos. She being my first true reader and editor in this work. To all the lunch breaks of sitting with me and helping me with the grammatical errors I had in my book. Going over each chapter and continuing to master the English language as I do today. As well as Gordon my other editor making this book a smooth read through.

I want to thank Melissa, Rachel, John, and Aprampar. For taking my initial book cover and making it into the beauty I've seen it becoming. I feel so proud of the work that you all have put into realizing my artistic vision. As well as giving this book the life and difference to others to stand on its own. I look at it now and see a cover that screams film.

I also want to thank my test readers; Nadene, Ana & Josie, and Chris who read through this novel. Giving me the great critical feedback and suggestions to help finalize and fine tune the story into what it is right now. Without your suggestions. I couldn't believe that my story could be more compelling then what I wrote initially. Thank you!

The second to last person I want to thank is myself. I started writing this story in 2006 and finally released it almost two decades later. To be honest, now is the best time. I am glad I found myself, and filled myself with the determination, endurance, and courage to complete this novel. From this completion I have given myself the proper discipline and determination for anything in life. I am proud of myself for seeing this to the finish line. No matter how difficult. It has happened, will happen, and continue to do so.

Finally, I want to thank you, the reader. The first step is your interest. The second, your intrigue into the novel and diving deeper. This being the last step reading this section also dedicated to you.

Your willingness to dive into this new story inspires me to write more. Your interaction, word of mouth and blessings of this here finding, thrills me. Being the self-published author that I became, and once being in your position. I am grateful you made it this far. If you are reading this, I feel you have enjoyed this story. With that feeling I believe you are looking for to the next event. To you I say there is more to come, and I am looking forward to sitting around the campfire and telling you stories from elsewhere.

Once again, to you–the reader. Thank you so much for your engagement. I hope I have made you a fan. Or inspired you to write your own story. As the storytellers of the past have inspired me.

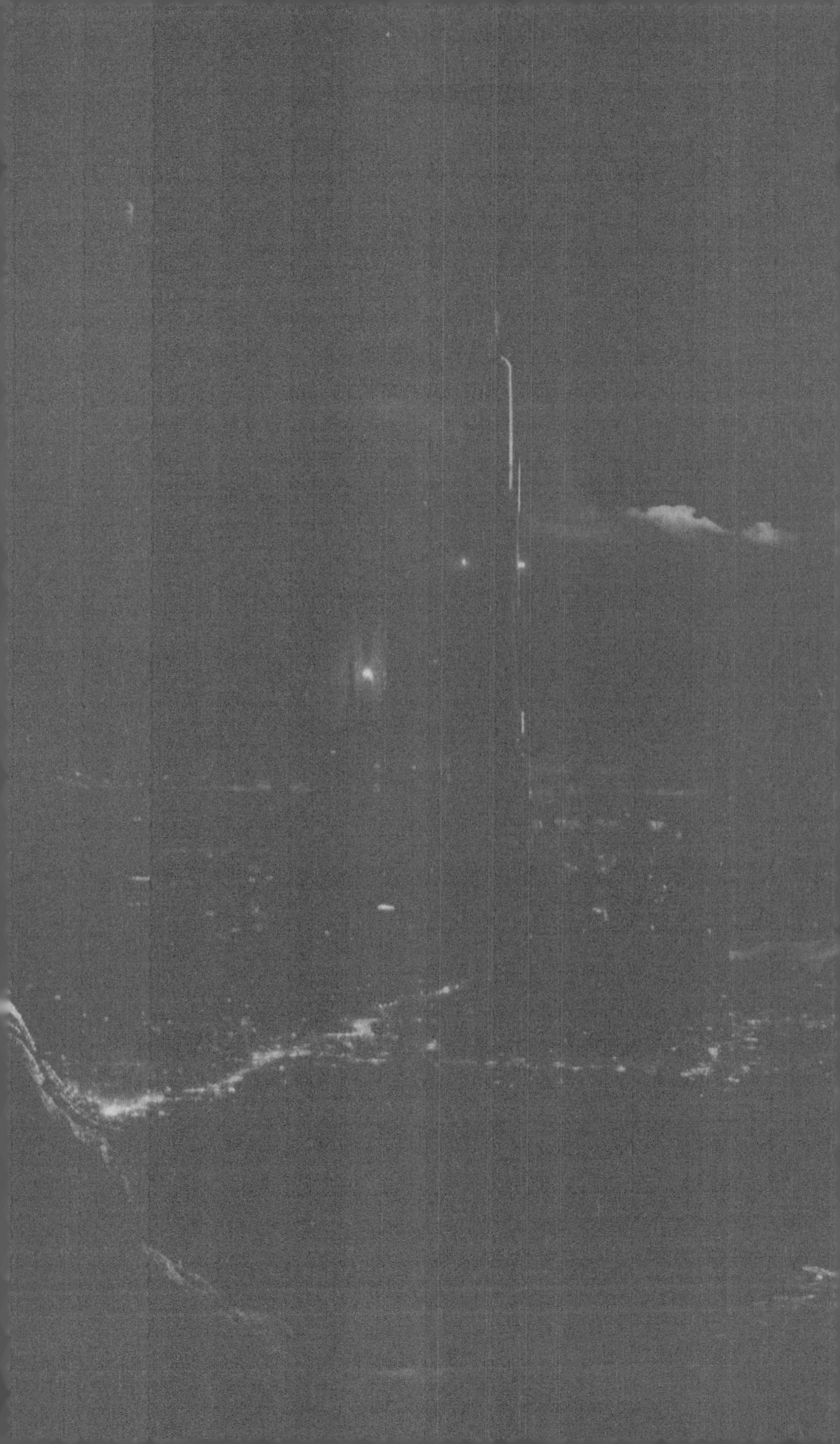

ABOUT THE AUTHOR

Photo by Jon Kim

Akil Smith was born and raised in Brooklyn, NY, and has lived in various different cities, from Frankfurt, Germany, to Montréal, Canada. He grew up in a geek-filled family of comic book and sci-fi fans. Growing up, he watched and read anime and manga, had a passion for art and poetry, and took up both expressive forms. What began his writing career was the support of his parents, the push coming from his mother. From time to time, he would tell her about his dreams of the characters and events he would see. She would tell him to write them down so that he wouldn't forget. Those tales are being told now. Alam Beginnings is the first of many. To stay in touch with Akil you can follow him on Instagram @ao.smithofficial and YouTube as "That Writer Akil."

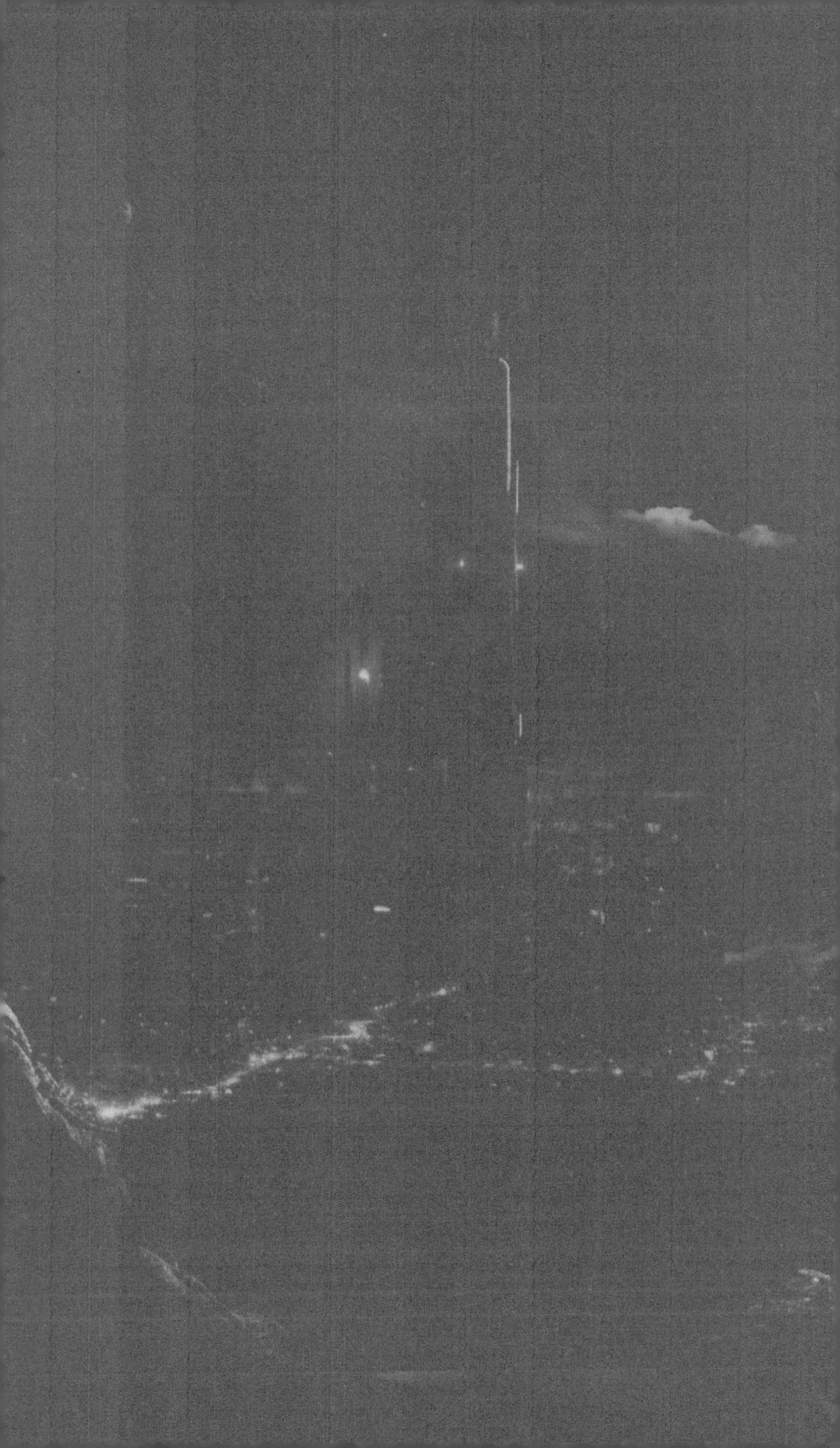